ARGYLLE

ARGYLLE

Elly Conway

BANTAM

NEW YORK

Published in the United States by Bantam Books, an imprint of Random House, a division of Penguin Random House LLC, New York.

BANTAM & B colophon is a registered trademark of Penguin Random House LLC.

Published in Great Britain in 2024 by Bantam Press, an imprint of Transworld Publishers.

Hardback ISBN 978-0-593-60001-6
Ebook ISBN 978-0-593-60002-3

Printed in the United States of America on acid-free paper

randomhousebooks.com

2 4 6 8 9 7 5 3 1

First U.S. Edition

For Mom and Dad, who have been beside
me every step of the way.

'Sometimes it is necessary to be lonely in order to prove that you are right.'

— attributed to Vladimir Putin

'The women laughed and wept; the crowd stamped their feet enthusiastically, for at that moment Quasimodo was really beautiful. He was handsome – this orphan, this foundling, this outcast.'

— Victor Hugo, *The Hunchback of Notre-Dame*

'The Amber Room represents to Russians many of the things we have lost.'

— Ivan Sautov, director of the Catherine Palace museum (quoted in *Forbes Life* magazine, 'Mysteries of the Amber Room', 29 March 2004)

Author's Note for New Edition

Note too long ago, I suffered a terrible accident that completely shattered my life. While I was recuperating and feeling sorry for myself, my parents would bring me movies and books to try to ignite my interest in something – anything – that wasn't about me and this terrible thing that had happened to me. One particular morning, my mother turned up with a book of photographs of beautiful landscapes. One of them was of a mountain range in southern Poland. It meant nothing to me, but as I looked at it I felt a tug of something and, that night, Aubrey Argylle came to me, fully formed, in a febrile dream, with his Nehru jacket and flat-top hair and buried sadnesses and his need to put right what the world keeps getting wrong. When I woke up he was in my head as if he'd walked right in the door and kicked off his shoes and made himself at home. I know writers roll their eyes when other writers say, 'The book wrote itself,' but this one really did (please don't hate me, guys). And in writing it, I gained a new purpose, and from that point on I began to heal. So I need to say thank you: to whoever took that photograph, to my parents, and most of all to Aubrey Argylle for bringing me back to myself and reminding me that sometimes the tools we need to fix ourselves are inside us the whole time.

Elly Conway, 2023

Prologue

THERE ARE FEW PLACES ON EARTH MORE DESOLATE THAN SOUTH-eastern Siberia at dawn on a bitingly cold March morning. The spiky pine forests of the taiga carpet the ground like a bed of green nails. Here there is no birdsong to pierce the minus-twenty-five-degree air. Only the whip of the wind and the plaintive howl of a distant wolf.

But a sound breaks the dead silence, a soft rumble growing louder, and now something appears, glinting in the early-morning sun. A high-speed train, its pointed nose spearing a path through the freezing air, plunging relentlessly onwards, as the thick forest gives way to swampy lowlands and windswept tundra.

In the standard carriages people lie on narrow berths, their faces to the wall, sleeping off last night's vodka, or else sit huddled on the bottom bunks eating *pirozhki*, watching the scenery through smeared and grimy windows. But at the rear of the silver streak there is something quite different. A carriage of gold, bearing the initials V F and I F intertwined in imperial purple.

The real-life VF and IF – otherwise known as Vasily and Irina Federov – are very much not intertwined. In fact, it would be hard to imagine two people sharing so confined a space in a more separate manner. Irina sits in a high-backed armchair which is really more of a throne than a chair, her left foot soaking in a porcelain bowl full of rose oil with petals floating on the surface, while a pinafore-clad woman kneels on the floor vigorously scrubbing the sole of her right foot with seaweed picked up fresh from the port in Vladivostok before the train departed.

Irina has a magazine in her hands, through which she flicks uninterestedly. The train will take six more days to arrive in Moscow and cellphone coverage is practically non-existent, for all that 'cutting-edge technology' they were promised. She cannot talk to her friends or her sister. Cannot complain to them that being trapped in this gilded carriage with her husband makes her want to claw off her own skin. Cannot tell them how his soft voice grates at her nerve endings and that when he fixes her with his colourless, lifeless eyes behind those rimless glasses she feels like a butterfly on a pin.

And even if she could talk to them, what would they say? That they had warned her against marrying an outsider, when she could have had her pick from the old Russian families. Generations as easily traceable as the veins on your wrist. That having made her misguided choice, she should console herself by spending his billions. A holiday home on Lake Valdai. An apartment in Knightsbridge. A villa on the French Riviera. Lavish furnishings. A new yacht. More liposuction. Longer hair extensions. By now she has had so many surgeries that when she stands in front of the mirror she doesn't recognize her own face. 'Careful,' he'd said the last time she came back from that private hospital in Beverly Hills, standing behind her at her dressing table as he pulled the still-tender skin on her cheeks back towards her hairline. 'If you stretch it any more, it will tear like an old paper bag.'

The beautician, who is now using a pumice stone on the tougher skin of her heel, presses too hard. 'Watch what you're doing!' Irina kicks out, unbalancing the woman, who puts out a hand to stop herself, nudging the porcelain tub and sending a small surge of water on to the plush carpet. 'Idiot!'

Across the carriage, almost as far as it is possible to be, Irina's husband looks up. But if he is angry at the disturbance, or concerned, or just curious even, it does not show in his flat, unremarkably featured face. He is sitting by the window in a matching armchair to his wife's, a polished wood desk in front of him, on which sits a laptop computer the size of a small briefcase. He is looking over his notes for the live televised debate he will take part in when he arrives in Moscow. They could have flown in, of course, on one of his two private jets, but it is all part of the campaign, this magisterial process through the parts of Russia most politicians ignore – sending a message to the dispossessed hordes in the rural backwaters that they have not been forgotten, not by him anyway, gathering up the populist vote one disaffected peasant at a time.

At first he had wavered about the golden coach. The last two winters have been hard here. People are hungry. 'I don't want to be accused of flaunting my wealth,' he had told his chief of staff.

The man had raised his eyebrows. 'With all respect, you are coming to power on a commoner's ticket,' he had said, 'the man who came from nothing to conquer the world. The people need you to embody everything they don't have. Why would they want to be represented by a man who has nothing they aspire to, by a man who is still just like them?'

Vasily Federov has gone to great lengths to prove his Russian credentials. He has invested hundreds of millions in technological infrastructure and national causes, has bought himself a mayorship and set about ruthlessly, systematically, cleaning up the streets of the city he ruled over with the aid of his own highly trained private militia. He has married the president's daughter, has steeped himself in Russian culture – bankrolling movies and plays and dance troupes that send him into paroxysms of boredom if he has to watch them for more than a minute at a time. Has endured hour after hour of language lessons so that he now speaks fluent Russian with only the faintest of accents. Yet still there are issues, like the golden carriage, that bring back to him the fact that he is still an outsider, remind him that he has yet to leave Christopher Clay completely behind.

The train is speeding through time zones – eight by the time they arrive at their destination. They have long passed Lake Baikal – the largest, deepest freshwater lake in the world – and Gulag Perm-36, the labour camp where so many dissidents had been held over the years. Federov has little sympathy. The Russian foundling who was unhappily adopted by Americans and grew up in the Midwest feeling like an outsider, an oddity, yearning always for his mother country, or perhaps just for his mother, he has no time for those who criticize and destabilize.

The train stops at various stations, and at each of them, in addition to the street hawkers and the travellers waiting to board, there is also a knot of people standing in the cold, the women with trousers under dresses under jumpers under coats, the men with red-raw cheeks where the wind has flayed them. They are waiting for him. Waiting for a glimpse of the golden carriage, and the man who rides inside it. The one who has promised them change. The self-made billionaire who started with nothing, with less than nothing, and made his fortune in America but will spend it right here. Not just in the cities where the oligarchs have their palaces, but in the bleak industrial towns and the neglected rural villages. The man who is saying what they want to hear – that mass immigration is a drain on resources and a dilution of Russia's national identity, that the metropolitan centres are sucking the country dry, leaving nothing for everyone else. That the Soviet Union can be rebuilt, stronger, re-absorbing all the people whose hearts are still Russian even though they might be forced to live under an Estonian or Ukrainian flag.

But there is always that question mark, isn't there? The accent he tries so hard to disguise. His soft hands and clean nails. His suit. His rimless glasses. He does not fit into the political narrative here. He does not come from old money and did not rise through the ranks of the Russian military. That's why they are here to see for themselves.

So at every station he must present himself in the doorway of the train, and Irina must put on her dark glasses and her small smile that is like a paper cut in her smooth face. And they must wave. And sometimes he throws out small gifts to the crowd – pencils with his name embossed in gold on the side, sweets for the children.

Now they are through the Urals and passing Yekaterinburg, where Tsar Nicholas II and his family were killed. Again Federov spares no sympathy. Everything has its day. As they get closer to Moscow, the scenery through the window becomes more industrial – belching factories and monstrous trucks, grey towns ringed by housing blocks.

Irina sits herself down at her dressing table and reapplies her make-up with a fat, soft brush.

'Remember to wear the bracelet,' Federov reminds her.

It is the first time he has spoken to her all day. She makes a face, though her reflection in the mirror hardly moves, thanks to the Botox injections her private physician gives her every three months.

The bracelet both enthrals and repels her, though she knows it's worth millions. It is made from heavy gold, crusted with diamonds, apart from one flat section which is engraved with random dots and squiggles that make no sense to her. 'It's called the Bracelet of Fidelity,' her husband had told her when he gave it to her, and as he fastened the clasp around her wrist it felt like a handcuff. She'd been appalled to find the initials NC engraved on the inside. Second-hand is anathema to her, the idea of wearing something that has rested on someone else's skin. But Federov is insistent, in that way of his. He doesn't raise his voice, but still her flesh rises up in tiny, frozen bumps.

She puts on the bracelet.

Irina is the daughter of a president, has grown up practically as royalty in a house where, as soon as you pick up your glass, someone darts in to wipe the table before you've had a chance to put it down again. She alone chose this man, Vasily Federov or Christopher Clay, so she can never admit that her soft-spoken, soft-palmed husband terrifies her. There is a black hole at the centre of him and she has no idea how deep it goes.

'Has he ever laid a hand on you?' her sister asked once, noticing how she flinched whenever he came near. And when Irina shook her head, she'd said, 'Probably because he is afraid of our father.' 'No,' Irina had corrected her. 'Because he can't bear to touch me.'

Approaching the capital, Federov puts away his portable computer and goes to stand by his case, which is open on the bed. She sees his hands, with those clean, perfectly shaped nails, reach into the pocket at the side and knows what he will be looking for. It disgusts her, this obsession of his. She has known men who have fetishes for feet, for bondage, for unspeakable sexual practices. But this thing of her husband's makes her skin crawl. The scrap of fabric that was once blue but now is grey and greasy with age and handling. His one link to the mother who rejected him not only at birth, when she left him in a phone box wrapped in the blanket of which this miserable scrap is all that remains, but again when, as a young all-American man still believing in happy endings, he flew to Russia and tracked her down to a tower block on the outskirts of Novosibirsk in the south-west of Siberia, only to have her slam the door in his face. After that he'd been half expecting the rejection from his former KGB officer father, but still the shock of it had eaten through the tender marrow of him like a cancer, cauterizing his emotions.

All this he told her at the beginning of their marriage, when there was still some softness between the two of them. Before confidences became weapons they could use against one another. Irina should have listened to her father. Birth is important. The purity of the blood that flows through your veins matters. Vasily Federov may be on the verge of becoming the most powerful man in the country. He may, as *The New York Times* commented last week, be the greatest threat to current world security, but deep down he will always be damaged.

There is a reception party waiting to greet them on the platform at Moscow's Yaroslavsky station. Not Irina's father, Vladimir Sokolov, but leaders of national far-right movements, including Russian National Unity and the Movement Against Illegal Immigration. Federov is gratified to notice also prominent figures from Austria's Freedom Party and from Italy's Lega Nord, even Vlaams Blok from Belgium.

He glances around, searching for the face he needs most of all. The one who will give most legitimacy to his push for ultimate power, the presidency of the greatest country in the world. He isn't here. Federov clenches his back teeth so hard that a muscle tics in his cheek. He has invested so much, invested everything.

'Where is he?' he hisses to Sergei Denisov. Denisov shrugs. Short and stocky with hair that has been transplanted so it sprouts from his scalp like new grass and then dyed chestnut, in stark contrast to his thick black eyebrows, Federov's right-hand man has a fleshy face into which his dark eyes are sunk like pebbles. Federov dislikes him, but he needs Denisov's reputation as a hard man and his long military record. 'The Butcher of Grozny', the Western press have dubbed

Denisov, after the atrocities committed in Chechnya under his command. But with fear comes respect, and Denisov's credentials go some way to counterbalancing the questions over Federov's own origins.

But now a buzz is building amid the crowd on the platform, and here he comes, unmistakable in his domed white headdress with the crest on the front and the golden cross on the crown. He wears flowing black robes with a heavy gold chain and is flanked on both sides by similarly robed priests. A public endorsement from the head of the Russian Orthodox Church is the single greatest boost to Federov's presidential hopes – worth the millions of dollars in charitable donations and the promise of an Orthodox Christian seat in the policy-making arm of government. As the two men shake hands, a hundred flashes go off from the assembled photographers. The photographs will be published all over the world. 'The new ultra-conservatism', the papers are calling it. Federov dislikes the term. There is nothing conservative about his vision to unite the disaffected groups on the margins of the political and social arena, not just in Russia itself but across the former Soviet states and onwards into the West, under a modern, populist, anti-immigration banner.

Does he see the irony, this Vasily Federov, Christopher Clay as was, of a man who grew up in the US saluting the Stars and Stripes, watching movies where the villains all had Russian names, now heaping the blame for all his mother country's ills on the outsiders, the incomers, the dispossessed? No, for he considers himself more Russian than those whose feet have never left Russian soil because he *chose* to come back here, to inject his vast wealth, extracted from the veins of America, into the ailing heart of America's greatest enemy. He feels himself to be Russian to the core of his being.

What he must do now is convince the Russian people of his commitment and patriotism, to allay their distrust. Which is why, after the photo opportunity at the station, he heads to the studios of Channel Rossiya, the network owned by his friend and political running mate Anatole Poletov. Or perhaps not friend, as Federov has never mastered the art of friendship, but certainly they are useful to one another and united in their zeal for the new world order they are forging.

In the make-up chair, he is uncharacteristically nervous and has to hold himself back from knocking away the arm of the make-up girl, who buzzes around him like an annoying insect. She has made him remove his glasses and he feels exposed and vulnerable, the world hidden from him behind a gauzy screen.

'Enough!' he snaps. He needs her to be gone so that he can concentrate on what he is about to say. What he is about to promise.

Under the studio lights he feels himself to be glowing, but in this he has the advantage over his opponent, Vice President Zhuravlev, who is openly perspiring. Federov feels his confidence return. The country – his country – is crying out for change. His father-in-law, Vladimir Sokolov, has allowed it to slide into chaos, too busy cosying up to the West – pipeline diplomacy that lines the pockets of the energy barons who support him – to notice his countrymen starving. There is a vacuum at the heart of Russian politics and it is this vacuum that Federov intends to fill.

But first he must prove himself to the people. And he knows exactly how he is going to do it.

The debate gets underway. They talk about domestic policies, about international threats. Federov sets forth his claim to be a modernizer but at the same time strikes a warning note about the rate of change in the country. He talks about drug use, and criminal gangs, linking them to the Uzbeks and Tajiks, and tries to turn his American upbringing to his advantage. 'I've seen first hand what the endless quest for self-fulfilment can lead to. I've seen how it can become a cancer that eats a society from the inside.' But in all this he is careful not to be too critical of the old regime, careful to pay lip service to Sokolov's achievements. This is still Russia, after all.

Sweat is dripping down Zhuravlev's forehead as he sees the momentum of the debate slipping away from him. He lashes out where his opponent is most vulnerable. 'As an outsider, perhaps you don't realize . . .' he says, and 'As an immigrant yourself . . .' Federov grinds his back teeth – his dentist will not be happy – but keeps his expression blank. He tells the camera about the town where he was found as a newborn, deep in the empty belly of Siberia. A Russian town, he says, where real Russians live. He doesn't contrast it to the

West-leaning metropolises of Moscow and St Petersburg, but the inference is there. He repeats his spiel about how he actively chose this country, in contrast to those who, born with a silver spoon in their mouths, choose to spend the wealth Russia gave them in the south of France or London or the Middle East. Here Zhuravlev, who spent seven months this year on his private island off the coast of Dubai, hooks a finger in the collar of his shirt to loosen it, which has the unfortunate effect of drawing attention to the sagging skin on his neck.

Zhuravlev feels the ground crumbling beneath him and casts around frantically for bones to throw to the people – intended tax cuts, an increase to the state pension. 'Not only do we deliver strong political leadership, we also take our job seriously as cultural custodians.' He lists the monuments his government has built. The museums they have endowed. He is building to a flourish. 'There can be no greater testament to our commitment to the cultural enrichment of our great nation than the magnificent exhibit we so recently unveiled, to international acclaim. I speak, of course, of the masterful replica – the culmination of twenty-five years of craftsmanship and at a cost of eleven million dollars – of that ultimate symbol of Russian greatness and glory, the eighth wonder of the world that was stolen from us by the Nazis six decades ago, only to vanish without trace. The incomparable Amber Room.'

As soon as the words are spoken Federov knows he has him, can taste the triumph on his tongue. Now it's time to press home his victory. 'Replica?' The scorn drips from his lips. 'How typical of this government to fob its people off with an imitation of the treasure that is rightfully ours. To show you how much I love this country – *my* country – to prove my commitment, I make the Russian people a solemn promise.' He turns so he is looking directly into the camera. 'If you give me your support, I pledge to restore to you not a replica, not a fake, an expensive imitation – but the *real* Amber Room.'

There is no studio audience, but the murmur of excitement that ripples around the television crew and the open dismay on Zhuravlev's sagging face tells Federov all he needs to know.

PART ONE

1

FOUR THOUSAND MILES FROM THE MOSCOW STUDIO WHICH IS THE scene of Vasily Federov's television triumph, at the point where northern Thailand meets Myanmar and Laos in an area of South East Asia commonly known as the Golden Triangle, a figure swings languidly in a hammock on the wooden verandah of a bamboo hut on the outskirts of Chiang Saen.

Aubrey Argylle is in his early twenties, all long limbs and broad shoulders, with clear eyes and a strong chin softened by a dimple, and dark, curly hair which he has tied back with a brown elastic band picked up that morning from the floor of the post office in town. The strands of hair that have escaped the band have ringleted with the heat. Yesterday the thermometer here passed one hundred degrees, and while today is a few degrees cooler the humidity is too high for the warm sweat to evaporate, so instead it forms a sticky coating on his skin.

One of Argylle's narrow bare feet is on the wooden floor, keeping the hammock in motion, but the rest of him is still. The notebook he was writing in just a few moments before rests face down on his stomach, the pen forgotten in his hand. He hasn't long returned from leading a small tour group on a hike up to Wat Phra That Pha Ngao, a Buddhist temple on a hilltop a few kilometres out of town. The temple itself is nothing special, but it provides a breathtaking view across the Mekong River and the mountain jungles beyond, into Laos. 'Is this it?' the tourists had asked him, straining to see in the other direction towards the rugged hills of Myanmar, although they still call it Burma. 'Are we in the Golden Triangle now?'

Argylle is used to managing the disappointment of tourists who have come here expecting to see mule trains laden with bricks of opium marching across distant mountain ridges. The opium trade that made the area notorious from the 1960s to the 1990s has now largely moved on to Afghanistan. There are still tribal gangs operating, particularly the warlords on the Myanmar side, and opium is still being funnelled from the poppy fields on the mountaintops down through Chiang Rai and Bangkok and then on to America and Hong Kong. But now the remaining traffickers tend to deal in methamphetamine, which is lucrative though it lacks the old-school glamour the tourists have come to find.

Argylle could tell them there is nothing remotely glamorous about the drug trade.

If you asked Argylle exactly how long he has been scratching a living here in this tropical backwater, he would give you a vague answer. 'A couple of years,' he might say, even though it has been more like five. He doesn't want to face up to the fact he has hit a dead end.

He knows why he came back here – in search of answers. But he has no idea why he has stayed.

He drags himself to his feet and drains his now-warm beer. Entering the hut, which consists of wooden boards laid across a wooden frame, bamboo walls and roof and glassless windows open to the muggy air, he crosses to a wooden board resting on two empty oil cans that serves as a bookshelf for a row of well-thumbed paperbacks – some standard airport fare, traded among long-stay backpackers, others more surprising. Camus, Kafka, James Baldwin. At the far end is a stack of notebooks, on top of which Argylle places the one he was writing in earlier.

Most of the notebooks are the cheap variety he buys in the town. Only the one at the very bottom is different, thick and leather-bound, with the tip of an integral satin bookmark ribbon just visible at the bottom. He doesn't have to open it to know what it says on the inside leaf: *The world is too wonderful not to write it all down.* A present from his mother, the Christmas before she died. He never even opened it, just muttered his thanks and forgot about it at the bottom of his case. Only months later, after everything that had happened, did he open it up and, smoothing out the thick, cream-coloured lined paper, begin to write – descriptions of things he's seen, little snippets of conversation. And he hasn't stopped. All these books full of words.

He is writing to her. He knows that. Writing her the world she is no longer able to see.

Argylle raises the hem of the mosquito net that hangs from a hook on the ceiling and retrieves a pair of jeans from the thin single mattress on the floor. The first time he went up into the mountains, he'd worn shorts. He hasn't made that mistake since. There's a pair of tattered old sneakers on the steps of the verandah – they don't smell so good so he keeps them outside – and he slips those on without bothering to untie the laces. A faded Johnny Cash T-shirt completes the look.

His plan is to take his motorbike north past Sop Ruak – the town where Thailand converges with Laos and Myanmar – and up into the hills. Technically, this crosses into Myanmar, still under strict military rule, but he has his cover story should he ever be stopped: a tourist guide scouting for new routes. It is not like the old days. Everywhere are signs that the region is moving on. Yet, despite the newly whitewashed image, Argylle is well aware of the dangers that still lurk here. Heroin might have given way to methamphetamine, but make no mistake, it is still a deadly trade. The rewards are staggering – billions of dollars – and so are the risks. International criminal gangs operate here in these jungles, despite the signs everywhere declaring the death penalty for anyone caught smuggling drugs. Warlords, triads – even the Russian mafia. These are not people you want to share a beer with, and it's not unheard of for a dead body to turn up, horribly mutilated. You venture on to a rival gang's turf at your peril.

And what is he really looking for, Argylle, as he scrambles his bike up the dirt track behind Sop Ruak? What takes him back into the jungle again and again, keeping him stuck in this holding pattern that is his life?

Ditching the bike, he begins his climb, following a just-detectable path through the increasingly dense undergrowth. Along with a couple of bottles of water, he has brought a small machete in his backpack, to hack back the dense vegetation. It is hot, unrewarding work, his feet kicking up red dust every step of the way. Through the canopy of the rainforest overhead, the sky is mud-yellow. Every now and then he comes to a thick whorl of barbed wire – Myanmar's attempts at demarcating its borders. He is heading for one of the Akha villages. The Akha are one of the hill tribes, displaced peoples from China or Tibet, unwelcome in any of the three countries that meet here. In the past the tribe was closely linked with the growing of opium poppies, but now they make their living from selling the artefacts they make and decorating themselves in order to pose for photographs with the tour groups that make the trek up here.

Argylle speaks Thai fluently, along with Arabic, Mandarin, Spanish, French, German and Russian, but the Akha speak a dialect all of their own and talking to them, asking his questions, is a slow process. He has the photographs of his parents in his pocket, the edges furry from handling.

But when he is still an hour's walk from the clearing where the tribe's distinctively thatched bamboo huts stand on wooden stilts above the earth, Argylle stops short.

Above the soft chirp of the frogmouth and the squeak of the emerald-green long-tailed broadbill and the call of a warbler in the high branches, above the thwacking of his sneaker soles in the dust underfoot and the cracking of dry leaves and twigs, there comes the low buzz of a light aircraft in the distance.

Immediately, Argylle is tumbling backwards through time to a tiny jungle airfield, just three or four planes, squeezed into a cockpit while his dad talks him through the instruments. The rush of adrenaline that first time the plane's wheels leave the ground, knowing it's all in his hands now. The airfields change – Brazil, the Philippines, West Africa, southern Spain, wherever his parents' import/export business takes them – but always there's a plane, and always his dad: impatient, mercurial, demanding, loving. Complicated.

Argylle steps into a clearing so that he can get a view of the plane.

Single-engined, maybe a six-seater, with a propeller on the nose and blue-and-gold markings. He has seen this plane before, on the tiny airfield in Mong Hsat across the border in Myanmar when he and his dad landed their Cessna there on a weekend jaunt.

'Is it true the CIA once ran a heroin-smuggling operation here?' one of Argylle's tour group had asked him earlier. Argylle had shrugged. It's possible, he told the group. The US wanted to keep Myanmar, Laos and Thailand free from the influence of communist China, just a few hundred kilometres away across the border. To this end, they'd backed the KMT, exiled Chinese trying to retake their country from the communists and funding their struggle with proceeds from the heroin trade. Whether the CIA was involved in that side of things, directly or indirectly, is anyone's guess but it certainly built radio masts in the area, and also helped fund that tiny airstrip, now largely disused, apart from by the odd visiting contingent from the CIA or DEA.

Argylle watches the plane track across the sky, still lost in the past. A different lifetime.

Crack! A deafening noise cuts across the peace of the jungle, causing the birds to fall silent. For a split second, the world stops, all life stilled. The small plane hovers soundlessly in the air. Then . . . the unmistakable sound of a stuttering engine.

2

AND NOW THE PLANE IS FALLING FROM THE SKY. ARGYLLE WAITS FOR the explosion, but these small planes carry little fuel so the moment of impact is muffled.

Now he is running, following the narrow plume of black smoke rising from the trees, belatedly recognizing that the crack he heard earlier wasn't an engine exploding. It was gunfire.

There aren't many gangs in this region with sufficient resources to count anti-aircraft weapons among their arsenal.

Sam Gor, aka 'The Company', is a Cantonese Chinese syndicate made up from members of five different triads and based in Myanmar's Shan State, although their reach extends beyond their territories. With a turnover reputed to run into the billions, they can afford the most sophisticated weaponry. This, paired with a legendary thirst for violence and brutality, makes them by far the most feared of the Golden Triangle cartels.

Argylle knows all about them from bitter experience. He wishes he didn't.

By the time he is approaching the crash site some thirty minutes later, Argylle is ragged from the heat, his breath torn in raw strips from his throat. If his hunch is right about The Company, and they catch him here, he won't be leaving, at least not on his own two feet. He slows his pace to pick a path stealthily through the trees, sticking to the denser vegetation, stopping to listen for signs of life.

He smells the plane before he sees it, feels the acridity of smoke in his lungs. It is burning season here in Thailand, when farmers raze their land in preparation for planting and the smoke lingers in the valleys and the trees, but this is something else.

From behind a tree, he can see two people, a man and a woman, stamping on blankets on the ground to put out the remains of the fire, and another man seated on the ground nearby clutching his head. All have smoke-blackened faces and dazed expressions. Behind them the plane is nose-deep into the undergrowth, one wing ripped off, debris strewn across the clearing. Argylle anxiously scans the surroundings but can find no sign of the gang responsible.

The woman is holding up her phone, looking for cell coverage. 'They've totalled the phone masts,' the man beside her says flatly.

'Quick, you have to get out of here.' The three battered passengers start as Argylle bursts from the trees. He tries again. 'The people who shot you down will be here any second. You have to go. Where are your guns?' Again, blank. 'Come on.' He loses patience. 'I know you guys are CIA. Where are your fucking guns?'

Finally, the woman speaks, and he notices for the first time the peculiar angle of her right arm, and how she is cradling it with the left. 'Not CIA. DEA. Charlie has a gun.'

Argylle looks at the two men, waiting to find out which one is Charlie.

'Not them,' says the woman tetchily. 'Charlie. In there.' She jerks her head towards the wreckage of the plane. 'But he's . . .' She shakes her head.

Argylle looks around. At any moment the Sam Gor could arrive. The federal agents are sitting targets. And if he's still here, he is going down with them.

What he *should* do, what any sane person would do at this point, is run, and abandon these poor schmucks to their fate.

Shit.

Although he knows this is the worst idea in the world, he runs towards the door of the plane – or rather the gaping hole where the door used to be – and swings himself inside. For a moment he stops, frozen at the sight of the pilot slumped across the dashboard, his skull caved in.

A soft moan jolts him out of his stupor. Strapped into the left-hand seat of the front row is a chubby middle-aged man he'd first assumed to be dead as well. Crouching in the cramped aisle, one eye on the window through which he can observe the three stricken DEA agents, Argylle says softly, 'Hey, Charlie. How you doing, man?' But he can see for himself exactly how Charlie is doing. See how the luggage rail has broken off and embedded itself deep in his abdomen.

There's no way he's going to make it. He notices the hilt of a gun by Charlie's hip, but getting to it means reaching around that thing in his stomach.

From the corner of his eye, he catches a movement outside, a flash of sun glinting on metal. Instinctively he ducks back into the cabin, the blood loud in his ears. Now there is shouting. A stint in Singapore as a child means he understands the voice speaking in Mandarin – 'Get down, get down' – but not the man yelling in Cantonese. A woman shrieks. Through the window he sees the three passengers from the plane lying face down in the dirt with their hands on their heads, surrounded by at least seven men, all with weapons drawn. The woman's arm is bent awkwardly underneath her. She gazes towards the plane and her eyes widen as she sees him. He puts a finger to his lips. He knows all too well what these people are capable of. Now the man speaking Cantonese yells something at a young boy, surely not more than fourteen or fifteen, gesturing in the direction of the plane, and Argylle ducks down. Have they seen him? His chest feels painfully tight, his mouth dry as dust.

The boy replies in high-pitched Mandarin. 'I'm not going in there. The whole thing stinks of gas. It's going to blow.' Argylle has already clocked the unmistakable reek of aviation fuel. He's trapped inside a tinderbox.

An argument breaks out between the boy and his boss. No prizes who'll win this one. Argylle scans around in a panic. One glance at Charlie confirms that he is now dead, his head thrown back, hands folded over the metal pole which skewers him. Behind him are two vacant seats, one on each side of the narrow aisle. And a single seat at the rear. There is nowhere to hide.

In desperation he squeezes himself into the compact space between the back seat and the rear of the plane. There is nothing to cover him, and no way that anyone walking to the back of the plane could miss him.

Through the gap in the seats, he sees the boy climb on board, his gun raised. He can see how nervous he is, his fingers shaking around the trigger guard. The smell of fuel is stronger now and the boy pulls his T-shirt over his nose to mask the stench. He hardly glances at the dead pilot with his head resting in a pool of sticky blood and brains, but when he gets to Charlie he stops. At first Argylle presumes it is shock that stalls him, but then the boy reaches down around the luggage pole and pulls out Charlie's gun. *This is it*, thinks Argylle. But the boy remains bent over the dead man, rummaging inside his clothes, finally giving a grunt of satisfaction as he straightens up, clutching a wallet which he shoves down inside the waistband of his trousers.

Outside, the man in charge is shouting. The boy, his T-shirt still covering his nose, glances wildly around the plane, his eyes coming to rest on the back of the plane. For a second Argylle is sure he will step forward – just two more paces and he will be fully visible. But then, without a beat, the boy turns and jumps from the wreckage.

Argylle sags with relief. He gets to his feet, unfolding his long legs, trying to steady his pounding heart. Through the window he sees the hostages, guns pointed at their backs, being herded into the jungle.

He squeezes down the aisle of the plane, only to hurl himself down behind Charlie's seat once more when he hears the fuselage of the plane creaking ominously.

Someone has come back.

The man who climbs on board is heavy-set, luckily for Argylle, as it is what had announced his approach. Behind the seat, he squeezes his eyes shut, waiting for the inevitable exposure.

When discovery doesn't come, he opens them again. Charlie's left arm is hanging down the side of his seat where the boy dislodged it. Argylle tries not to look at his wedding ring, tries not to think about his wife, perhaps children. There's a crack in between the arm and the seat through which he can see the thick-set man still standing in the nose of the plane where he boarded. He is leaning over the dead pilot to wrench something from the dashboard, a small, square black box with an antenna protruding from the top that Argylle recognizes immediately as the plane's transponder.

The portable transponder will be encoded with the aircraft's unique squawk code, so air-traffic controllers can track its radar signal and ensure it doesn't crash into anything else. The man fiddles with the knob and Argylle, after all those hours spent flying with his dad, knows he will be turning the mechanism off so that it can no longer transmit signals that might give away its location.

Now the man glances over at Charlie, and Argylle feels queasy, guessing that, like the boy, he will be thinking about the wallet Charlie will most likely be carrying in his inside pocket. If he takes another step in this direction, Argylle is finished.

A shout comes from outside, but still the man doesn't move. The moment seems to stretch on for ever, the man's eyes hard and black and staring right at the spot where Argylle crouches. Then a second, louder shout jolts him into a decision and he turns, muttering, to drop heavily from the plane.

The relief is so tangible Argylle can taste it.

Once the group has gone from the clearing, the men using their guns to prod the Americans ahead of them, Argylle makes his way to the front of the plane. He should leave. Run in the opposite direction. He knows the CIA will have been tracking the plane so back-up is probably on its way right now.

He also knows that by the time they arrive, it will be too late. The jungles around here are dense, and only one side knows its way around.

It isn't his problem. He doesn't owe these people anything.

He pictures the woman lying on the ground with her broken arm bent underneath her and one tear trickling down her cheek.

He picks up the transponder.

3

FRANCES COFFEY TAKES A LONG, UNSATISFYING DRAG ON HER nicotine inhaler. Whoever decided a plastic tube was a good substitute for cigarettes had clearly never been a smoker.

I am a person who doesn't smoke, Coffey reminds herself, as her therapist has instructed her. *I am a person who doesn't smoke . . . but I would really kill for a Marlboro Light.*

'Tell me again exactly when we lost signal?'

Mike Randall turns back to his monitor. 'That'd be six minutes ago . . . seven now.'

'What the hell happened out there?'

Randall shrugs and darts a look across at his colleague and buddy Agent Joe Quintano. Privately, they've both admitted that, despite their combined twenty-one years of experience in the Agency, sometimes the boss makes them feel like they're back in class, trying to cover up the fact they don't know the answer. It's something about the combination of her encyclopaedic knowledge from years of working the archives and an acute emotional intelligence that makes her able to second-guess how players in any given scenario might react.

'It took off from Mong Hsat as scheduled. One minute it was tracking along as normal, and the next it was falling from the sky.'

'Accident?'

'Possible,' says Quintano, tapping his fingers against his chin. 'Engine failure, perhaps. But –'

'– why did the transponder suddenly cut off after the plane came down?'

In the clandestine CIA headquarters beneath an agricultural chemicals plant in rural Delaware, Frances Coffey, the CIA's Chief Operating Officer – five feet four with a neat brown bob and tortoiseshell glasses and a way of fixing a person with her soft grey eyes that makes them want to do better, *be better* – pulls hard on her plastic cigarette again.

'I think we have to assume it was brought down deliberately,' says Randall.

'Do we know what syndicates operate in that region?'

Quintano turns to his computer and keys in some commands.

'It doesn't look good, boss,' he says, his expression grim.

Coffey steps forward to look at his screen. Her face, always pale, noticeably blanches.

'Who?' asks Randall.

'Sam Gor,' Quintano replies. 'The Company. Their top man, Tse Chi Lop, makes Pablo Escobar look like Mary Poppins.'

'And you think that's who the DEA were scoping out?'

Coffey nods. 'Must be. I don't need to tell you we're in the grip of a methamphetamine epidemic here in the US and most of that meth is cooked up in overseas labs headed by syndicates like—'

'Sam Gor,' says Randall. 'I get you. So you think this Tse took down our plane because the DEA were asking too many questions?'

Coffey nods. 'Looks that way.'

The three of them fall silent, imagining what this means. Then Coffey squints at something beeping on the screen through her varifocal lenses.

'What's happening?'

Quintano swings around.

'What the— The transponder is back on. The plane appears to be moving.'

'Flying?' The only outward signs of Coffey's excitement are the bloodless knuckles on the hand gripping the back of Quintano's chair.

Quintano shakes his head.

'But you said the plane was moving?'

'It is, but . . .'

'But?'

'It's moving as if it's . . . *walking*, ma'am.'

Coffey's mind whirs, working out the possibilities. Absently, she reaches into her jacket pocket for her cigarette pack, sighing when her fingers encounter only empty space.

I am a non-smoker, she reminds herself as she follows the progress of the blipping signal across the screen.

What the hell is going on?

4

DEEP IN THE TREACHEROUS JUNGLE OF SHAN STATE ON THE WRONG side of the Myanmar border, Argylle is tracking the hostage group while holding the transponder tucked under his arm.

After five years in this part of the world, Argylle is used to the terrain and the insects and the heat that sits on your skin. The air is always thick in February and March, when a combination of forest fires and farmers burning the dregs of the last harvest to prepare for a new crop sends pollution levels spiking, and his body feels as if every single cell wants to shut down. He is used to the dense vegetation that requires him to stop every few metres to hack at it with his machete, but not when he is trying to be silent, carrying a black box that, while smaller than a shoebox, is nonetheless heavy and slippery in the sweltering heat.

This area is new to him, one of the uncharted swathes that would have his Thai friends pointing at the map and shaking their heads in warning.

You don't wander around in these parts. You don't take photographs.

This is where the drugs labs are, run by gangs who have their own militias. The authorities tend to turn a blind eye in exchange for military back-up and a cut of the profit.

Argylle knows that if he is discovered here he will most likely end up one of the many disappeared – people who stray too far into the grey area of the map, and are never heard from again. Or who turn up in pieces. An image comes to him. Two coffins, side by side. He bats it away.

What is he doing here, risking his life for a group of strangers? He can't answer. All he knows is that for the last five years he has felt as though he has been living in a padded room where nothing quite reaches him, numb to what is happening around him. But now, in this very moment, he is finally alive.

The trees ahead are thinning out, and he slows before a clearing in the jungle, where he can just make out a knot of people in front of some kind of building. He hears a lot of shouting and feels the prickle of fear as the full danger of his situation becomes clear. If this is a lab that the gang have brought the hostages to, no one's getting out of here alive. There's too much at stake. If his transponder gamble has worked and CIA back-up is on its way, they will be walking into a death trap.

He looks around, assessing his situation, until he spots a gnarly old tea tree which would give him a vantage point. Hiding the transponder in the undergrowth, he hoists himself up the rough, spiky trunk, sending out silent thanks for the jeans that protect his thighs from being torn to shreds. His hands are not so lucky, and by the time he reaches the upper branches his palms are scratched and bleeding, but he still can't quite see into the clearing from where the voices are coming. Lying almost flat, he inches along the branch ahead of him, praying it will take his weight. There's a moment where it dips alarmingly under him and he feels sure it will break. His stomach lurches but, incredibly, the branch remains intact.

From halfway along, he has a view over the top of the tree in front of the clearing. Relief floods through him as he sees not the tell-tale signs of an industrial lab but a handful of ragged huts, a makeshift camp.

The hostages have been made to sit on the ground while the armed gang members talk excitedly with three others who have emerged from the huts. The DEA agent who'd been on the ground when Argylle first arrived is in a bad way. As Argylle watches, he topples so that he is lying on his side. The gang members laugh. The boy who'd seemed so young and nervous when he stole Charlie's wallet in the plane earlier swaggers over and casually kicks him in the stomach.

The woman, still holding her arm gingerly, looks away.

Some of the drugs cartels in the area don't want any trouble. Some of them, realizing that the US government is tracking their organization, might have set up shop elsewhere.

Not these guys.

Argylle knows to his cost what this group does to people they think are encroaching on their patch.

He glances down to the undergrowth that conceals the transponder and fights off a wave of despair. His plan seems now to be a long shot, dependent on the CIA tracking the plane and the signal being reliably transmitted.

The gang members, he sees now, are a motley bunch. Several are missing teeth, their skin angry and ravaged with sores, their eyes wide and wild. They definitely didn't get the 'don't get high on your own supply' memo. Though most of the drugs manufactured in this region get shipped out, enough remain in local circulation for Argylle to recognize the signs of meth addiction. The bad news is that meth addicts are notoriously unpredictable and prone to bouts of extreme violence when they're on a comedown.

He looks at the boy, his adolescent skin marred by acne and drug use, and feels an unexpected surge of pity and hopelessness at what lies ahead for him.

The man on the ground moans, and the other male DEA agent, who has a beard and a distinctive white patch in his dark hair, turns to a short, squat man who is clearly the leader of this group. 'He needs help,' he says, gesturing. The other man nods, then walks over and calmly shoots the prone American in the head.

Oh shit. Oh God.

Argylle shuts his eyes to dispel the image. When he opens them again, he sees the woman has been sprayed with her colleague's blood and has some grey gunk caught in her hair and on her clothes.

Again he glances at the low bush where the transponder is hidden. It seems increasingly likely that no one is coming. Could the transponder have run out of power? A crushing dejection comes over him. Yet he cannot bring himself to turn and walk away.

Minutes pass. As Argylle steels himself for the bloodbath he feels sure is coming he hears a faint rustle in the undergrowth immediately below his vantage point. To his astonishment he sees that the ground beneath his tree is crawling with camouflaged figures edging towards the clearing, clutching assault carbines. One of them holds the transponder, recently liberated from its hiding place.

Judging by the sweat running down their faces, they've already trekked some distance. He looks around for a way to alert them to his presence, not wanting to surprise them.

The leaves of the tea tree in which he is sitting are bigger than a man's hand. Edging backwards along the branch, Argylle tears one off and drops it on to the head of the man directly below. Instantly he has several guns pointing up at him, and he raises his hands to show he isn't armed. He points to the transponder then at himself. The man nods. All this time the voices of the gang have been a low hum, but now a bark of laughter comes from beyond the trees. 'How far?' mouths the commander.

Argylle points to where he can just about see the tops of the huts and holds up both his hands, pulsing twice. 'Twenty metres?' the commander mouths. He points at two of his men and signs an instruction that Argylle doesn't understand. They nod, and one of them withdraws a grenade from a pouch in his army-issue jacket.

The commander makes a circling motion with his hand and the men disappear silently into the undergrowth. He sends another group in the other direction. Unlike the commander, the men look Thai. Argylle wonders where they came from, remembers the rumours of an off-radar 'black' prison somewhere in the Thai jungle where the Americans take any prisoners they want to interrogate, out of sight of the world's watchful eyes.

Now the commander beckons Argylle down and points behind him. Argylle shimmies down and takes a few steps back. His heart is in his mouth. He knows the hostage-takers from the plane are armed, but the rest of the gang don't seem to be. Why would they be, all the way up here, with nothing to guard other than a few huts and canvas tents? With the element of surprise, the newcomers might just be able to take them. But they have one chance only. If the gang have time to arm themselves it will be carnage.

Even though he is expecting it, the explosion from the far side of the camp, closely followed by a second explosion from the other direction, sends a jolt of shock through Argylle. Sometime in the split second between the two blasts, the rescuers charge forward. After that, everything is a blur of shouting and gunfire. Argylle hates feeling useless but knows he'd be more of a hindrance than a help, so he conceals himself at a distance and waits, every cell of his body tensed.

It seems as if the fighting goes on for hours, although it can only be a matter of minutes. From his position well back from the action, Argylle hears a man shouting something in Cantonese that is cut short by a loud crack that sends the leaves of the trees quivering.

Finally, through the trees comes the male hostage from the plane, the DEA agent with his dark beard and the white patch in his hair, and close behind him is the woman, still clutching her arm. And now come the rest of the rescuer group, two dragging between them the slumped form of the murdered DEA agent. From his hiding place, Argylle wills them to hurry. The explosions will have alerted the rest of the cartel and he definitely doesn't want to be around when they arrive.

Argylle keeps himself hidden behind a tree, even though he sees the commander casting around him and knows he is wondering where he is. As soon as he is sure the group are headed in the right direction, he slips away, melting back into the jungle.

He has his reasons for wanting to stay lost.

5

One year before Federov's promise to the Russian people

IN PRIVATE, FEDEROV'S INNER CIRCLE REFER TO HIM AS THE BLACK Hole, in reference to how he absorbs everything around him – light, life, information. That endless gap between you telling him something and him reacting, where it feels as if he might suck the very marrow from your bones through his flat, dead eyes.

So his secretary shouldn't be surprised, when she passes on the message that his biological father is dead, that his face remains as smooth and blank as soap. And yet still it takes her aback. This lack of human response.

The half-sister Federov has never met called his office to let him know the news. His two half-brothers do not know she is doing it, would not approve, but she thinks it's only right. It's out of the question for him to come to the funeral, but perhaps he would like to visit the home where she nursed her father through his final years.

So it is that Vasily Federov finds himself waiting outside a door on the fourth floor of a well-kept apartment block in the Moscow suburbs. He has been here once before, as a teenager, still hopeful even after a bruising rejection from his birth mother. Though young, he'd already shown signs of the entrepreneurship which would eventually make him a billionaire, buying up broken word processors – the early precursors to computers – fixing them and selling them on to his

Midwestern neighbours. With his earnings he'd paid a private investigator to track down his birth parents and then bought himself a return plane ticket. As soon as he'd landed in Russia he'd begun calling himself Vasily Federov after his father, shaking off the miserable childhood of Christopher Clay. But things hadn't gone exactly to plan.

His mother, now a jaundiced alcoholic living in squalor on the thirteenth floor of an elevatorless housing estate in Novosibirsk, had blocked the doorway and called him a 'fucking liar'. Her hair was thin and greasy, but her eyes, the whites turned the colour of morning piss, looked afraid. A man with curd-like flecks in the corners of his mouth, his cheeks etched with livid purple veins, had shuffled into the hallway behind her wearing a greying vest that didn't quite cover his belly. 'Who the fuck is that?' he'd asked. 'No one,' she'd replied, slamming the door.

He'd locked that memory away and buried it so far inside himself no one would ever find it.

Even so, he'd thought he might have more luck with his father. He'd learned from his investigator that his father was a married KGB officer temporarily stationed in Siberia to oversee the Siblag correctional labour camp, part of the Western Siberian Gulag, when he'd had a brief affair with the young woman who came in at 6 a.m. to clean the camp offices. When he'd been transferred back to Moscow, he hadn't even known she was pregnant, and when she tracked him down months later, asking for money, he denied the baby was even his.

But he'd been a younger man then, with a wife and three children of his own. Now his wife had been dead five years from breast cancer and the children were grown. He lived in this respectable apartment block on a disability pension from the government, owing to an injury he'd sustained in Afghanistan. He had nothing to lose by acknowledging this long-lost son.

After his humiliating experience with his mother, Federov had played things differently this time, writing to his father first to alert him to his existence and his wish to meet, assuring him he wanted nothing from him. His spirits had soared when he'd received a one-line reply inviting him to visit. But when his father had opened the door, he wasn't smiling.

'I just wanted to take a look at you,' he said, once he had grudgingly allowed him into his overheated, overfurnished living room, his mean eyes raking up and down Federov's lanky teenage body. 'And now I have, I can see you're no son of mine.'

Federov, sitting on the edge of an uncomfortably upright armchair, held his nerve as he looked into his father's face that was also his face – curiously flat, its features making little impact. 'I'm your son.'

His father shook his head. 'I have two sons. One is in the army, fighting for his country; the other is a policeman. Those are Federov men. You are nothing like them.'

Federov had cast around the stuffy room, taking in the family photographs on the sideboard, the medals in a glass-fronted cabinet, the brown patterned carpet that clashed with the floral wallpaper. There was a Persian-style rug hanging on the wall in pride of place, and the windows were festooned with nets. His gaze had alighted on a glass-topped side table, covered in a lace cloth, on which a notebook lay open, the visible page half filled with small, neat writing and a pen laid across it, as if someone had been disturbed mid-sentence.

'You're working on something?' he said, trying to spark a conversation.

'I am carrying out vitally important research.'

'Into what?'

'Into something that will make the name Federov known across Russia, the ultimate legacy to the motherland.'

'But what is it?'

His father's expression had closed up, as if a shutter had come down.

'You think I'm going to share my life's work with a stranger?'

By this stage, Federov should have been used to rejection, yet that word 'stranger' sent a splinter into his heart that could never be removed. As Federov was leaving, a young woman had appeared from a room along the corridor, starting when she saw him as if she'd seen a ghost.

'Go back into your room, Yelena,' his father had ordered.

That was twenty years ago. And now here he is again, outside that same door on the fourth floor, where he had vowed never to set foot again.

'I'm sorry,' says Yelena Federova, his half-sister, who must now be in her forties but looks two decades older. 'I knew you were my father's son as soon as I saw you all those years ago. My father wouldn't talk about it. He turned off the television every time you came on. He was ashamed.'

'Of me?'

'Of himself.'

They stare awkwardly at one another, hoping for a spark of connection, but there is none.

'I'm afraid you cannot stay long. My brother Dmitri will be here shortly.'

Federov looks around.

'Where did our . . . your . . . father spend most of his time?'

Yelena gives a mirthless laugh. 'That's easy. In his study. He practically lived in that room by the end.'

'Can I?'

Federov smiles as if unseen fingers are stretching out the corners of his mouth against his will, and an icy chill flutters across Yelena Federova's chest. She can see he is his father's son all right, and that disturbs her. Her life with her father was not easy.

The study is a small, airless room, containing a polished wood desk, piled high with files, and a glass-fronted cabinet filled with carefully labelled boxes. There's a sepia-tinted photograph on the wall which he recognizes as Tsar Nicholas II with his family. The moustachioed tsar is posing next to his wife wearing a brass-buttoned uniform and is surrounded by his daughters, all white dresses and long hair and ribbons. None of them with any clue what horror lies ahead.

Federov sits down at the desk in front of two more photographs, in silver frames. The first shows his father flanked by a pair of broad-shouldered men who share his small eyes and square chin. In the second he is far younger than Federov is now, standing with a group of men in uniform outside an austere-looking building.

'He was in the army after the war and then joined the KGB at the beginning, rising to Lieutenant Colonel. As he spoke fluent German, he was part of the taskforce who tracked down and interrogated Nazis who'd committed war crimes against the Soviet Union.' Yelena

Federova is standing in the doorway. A note of pride has crept into her voice.

'Did he talk about his work?' Federov has picked up the nearest file and is flicking through what seems to be a wad of genealogists' reports on various women purporting to be Anastasia Romanov, long rumoured to have escaped the massacre that killed the rest of her family.

'Sometimes, particularly when he had had a drink. But only to me. We lived together for many years.'

'You were close, then?'

'You don't get close to a man like Papa, but we kept each other company.' Yelena glances at the plastic clock on the wall. 'Will you be long here? Only you need to be gone by the time Dmitri comes.'

'Not long,' says Federov, opening up another file. 'I only want to get a sense of who he was. You know he told me, that time I was here before, that he was working on something of great importance.'

Yelena rolls her eyes.

'Why doesn't that surprise me? Well, it's all there.' Her pale eyes flick towards the stack of files. 'The great quest that was going to write his name in the history books.'

There's little warmth in her voice.

'And what was it? This great quest?'

'Our father thought he would succeed where hundreds of people and scores of government agencies have failed and find the thing that's been missing for decades.

'He thought he could bring us back the Amber Room.

'I really think you ought to leave now. Dmitri is on his way.' Yelena Federova has been lurking in the doorway, growing ever more agitated, but her new-found half-brother is in no hurry.

'Don't worry about me. My security guards are outside.'

Yelena doesn't tell him that it's not *his* safety that concerns her. Dmitri too is not an easy man.

'What's that you're reading?'

Vasily Federov is engrossed in a printed document, several pages thick, and a flicker of irritation crosses his face at being disturbed, but he doesn't look up.

'A transcript.'

Yelena nods. 'Ah yes. Rudolf Naumann. One of the top-ranking Nazis, responsible for all the rare art and antiquities the thieving Germans stole during the war. It was he who started Papa's whole obsession with the Amber Room. Papa interrogated Naumann nine years after the end of the war. Because he shared a surname with two other SS officers the Allies mistakenly thought he was accounted for and he managed to evade capture for all that time, but he was finally traced to Austria.

'Papa had his . . . *techniques* . . . for getting people to talk, and Naumann, by all accounts, didn't put up much resistance. Through his information they recovered a Leonardo da Vinci no one had ever thought they'd see again.' Again that note of pride. 'So why not the Amber Room?'

Federov is leafing impatiently through the transcript.

'They were getting there. See where he talks about moving crates in the dead of night, and about his excitement when they reassembled it? The part where he says that thing about how standing in the room was like being close to God?'

'Yes, but *where* was the room? Why isn't that in here?'

'Because he died. Naumann. Heart attack. Just as he was about to tell them the name of the place. That happened sometimes during the questioning. Papa didn't always know when to stop.'

She gazes pointedly at Federov as if waiting for him to ask her more, but he doesn't.

'But your father must have researched Naumann, surely? To find out where he was based during the war.'

'Of course. Except he wasn't based anywhere. He travelled around Europe to every place the Germans occupied, making lists of stolen art, deciding what to send to the private galleries and collections, what was degenerate and needed to be destroyed. He could have been talking about any one of them.'

'Why does it say "pause", here and here and, again, here?'

'He was rambling. Well, no wonder. Afterwards, they discovered he was riddled with a dirty disease. *Syphilis.*' She whispers the last word. 'So they put in "pause" whenever he started talking about something irrelevant. He kept saying a woman's name, apparently, over and over. Maybe that's who gave him the clap.'

'Can you remember the name?'

'It's in there somewhere. After he became fixated on the Amber Room, Papa wrote it down. Turned out to be a French actress, but she died a long time ago.'

Federov is scanning the margins of the typewritten pages, stopping when he comes to a handwritten note.

'Nathalie Chabert? Is that it?'

Yelena shrugs. She has again grown agitated, glancing more and more often at the clock.

'Probably. Now you really must leave.'

For a moment, Yelena Federova thinks that this stranger, her half-brother who shares the face of the father who made her life a living hell, will refuse to go. She had hoped that inviting him here might be a new start for her. He is rich. He is family. But the longer he stays, the more she wants him gone. Not just because of Dmitri but because of how the air in the apartment feels now he is in it, close and sticky and hard to breathe.

She is relieved when he gets to his feet, but in the narrow hallway, he hesitates.

'What else?' he asks.

'I don't understand.'

'The pauses. What else was in them?'

'Nothing, just the name. Nathalie whatever her name was. You wrote it down.'

'There must have been something more.'

'No, I—'

'Think!' It is the first time he has raised his flat, soft voice and it startles her.

'The name. That's all. Oh' – something else comes to her – 'he did say another strange thing. *Bracelet.*'

'Bracelet? What bracelet?'

'That's all. Just the name and the word "bracelet". Now, please, you must go.'

37

6

'SO WHAT CAN YOU TELL ME ABOUT THIS GUY? APART FROM THE fact that he disappeared off the face of the planet after saving two of our operatives' lives?'

When Frances Coffey asks you a question, she does it in so benign a fashion, her eyes myopically large behind her glasses, an encouraging lift at the corner of her mouth, that you might imagine yourself to be having a conversation, might even decide there is no imperative on you to get it right, or even to answer at all.

That would be a mistake.

Coffey could not have hauled herself to the top of this male bastion – battling every rung of the way from the archives where she began, possessed of neither influence nor beauty, just an unshakable belief in doing the right thing – without a core of steel running through her beneath the nondescript navy-blue jacket and trousers and the sensible low-heeled, rubber-soled shoes.

Mike Randall has learned the hard way not to underestimate the boss. He has seen people think they can get away with just showing up and turning on the charm, only to find themselves heading the wrong way down the CIA ladder.

He has also learned what satisfaction there is to be gained by winning her respect. The little nod she gives at a job well done. Right now he is sitting on the edge of his seat, knowing that the answer to this particular question is explosive.

'It's a weird story, boss.' He can't hide the thrill of excitement in his voice at what his research has uncovered. 'For a start, we're not sure Argylle is actually his name. His parents had a ton of aliases – Derwent, Nielsen, Buckley. Unfortunately for him, it seems like Aubrey *is* his actual first name. Who'd do that to a kid?'

'Perhaps they were Aubrey Beardsley fans?' suggests Coffey. She is met by a blank look.

'The fact is they were big-time dope smugglers,' Randall presses on. 'The DEA has a folder as thick as your arm on them. Originally from California, they dragged the kid all around the world – Africa, Asia, South America, Europe. By all accounts, they were a pretty tight family, devoted to each other, and even though the boy hardly had any formal schooling he was super-bright. He speaks six or seven languages fluently.'

'And yet he's ended up living in a north Thailand backwater.'

'That would seem to be the case, boss. His parents died there five years ago, when the boy was seventeen, probably killed by the Sam Gor, ironically enough. By then they'd packed him off to some ritzy boarding school in England, which he hated, from what we've been able to gather.'

'Did he know where the money came from?'

Randall shakes his head. 'Not at the time. Their cover story was that they were in the import/export business, textiles mostly – and we believe that's what they told the boy too. That's how they explained why his dad had his own small plane, and why they kept moving around so much.'

Coffey nods. 'And I guess when he got old enough to start asking questions, they shipped him off to school.'

'I feel sorry for the kid. It's clearly screwed him up. Well, that and being called Aubrey.'

Coffey looks thoughtful.

'And yet this *damaged* young man put himself in danger to save the very people who hounded his parents. *And* had the ingenuity to use a mobile airplane transponder to lead us to the cartel.'

Randall doesn't like the way Coffey is looking at him, her eyebrows raised over the top of her glasses, as if they are both sharing the same thought and, furthermore, find themselves in full agreement on it. When she opens her mouth to speak, he knows what she is about to say even before the words come from her mouth.

'I think we should have a little chat with young Mr Argylle.'

7

ARGYLLE IS IN THE BAR.

The Bar has a Thai name, but Argylle and his friends just call it The Bar. It seems to work pretty well. Unlike the smarter tourist places along the banks of the Mekong, The Bar is hidden down a side street at the back of town, serving locals and the odd back-packer who wanders in, drawn by the pool table in the centre and the bamboo bar with red vinyl stools, and the Formica tables where the girls from the massage parlour take a break, nursing their sodas without being hassled. The lighting is dim – two low-hanging lamps over the pool table and strings of red-and-blue fairy lights stuck to the ceiling and woven around the bamboo posts of the bar. The walls are lined with cardboard egg boxes in a half-hearted attempt at soundproofing, broken up by tourism posters of Thai beaches and temples, framed by red-and-green tinsel left over from a long-past Christmas. There are two plastic fans on each side of the pool table, blasting out cooler air on rotation, and postcards Blu-tacked over the bar from past regulars, beneath which Paitoon, the barman, perches on a stool, engrossed in whatever soap opera is playing on the small television screen in the corner.

Tonight Argylle is at the pool table with his friend Somchai, who teaches English in the local high school, sending money back to his family in their home village, hundreds of kilometres away. The two have developed a routine where they meet every evening at 8 p.m.

and play for a couple of hours, with Somchai speaking in English and Argylle responding in Thai. Their life experiences have been very different, but they're both looking to re-create some sense of home.

It is six days since the plane was shot down and already it has begun to seem to Argylle like something he hallucinated after drinking too much of Paitoon's 'special' hooch.

Chiang Saen is a small, sleepy town, but because of its position nine kilometres from the Golden Triangle, where the borders of Thailand, Laos and Myanmar converge, and its views across the mighty Mekong into Laos, it has its share of tourists. Many of these are on organized tours, but it also attracts lone backpackers, fresh from the party beaches in the south, looking for adventure and drawn by Myanmar's tantalizingly closed borders and the glorifying Golden Triangle mythology.

Tonight, one such individual comes through the door. On first glance he appears four or five years older than Argylle, broad-shouldered in a loose-fitting cotton shirt that is faded blue and in need of a wash. Beneath a close-shaven head, his skin is the regulation nut-brown of the long-term Thai tourist, his jaw uncompromisingly square. In a country where five feet nine is considered tall, the newcomer towers above most people in the bar. Argylle at six feet one is used to feeling like an ungainly giant, but he judges the man to be at least on a level with him and, now he looks closer, built like a tank.

Leaning over the pool table to take a shot, Argylle pauses to watch the imposing stranger cross to the bar, passing the table where four girls from the massage parlour are grouped. The girls are in their work uniform. What there is of it. Like Somchai, they are here to earn money to send home to their villages, but without the benefits of education they are more limited in their choice of career.

The newcomer barely glances at the women, his gaze sliding over them as if they are slicked with oil.

Interesting, thinks Argylle, sending his ball into the pocket.

'How about a game when you guys are done?' Having bought a beer, the stranger has wasted no time in coming over.

Argylle and Somchai exchange a shrug. 'Sure,' says Argylle.

'My name's Scott. Scott Novak.' The man's hand, when Argylle shakes it, is the size of a baseball mitt.

The first game goes to Argylle, who knows just how to compensate for the dip in the table. The next four games in a row go to Novak.

Competitive, thinks Argylle, despite his laid-back schtick.

Somchai heads out. He has to get up early for school in the morning. So now it is just Argylle and the big man. By this point they have switched from beer to spirits. Argylle is drinking Mekhong, a Thai drink that purports to be whisky but tastes like rough rum. He declines to join Novak in ordering the imported premium brand Johnnie Walker. Not just because it's twice the price but also because he happens to know that Paitoon mixes it with something else out the back. It is not for the faint-hearted. Novak looks like he can take it, but still Argylle feels duty-bound to warn him. 'That isn't the same stuff you're used to back home.' Novak smiles. 'Dude, do I look like a guy who can't handle his drink?'

He is so sure of himself.

Seated on the vinyl stools, they fall into wary conversation. Novak describes how his fiancée dumped him for his best friend so he used the money he'd saved for the wedding to take the trip of a lifetime. For the last two years he has travelled all over southern Asia. India, Indonesia, Cambodia, Vietnam. By now he is slurring a little, and he gets out his passport to remind himself where he's been, flicking through the various visas. 'Full Moon party, Koh Pha-ngan. Man, that was a trip. PADI Master dive course on the beach in Vietnam.'

Argylle, a few drinks behind his new friend, finds his attention snagged by one of the visas, but says nothing. Novak ploughs on.

Argylle is used to travellers who list the places they've visited, like entries on a spreadsheet. 'I did Malaysia,' they tell him. 'I've done India and most of Africa too.' They want him to be impressed and take issue when he isn't. But Novak isn't like that.

Novak wants to know about Argylle's story. How did he end up here? (Argylle wishes he knew.) What happened to his parents? (Argylle often wishes he didn't know as much as he does.) What are his long-term plans? (To get to the end of the night, and wake up

43

tomorrow and get to the end of that too.) Argylle doesn't say any of this. Instead he is friendly, but dodges the questions. It's something he learned very early on. 'Family business stays in the family' was a motto while he was growing up.

'Textiles export?' Novak says. 'That sounds cool. It must have been tough, though, being dragged all around the world.'

'I got used to it,' Argylle says. He doesn't feel like telling this entitled American anything real, like how, rather than resent the endless moves, he came to love that feeling of waking up somewhere completely new. The thrill of exploring a different neighbourhood, listening to the sounds of a language that was completely alien to him, challenging himself to pick out repeated words, starting with 'yes' and 'no' and then going wider.

One of the girls gets up from the table in the corner and walks over to them. She is beautiful, with long, black, shiny hair that she wears in a high ponytail that swings when she moves and a strapless figure-hugging dress over a narrow, graceful body.

Novak tenses.

'Don't worry, I'll get this,' he says, putting himself between Argylle and the girl. Standing at his full height, he dwarfs the slight figure in front of him.

'Sorry, sweetheart. Not now. My buddy and I are having a private conversation.'

The girl gazes up at him contemptuously from her wide brown eyes. Then she pushes past him.

'Argylle. You lend me your phone again, please. The street phone is kaput and I need to call my honey.'

Somchai isn't the only one in this town who uses Argylle for English practice.

'Sure, Ning.'

He digs in the pocket of his shorts, finds his flip phone and hands it over.

Novak stares after her, incredulous, as she leaves the bar. 'Look, bud, what you do with your money is your own business, but cell-phone calls can't be cheap in a place like this. You seriously gonna let a hooker go off with your phone to call her boyfriend?'

'You're right, it isn't your business,' says Argylle smoothly. 'And it's not her boyfriend, it's her son. He's two years old and he lives with Ning's mother, four hours' drive from here. Ning sends all the money she makes here back to them.'

'She doesn't look old enough to have a child.'

'She claims to be nineteen, which means she's probably at least two years younger.'

Novak has the grace to look shamefaced. And when Ning comes back in with Argylle's phone he presses a ten-dollar bill into her hand. 'For your honey,' he mumbles.

'Paitoon, another double for my friend here,' says Argylle.

Argylle doesn't know what exactly Paitoon mixes in with the premium-brand bottles, but by the time the bar closes up Novak is almost incoherent.

'Let's get you home, *buddy*,' Argylle says. This is a bigger ask than it sounds. Novak is built like a truck. Luckily, 'home' turns out to be close by, a guesthouse on Sleeping Buddha Road – that's not its real name, just what Argylle calls it, owing to the vast recumbent stone figure that dominates one section of the otherwise residential street. It's what he loves about this place – the way roadside bars butt up against ancient temples and market stalls spring up among the palm trees and the statues.

His new friend has a room in a guesthouse that backs on to the river with its own small porch adjacent to the road. Inside there's a bed against the wall and a square television mounted inside a metal cage so it can't be stolen. There's an open rucksack on the gaudily tiled floor stuffed with defiantly unfolded clothes.

Argylle deposits Novak on the bed, his shoulder creaking in relief.

'Maybe ease off the protein shakes,' he mutters.

Six hours later, Argylle awakes on the porch to a stray dog sniffing at his neck. He stretches out his complaining limbs. Though he'd brought the thin cushions from his own porch to sleep on, they were no match for the damp heat rising through the wooden boards and he feels stiff and achy.

'What the *fuck*?'

The sound echoes down the deserted street, momentarily silencing the chickens in a nearby yard.

'What the actual *fuck*?'

This Novak sounds very different to the one who'd tried to buddy up to him in the bar last night.

The door bursts open and there's his new friend, with a shiny, pink bedspread fetchingly wrapped around his bulky frame. 'Where are my fricking clothes?'

'I took them back to my place for safekeeping.'

'Well, you can bring them the hell back.'

'I certainly will. Just as soon as you tell me who you are and what you want.'

Novak glowers at him. Up close, Argylle can see the toll Paitoon's 'special edition' Johnnie Walker has taken in the livid semicircles under his eyes and the greenish tinge to his skin.

'I don't know what you're talking about. And you can tell your little pal behind the bar that I hope he has insurance, because he's gonna need it when I send the health-and-safety inspectors round. He can't go around poisoning people. Just wait until I pay him a little visit . . .'

Argylle moves aside to let Novak through the steps on to the street.

'Be my guest. Only I should say the Thais are pretty hot on public decency. There are holy temples all over the place here, and if you're caught out near one of those dressed like that . . . Plus, I feel it's only right to tell you it's illegal in Thailand to go out without underwear and, while I don't want to presume, I'm fairly sure you're commando under that fetching pink skirt.'

Novak steps towards him at the same moment as the screen door of the neighbouring room opens and a young Thai couple emerges, smiling and pressing their hands together in the traditional *wai* greeting. The woman's smile falters when she catches sight of the hulking figure in the pink satin bedspread.

After they've gone, Novak sits down heavily on the step.

'What do you want?'

'I told you. I want to know who you are.'

'My name's Scott Novak, I'm a—'

'Who you *really* are. And don't show me that fake passport. Maybe you don't know that foreigners like me have to leave the country every ninety days to extend our tourist visas. Normally, I go to Vietnam, so I'm very familiar with what a Vietnamese visa stamp looks like now, and what it looked like two years ago when you say you did your PADI course. Did you know they changed the design? I'm guessing not or you wouldn't be claiming the current stamp is what got you over the border back then.'

'So, I got my dates wrong. Dude, the stuff that barman was giving me, I'm surprised I remembered my name.'

'*Semper Fi.*'

'I beg your pardon?'

'*Semper Fi.* It's engraved on the back of that silver signet ring in the pocket of your rucksack.'

Novak springs up. 'Have you gone through my stuff? That is seriously uncool, man. I hope you get along with your little barman buddy, because the two of you are gonna be getting on intimate terms in that jail cell.'

In his state of animation, the big guy has loosened the grip on his bedspread and Argylle turns discreetly away, addressing his next remarks to the dog, which has reappeared in search of food.

'*Semper Fi* is the motto of the US Marines, as I'm sure I don't need to tell you, especially not as you used to have it tattooed across the top of your left butt cheek, I believe.' He gestures to a patch of skin where the silvery ghost letters of the Marines' motto are still just about visible. 'Funny how you forgot to mention that part while you were telling me your life story in the bar last night. So I'll ask you again. Who are you? DEA or CIA? Take your time. I've got all day.'

8

'SO LET'S GET THIS STRAIGHT. YOU WERE BARELY THERE A COUPLA hours and he burned you? Wow, Wyatt, you're losing your touch.'

Woody Wyatt holds up his ham-like hands to Mike Randall in surrender. He is trying to be a good sport, but does the guy have to sound so gleeful about it? Wyatt would like to see Randall do any better. The guy never even leaves his desk – the nearest he gets to actual danger is a paper cut from opening the mail.

'Tell me about it. Dude, whatever was in that hooch they served me, I'm telling you, we should patent that shit. It's been three days and I'm still spitting up my internal organs. Who needs WMD when you can unleash a fucking Thai barman on the enemy?'

Frances Coffey coughs and Wyatt straightens up. He'd forgotten for a moment that the boss was here. It's those kinds of slip-ups that kept getting him hauled up in front of the disciplinary committee in his Navy SEAL days.

'Sorry, boss. I guess I'm just embarrassed. He walked all over me.'

Coffey takes out her nicotine inhaler and stares balefully at it before replacing it in her jacket pocket unused. A reluctantly reformed smoker himself, Wyatt feels for her. He likes Coffey. She doesn't suffer fools. Sure, she can seem overly forensic at times, insisting they hold back until every angle is covered – once a librarian, always a librarian – when he would prefer to charge right in, but at least she's straight with everyone.

'Tell us your impressions of him, Woody. He's a bit of a languages geek, I gather?'

'I guess. His friends seemed to understand him well enough, though, frankly, boss, he could be speaking ancient Greek and I wouldn't know. Languages were never my strong point.'

'What about his character? I mean, this is a guy who risked his life to save the very people who tried for years to put his parents behind bars. He's never been trained and yet he knew how to use a transponder as a makeshift GPS. And he blew the cover of one of our most promising operatives in less than twenty-four hours.'

Wyatt looks sheepish. He is starting to realize it will take a long time to live this down.

'You don't want to go near this one. Trust me. His parents were drug dealers. He makes his money helping thrill-seeking tourists nearly get themselves killed and spends the rest of his time smoking dope, drinking beer and hanging out with hookers. He's lazy, he's unprincipled and he distrusts authority.'

'But does he have what it takes?'

Wyatt is tempted to say no. He grew up in a military family in Illinois, following his father into the US Marines just the minute he was old enough, fighting his way up through the ranks to join the Navy SEALs and seconded from there into the United States intelligence agency. That long-haired bum he'd encountered playing pool, in a backstreet bar in a remote town in the Thai jungle known principally for its links to large-scale drug production, is everything he detests. But Woody Wyatt is nothing if not honest.

'Yeah. He's good. But, boss, if you're thinking of recruiting him, you'd be wasting your time. He's carved out a comfortable little life for himself there, shooting pool, getting wasted.'

'But not living the high life? No sign of the money his parents must have stashed away?'

Wyatt shakes his head.

'Even so, he seems happy enough there. And don't forget the DEA might not have killed his parents, but they certainly made their lives a misery. We're the enemy as far as people like Argylle are concerned.'

'Still. He might not turn down the chance of an all-expenses-paid holiday to the States.'

'To Delaware?'

Coffey makes a face.

'Perhaps not. But I will be in Manhattan next week. Perhaps that will be more to Mr Argylle's taste.'

Ten days after Scott Novak's visit, life in Chiang Saen has slipped back into its usual lazy rhythm, and Argylle is struggling again to believe any of it happened at all. When he lies in his hammock on the porch of his bamboo hut in the clammy afternoon heat, the scene up there on the mountain with the shot-down plane seems like a dream he once had, nothing to do with him.

So it is a shock when he pays his weekly visit to the town post office to pick up his mail and finds an official-looking letter with a typed address and a US postmark waiting for him. Crossing the wide, tree-lined road outside, dodging a moped with an umbrella-shaded sidecar loaded with watermelon, he rips open the envelope. Inside is a sheet of stiff paper, folded into three, bearing the logo of the United States Foreign Service.

Interesting, he thinks.

In the shade of a restaurant awning, he scans the letter. It thanks him for his quick-thinking actions, which helped save the lives of US government employees, and, noting his proficiency in languages, invites him to New York to discuss possible interpreting opportunities within the Service. All expenses paid.

Argylle laughs out loud. He is no fool. He knows who was on that plane, and why. Just as he knows that Scott Novak, or whatever his real name turns out to be, was some sort of federal agent. He knows that what he did up there in the mountains on the Myanmar border has brought him to the attention of the US intelligence services, and now they want to check him out.

He also knows that the same US government that is offering him these 'opportunities' would happily have locked his parents up in a maximum-security jail and thrown away the key.

All the way home, he chuckles to himself, wishing his dad was here to appreciate the delicious irony of it all – the idea that he, the son of drug smugglers, brought up to question all authority, might end up working for the American establishment. But by the time he steps on to his porch, he has stopped finding it funny and is instead churned up with that familiar mixture of grief and anger.

In the end, it's all such a waste.

Pausing in the doorway, he crumples the letter into a ball and lobs it across the room into the cardboard box that serves as his waste-paper bin. *GOOOAAAAL!* Then he gets on his bike to go and swim at the local waterfalls, where the shock of the cold water drives the whole thing from his mind.

But two days later, something happens that makes him think again.

He is on his porch, writing in his journal, when he is surprised to see a familiar figure hurrying along the unmade track towards him. Argylle can't remember the last time he saw Ning outside of either The Bar or the massage parlour and, judging by her serious expression and the determined swing of her black ponytail, she isn't here for a social call. Up close, her brown eyes are pink-ringed and anxious and when she speaks to Argylle in Thai instead of using him for English practice as she usually does, he knows something is very wrong.

'My cousin Kasem. He is a shit-for-brains. Even my auntie says so. He works for very bad people.' Ning's voice runs on when she speaks Thai, as opposed to English, where she is slow and precise. Even so, she stops and looks around fearfully before lowering her voice to continue. 'Drugs gang.' She turns her head and mimes spitting on the floor. 'He told me last night that the Sam Gor shot down an American plane in the mountains, and a local *farang* led the American soldiers to the Sam Gor camp and plenty of Sam Gor ended up dead, good riddance' – again the head-to-the-side spitting gesture – 'including San Yuan Lai's youngest brother.'

A hard lump of ice drops into the pit of Argylle's stomach. Everyone knows San Yuan Lai in this area. The right-hand man of Tse Chi Lop, Sam Gor's legendary head, Lai has an unrivalled reputation for brutality and for the imaginative ways he disposes of those who try to leave the gang or, worse, who betray him. Tongues sent in the post to grieving relatives, messages spelled out in entrails.

'Lai has offered a big reward to anyone who can find the *farang* and bring him to him – *alive*. That idiot Kasem says the *farang* has long hair, like a girl.' Ning looks pointedly at Argylle's unruly ponytail. 'Kasem is still in town sleeping off his hangover, but his friend left early. He knows it's you, Argylle. And when he gets to the camp, they'll all know. I guess you have about eight hours. Nine if you're lucky.'

The ice has got into his veins now, spreading into his arms and legs.

'But this is my home.'

Ning's eyes blur over, but still her voice has the brusque tone of one who has learned the hard way that sentimentality achieves nothing.

'Not any more, Argylle. You have to leave. Whatever they did to your parents, they'll do far worse to you. And your friends too.'

Of course. Shame engulfs him. In his concern for himself, he momentarily forgot that his presence here also endangers anyone who knows him. Just by coming to warn him, Ning has taken a terrible risk.

'I have a son, Argylle.'

She doesn't need to say more.

'I'll take a taxi, go straight to the airport. Book myself on to a flight. Leave a trail.'

Ning nods, knowing that's the best chance of keeping the Sam Gor away from Chiang Saen.

Argylle watches her leave with a heavy heart, cursing his own idiotic heroics. Despite his parents' violent deaths, he has always felt safe here in this little town, far from the drugs labs up there in the mountains.

Not any more.

He crosses to the back of his hut, where a door leads to a rudimentary outhouse – really just a shower attachment fed by a black garbage bag of sun-warmed water suspended from an overhanging tree, and a squat toilet with a bucket next to it. In the corner a rusty, disconnected pipe juts from the ground. Argylle unscrews it and shakes out a plastic bag. Back inside, he tips the contents on to his mattress. Twenty-two dollars and fifty-nine cents.

When Argylle's parents were killed, they had left behind instructions to be followed in the event of their death. And a Swiss bank account, supposedly containing enough money to set their son up for life, along with the name of a financial broker. But when he'd contacted the broker, he'd been told there were only five thousand pounds in the account. And since the funds had been invested through a complicated offshore trust to avoid both tax and difficult questions from the authorities, there had been no way to prove otherwise.

These twenty-two dollars and fifty-nine cents are all that remain of his inheritance.

Argylle knows he needs to get away. And stay away.

Twenty-two dollars and fifty-nine cents aren't going to get him anywhere near as far as he needs to go.

For a moment he stares down at the paltry collection of notes and coins on the sheet, while his pounding heart sends blood crashing around his ears like the sea. Then he crosses the room and reaches down into his cardboard-box wastepaper bin, fishing around until he brings out the crumpled letter he'd tossed in there two days before.

Shaking loose some pieces of orange peel that have collected in the folds, he smooths it out.

9

Three months before Federov's promise to the Russian people

THE ATMOSPHERE IN THE HALL IS ELECTRIC, THE AIR CRACKLING with money and avarice.

Already in this Important Jewels auction, records have been broken. A rare diamond-and-emerald Tiffany necklace went for nearly twelve million dollars. A 1920s Cartier watch, once owned by Jackie Kennedy, just fetched three times the guide price.

In the rows of seats facing the auctioneer's block, smartly dressed men and women sit up straight, taking furious notes or photographs or texting on their phones, fingers flying. Or they leaf through the auction catalogue or whisper to each other, or gaze at the banks of phone bidders lining the sides of the room, trying to guess who is on the other end of the line. There are rumours that Larry Ellison, the Oracle tycoon, has an interest here, and Prince Al Waleed bin Talal Al Saud, one of the world's richest men.

The final lot sends a ripple of interest around the vast hall, mercifully air-conditioned against the steamy Hong Kong afternoon.

'Here we have a completely unique piece, one of a kind,' says the auctioneer. He indicates the screen to the right of him featuring a close-up of a gold bracelet against a plain black background. 'This stunning bracelet was created by the famous house of Mellerio, inset with diamonds – both brilliant and rose cut – and bears a mysterious inscription on the inside rim, "15.X", alongside the Latin word *fidelis*. It also has these two distinctive grooves on either side of the rim. Dating from nineteenth-century France, we know it was commissioned by the Emperor Napoleon III as a gift for his wife, the Empress Eugénie, but the meaning of the engraved digits on the inside and the intricate pattern engraved into the outside remains tantalizingly elusive. The empress was known for changing her clothes and jewels three or four times a day, so this was one piece among many, and no records exist to explain its singular design. It was in the possession of the French movie star Nathalie Chabert for many years – hence the initials *NC* also engraved on the inner part, a later inscription that experts have dated back to the mid-twentieth century. The bracelet formed part of Madame Chabert's estate when she died in the 1970s and now, thirty years later, her daughter Isabelle brings it to auction. Despite the mystery that surrounds its design, it remains a breathtakingly fine example of nineteenth-century antique jewellery, which is why we have set the opening bid at six hundred thousand US dollars.'

The bidding begins. A handful of the phone bidders are fully engaged, plus a smattering of people around the hall. Eight hundred thousand is reached. A million. Now the initial interest has been whittled down to just four diehards. 'One million four hundred. One million and a half . . . Two million.'

Now just two committed bidders remain, and one of those is hesitating. It seems the lot has been won by a phone bid communicated by a young woman in a severe black jacket at odds with her round, smiling face. 'Going once for two million, twice—'

'Five million.'

A gasp travels around the room. The bid has come not from a phone bidder but from the back of the auditorium. People crane to get a look and are puzzled when they see not one of the usual collectors or their representatives who do the circuit of jewellery auctions, or the celebrities who sometimes turn up looking for baubles on which to spend their millions, but an unremarkable-looking man with rimless glasses and a wide, shallow face so devoid of expression he might just as well have been tossing out coins for a newspaper rather than committing to pay five million for a bracelet valued at one fifth of that amount.

In the raised banks of seats where the phone bidders sit, the young, round-faced woman is no longer smiling. Instead she is talking urgently into her telephone. The auctioneer, who seems as much in shock as the rest of them, looks at her askance. 'As I said, this item is truly one of a kind. Do we have any advances on five million?'

The young woman shakes her head, the phone still clamped to her ear.

After the bidding ends, the mystery bidder's neighbour – an art dealer working on behalf of the Victoria and Albert Museum in London – turns to him with her eyebrows raised.

'That was a bold bid,' she says admiringly. 'But aren't you worried you paid too much?'

The unknown man looks at her, and she regrets having spoken when she sees the lack of warmth in his expression.

Still, he answers her civilly enough.

'It was a gift from a devoted husband to his wife.' The smile he gives her doesn't reach his pale, almost lashless eyes. 'What price can you put on love?'

10

THE HULKING ART DECO BUILDING BETWEEN THE JUNCTIONS OF Varick Street and King and Hudson and West Houston Street on the west side of Lower Manhattan appears as unwelcoming as it is anonymous. Occupying an entire block, its brownstone facade is broken up only by a handful of Stars and Stripes banners hanging from flagpoles and signs advertising various unglamorous federal departments – post office, veterans' affairs, passport services. Looking up, a passer-by would find twelve storeys of featureless office windows. Nothing to see here.

As he comes up Houston Street subway, emerging into the greasy Manhattan air, Aubrey Argylle wonders yet again just what the hell he is doing here.

When he passes through the uninspiring entrance and a receptionist asks him his business, it's all he can do not to reply, *Not a clue*.

The man who comes to meet him in the lobby has one of those clean-cut faces that could be mid-twenties or mid-forties. He introduces himself as Mike Randall and gives a job title so instantly forgettable that Argylle suspects it must have been deliberately created that way. In the elevator Randall asks him about his flight and his hotel and what he has been doing since he arrived the previous evening, leaving no space for Argylle to ask any questions of his own.

They get out on the tenth floor and then Argylle follows Randall through a doorway that leads to a set of stairs and they ascend to the next level. Everything is beige. Unremarkable. One corridor much like the next. They finally come to a halt outside a door as non-descript as all the other doors.

Randall opens it and they enter a cramped open-plan office with five or six desks. No one looks up. At the back of the office is a second door. Randall pauses before he knocks, and Argylle notices how he pulls himself up straighter. This is someone he wants to impress.

Argylle follows Randall into a modest corner office with two windows that provide a sectional glimpse of the dirty grey New York sky through the vertical slatted blinds.

We don't always recognize the people who will be most important to us in our lives, but something about Frances Coffey stops the breath in Argylle's throat and brings a rush of warmth to his chest. Years later, people will try to suggest he was a motherless boy trying to fill the hole in his life, but Argylle loved his mother and isn't in the market for a replacement.

Coffey gets up to shake his hand, and her eyes behind her glasses are magnified so he is able to read there both shrewdness and intelligence, as you'd expect, but also a compassion that takes him by surprise.

She asks him to sit and they shoot the breeze about how cold March in Manhattan feels after the tropical heat of Thailand and how even though Argylle has never been here before it feels familiar because of all the film backdrops. They get on to his family. Argylle trots out the script. His parents were in the import/export business. Yada yada yada.

The thing is, he knows that she knows what his parents really did. The same as she knows he knows he isn't here about any embassy job.

'Family business stays in the family.' His father's motto rears its head again. Argylle had loved his father and never doubted he was loved right back, but it was a more complicated love than with his mother. Where she was quiet and watchful, an observer of life, his father took up all the oxygen in the room. Charming and egocentric, sure that his way was the right way. Argylle didn't doubt that the life they led was his dad's doing. His father had never made a secret of his conviction that legalization of cannabis was just around the corner, and papers Argylle found after his parents' deaths made it clear they believed themselves to be pioneers rather than lawbreakers.

'It's not addictive, like opium and cocaine,' his father had written in his 'in the advent of our sudden death' letter. 'It doesn't make people violent and antisocial, like alcohol. We haven't even begun to tap into the full extent of its healing properties. We could have quadrupled our income if we'd branched out into other narcotics, but we're not criminals. We're just ahead of the curve.'

Coffey smiles at him over her steepled hands. Argylle looks at the ragged skin around her thumbnail and understands that her calm demeanour is self-taught rather than innate, and that it comes at a cost.

'That was quite the rescue mission you pulled off there in Myanmar,' she says. 'You're a brave man, Mr Argylle.'

Argylle shifts in his seat. How can he explain that it wasn't about bravery, it was simply about answering the question 'to act or not to act?' How can he make her understand that his whole life for the last five years has been about not acting, about treading water, and he has had enough. He thinks back to that sultry, soupy day when a small plane fell out of a yellow sky and he wonders how he could have done anything different.

'Two of your guys still died,' he says. 'That doesn't feel like a success to me.'

'But two others made it because of you.'

They both fall silent. Argylle wants to ask about the woman with her broken arm, but he guesses it's probably better not to know.

'I'm conscious I'm detaining you when you've probably got a whole list of things you want to see and do here in the Big Apple,' says Coffey, as if he is here on a sightseeing trip. 'Shall we lay our cards on the table, do you think? You've probably worked out by now that we're not interviewing you for an interpreting job. I'm with the CIA and we are very interested in making you part of our organization.'

Argylle laughs. He can't help it.

'I assume, being the CIA, you know who my parents were and what they really did for a living?'

'Quite correct.' Coffey smiles at him, as if they are discussing something completely legitimate and salutary rather than large-scale marijuana smuggling. 'But you weren't told what they did when you were growing up, and even if you had known, what could you have done about it? You were just a child.

'I'm sure it won't surprise you to know we've carried out a little due diligence and we now know you haven't gained financially from your parents' illegal activities, which might have made things more . . . complicated.'

Argylle stops laughing abruptly.

'Glad my being broke simplifies things for you.'

'So what do you say?'

This is real, then, this preposterous invitation? All at once he finds he is angry. He might not have known what his parents were really up to, but he had heard their whispered arguments, knew that sometimes his mother was afraid for no reason and would hug him to her and tell him to always remember how much he was loved. The last time he'd seen them, when he was back for the Christmas holidays, they'd been so jumpy. Not their usual selves at all, she noticeably thinner, her collarbone pressing through her skin.

Afterwards, he'd discovered that his dad had gone behind his mum's back to do a deal with the Sam Gor to use their supply route, after being let down by their usual contact. Something went wrong and the debt was never paid.

This much Argylle knows. What he still doesn't know is what was done to them. Whether they suffered. How long they were kept at the camp before their bodies were dumped by a waterfall to be found by the next tour group that hiked up that way. At the time, Argylle had been away at school, and by the time he got to Thailand the case was already closed.

'Better you don't know,' the police chief would tell him, when he asked. Viewing the bodies was out of the question.

That's why he spends his free time roaming the jungle. Looking for answers that, deep down, he realizes he might not want to find.

It was because of agencies like Frances Coffey's hunting them down that his parents were driven into the arms of the Sam Gor and decided to send Argylle away to school rather than put him at risk. How he'd hated that school, hated being sent away, hated the hard rock he carried around always in the pit of his stomach.

'I'm sorry,' he says, standing up suddenly. 'I thank you for the flights and the hotel and for the invitation, but I'm not the person you're looking for.'

Coffey's smile doesn't dim, although he sees her hands go to something in her pocket that she turns over in her fingers like a talisman.

'That's a pity. You have all the makings of an excellent operative. But of course it is your decision. Enjoy the rest of your trip, Aubrey Argylle.'

Already, as he turns to leave, he is stung with regret that he won't see her again.

A few minutes later he is back out in the street, amid the blaring horns of the yellow cabs and the idling of the courier vans. There's a Mexican fast-food outlet over the road and he crosses, intending to get himself some lunch, but changes his mind and instead heads up Seventh Avenue, in the direction of Times Square. As he walks, the anger that propelled him through the latter part of the encounter with Frances Coffey, flooding him with unshakable belief in his own righteousness, dissipates into the petrol-fumed air and he is left with a hollow feeling, as if someone has taken a long spoon and scooped out his insides.

On he walks. Block after block. Passing a junction where the Empire State Building looms off to the side like it does in a hundred Hollywood movies, he tries to summon up his earlier rage, but it will not come. Approaching Times Square, he notices more and more hunched figures sitting on the sidewalk on sleeping bags or flattened cardboard boxes. Some have signs: *Hungry, please help* or *Army vet, I risked everything for you. Please help me.* Or *Seeking Human Kindness.*

Argylle feels a drawstring pulling tight across his heart. The line that separates him from these people is gossamer thin. He cannot go back to Chiang Saen. And he has nowhere else to go. Will he end up here? On these streets or some just like them?

A block from the lights and bustle of Times Square itself, he comes across a young kid, seventeen or eighteen, sitting on a colourful blanket, leaning against a wall. In contrast to the others, who have that fixed, unfocused stare of people who have given up hope, the boy is gazing around him as if drinking in the city that surrounds him.

Argylle fumbles in his pocket, drawing out a fifty-dollar bill from the wad he was given as 'spending money' by the woman who'd met him off the plane when he arrived. Delighted, the boy springs to his feet. 'Hey! Don't rush off. Stay and talk to me, man.' Argylle squats down beside him. The boy is excited. He has only recently crossed over from Mexico. 'I'm good at computers. Here I can get rich. Away from the gangs.' Argylle feels a long splinter of guilt. His parents had truly believed the drugs they dealt in were harmless – helpful even. But had they ever considered the human collateral involved in getting them to the people who wanted them?

'My mom saved five hundred dollars and gave it to me, so I can have a better life,' the boy tells him.

'Weren't you scared?'

'Are you kidding? I was crapping myself, man, but you know you should always do the thing that frightens you.'

And now Argylle hears his mother's voice, soft as summer rain, coming to him through the years. 'When you're faced with a choice, pick the option that scares you most.'

And he realizes what he has known deep down all along. That it wasn't anger that saw him walking out on Frances Coffey's offer, it was fear. Not fear of physical danger. He can deal with that. But leaving the past behind and stepping back out into the world? Accepting, finally, that his parents are gone and he needs to forge his own path? That's something else.

He gets to his feet and shakes the kid's hand, hoping the big city will be kind to him. Taking from his back pocket the small rectangular card Coffey gave him before he left, he dials the number, which is the only thing printed on it. As the ringtone sounds, he turns around in the direction he has just come from and begins to retrace his steps.

'It's me. Argylle. I'm on my way back.'

11

Two months after Federov's promise to the Russian people

'WHAT EXACTLY ARE YOUR QUALIFICATIONS, MR DUBININ? ONLY I HAD specifically requested Russia's foremost expert in rare and antique jewellery and your name came up, and yet you have had my bracelet for six weeks now and can tell me no more about it than I already knew.'

Pavel Dubinin bites down on his lower lip. As director of the renowned Hermitage Museum Foundation in St Petersburg and one of the world's leading experts on Fabergé and French antique jewellery, he is used to being deferred to. He is not used to being spoken to like this – and in his own office too. And yet Vasily Federov is a powerful man. He could be a very useful donor to the museum. And now that he is running for office, with the unofficial endorsement of his father-in-law, so rumour has it . . . well, wouldn't Dubinin be a fool to alienate him?

'It's a beautiful piece, Mr Federov. Really, the kind of thing only the most discerning buyer would know to pick out. Napoleon III himself had it made for his w—'

'I am not paying you to regurgitate what the auctioneer already told me.'

Dubinin would have liked to point out that he hasn't yet been paid a single kopek, but he holds back.

'I've committed considerable time to your search, tracing back the ownership of the bracelet. As you know, the bracelet was in the possession of the French actress Nathalie Chabert, who was very well known in the 1940s and early fifties, although her star waned after that and by the time she died in the 1970s she hadn't had a film role in sixteen years.'

'Did she travel here to Russia, do you know, before the war?'

Dubinin is taken aback by his left-field question.

'Not that I know of. In fact, I'm certain she did not. Her biography said she remained virtually unknown outside of her native France, and she would tell people she was proud of the fact she'd die without leaving the country where she was born, the country that gave her everything.'

Federov's mood is growing worse, the air between them souring.

'So she didn't travel to Germany either,' he mutters to himself. 'And yet there has to be a connection.'

Is he perhaps regretting the five million dollars he has spent on a hunch? A hunch based on little more than a dying Nazi's final, tortured words and his late father's conviction that those words could solve the riddle of the Amber Room's disappearance?

Impossible to say.

'I did talk at length to Isabelle Chabert, Nathalie's eldest daughter. It was she who put the bracelet up for sale. Putting two and two together, I think she needed the money, so I don't need to tell you how grateful she was that you paid so handsomely.'

'You're right, you don't need to tell me.'

Dubinin looks up sharply. Is Federov making a joke? But one glance at his expression disabuses him of that idea.

'Madame Chabert told me her mother never wore the bracelet and was very secretive about where it came from. When the subject came up she'd say she couldn't remember. That it might have been a present from a grateful director. She said it was unusual for her mother to be so vague. Normally she was very precise.

'It seems the mother was married twice, and there was no love lost between her two sets of children. Isabelle believes her mother's entire estate should have gone to her and her brother, instead of being split evenly between all three Chabert offspring.'

Federov says nothing, though he of all people should understand how messy things can get between half-siblings.

'Is the younger child a son or a daughter?'

'Daughter, I believe.'

'You believe? You haven't tried to contact her?'

'You asked me to find out more about your bracelet, Mr Federov. The younger Chabert daughter has nothing to do with it. In fact, the two sisters have only met on one occasion – their mother's funeral.'

'Still, her mother might have told her where the bracelet came from. I'm surprised you did not think it worth following up.'

Finally, Pavel Dubinin's patience snaps. He earns a good living from his role with the foundation. He is well regarded. He does not need to put up with this. Even so, he doesn't quite dare meet Federov's eyes when he tells him:

'I think perhaps you misunderstood, Mr Federov. I'm an art historian, not a private detective.'

'It is of vital importance to me to discover the exact provenance and history of my bracelet, Mr Dubinin. I thought I'd made myself clear. You're to leave no stone unturned.'

Dubinin bristles. Does he think he's talking to some minion he can order around at will?

'Is this connected to a certain promise you made in the presidential debate?'

He hadn't intended to mention the Amber Room, though of course he made the connection right away. Federov's urgency, the staggering amounts of money he's offering as a reward for information. He'd known instantly this was about more than a bracelet, though he can't for the life of him see how the two things are linked.

'My reasons are my own.'

The man is so infuriatingly superior.

'Of course. I only hope your promise doesn't turn out to be premature.'

Federov turns his blank gaze on him. 'No matter. I'll find someone more qualified. You take care now, Mr Dubinin.'

A chill blows across the surface of Dubinin's skin, light as spider legs.

12

THE TEAM ARE PINNED DOWN. UP AHEAD, TWO IRAQI TANKS GRIND across the oilfield, their tyres churning up the dust and dirt into a gritty brown cloud. From a nearby bunker comes almost incessant gunfire, while behind them armed Iraqis pour out of a bombed-out compound. In the distance, black smoke belches into the sky. Basra is burning.

Argylle casts around. Fifty metres away to his left there is a tank, its occupants killed some minutes ago in a barrage of machine-gun fire from their team. If Argylle can reach it, he could drive it back and scoop the others up before the Iraqis close in.

'Cover me!' he shouts to the man next to him, dust whipping into his mouth and his eyes.

'What? No way.'

'I can get there, but I need to go now.'

'Quit with the heroics.'

Argylle feels his heart hammering in his chest.

'Fine. I'll do it without you.' He sets off at a sprint, his eyes trained on the gap ahead, his breath short and shallow.

The noise of the impact when the artillery fire hits is ear-splitting.

'Down! You're fucking down, Argylle!' Wyatt yells at him.

'STOP!'

The command cuts through the noise of the shelling and the distant bombing. Argylle wrenches off his VR helmet in disgust.

'Argylle, Wyatt, get over here. Now!'

Wyatt throws down his simulator. The two men don't so much as glance at one another as they make their way towards Will Hooper, the training operations instructor.

'Just what the hell is going on with you two?'

'He has no idea about combat protocol, sir. He's had next to no training. He's just a liability.'

'I could have made it, sir. I had a clear path.'

Hooper holds up his hand. He is more than a head shorter than Wyatt but just as broad, a dense cube of a man, packed tight with muscle and sinew and a barely suppressed rage.

'All of you, come over here.'

The other twelve put down their simulators and remove their VR headsets. The room is thick with ill temper.

'I shouldn't need to tell you this, but it looks like we have to go straight back to kindergarten with you bunch of losers, so get yourselves into a circle, put your thumbs in your mouths and listen up. This SOG wasn't assembled because Frances Coffey thought you guys looked cute together, it was very carefully selected. You are a team. Got that? And you're a team because I say so. Each of you has skills that the others don't, though Christ knows they've gone AWOL today. So I want you to forget you ever knew Glenn Dabrowski. Forget about Isfahan. Start remembering why you're here and who you're working for.

'And as a first step you can take yourselves out this evening for a beer and a pizza. Together, as a team.'

There's a rumbling of discontent, people shooting each other side glances. No one looking directly at Argylle.

'That's not a suggestion, by the way.' Hooper has a way of looking at you as if he is an airport scanner, seeing through the exterior to what's going on inside. 'It's an order.'

13

ARGYLLE DOESN'T KNOW WHERE THE HELL PERILLI'S IS. THE OTHERS have been in and out of this facility for months, if not years. They know every last bar and food outlet within a twenty-kilometre radius of the base's heavily guarded gate, but no one has seen fit to tell him where they are supposed to be meeting for pizza.

Not that he's remotely surprised. No one has exactly been slugging it out to be his best buddy since he arrived here at Harvey Point. After he said yes to Coffey's offer, everything happened so fast. A call to Somchai back in Chiang Saen to explain and tell him to take whatever he wanted from the bamboo hut, and then straight to Virginia for six weeks' intensive training down at Camp Peary. And directly on to this team induction programme here in North Carolina. There are fourteen of them here, though Coffey has explained that individual missions might call for a much smaller core team. For Argylle, who didn't attend school until he was sixteen, the whole group thing doesn't come naturally, but at least he's willing to try. Unlike the rest of them.

He tells himself he doesn't care. He's used to being self-sufficient. It's what he knows.

He and Wyatt have been avoiding each other. Which suits him fine. The big guy didn't even bother disguising his disgust when Argylle was foisted into his team to replace the missing Dabrowski. Argylle has no idea what went down in Iran. All he knows is that the team were dispatched to investigate the nuclear facility at Isfahan

68

and something went belly up. They were ambushed before they even got close. And now the wildly popular Dabrowski has been jailed for espionage offences, and Argylle has been drafted in despite having undergone only a fraction of the training the others had to do, and everyone hates his guts.

'They'll come around to you,' Coffey had told him when she called at the weekend two days after his arrival here in North Carolina and he told her he'd made a huge mistake in coming.

Argylle has been surprised by the personal interest the CIA's Chief Operating Officer – which he now knows to be the highest-ranking non-political office in the organization – has shown in him since her first phone call back in March. When he'd asked her whether she made fortnightly calls to all her new recruits she'd laughed her ripped-from-the-throat laugh and he'd understood from her long intake of breath that she was taking a drag on her nicotine inhaler. 'The truth is you remind me of myself. I too was an outsider. When I started in the 1970s, I worked in the library. Imagine, no military academy schooling, no armed forces background, no Ivy League college languages degree. Just me in the archives for year upon year. But you know what's in the archives, Aubrey?' No one has called him Aubrey since his parents died. It's the name that saw him teased mercilessly at school. But to his surprise he finds he quite likes Frances Coffey saying it.

'Knowledge. That's what's in the archives. I absorbed everything. I drank it all in. And more than that, I learned all the things the Agency has tried to bury over the years the secret missions, the assassinations we always denied. The missions that never officially existed. The missions that went catastrophically wrong.

'Knowledge is power, and that power was what propelled me up the ranks here. But let me tell you there were a lot of people none too happy about that. It took me a lot longer to win my place here than it's going to take you, I can guarantee you.

'But here's the thing, Aubrey. Everyone has moments of feeling they don't belong. Even the Woody Wyatts of the world.'

At the mention of Wyatt, Argylle's mood had dropped.

'He hates me.'

Coffey hadn't disagreed. 'What do you expect? Dabrowski was his buddy and now he thinks you've been brought in to replace him. Plus, you made an ass of him out there in Chiang Saen. But you know how we know that?'

'Because you were bugging him?'

'Wrong. Because he came back here and told us so. That's the thing about Woody. Underneath the front and the wisecracks he's as straight as they come. He didn't sugar-coat things to make himself look better. He put his hands up. But that doesn't mean he liked it. It'll take a while to earn his trust but, once you do, you'll have a friend for life.'

There is precious little evidence of this promised friendship when Argylle finally shows up at Perilli's in the small town of Hertford, ten miles from the base.

The others are there before him, deep in a conversation which falls silent as he walks in. Argylle taps out the Morse for SOS on the side of his leg, something his mother taught him. 'You'd be amazed how often it turns out you can answer your own call for help,' she'd said.

Not this time.

Argylle casts around the long table, looking for a friendly face, or failing that a spare seat. But it seems like all the chairs are taken. He spots Brandon Reynolds, just out of college, and Mia Matsyuk, tall and willowy, with wrists so slim Wyatt could snap them with his bare hands. There's the sad-eyed Canadian Alex Kellerman, and balding mechanic Jim Ryder. And down the far end, the one with the scars on his cheek is Eric Lawler, a jumpy Afghanistan vet, his injuries sustained in an attack that apparently left half his patrol dead or captured.

Just as he is considering turning on his heel and leaving the way he has come, there's a movement from the far end. A compact, muscular young woman with a shock of tight, dark curls and a beat-up biker jacket has stood up and is wordlessly lifting a chair from the table behind. 'Scoot up, Schneider,' she says to the sallow-complexioned man next to her, who does as she asks, though if there was an award for complying with bad grace, he would win hands down.

She glances over to Argylle and nods. As he joins her, hoping his gratitude at being rescued isn't written all over his face, he tries to remember her name but comes up blank.

'Thanks,' he mutters, taking his seat.

'Well, with everyone fighting over who gets to sit next to you, I'm just honoured you chose me,' she says, straight-faced.

'Right. Well, thanks anyway. I think.'

He picks up the menu.

'You have no idea who I am, do you?'

'Sure I do. You're . . . Karla?'

She flashes him a disdainful sideways glance. 'You know we were told you were this whizz-kid. Fast track. Mr Hotshot. And you can't even remember my name? Way to make a good impression, New Boy.'

Argylle feels chastened. She's right.

'Sorry.'

'For your information, it's Keira. Keira Carter. I'm with the CCI.' She sees his blank look. 'That's the Center for Cyber Intelligence to you. But somehow I ended up getting seconded to this bunch of dead weights. Not that I had a choice.'

'So you weren't on the Iran mission?'

'Nope. Because if I had been, maybe it wouldn't have been such a shit-show.'

Argylle stifles a smile. Carter has a big energy, but she's pocket-sized.

'I see the way you're looking. You gotta work on your poker face, New Boy. The truth is that Isfahan fell apart because our intel could be decrypted by a ten-year-old child with a *Coding for Dummies* book. That's why I landed here a couple of months ahead of you.'

Ah, so Carter is the techie. It makes sense. Argylle knows his way around a computer, but the ins and outs of coding and encryption are way outside his comprehension.

'Actually, you've got that wrong.' Matt Schneider's disconcertingly close-together eyes flick between Carter and Argylle. 'The mission to Isfahan fell apart because the Iranians were one step ahead of us every step of the fucking way. Because there was a

71

fucking mole in the team, feeding back all our fucking movements to their Russian ubermeisters.'

After he finishes speaking, the table falls silent and Argylle is uncomfortably aware of thirteen sets of eyes turned in his direction. And not with any discernible friendliness either.

'Just as long as we're clear there's no way that mole is Dabrowski.'

Wyatt has been holding court down the other end of the table all this time, laughing and joking. But now his expression is deadly serious.

'Yeah, so how come Dabrowski is doing time in Super Max, then?'

Matt Schneider isn't as imposing as Wyatt, but there is a hardness around his sharp, ferrety features that gives him the look of someone you would not want to cross.

'Dabrowski was set up.'

Coffey wasn't kidding when she said Wyatt was loyal to his friends.

'And quit bitching about the team to outsiders,' Wyatt adds, gesturing towards Argylle.

Argylle bites down on his lip. Every time he tries to give the guy the benefit of the doubt Wyatt finds a new way to piss him off.

'Come on, Wyatt,' says the woman to Wyatt's left. 'Carter and Argylle are part of the team now. Give them a break.'

Argylle has noticed her before. Five feet seven or eight with strong, dark brows above eyes that change colour from brown to green depending on the light, and a long, thin nose that bisects her narrow face, she is not conventionally attractive. And yet he likes looking at her. Likes the way her mouth twitches before she laughs and how she teases the others without ever being cruel.

He nods his thanks and is rewarded with a fleeting smile before she looks away. Wyatt, observing, frowns.

'Well, I for one am delighted to have fresh blood in the team,' drawls a voice from the centre of the table in a musical Southern accent. 'Y'all were just about boring me to death. No offence.' A face appears, leaning over the chequered cloth, and an elegant hand waves desultorily in Argylle's direction.

Argylle has noticed him before too.

How could he not?

Six feet seven, with a lithe, graceful build and a shaven head, Noah Washington would stand out anywhere, let alone in the macho environs of the Harvey Point training camp.

At first, Argylle had taken him for a newcomer like himself, sure someone so distinctive couldn't survive long in a programme with so many rules and demands. But the very first test mission had disabused him of that notion. Washington is without doubt the best shot among them. Not only that, he has a unique combat style that mixes balletic strength and agility with lethal accuracy. Argylle – who also has a technique that is all his own, mixing elements of Muay Thai, Eskrima, Vo Thuat and Pencak Silat picked up in the various South Asian countries he lived in as a child – tried once to congratulate him on it, but Washington was having none of it. 'Honey, when you look the way I look and you come from where I come from, you learn to fight fast, and you learn to fight good.'

'Nothing wrong with fresh blood,' interrupts Schneider. 'Even Carter here has paid her dues, right? We all know why she's here. But this guy? Six weeks of physical training. Zero training missions. You got a Sugar Mommy thing going with Coffey, Argylle? That it?'

The arrival of pizza saves Argylle from having to reply. While they're eating Wyatt tells a story about going on a blind date and, when he turned up, all six foot one and two hundred and fifty pounds of muscle, the woman had looked him up and down and said, 'No offence, but I prefer men who are a bit less . . . *obvious*.'

As the others laugh, Argylle remembers what Coffey said about Wyatt reporting back on his own humiliation in Thailand. For a moment he wonders if he's read him wrong. But just because someone can tell a joke against themselves doesn't mean they're not a major asshole.

'She's got a point there though, bro,' says Wyatt's opposite neighbour, an older guy with a white streak in his brown hair and deep grooves down his cheeks who keeps himself to himself. 'Sometimes women just want a little bit of understated sophistication.' He straightens an imaginary bow tie.

'Dream on, Corcoran.'

'So what's with all the writing you do?' Carter asks Argylle, holding up a slice of pizza as big as her head and catching the strings of mozzarella in her mouth. 'There's a rumour you're actually an undercover journalist writing an exposé on us. If it's *Vanity Fair*, I demand a stylist and photo approval.'

Argylle shrugs. 'It's just a habit.'

For a moment he considers telling her the truth, but he can't face the questions.

'Of course, the odds-on explanation is that you're writing everything down to feed it back to Coffey.'

'Why would I do that?'

Carter tosses a garlic dough ball into the air, catching it in her mouth.

'Because you're a stooge sent in to sniff out what really went wrong with the Iran mission. That's why you've skipped the training we all had to slog through.'

It shouldn't sting, but it does.

'They know what went wrong with the Iran mission. Dabrowski betrayed us. That's why he's in the slammer, where he belongs.'

'I know that, Argylle. And deep down the others know that too. But that doesn't mean they like it. The whole thing has made everyone suspicious of everyone else. And you, my friend, are at the very top of the suspicious persons tree.'

'Should I be worried?'

Carter grins, a wide, toothy smile that splits her face in half.

'Just keep your back to the wall, that's all.'

'They think I'm some sort of patsy, reporting back to you. I've got no chance here.'

'Relax, Aubrey. They're just playing you. There's no need for anyone to report back to us. We got our guy. There was a full investigation and there are zero doubts who sold them out. Glenn Dabrowski is going to be in jail for a very long time.'

Argylle kicks the ground savagely. He is pacing around in the pine woods outside the team's allocated sleeping quarters – a fancy term for what amounts to two long, corrugated Quonset huts (male and female) lined with bunks, each with a spartan bathroom at one end. Harvey Point – a five-square-kilometre spit of land projecting out into the vast Albemarle Sound estuary in Perquimans County, North Carolina, on the brink of the North Atlantic Ocean – was used by the US military during the Second World War to mount anti-submarine surveillance and launch seaplanes. Since then it's been a top-security government facility, its geographical remoteness, plus its two airfields and expanse of fields and woodland, making it a perfect setting for anti-terrorist and explosives training. It's cut off from the rest of the world. Which only increases Argylle's sense of isolation.

'Firstly, for Christ's sake, don't use my first name when the others are around. They've got enough ammunition against me, they don't need any more.'

'Of course. If that's what you want.'

'You bet it is. And second, it doesn't matter if they're playing me. What matters is you're asking me to potentially put my life in the hands of a bunch of assholes who hate my guts.'

He taps his thigh, but it doesn't help. What he really needs is a spliff, but Coffey has made it clear that is not happening any more, not if he wants to stay part of this organization anyway.

Which, at this moment, is not something he is at all sure of.

14

ARGYLLE IS LYING ON HIS STOMACH IN THE BAKED EARTH, HIS NOSE and mouth full of dust. 'Go,' hisses Wyatt in his ear.

Argylle doesn't reply, just gestures to Wyatt to stop. He needs to get his head straight. From his position behind a scrubby bush he can just about make out the slumped figure of Keira Carter handcuffed to the front post of a wooden hut in a particularly remote area of the facility. It's a warm May day and the combination of the sun and lack of sleep means he has to summon every ounce of focus.

For the last few days and nights on this training exercise they've been pushed to their physical limits, running miles with packs on their backs, sleeping in forty-minute spurts, hiding out for hours at a time in cramped and uncomfortable positions. For the old hands, with months or years of training and completed missions behind them, it has been gruelling, but for Argylle, who had only the most basic preparation, it has taken every bit of resilience and pig-headed determination. They were divided into teams at the beginning of the exercise, told only that they needed to recover a memory stick hidden somewhere inside the enemy team's HQ and that the objective was to try to get it without being taken hostage, like Carter.

Argylle has been put in charge of their team, which has enraged Wyatt.

'Go for it,' he hisses in Argylle's ear now. 'What the hell are you waiting for?'

Argylle, who, despite his minimal training, learned about instinct and intuition from parents who were always watching their backs, tries to block him out.

As he focuses on Carter's drooping head, he is running in his mind through the last known positions of the opposing team members.

'There's someone still in the hut.'

Wyatt is scornful. 'No, there isn't.'

'I think it's an ambush.'

'We watched them leave.'

'They could have looped back.'

The hissed exchange has grown increasingly bad-tempered. This exercise has been running for three days now and their nerves are shredded. They are running on coffee and adrenaline.

'If you don't, I will.'

Argylle glares over his shoulder. Wyatt glares right back. For a moment this is all there is, a silent locking of horns. Then Argylle makes his move, scrambling to his feet and sprinting for the door, knowing even before he is upright that this will turn out to be a mistake.

Sure enough, the door flies open.

'Take out your gun!' Wyatt shouts.

Argylle's hand goes to the Glock in his belt, but he doesn't draw it, not even when Schneider comes barrelling out of the hut, followed by the rest of his team – first Martin Casner, a beefy Texan, then Brandon Reynolds, looking younger than his twenty-two years, and slender Mia Matsyuk.

'What are you doing, dude? Draw your damn weapon.'

Instead Argylle goes in with his feet and his fists. All CIA recruits learn elements of Krav Maga – the lethal Israeli combat system that combines martial arts with boxing and wrestling – but Argylle rolls it up with the martial arts he learned as a kid.

Even though his parents were pacifists, they instilled in him the need to defend himself. Pradal Serey, Lethwai, Muay Thai. He learned them all. Now that he knows more about his parents' secret life he knows why, but as a child he didn't think to question it. He just enjoyed the physicality of each discipline, the way one action bled into another. It was like chess – once you knew the different sequences, and how your opponent might combat them, and what response you might make, the various permutations open to you, it became like a formal dance.

If both of you knew the rules.

Schneider does not know the rules.

Within seconds of Argylle's whirling attack Schneider is on the floor, the gun he was toting kicked from his hand into the dirt a couple of metres away. But Argylle, kneeling on Schneider's arms, pinioning him to the ground, cannot take on the rest of the enemy team who have followed close behind their fallen leader. As well as Casner, Reynolds and Matsyuk, there is also Asif Samra, the softly spoken engineer.

Wyatt, following close on Argylle's heels, might have had a chance of a shot if his eyeline hadn't been blocked by Argylle and Schneider. Instead he has no option but to launch himself bodily at Casner, who already has his revolver raised.

A split second later Argylle hears the explosive pop that means someone has been shot. Glancing around, he sees the tell-tale blooming of the red ink pellet on Wyatt's camouflage vest.

'What the fuck!'

When you're hit, the rules are you go down, but Wyatt is very much not down. In fact, he is pacing around, his face puce with anger. 'What the actual fuck, Argylle.'

Everything grinds to a halt. Those who were fighting a minute ago now start arguing instead. No one has slept and tempers are frayed.

There's a lot of shouting, in the middle of which Erin Quinn appears, looking remarkably relaxed and waving something around in the air.

Something small and memory-stick-shaped.

'Way to go, Escobar,' hisses Wyatt.

Coffey has already assured Argylle that only a handful of people at the Agency know the truth about his background and his parents' real occupation. But the fact that one of them is Woody Wyatt infuriates Argylle. Who is this dumb man-mountain of macho bigotry to judge Argylle's family? He knows nothing about them.

Suddenly it is all too much. That his mum and dad are dead, that he misses them, that they weren't who he thought they were and yet they were still his parents, and now he has wound up here, having to defend them to people who will never ever understand. In frustration he turns, gathering energy as he does so from the deepest part of him, funnelling it through his body as he rises off the ground and letting it all come out in the elbow he drives straight into Wyatt's meaty neck.

The big guy staggers, caught by surprise, and it looks like he will go down. Argylle momentarily exits from his own body, observing the scene, as if he is somehow watching himself in a movie. But now Wyatt is back upright, roaring like a bull. *Oh shit*, the out-of-body Argylle just has time to think before he is hit by a force that slams him – *whoomph* – to the ground. And now there is nothing except the crushing weight of Wyatt on top of him, forcing all the air from his lungs.

'What the *hell* is going on here?'

Will Hooper, who has been supervising the exercise from one of the wooden lookout posts that dot the landscape here, has broken cover to haul Wyatt off. Argylle sits up, clutching his bruised ribs.

'Do you think you're back in the schoolyard, huh? Does this seem like a game to you?'

Hooper is looking from one to the other, chin jutting, eyes bulging.

'Well?'

'No, sir.' Wyatt and Argylle both study the ground, shoulders hunched, just like the schoolkids they're accused of being.

'Both of you, my office. *Now.*'

Argylle feels sick. He doesn't normally lose his temper so easily. He's always been one to watch and weigh up. How can this be the right place for him, if it makes him act so unlike himself?

Hooper's office is a prefab hut near the canteen. There's a desk and a computer that, judging by the papers piled on the keyboard, looks like it doesn't get much use.

'What in the name of Jesus just happened here?' When Hooper is angry, a vein stands proud on his forehead.

'I'm sorry,' Argylle mutters. 'I started it.'

Wyatt is not having this.

'Because I provoked him,' he says, as if not wanting Argylle to claim credit. But when Hooper asks him what he'd said, he remains tight-lipped.

'Why didn't you draw your weapon, Argylle?' demands Hooper.

Argylle shifts his weight from foot to foot, not looking at these men who, with their square jaws and broad shoulders, came up the hard way. Argylle has learned that Hooper too was a Navy SEAL before joining the Special Activities Division.

'I didn't grow up in a gun-loving household,' he begins at last. 'My parents were pacifists.'

Beside him, Wyatt makes a snorting noise. Argylle feels his face burn but hears his father's voice. 'The arms industry is responsible for so much misery in the world.'

'Pacifists?' Will Hooper articulates the word as if it is a foreign term that he is struggling to pronounce. 'And yet you decided your calling was the CIA? What is it you think we do here, son? Bake cookies?'

Argylle tries again. 'They understood that the world isn't perfect and you have to defend yourself, but they felt that hand-to-hand combat was . . . *nobler*, I guess.'

Even as the word comes out he is regretting it.

Hooper positions himself in front of Argylle so their faces are just inches apart. Though the instructor is shorter, there is a power compacted inside his muscle-strung body that makes him an imposing presence.

'This is the CIA, Argylle. We don't do "noble". We do "successful", we do "get the job done". If Frances Coffey hadn't vouched for you herself, you and your Bruce Lee bullshit would be outta here so fast you wouldn't know what hit you. As it is, you have two hours' extra weapons training every evening after the rest of them kick back for the night. Got it?'

As Argylle and Wyatt leave Hooper's office the atmosphere between them is as sour as halitosis.

'Go on,' says Argylle. 'Spit it out. Whatever you're going to say.'

Wyatt glances over. Shakes his head, then immediately thinks better of it.

'I don't want to speak ill of the dead, but your parents were fucking hypocrites, man. It's cool for them not to want to get their hands dirty handling weapons, but what about the other guys in the chain? What about the poor Mexican kid whose only way of making a few pesos is working for the drug gang? Do you think he has the luxury of principles? So, you know what I think, *Aubrey*? What? You think I didn't know everything about you before I got sent off to meet you in that backwater bar in Thailand? What I think is that your parents were full of shit.'

Argylle feels the energy build inside him. He glances over at Wyatt, fixes on a point on his nose and imagines the crunch of cartilage and gristle as his elbow connects. Walks abruptly away.

His anger propels him deep into the pine forest, where the air temperature drops because of the thick shade. His hands are balled into fists in his pockets. Wyatt is the one who's full of shit. He knows nothing about Argylle's life or his family.

But as his rage recedes, the doubts creep in. Doubts he has managed to keep at bay over the past years since he returned to Thailand to bury his parents and a not entirely unsympathetic police chief had informed him that he was not after all the son of textile exporters and that his whole life had been a lie.

Because Wyatt is right, isn't he? His parents were hippies at heart, convinced the marijuana they were trafficking did more good than harm, and that sooner or later the law would catch up with their way of thinking. They were outspokenly pro-legalization, anti-violence. He remembers in a street market in Hanoi, his mum, with her muscovado-soft eyes, explaining to him about the Vietnam War, the American boys drafted in to fire on unarmed civilians for reasons they never understood.

Yet at the same time his parents were running a drug-smuggling operation worth millions. They must have known, mustn't they, that even if they considered the drug itself benign, the process of getting it into the hands of those who wanted to buy it was soaked in blood?

He stops under a tree and bends down, feeling suddenly nauseated.

Snapshots from his childhood flash through his mind, but for once there is no comfort in them. All that time his parents were pretending to be people they were not. And now he will never know the people they actually were.

Now it comes back to him. The scene that at the time seemed so unlikely that afterwards he'd half thought he had dreamt it. During what was to be Argylle's last term at school, shortly after his father had paid him an unexpected visit while he was in the UK 'for business', the headteacher had told him two men had been in, asking for him. 'But the weird thing is they used the surname Major,' Argylle reported back to his father on the phone, referring to the family name that had changed some years back. His father had glossed over it, but a week later, a cryptic postcard had arrived from Thailand. 'If anything happens to us, the Kingsman Arms does an excellent Cosmopolitan. Forget the ingredients – the twist is to die for.'

It made no sense that his dad, who hardly drank, should have even heard of the down-at-heel village pub near the school, and Argylle had made a note to quiz him about the mysterious message the next time they spoke, but then had come the bombshell call to say his parents were dead.

The following days passed in a blur of arrangements, but on the eve of his return to Thailand, a still-reeling Argylle remembered about the card and slipped away to the village.

Stepping inside the pub that night straight from school was like crossing from one world into another. Inside there were little round tables overhung with red-shaded lights and walls lined with wood panels. There was a dartboard and a blackboard advertising 'the best Sunday roast in England'. The few customers, mostly men, were all glued to the television where Arsenal were being thrashed by Chelsea. They hardly looked at Argylle when he came in.

Still, he was wary. You didn't order fancy cocktails in a place like this. A glance over at the barman did little to quell his nerves. Tall with a strange high-collared jacket and a bizarre haircut that rose up high from his forehead before being flattened off at the top, the man was as imposing as he was unusual.

Swallowing, Argylle sat down on a ratty red plastic bar stool in front of a tap dispensing draught Guinness.

'Cosmopolitan with a twist, please.'

The barman looked over, his green eyes amused, and Argylle was conscious of his scrawny seventeen-year-old frame and the long, unruly hair that the school insisted he tie back with an elastic band.

'Does it look like we're in a club or a pub?'

But there was no malice in the older man's voice.

'Fine. Hold the vodka, the Cointreau and the cranberry juice. Just the twist.'

Argylle was glad he'd looked up a Cosmopolitan before he set off. Forewarned is forearmed. Even so, he held his breath waiting for the barman's response, relieved when a smile twitched at the corners of his mouth.

'Coming right up.'

The barman reached under the bar and, to Argylle's surprise, produced a small, slim box, which he slid across to his underage customer.

'You must be in a lot of trouble if they sent you to me, darling. What's your name?'

Argylle wasn't sure if he was more shocked by the 'darling', or by what the man said.

He tried to stop his fingers shaking as he opened the box, but he couldn't control the gasp when he caught sight of its contents.

'Aubrey,' he said faintly, his eyes fixed on the gun nestling inside the box in front of him. 'Aubrey Argylle.'

A customer got up from a nearby table and the barman casually snapped shut the lid of the box.

'Well, Aubrey,' he resumed when the customer had passed through to a narrow door at the back marked Gents, 'you should probably take your new toy and get going.'

But during that brief interlude Argylle had come to a decision.

'Thank you, but I won't be needing this,' he said, as firmly as he could, pushing the box back across the bar.

The barman raised an eyebrow and stared at Argylle with interest, and something seemed to pass between them. Then he shrugged and swiped the box from the bar, returning it under the counter.

'As you wish, sweetheart.'

Argylle remembers that his heart was hammering as he left the pub but that for the first time since he'd heard the news about his parents he'd felt a sense of control. Until he arrived back in Chiang Saen, he didn't have the first clue what that scene was about, but he knew he'd faced a fork in the road back there and the route he chose would have repercussions on the rest of his life. And while his father might have been trying to protect him, he knew his mother would have approved of the choice he'd made.

And now he's reached another fork.

And he is about to make a different choice.

His parents are dead. He doesn't need to live his life constantly in reference to theirs – what they would or would not have done. He will forge his own path.

But that doesn't mean renouncing them and everything they gave him.

Later that evening, he places a call to Frances Coffey.

'What I said about not calling me by my first name. I want you to forget it.'

'Are you sure? There are some who might use it against you.'

'Let them. Wyatt already knows anyway.'

'Yes, but he hasn't—'

'I'm done with being ashamed. My parents were far from perfect. I know that. But I loved them, and I won't apologize for that. Christ knows, I have little enough to remember them by. I'm damned if I'm going to ditch the name they gave me in case some little nobody like Matt Schneider takes the piss.

'Look, for all I know, you're about to kick me out anyway, but if I stay, I want to stay on my terms. And if the rest of them don't like it, they can, as Wyatt would say, kiss my ass.'

15

SOME HOURS LATER, WOODY WYATT IS UNHAPPILY BACK IN WILL Hooper's office. He has been dragged out of what seemed like a very promising encounter with Erin Quinn. Not that Wyatt would ever make a move on someone from his own team. It's very much a no-go area, plus he's been involved in enough bitter break-ups to understand that it's preferable if the person who's supposed to have your back doesn't actually want to stab you in it. But this is an inter-Agency team and when the mission is over they will most likely be disbanded again, and that means open season as far as he's concerned.

He and Quinn had been sitting behind the women's barracks, sharing a beer that she'd somehow smuggled into the barracks. This part of the training focuses on physical resilience and fortitude, and bottles of Coors don't feature. But Erin Quinn has her own secret ways. Born into a family that's steeped in the culture of the CIA, her recently deceased dad an Agency hero who was blown up by a suicide bomber in the early days of the US involvement in Iraq, she knows her way around the Point and most of the other CIA outposts. When they head into the local town, the barkeeps and waiting staff call her by name.

So he hadn't been thrilled to find out from Asif Samra, the team's mild-mannered engineer, that Hooper was on his trail.

Still, here he is. Also in attendance are Mike Randall and Frances

Coffey, beamed in from Delaware courtesy of Bright Eyes, the Agency's highly encrypted, classified video-conferencing system with a dedicated server so secret there's no trace of it anywhere on the Web.

Hooper is bringing the other two up to speed on what happened earlier and making it clear that he considers Argylle to be unsuitable for the mysterious mission they have ahead of them. 'Maybe he'd be okay at something desk-bound,' he says. 'But without proper weapons training, the kid's about as much use to the team as a chocolate griddle pan.'

Coffey looks solemn, her lips pressed bloodlessly together.

'You said he had Matt Schneider on the ground?' says Randall. He is taking notes as they speak, and Wyatt knows without needing to see that his writing will be neat and exact, the opposite of his own.

'Look, I'm not saying the kid hasn't got some skills when it comes to unarmed combat,' says Hooper. 'In fact, I wouldn't mind him teaching me some of those moves he had out there.'

'But that means jack shit if he won't pick up a gun when our backs are against the wall,' interrupts Wyatt.

'I see that,' says Coffey slowly. 'But you've told him to report for extra weapons training, Will? Surely it won't take you long to bring him up to speed.'

Hooper shrugs. 'Only if he'll agree to it.'

'Wouldn't want to compromise his *principles*,' says Wyatt, who is still smarting from having lost the exercise earlier. Wyatt can be relaxed about most things, doesn't take himself too seriously. But he has a competitive streak that sometimes takes even him by surprise. It's always been like that – he was the kid who goofed around in the back of the class, but put him on a football field or a racetrack and it was a whole different story. Looking up into the rafters, hoping to catch a glimmer of pride on his father's face. He thinks most of them are like that in the Agency. It's practically a requirement of the job. But Argylle? He still isn't sure whether it's competitiveness that drives him or something else. Not patriotism – he's a man who grew up without a country. Not his dead hippy parents. So what exactly is it that has brought him here and, having brought him, what has kept him?

'What's your verdict, Woody?' Coffey asks him now, her jaw moving as if she is chewing on the inside of her cheek.

There is something about the way she asks him, as if she is genuinely putting her faith in his judgement, that makes Wyatt decide to set his personal dislike aside.

'Either he's going to turn out to be the best recruit you ever had . . .' He tails off, thinking how best to phrase what he wants to say.

'Or?' she prompts.

'Or he's going down at the first fence – and taking us all with him.'

16

IT'S TWO HOURS BY HELICOPTER FROM THE POINT TO THE UPPER Gauley River, which feels twice as long when no one is talking to you. Argylle tells himself he doesn't mind. He has spent his entire life as an outsider. Why should it start bothering him now?

The Special Ops chopper has seven rows of double seats down each side with an aisle in between. From the back, he can hear Wyatt talking in a low tone to Erin Quinn and then her laughter. Every seat has two people on it except his. *Good*, he thinks. *More room for me.* To demonstrate, he stretches his long legs diagonally across both high-backed canvas seats and leans back with his arms behind his head. Across the aisle, Mia Matsyuk gives him a small, private smile. She's something of an enigma. Self-contained, slightly aloof. He has heard that she lived in Russia for seven years and, like him, speaks the language fluently, but she doesn't encourage personal conversation. Next to her, Eric Lawler sprawls into the aisle, his left foot tapping restlessly on the chopper floor. Like Matsyuk, Lawler is not hot on small talk and Argylle suspects the scars from his time in Afghanistan aren't just physical.

Argylle closes his eyes and finds himself thinking about the six months he and his parents spent living in Pondicherry in India. The pastel-coloured French colonial villas with their colonnaded balconies and bougainvillea-clad walls. The heady smell of fresh jasmine buds sold from great tubs at the roadside and the chorus of beeping motorbikes. He thinks of a particular evening, the three of them watching the sun set from the seafront promenade, the breathtaking majesty of it all. His mother turning to him, her face made golden by the setting sun. 'I want you to remember this moment, whatever happens in the future, whatever you may think of us, and try not to judge us too harshly.'

At the time he hadn't understood, had just thought she was getting emotional, as she sometimes did when confronted by the enormity of nature in all its glory.

Why had they kept so much hidden from him?

He shifts in his seat, trying to dislodge the memories.

After they've been in the air an hour he becomes aware of something looming over him.

'Move over, Argylle. Don't you know being comfortable is against Agency policy?'

Keira Carter pushes his feet to the side and sits herself down next to him. 'Casner was snoring so you get the pleasure of my company.'

They start to talk. Argylle has become expert in the art of asking people so many questions they don't have the opportunity to ask any of their own. But he finds he is genuinely curious about how someone like Carter, who, like him, seems something of a loner, ended up here, on this bus, on the way to yet another team-bonding exercise, this time white-water rafting.

'You think you got a monopoly on being a loser misfit, Argylle? Is that it?'

After more digging he discovers that Carter's parents are first-generation immigrants who had high hopes for their only daughter, which seemed to be realized when she got a scholarship to Yale to study computer science. 'They'd have preferred a doctor or a dentist, but still I was the first in my family to go to university. Man, you would have thought I'd split the atom, the amount of bragging they did about it. Just about broke their hearts when I dropped out.'

Carter had been headhunted by the CCI while still in her sophomore year. As she's unable to tell her parents much about what her new career entails, they are under the impression she gave everything up for a glorified office job.

'Dad is all about the easy life, but I've always been a

disappointment to my mother, from the minute I first refused to wear the pink, frilly dresses she liked to buy for me.'

'Last year, then?'

'You're a funny guy, Argylle. She never understood me. Never wanted to try. Going to Yale was the first thing I did that made her proud – I guess I was living the life she never got to have – so you can imagine how happy she was when I dropped out.'

Throughout the journey the clouds have been building through the tiny chopper windows. The white-water kayaking exercise had been supposed to happen two days after the memory-stick-retrieval exercise came to its abrupt conclusion, but a summer storm has put them a day behind. All yesterday, torrential rain and gale-force winds had battered the camp, the team forced to stay inside, waiting for the storm to pass.

This morning dawned clear and fresh in North Carolina, but the sky has grown progressively overcast and as they approach their destination they can see evidence of yesterday's mayhem below. Branches broken off trees and strewn on the highway, a flooded field.

It's already raining when they disembark. 'This'll ruin my blow-dry,' mutters Carter, whose thick curls look as if they've never seen a hairdryer, as they stand, already soaked to the skin, waiting to pick up their life vests and kayaks.

Argylle smiles. He still wears his own hair long – much to Hooper's derision – and it is plastered to his head, the ends dripping down the neck of his T-shirt. But after his years in the tropics he is used to this weather. Hot rain peppering the baked ground like gunfire, clothes permanently damp with humidity.

He is also, though he hasn't seen the need to share this with the group, very used to white-water rafting. In his former life he regularly took small groups of tourists down the Mae Kok River, where sometimes the bamboo rafts had to skirt around elephants bathing. He understands how the river changes according to the time of year, how much more respect it demands during the rainy season, when the water level rises and the rapids are faster, the currents stronger.

In early summer, the Upper Gauley is usually a warm-water river, but the recent rainfall and the churning of the wind has lowered the temperature considerably. 'You probably won't die of hypothermia, but it won't be a whole barrel of laughs,' says Hooper as they set off. They aren't in teams for this exercise, and Hooper impresses on them that they're not racing each other but rather making sure the entire group gets down as quickly and safely as possible.

An athletic-looking man with a weather-corrugated face and wearing heavy-duty waterproofs gives them instructions about the lie of the river, which has some grade-five rapids – the most danger-ous regular classification. 'Normally the river would be packed with other rafts so someone would always be on hand to pull you out if you ran into trouble, but you're the only ones crazy enough to come out today. So don't pull any stunts.'

He talks them through the rapids, which channels to look for, which to avoid, where the undercuts are – rocks overhanging the surface, threatening capsized boaters with being sucked underneath – or the sieves, where a boater could be dragged through a hole formed by a pile of rocks. 'The water level is unusually high, so some of the rocks you'd normally be able to spot a mile off are completely sub-merged. Just bear that in mind – there are some big mothers out there.'

Argylle listens intently, but notices that Wyatt spends the whole briefing joking with Schneider. No doubt, as an ex-Marine, he thinks he understands water. Rookie error.

The first rapid is called Initiation and is a wide, fairly shallow set of drops, and all of them find the easiest, most direct lines without too much trouble, though the surf smacks the bows of the kayaks with a force that elicits a chorus of 'yeah's and 'whoah's. Argylle has forgotten how exhilarating it can be. Slamming straight into nature itself.

The next few rapids pass in the same fashion, everyone growing more confident, despite the worsening weather conditions, hugging the bends tighter, risking the faster-flowing channels. Erin Quinn pulls up beside Argylle as they wait in a recovery pool for the rest of the team to catch up.

'You've done this before,' she says. Even with the regulation hard

91

hat and orange waterproof her smile goes right to something in the heart of him.

It is on the twelfth rapid, Pillow Rock, that the first signs of trouble start. The rapids here drop nine metres and there's a sharp bend in the river where a large boulder is wedged. Argylle spots the line immediately, sticking to the left-hand channel then veering out right to avoid the boulder. But as he is heading down, the spray thick in his face, he is conscious of something coming up on his shoulder. Wyatt is bearing down on him, with a wild look of excitement on his face. 'See ya, sucker!' he calls as he noses his kayak past in the middle channel, forcing Argylle to cling to the left far longer than he had intended.

Whoomph! Argylle is momentarily distracted and his boat hits the boulder with sickening force. Though it is saved from smashing to pieces by the pillow of water that forms on impact, it is sent spinning into the eddy of the river. Ejected into the churning water, Argylle can do little except follow the upturned boat around the bend and as it crashes down the rapids. Because of yesterday's storm, the river is full of debris – branches torn from trees and larger dislodged logs. As he descends, swallowing water as he is pushed under again and again, something slams into his shoulder, causing a burst of pain.

When, heart thumping with exertion and adrenaline, he finally reaches the calmer water of the recovery pool at the bottom right, Wyatt has hold of his kayak. 'Good swim?' he asks as Argylle heaves himself out of the water.

Asshole, he thinks.

'Asshole,' he says, when he can talk.

'Don't pay no mind to Wyatt,' says Washington when they pull up at the next set of rapids. 'He's like a big kid. A day stuck inside while that storm was raging has him all pumped up with excess energy just looking for an outlet. Don't take it personal.'

But Argylle, whose shoulder is pulsing with a dull, persistent thud, takes it very personal indeed.

The next few rapids pass fairly uneventfully, but there is an atmosphere that nudges its way through the relentless rain and the spray until it hangs thickly over the group like an extra cloud they carry with them. Only Wyatt seems unaware, charging forwards, whooping and shouting, waving his paddle in the air as he flies over the rapids, his kayak soaring into the damp air.

The next grade-five rapid is named Lost Paddle and, though wide and not as steep as some of the others, it's four hundred metres long, with plenty of undercut rocks. Coming directly after a junction where a second river has come thundering in to join this one, Argylle knows the water will be fast and high.

As he skims down over the urgently flowing rapids at the top, Argylle looks in vain for Six Pack Rock, which their instructor warned them about before they set off. He knows it is bang in the centre of the fastest-flowing section of the rapids, where a vicious whirlpool funnels surf down under the current and a huge boulder looms hard on its heels over on the right.

Argylle is the first down. Realizing that the rock must be entirely submerged, he makes instantly for the far-left channel so he can be sure to avoid it, even though this is the longest and least obvious line. He is conscious of the others following behind as he battles through the eddying flow. The rain is driving down now, blown into their faces by the wind. When he finally makes it to a safety pool part way down, he sees that the others are valiantly struggling to hold to that same left line.

All except one.

Dear God, tell me he's not . . . Wyatt comes flying down the centre of the run, his paddle raised above his head, a Greek god in a winged chariot.

A Greek god who doesn't know there's a fucking great concealed rock in his path.

All of a sudden the kayak lifts into the air as it impacts with the stone. Wyatt is flung clear, crashing back down into the water dangerously close to the hulking boulder over to the right. The one Argylle knows to be hiding an undercut where a person can be sucked underneath and held for Lord knows how long, only to be spat out, half drowned, the other side.

Sure enough, Wyatt, who has been thrashing about, using his paddle to stay afloat, abruptly disappears under the surface. 'He had that coming!' says Carter, who has come up on Argylle's left. They wait for him to reappear, but even before it becomes obvious that Wyatt is not re-emerging Argylle has started to move, pushing against the current towards the back side of the boulder under which Wyatt has been dragged.

He knows that when an experienced boatsman like Woody Wyatt doesn't come back up again it's because something is stopping him. Entrapment, they call it on the river. Rocks, tree trunks, debris. Anything a person could catch a foot or a leg in.

Argylle dives down and sees Wyatt immediately. His first thought is that he's playing a joke on them, as he appears to be fully through the underhang of the rock. Anger is a bitter taste in Argylle's mouth. *Does he think it's funny?* Then he notices that one of Wyatt's feet is still wedged behind him on the other side of the rock. The big man is grappling to reach it, but the weight of the water pushing downstream makes it impossible for him to twist enough to reach back through the underhang to get it free.

Argylle surfaces and hauls himself on to the rock under which Wyatt is stuck, scrambling to get to the top, battered by the spray sent up by the water smacking against the stone. The noise of the river is almost deafening here. He thinks he hears the others shouting, but he is focused on getting to the other side so that he can free Wyatt's leg from whatever is trapping it in place.

Argylle is usually able to clear his mind so that he can act without overthinking. But even he hesitates for a moment on that rock, looking down into the swirling mass of water.

In that split second of hesitation, he becomes aware of a blur of movement at his shoulder, and there is Erin Quinn, drenched and pallid-faced, clambering up the rock to knot a kayak rope around his waist, passing the end of the rope to Washington behind her, who in turn passes it to Schneider and Casner and Corcoran, Reynolds, Lawler, and the whole team, in a human chain, even reed-thin Mia Matsyuk, all the way back to Carter, standing on the bank, wedged in behind the trunk of a tree. And now the time for thinking is over and he plunges in, the shock of the cold water momentarily blocking out the pressure of the current, until with a jolt he is back in the moment and being bashed against the rock, his entire left side scraped raw and only the reassuring grip of the rope tethering him to the solid, safe world.

He forces himself downward against the weight of water that tries to drag him under the rock. With the undercut now being blocked by the hulking figure of Woody Wyatt, he risks being propelled out into the dangerous middle channel, where there is a whirlpool sucking everything down into a deep vortex of debris.

And now he sees what has happened. Thanks to the storm, an array of debris has built up that is too big to pass under the boulder. A huge branch, probably dislodged by Wyatt as he was sucked underneath, has tried to follow him under and become stuck diagonally across the entrance to the channel below, trapping Wyatt's foot between it and the pile of smaller loose rocks on the riverbed.

A pressure is building in Argylle's lungs, a water-filled balloon inflating in his chest. God knows how Wyatt's lungs are bearing up. Diving down, Argylle tries to lift the branch away to free Wyatt's trapped foot, but the pressure of tens of hundreds of cubic metres per second of water keeps it pinioned in place. So now he must go down further to try to dig it out from the bottom, even when everything in him is telling him to head the other way, up to the surface, where he can breathe.

The rocks underneath Wyatt's foot are loose, probably washed here from further upstream before being snagged by the boulder. Argylle scrabbles with his hands to get a grip on the topmost rock, panic taking hold as it refuses to budge. He grabs a small branch that has also become stuck and tries to lever it into the gap between the top rock and the one under it, but it snaps almost immediately.

His chest is burning now, a pressure cooker about to explode. The desperation to open his mouth and take a breath almost unbearable.

He grabs a second branch. This one is stronger, and he manages to wedge it into the narrow gap between the rocks, pressing on the end with everything he has. The top rock shifts but doesn't fall. He does it again, knowing this could be the last attempt. The balloon in his chest has pushed out his ribs, bowing them until he knows beyond all reason that they will surely snap.

As the water pummels him relentlessly, he pushes down once again on the end of the branch, which duly breaks – but not before it has dislodged the top rock, sending it off to the riverbed on the side and freeing Wyatt's foot. The sudden funnel of water created by the new vacuum sweeps Argylle along with it, and he just has time to register that he is about to follow Wyatt in being sucked underneath the boulder before the balloon in his chest bursts and everything goes black.

17

OUTSIDE THE MAIN DOOR OF THE MILITARY HOSPITAL, ARGYLLE stops to gulp in the fresh air. He wonders how long it will take to forget that feeling of not being able to breathe, how long before he can feel his lungs inflating and deflating without panicking that they might suddenly stop.

Over the two days he lay in his hospital bed he has pieced together some idea of what happened after the world went black. Him being yanked, unconscious, out of the water by his teammates, coming to next to a blue-lipped Wyatt undergoing CPR from Will Hooper, all the compacted energy in those densely muscled arms pressing down into Wyatt's broad ribcage.

He has a vague memory of Erin Quinn sitting next to him in the ambulance, and of finding it a comfort to have her there.

Then blackness.

Information on the man whose life he saved was brought to him in snippets, relayed by a moon-faced nurse with a laugh like a drain. Wyatt is alive. Now Wyatt is conscious. Now he is flirting, and doesn't he have gorgeous eyes? Only when the news came that Wyatt was being discharged before him did Argylle resent the unasked-for updates.

He had visitors. Will Hooper came and talked for a long time about protocol and the dangers of heroics until the nurse said firmly that it was too soon. One time he briefly awoke from a deep sleep to see Erin Quinn sitting by his bedside, but when he opened his eyes again maybe minutes or perhaps hours later she was gone, leaving behind the newspaper she'd been reading. He recognized the impassive face of Vasily Federov staring out at him from the front page under the headline: IS THIS THE MOST DANGEROUS MAN IN THE WORLD?

Now, finally, he is returning to the Point. The thought both excites and depresses him.

True, he'll be glad to leave behind the hospital with its twenty-four-hour noises and bleach-stinking corridors. But to be going back to that team, and that atmosphere of distrust, walking into noisy rooms that fall instantly silent when . . .

'Well, get in, then.'

Argylle doesn't move, eyeing the *thing* that has just pulled up in front of him – long as a bus, with a huge dent in one side and a side door that belongs to a completely different vehicle. Rust-coloured, although on closer inspection that might actually *be* rust . . .

'Impressive wheels, Carter. Did you make this mean machine yourself?'

'One of my brothers built it out of three different wrecks. Now, you getting in, or you want me to draw you a map? It's sixty-eight klicks so you'd better get moving pronto if you're walking.'

There is to be a meeting this evening with Frances Coffey herself, who has just flown in. Argylle won't even have time to drop his gear at the barracks, Carter tells him.

'Are we being disbanded?' Argylle has been considering this possibility. That Coffey will decide the team isn't working and send him back. Trying to work out if the idea makes him disappointed or relieved.

Carter shrugs, but her expression is tight. 'You know, it's funny, I thought I wanted to go back to the CCI, but turns out I'm not ready to go back behind a desk.'

Argylle thinks of his hut and his hammock in Thailand. Thinks of leading tour groups into the jungle, always one who wants to prove himself, thinks of the days going past, and the months, and now five years are gone and he hardly knows where. If it wasn't for the Sam

Gor, would he still be there in another five years? In ten? Stuck in a holding pattern in the last place he felt any sense of belonging?

When he follows Carter up the steps to Hooper's office, his feet drag. Not just because any movement still tires him out, but because he can hear the buzz of conversation and knows they are all in there.

But when he walks inside, through the door Carter is holding open as if he's an invalid, for Christ's sake, there is a spontaneous burst of applause. The entire squad are on their feet. He sees Matsyuk, normally so reserved, clapping her hands above her head, and the taciturn Lawler putting both pinkies in his mouth to whistle.

Mortified, Argylle is relieved when Hooper quietens them down. He slides into an empty seat, aware of Wyatt at the back of the room and of Frances Coffey in a chair by the window, leaning forward with interest.

Hooper stands up and Argylle can tell from the set of his jaw that he isn't about to give him a pat on the back. Sure enough, Hooper launches straight into the importance of following instructions (with a look to Wyatt) and of observing protocol when things veer off course (with a look to Argylle). 'We don't want mavericks in the CIA. We don't want cheap heroics. We want team players. Is that understood?'

A chorus of 'yes, sir's greets the stinging rebuke.

Now Hooper goes through the exercise in detail. The mistakes that were made. The rules that were broken.

Argylle comes in for some criticism, but most of Hooper's disapproval is reserved for Wyatt. His recklessness, his unforgivable rivalry towards a member of his own team. When Hooper has finished his tirade, he asks Wyatt to stand up.

'Your actions endangered the whole squad. If you'd done that in the field, you'd have put the entire operation at risk. Now, I wouldn't blame Chief Coffey if she were to cancel this entire team as of this moment, but in the event she gives you lame bunch another chance, I want you to step outside so the rest of the team can take a vote on whether to kick your sorry ass out, which, incidentally, is what I'll be recommending.'

Wyatt stands up and heads towards the door, but when he passes in front of Argylle, he stops.

'I know I deserve whatever's coming to me,' he says, and his voice sounds different without its usual swagger. 'I was a prize jerk. But I want to thank you, in front of everyone, for what you did back there. You saved my life.'

Argylle wants to make a joke about that adage that saving someone's life makes you responsible for them, and how if he'd remembered that he wouldn't have done it, but he finds his mouth as dry as gravel.

After the door closes, Hooper recaps on Wyatt's crimes, just in case anyone was in any doubt. 'I can't stress enough the importance of team trust. Ask yourselves this: can you truly trust a guy who put you all in danger, just so he could beat you to the finish line?' Next he reminds them their decision could have repercussions for them all. 'We won't send you out on a mission if we consider there to be a weak link in the team.'

Only then does he ask for a show of hands as to who still wants Wyatt to stay.

The first hand that goes up is Schneider's, then Quinn's, closely followed by everyone else in the team. Hooper glares at Argylle's raised hand. 'He almost got you killed. You do know that? Just because he's the muscle of the team—'

'He's not just the muscle, though, sir,' says Washington. 'He's also the heart of us.'

There's a split second of silence, and then Will Hooper shrugs and turns away, but not before Argylle has seen a flicker of what looks a lot like relief pass over his craggy face. He nods at Carter, who is nearest the door, and she gets up to summon Wyatt back inside.

The big guy looks pale as he makes his way to the front of the room.

'Y're in luck, Wyatt. These other thirteen idiots in your team have voted to keep you in. Go sit. But be warned, if you ever pull a stunt like that again, you'll be out on your dumb ass so quick you won't know what hit you.'

Wyatt takes his seat at the back, head bowed.

And now Frances Coffey is getting to her feet. She doesn't look at Argylle, and he braces himself to hear that the team is being disbanded. He is surprised, now that the moment is here, by how much he finds he minds. A band tightens around his chest as he waits for her to speak.

'I'm not going to go over what Will has just said. I think he made himself crystal clear, and I trust you have all taken it on board. Instead, I'm here to tell you about your next mission.'

Argylle's head shoots up. All around are murmurs of surprise and disbelief.

'But the rapids?' says Erin Quinn. 'I thought . . .'

'Will Hooper is absolutely right that what happened at the Upper Gauley should never have happened. But—' She looks around the room, her eyes – soft behind her glasses in contrast to the sharp cut of her hair – finally coming to rest on Argylle. 'When you were really up against it back there by the river, when everything was about to be lost, that's when you finally pulled together as a team. Forming a human chain, no man or woman left behind. It's what we've been waiting for, what we'd worried might never happen.

'Don't get me wrong, there are still an awful lot of rough edges. And the scars from Isfahan still have a long way to heal. But it's a start.

'Right. Notebooks out while I explain about the mission. How's everyone's French?'

PART TWO

18

THE TERRACE OF THE BAR AMÉRICAIN IN THE HÔTEL DE PARIS IN the heart of Monte Carlo, from where Argylle gazes out through the palm trees at the early-evening sun pooling on the surface of the navy-blue Mediterranean, feels like a long way from Chiang Saen or even the camp at Harvey Point. The inaugural Laval Ball feels even further.

This glittering international event, the brainchild of Prince Florestan, playboy son of the ruling family and his American bride, A-list actress Jennifer Martin, is ostensibly a fundraiser for the principality's newest cultural offering – the dazzling Monte Carlo Jewellery Museum. What better showcase for the world's most valuable, beautiful or historic jewels than this tiny mecca of wealth and finery? From ancient bronze brooches unearthed in the ruins of Roman palaces to star sapphires from the Mogok mines in Myanmar and a pearl necklace owned by Marie Antoinette, the new museum promises to mix antiques steeped in blood and history with the glamour of Hollywood – jewels bought by Richard Burton for Elizabeth Taylor, the engagement ring worn by the principality's own princess, Grace Kelly.

The Salle Empire off the hotel's lobby, with its gold-leafed ceiling and crystal chandeliers, its marble pillars holding up frescoed arches, has been turned into a temporary exhibition of some of the most famous items of jewellery in the world. The exhibits have been borrowed from private individuals or collectors for this one night only and are guarded by the most extensive security operation the principality has ever mounted. Some of the pieces have never before been seen by the public, and it is a measure of the prestige of the occasion and the setting that they have been released. Everyone who is anyone wants to be here. And the guests will be expected to dig deep. In addition to the €2,500 per head ticket price, the tables arranged outside in the casino gardens, under awnings of silk studded with thousands of tiny lights to give the impression of a canopy of stars, cost upwards of two hundred thousand euros each.

A stage has been rigged up at the end of the gardens closest to the casino itself. Already the hundred-piece orchestra is warming up, the musicians dressed according to the ball's 'Metallica' theme in shades of silver, bronze and gold. There will be various globally famous artistes performing at various points in the evening. Earlier, a buzz of excitement rippled through the guests on the terrace as a cavalcade of black cars made its way up from Port Hercules where the one-hundred-metre superyacht *Hope* has been berthed all day. Elton John was rumoured to be in the first car, one of the top-tier artistes due to perform here.

Argylle heads inside. He likes the bar, with its wood-panelled walls and old-fashioned leather stools that make one feel that little has changed since Charlie Chaplin and Winston Churchill were frequent visitors many decades ago.

These days, the clientele is different. Argylle hears a lot of Russian spoken here, and Arabic and Mandarin. The whole of Monte Carlo, this tiny jewel in the kingdom of Monaco, has been closed off for the duration of the ball, creating an exclusive playground for those with the deepest of pockets.

He asks for a whisky and soda and settles himself into a leather armchair from where he has a view of the door, as if this is his natural habitat, although the truth is Argylle has no natural habitat, equally at ease everywhere and nowhere.

In the two months since the white-water-rafting incident, Argylle's physical appearance has altered. Intensive training has bulked him out, filling in the lines that before were faint or blurred. He is still watchful, still wary, but every now and then he leans into the world as if he is engaging with it, rather than sitting back observing.

Gone is the long, dark hair he used to tie back with an elastic band to stop it getting in the way. Instead, he sports a new flat-top style, with short sides as soft and smooth as suede. His faded jeans and old T-shirt have been replaced by a suit of raw silk in a midnight blue threaded with silver, in deference to the theme, so that it shimmers in the light. The jacket is cut in a Nehru style, hip length and tailored to fit, with a mandarin collar and a silver silk square in the pocket.

When he'd been tasked with reinventing himself for this mission, the distinctive-looking barman from the Kingsman Arms back in the UK had come into his mind and lodged there, refusing to shift.

'Looking fly, Argylle.'

Argylle affects disinterest.

'Yeah, well, you might have made an effort, Quinn. I feel bad eclipsing you.'

Erin Quinn stands before him, hand on hip, looking like she has just stepped out of the pages of a fashion magazine in a strappy gold dress that dips in the front and plunges in the back, her skin glowing.

'To think I even brushed my hair specially.'

They smile at each other, suddenly awkward, even though the two of them have spent the last few weeks, since being partnered up by Coffey, practically glued to each other's side, creating elaborate new identities and back stories of how they met and fell in love. Argylle is Ben Armstrong, son of a British multimillionaire who made his money in antiques, while Quinn is Kate Parry, an art-history graduate and trust-fund babe with a passion for jewellery. They met at university (Oxford), where Kate was on a year's exchange programme from Stanford, and plan to marry on the Amalfi Coast in October. They have come here looking for ideas for a ring which Kate intends to design herself. She wears on her finger a three-hundred-thousand-dollar engagement ring designed by Garrard's of London that the Agency has hired for the occasion and which must be placed in the hotel safe overnight before being returned tomorrow by a courier driving an armoured van. They have even been taking dancing lessons so that they can appear to be what they profess to be – an ambitious young couple born into money, as comfortable in a ballroom as in a festival tent.

Quinn looks around as she takes a seat opposite Argylle, but they have the bar largely to themselves. The ball doesn't start for another hour and most guests are still getting ready.

Argylle sometimes thinks he has an intolerance to extreme wealth in the same way other people are intolerant to lactose or pollen.

'You good?' Quinn asks, her face tilted, eyes appearing amber in the glow of the flickering candle on the table.

'Me? Sure. Just counting the minutes till I get to show off my quickstep.'

Quinn puts her hand over his on the tabletop and leans in so their talk can't be overheard, just the murmuring of a couple in love. Argylle tries to concentrate on playing his role, but he is distracted by the touch of her fingers and by her rose-scented perfume.

'Is it there yet?' he asks her.

She shakes her head, smiling as if he's said something cute.

'I saw Wyatt earlier and he says all the others have arrived but the Duchess is still missing.'

Woody Wyatt has enjoyed a different kind of preparation period. Not for him the dance classes, or the immersion in British upper-class culture, nor the pizza nights with Erin Quinn in Perilli's meant to bond them as a believable couple. Instead, he has had a crash course in security, working first on the door of an exclusive jeweller's in Manhattan, then at the flagship Cartier store in Paris, before being selected by the world-famous jewellery house to come here to Monte Carlo, accompanying the historic jewels on loan for the night. Currently he is standing guard downstairs in the Salle Empire with the rest of the security detail.

With some of the world's most expensive, even priceless, jewels brought together in one place, the organizers have taken no chances when it comes to protection. Because the nature of the occasion, with guests wandering in and out, makes alarms or lasers impractical, each exhibit boasts its own security guard. They are positioned discreetly around the edge of the room, wearing suits as befits the occasion but identifiable by their lack of adherence to the metallic theme, and by the fact that most have necks as wide as the female guests' waists, and visible earpieces.

'Let's hope she's planning to make a dramatic entrance,' Argylle says, matching Quinn's smile. But inside, the first twinges of alarm are plucking at his nerve endings.

The Bracelet of Fidelity, codename the Duchess, a dazzling jewel made from heavy gold inset with pinpricks of diamond, beautifully and mysteriously inscribed, is the entire reason they are here, the cause of the dance classes and the haircut and the suit and Erin Quinn pressing on his hand and murmuring into his ear.

And the truth is that, though he has enjoyed all of the above, Argylle still feels uneasy about this mission. All this effort and expense, just to steal an expensive bauble? It doesn't sit well.

Sure, they've been told who that bauble belongs to – Russian presidential hopeful Vasily Federov, a man whose dark reputation has spread far beyond Russia's borders. This is the man responsible for rounding up twenty thousand alcoholics and homeless people from the streets of Omsk in south-western Siberia, never to be heard from again; the man who insisted on storming a theatre in which a hundred and seventy-five children were being held hostage by Chechen revolutionaries, ignoring the hostage-takers' repeated threats to blow the whole place up – as they duly did. Despite there being no survivors, Federov had later insisted he'd make exactly the same decision again. Irina Federova, his wife and the wearer of the bracelet, is herself the subject of several lawsuits alleging abuse and ill treatment brought by former aides and domestics. So there can be little sympathy for the couple they are about to rob.

It's just not what Argylle had envisioned for his first mission. Of course, he hadn't been expecting to fight some epic battle, but he had imagined some sort of meaningful undertaking, something worthwhile.

Coffey has been unforthcoming about the reasons behind the mission, which for logistical reasons involves a reduced team of eight. 'Sit tight. It'll become clear later on,' she's told them. With anyone else, Argylle would have pushed for more information, his ingrained distrust of authority coming to the fore. 'Always question everything,' his dad had told him. But somehow, with Coffey, he's learned to bite his lip.

All they know is that Federov has agreed to a request from the ball's organizers to display the bracelet. Perhaps he has been persuaded that having one of his possessions on show amid those of royalty and film stars will strengthen his position as a global player. Perhaps he just wants to show off his latest toy.

The plan for the actual theft has been endlessly gone over, every eventuality played out. Ivan Volodin, the Russian security guard charged with protecting the bracelet, has already been identified and thoroughly checked out. The team know his likes and dislikes, the names of his children, the fact he's not averse to a toot of cocaine to get him through a shift.

Wyatt is already on first-name terms with Ivan and the rest of the security detail. Of course he is. He's that kind of guy. He and Ivan have already partaken of a pick-me-up in the staff toilets. The Russian is delighted to discover that, unlike him, Wyatt has come directly from Paris, the contents of his luggage not subject to airport drug-sniffer dogs.

The two have already worked out a signal to slip away for a synchronized comfort break. What Ivan doesn't know is that the cocaine in the second wrap has been cut with Rohypnol. Wyatt, bent over the toilet lid with a rolled fifty-euro note, will sweep his line down the collar of his shirt, leaving the bigger one for a very grateful Ivan.

Back in the Salle Empire, as Ivan starts to sweat and sway, Wyatt will move in to help while actually ensuring that when Ivan eventually falls, he does so into the display case, sending it crashing to the ground. And when it does, there's Argylle and Quinn, ready to help pick up the bracelet – or rather the replica Argylle has in his pocket. This fake bracelet is the product of weeks of work by one of the world's foremost jewellery forgers, employed by the Agency to work from the photographs and description in the Hong Kong auction house catalogue to create an identical copy of the Bracelet of Fidelity. Or nearly identical. The quality of the pictures made it impossible to exactly reproduce the bracelet's intricate pattern of dots and squiggles. And of course none of them knows yet what it is about the original bracelet that makes it so precious to Federov, and that's the part that not even the best forger could replicate.

It's a complicated plan, and much can go wrong, but the team have role-played this a hundred times and now they know Ivan has taken the first bait, the biggest uncertainty has been removed.

There's just one problem. As yet, there is no bracelet.

By now the bar is filling up with guests – Argylle has never seen so many couture gowns, so many diamonds, so many sets of perfect, gleaming white teeth. Among the older guests – well, those over thirty – there is a certain uniform look sculpted by Botox and fillers. Both women and men sport those high, rounded cheeks, those lightly slanted eyes. Everyone is alert with anticipation and recreational pharmaceuticals.

'Shall we take a stroll?' Quinn asks, as if they are just another golden couple seeking distraction from the relentless leisure of their golden lives.

They cross the arched, marble-columned lobby, passing underneath the huge central ceiling rose with its intricate glass petals and the vast, dramatic chandelier. A pianist is playing a grand piano in the corner and they pause at one of the tables that line the edges of the lobby, as if soaking in the atmosphere. Through the open doorway to the Salle Empire, Argylle can see Wyatt staring grimly ahead, and two metres away from him, a display case, empty apart from the green velvet cushion on which ought to be nestling the Bracelet of Fidelity. Wyatt catches his eye. Gives an almost imperceptible shake of the head.

Argylle has seen very little of Wyatt since that team meeting in Will Hooper's office back at Harvey Point. And when they have met, though relations have been noticeably more cordial, they have not been easy. There is a stiffness between them. Which is fine by Argylle. He's not in the market for friends.

'Let's go back up to the room,' says Quinn, playing the flirtatious fiancée just a little too well.

He doesn't need asking twice.

Apparently modest by the hotel's standards – the Princess Grace suite, for example, has two storeys – it's by far the most luxurious room Argylle has ever stayed in. When he travelled with his parents, they stayed under the radar in small, quirky hotels or digs. Their relatively modest lifestyle was another reason Argylle was blindsided when he learned what his parents really did for a living.

This hotel room has a plush blue carpet and a small balcony with ornate wrought-iron railings overlooking the twin towers of the famous casino of Monte Carlo. It is dominated by a huge bed with a pale blue-and-white bedspread and matching cushions that Argylle tries hard not to look at in case Erin Quinn might guess what is passing through his mind. The windows are draped in vast swathes of material that matches the bed cover.

There's a small writing desk in front of the window at which Quinn is sitting, already on the phone. 'Yes,' she says. And 'I understand.' She looks serious, and Argylle gets a horrible feeling that everything is about to go very, very wrong.

19

'DAMMIT,' SHE SAYS, THROWING HER PHONE DOWN ON TO THE DESK.

Argylle waits.

'According to Wyatt's new best buddy, Ivan, the Federovs had a change of heart and have decided not to put the bracelet on display. Instead, Irina Federova will be wearing it.'

'You've got to be—'

'Precisely.'

Argylle slumps down on to the bed.

'So now we have to improvise. Coffey and Randall are running through everything they know about the Federovs to try to find a way to get that bracelet off her wrist. We just have to wait for instructions and, in the meantime . . .'

For one wild, stupid moment he thinks she is going to suggest the very thing he has been unsuccessfully trying not to think about.

'. . . Let's go dance,' she finishes. 'Coffey wants us in position down in the gardens. Don't ask me why.'

Outside, dusk has arrived and Casino Square and the gardens look like the setting of a fairy tale, the palm trees and overhead canopies hung with lights under which hundreds of beautifully laid tables glimmer with the flames of thousands of candles. Against this background, the guests glitter and dazzle in their metallic costumes – gowns of overlapping sequins in silver and bronze, tiaras winking

113

with diamonds and rubies, elaborate hair sculptures threaded with golden flowers.

On the stage at one end, the orchestra is playing as a never-ending cavalcade of luxury cars – Bentleys and Ferraris and a gleaming Rolls-Royce Phantom – pull up to deposit their precious cargoes at a red-carpeted landing stage, greeted by liveried staff.

The heat of the day has ebbed, leaving behind a warm glow and the promise of an evening delicately fragranced with jasmine and orange blossom. Even the whirring of the odd helicopter on the periphery – Monte Carlo itself has been declared a no-fly zone for the duration of the ball – bringing in a guest from Cannes or the Italian Riviera doesn't disturb the heady atmosphere.

Argylle and Quinn stroll hand in hand on to the dance floor, which is open to the sky so that the stars seem like a continuation of the fairy lights strung over the tables. The orchestra breaks into a soft samba version of 'Can't Take My Eyes Off You', and Argylle grimaces.

'Just don't overthink it, Argylle. You got this,' says Quinn.

He tries to ignore the schmaltz factor and instead lets the music guide him, moving his feet as he's been taught, spinning Erin Quinn around under the sparkling sky.

All the time, he is scanning the tables and the steady stream of cars pulling up outside the hotel to disgorge the glittering guests. He spots Schneider, wearing the black suit and lanyard and earpiece of one of the official ball stewards, patrolling the perimeter of the dance floor. Their eyes meet, and Schneider nods and immediately tracks away. Argylle and Quinn wait a beat before following, laughing to each other as if this is all just frothy, expensive fun.

They catch up with Schneider in a narrow side street between the Hôtel de Paris and the Sporting d'Hiver building.

'It's all gone to shit,' he says, while nodding, as if they're asking him something, and then turning to point back the way they came.

'So there's a new plan that revolves around the strobe lighting show that's due to kick off the fireworks. I'm afraid you lovebirds are gonna have to tear yourselves away from the cha-cha-cha or whatever the fuck it is you were doing and listen up . . .'

'It'll never work,' Argylle hisses in Quinn's ear.

'You got a better plan?'

The two of them are heading towards the command tower for the lighting display.

'Have you ever heard of it?' he asks her. 'Flicker vertigo? Jesus. We're grasping at straws here. Also, don't you think it's unethical to take advantage of someone's medical—'

'Get over yourself, Argylle. Did you read through Irina Federova's file? If you had, you'd know that she once threw boiling water over a seventeen-year-old maid who spilled a couple of drops of milk on her ivory-inlaid table. The girl had second-degree burns all the way up her arm and had to have a skin graft. An ex-boyfriend who dared to break up with her disappeared and was found in the Volga River the following spring once the ice melted, with his throat cut. This won't hurt her. She won't even remember it once she comes around.'

Research has revealed that the Federovs' team have demanded that the lights operate within safe flash frequencies – four to six flashes per second – on account of Irina's rare condition.

'So all you have to do is get up to the lighting tower and reprogramme the lights,' Schneider had told them. And before his ferrety face reverted to its default scowl, Argylle could have sworn he was smirking.

Asif Samra has become one of Argylle's closest allies in the team. A short, slight man with a serious expression through which his smile erupts as unexpectedly as lava bursting through rock, he is the engineer of the group. Faced with an obstacle or a problem, he brings the full force of his considerable logistical powers to bear on finding a solution. Argylle envies him his calm, methodical approach to life. And the wife and two small daughters whose photograph he carries in his pocket.

I would like that some day, Argylle thinks. And the realization takes him by surprise.

Samra and Carter are holed up at the Ibis at Nice airport, which is the team's temporary HQ, keeping track on what is happening via multi-band radio and computers. The discrepancy in their standards of accommodation has not been lost on Carter. 'Wait up,' she'd said earlier. 'You're swanking around in the Hôtel de Paris, swigging champagne and eating lobster and staring into Erin Quinn's eyes, and I'm stuck with Samra in a fifty-euro-a-night room with a view of Terminal 1, inhaling lukewarm McDonald's straight from the bag?'

'Yeah, but you're not running the risk of being scalped by Sergei Denisov.'

'No offence, but that haircut needed to go anyway.' The two were communicating via a basic Lai-Massey code system back in Argylle's room, but even so he looked around to check Quinn hadn't heard the part about him staring into her eyes.

It was Samra who came up with this new plan, as everyone else panicked around him. Over the last weeks the team have learned everything there is to know about Federov and his wife. What they like to eat, where they shop, who their friends are – or at least the people who purport to be friends. They know about Vasily Federov's unhappy childhood as Christopher Clay. How his parents refused to talk about his Russian background, insisting, 'You're an American now.' How his adoptive father would tell him how obvious it was that they were not blood relatives because the boy had no interest in sports. They know about his overnight windfall after he created the phenomenally successful TradeOff website, enabling people world-wide to swap anything from sofas to cars. How he met his wife at a party fundraiser in Moscow where he shocked even the wealthiest oligarchs by bidding seven million dollars for a date with the president's daughter. And they know about her too. About her temper and her tantrums and the long list of people paid off to keep quiet about their mistreatment at her hands. They know about her unhappiness within her marriage. And they know about her flicker vertigo, diagnosed two years ago and kept a close-guarded secret by her husband, who detests all signs of weakness.

There are two people in the lighting control tower, they've learned. A technician, plus the 'world-renowned lighting maestro', as he is billed on the programme, who is responsible for tonight's 'extravaganza for the senses'. According to the official ball literature, the show will feature patterns of light reflected on to the trees and the grass and the facades of the buildings that surround the gardens in exact tandem with the orchestra playing a specially composed score, building to a dazzling crescendo of crashing notes and flash lighting.

The whole thing will take six minutes, timed to coincide with the Federovs' arrival. As guests of honour, having contributed more than any other single donor to the museum, the couple will be met at their car by Prince Florestan himself and his new bride, Princess Jennifer, and escorted from their car down the Grand Avenue, the cue for the light show to start – the light show that has been painstakingly devised so as not to trigger Mrs Federova's exceedingly rare form of vertigo. The finale of the light show is exactly timed to coincide with the party arriving at their seats, at which point the fireworks will begin.

'So all we have to do is climb up there and work out how to reprogramme the lights and then persuade two complete strangers to carry on with the light show as if everything is completely normal,' Quinn whispers as they survey the command post, a tall, scaffolded tower with an enclosed control room some twenty metres off the ground. 'No sweat.'

The lighting rig is at the bottom end of the fenced-off gardens, set back from the main thoroughfare, so there are no other guests around.

'You wait here while I go and take a look,' says Argylle, moving away before she can protest.

He starts climbing up the inside of the rigging, affecting a confidence he doesn't feel. He feels the mission slipping away from them and, far from being ambivalent about it, as he'd imagined he might, he finds he minds acutely. For five years he has been treading water, and now he has finally pushed himself to act it seems inconceivable that it might turn out to be all for nothing.

He knows from experience it's best not to look up when scaling a height, so he keeps his focus on the metal rungs in front of him, which is why he doesn't notice the man approaching until a hand grips his ankle, yanking him so that he slithers gracelessly down to the ground.

Think, he commands himself. *Think*.

'*Qu'est-ce que vous faites, Monsieur?*' The French security guard is polite enough, but his smile seems mocking and his hand hovers over his hip, where Argylle can see the bulge of a gun. Though Argylle speaks French fluently, he replies in English, slurring his words. 'Wanna go up there,' he says, gesturing expansively with his arm towards the lighting control room. ''S fun to be up there. See for miles.'

From the corner of his eye he sees the shimmer of Quinn's gold dress in the trees as she slips away.

Woody Wyatt's face lights up when he spots Quinn in the lobby, discreetly trying to get his attention. Despite the adrenaline pumping around his system, his muscles thick knots of nerves, a separate part of his mind still appreciates how good she looks in that gold dress. Signalling that he is taking a toilet break, he joins her in the crowd of guests grouped around the pianist, who is playing something classical. Though Wyatt would have preferred a bit of Foo Fighters, he pauses, pretending to be lost in momentary enjoyment of the music. As the pianist thunders up and down the keyboard, Quinn gives Wyatt a condensed version of what's needed and he nods so briefly he could be bowing his head to the music.

Out he goes through the staff exit that leads to a small courtyard. At first he thinks he has missed him, but then he spots the orange end of a cigarette in the far corner and finds his new best friend, Ivan, sitting disconsolately on a wall. As the Federov bracelet is a no-show, his presence here is redundant, but still he is eking out the last moment of glamour from the evening before he heads to his shitty motel.

'Ivan, my man, I need you to cover for me for half an hour. I can make it worth your while.' He shows him the original wrap of coke.

Ivan seems to have forgotten their earlier bonding session in the toilets and regards him with suspicion.

'Why you ask me this? How I not know you are with police?'

At that moment, there's a shimmer in the shadows at the side of the patio, and Erin Quinn steps into a pool of light, her bare, tanned skin glimmering under the straps of the gold dress. She runs a hand up Wyatt's arm.

Ivan's attitude instantly alters, his shoulders relaxing and a smile breaking across his fleshy face.

'Okay. Now I understand. Yes, my friend. You go.'

Exiting the hotel, Wyatt follows the golden figure of Quinn, his eyes fixed on the gleaming ridge of her spine. An observer would never have known they were together, but as they approach the lighting tower Quinn slows, gesturing towards the two figures at the base of the scaffolding, where Aubrey Argylle is being detained by the security guard.

Wyatt nods, understanding immediately what needs to be done.

'Dude, you need to get your ass outta here quickly,' he tells the guard, running up and panting as if out of breath. 'There's something going down in the Salle Empire. I've just come from there. They're asking for you.'

The guard assesses Wyatt's uniform, his security lanyard, his impressive size. And if he wonders why this American has been sent to fetch him, that thought is overwhelmed by the seduction of being needed, being personally summoned. He originally requested a security detail inside the hotel itself, wanting to be at the heart of the action, where there would be more chance to brush shoulders with celebrities and more potential to impress his superiors. Being stationed out here in the wilderness, patrolling the perimeters of the event, had felt like a rebuff. But now he is being given a second chance.

'Don't worry, I'll take over here,' says Wyatt firmly. And the guard drops his hand.

While Quinn and her impractical gold shoes remain reluctantly on terra firma, ready to misdirect the security guard should he return, Argylle and Wyatt scale the scaffolding. All three are painfully aware of the ticking clock. Argylle feels the countdown to the Federovs' arrival keeping time with his own heartbeat.

But when they burst into the control room, instead of the two people they'd been expecting, there is only one.

'Oh, thank God. I've been going crazy. Is he here? Please tell me you've brought him with you?' The heavy-set man in the Hawaiian shirt sitting at the control board stares at the door behind them, his lightly perspiring face registering first hope and then disappointment as no one else appears.

'Who?'

'Josef Koller.' His face registers disbelief when they seem not to recognize the name. 'The most famous lighting choreographer in the world?'

From the man's accented English and Koller's name, Argylle guesses the two are an established team, probably from Austria or Germany.

'He hasn't arrived?'

The man shakes his head mournfully. 'He is staying at the Chèvre d'Or up there in Èze – *ja*, sure they put him there, and I am in a shit-hole with a shared bathroom thirty kilometres away. And now I find out there has been an accident in the town, completely blocking the road up to the hotel, so the car they sent cannot reach him. You know how that town is – right up there on that hillside and the centre only accessible by foot. So he is stuck there, and the whole light show must be be cancelled, after we worked on it nearly a year.'

Argylle can't quite believe their bad luck. The whole mission feels cursed, particularly when the man stops suddenly, his eyes narrowed.

'Say, who are you guys? I thought you were bringing me a mes-sage.' He glances down to the side of the lighting board and Argylle sees a phone there.

He nods to Wyatt, who doesn't need telling twice.

'Sorry, dude,' Wyatt says, grabbing the phone. 'You seem like a nice guy, so please just do what we say. What's your name, bro?'

The seated man takes a good look at Wyatt's arms, thick as lamp posts. 'Max,' he says, and he swallows. Loudly.

20

ARGYLLE MAKES HIS WAY FROM THE LIGHTING TOWER AND BRIEFS
Quinn before melting into the throng of guests, talking to Carter
through his earpiece. 'Good of you to break off from your champagne and caviar,' she says with heavy sarcasm. 'To what do I owe
the pleasure?'

'I need you to identify one of the helicopters circling around and
hack into their camera feed,' he says.

'I'm busy, Argylle. I'm requisitioning an ambulance.'

'What? Why? Never mind, there's no time for that. Just do it,
please. It's urgent.'

Seconds later, Carter comes back. 'There's a French TV helicopter
up there, for Canal Plus, getting as close as they're allowed, recording footage of the celeb arrivals.'

'When it next circles inland I need you to tell me what's going on
in a place called Èze. It's up a mountainside about ten klicks from
here.'

Argylle himself is heading for the slip road where the luxury cars
that deposited the VIP guests are parked up, their drivers standing in
groups, smoking, or else sitting at the wheel, snoozing or listening to
the radio.

If you were to ask him straight, Argylle would tell you that he is
unmoved by fast cars, that he finds the whole notion of spending
hundreds of thousands of dollars on what is just a means of getting

121

from A to B obscene. And that's true . . . up to a point. Yet standing looking at the array of vehicles, the Porsches and the Lamborghinis and the Bentleys, he feels the pull of desire.

In his ear, Carter whistles under her breath. 'Nice place, this Èze. Kinda like a warren of ancient walkways, no cars or anything, stuck up on top of a hill and surrounded by high walls. The view must be phenomenal.'

'I'm not going on bloody holiday there, Carter. Just tell me why the most famous lighting choreographer in the world can't get to the ball he's been rehearsing for for months.'

'The most famous what? Never mind . . . Okay, there's some sort of pile-up blocking the one road that links the new town to the old part. Looks like a tour bus went into a car. All the traffic is backed up. No one is going anywhere.'

'So why can't he walk to the main road or something and pick up a ride there?'

'The old town is up a really steep hill and completely cut off. He'd have to abseil down the walls.'

'What about the other direction? Check the map to see if there are any smaller roads leading directly down to the coast where I could come and pick him up.'

Argylle has his sights set on a gold Maserati whose driver is stretched out in the passenger seat.

'None that go all the way. Although there is something . . .'

Already Argylle is moving forward towards the gold car: fifty metres, twenty-five . . .

'Dammit, it's a footpath, not a road. Narrow and rocky and hellish steep. You'd need to be a goat to get up there.'

Argylle comes to an abrupt stop. Reluctantly, he tears his eyes from the Maserati and starts scanning along the line of beautiful, gleaming cars, giving an unhappy nod when he finds what he's looking for.

'Not a chance you can make it that way, Argylle,' Carter continues, oblivious. 'It's even called the Chemin de Nietzsche, I'm not kidding – and if that's not an omen . . .'

*

122

The motorbike is set apart from the fleet of luxury cars. Not that it isn't a spectacular machine in its own right, gleaming flame red, but it doesn't fit with the aesthetic of the others. The driver's helmet rests on the broad leather seat while the driver himself leans against a wall nearby talking on his phone with his back to his vehicle. As Argylle approaches, he sees that the keys are in the ignition and sends up a silent prayer. *Finally, something going right.*

He has almost reached it when the driver turns around, shoving his phone into his pocket. 'I'm sorry,' says Argylle in French, approaching the man.

'What for?'

'This.'

The driver still has a half-smile on his face when Argylle spins and plants a dropkick straight in his temple, sending him crashing to the ground. Argylle drags him behind the wall, reaching into the inside pocket of his jacket to remove his official documentation.

For a heart-stopping moment Argylle is sure one of the drivers chatting in a nearby group has noticed, but then he turns back to the others, laughing, and Argylle can breathe again.

And now Argylle is on the bike. Though he knows his way around a motorbike, having used a chunk of the five-thousand-pound legacy from his parents to buy one second hand, this is certainly the most powerful one he has ever ridden. Four cylinders and over two hundred horsepower.

At the checkpoint, he flashes his documentation at the guard without removing his helmet and is waved lazily through. He pulls up further along the road and takes a selfie on his phone to send to Carter.

'Are you kidding me?' says Carter in his ear, when he resumes contact. 'Are you actually kidding me?'

'Just pick me up on your camera feed and guide me up.'

'I just hope you updated your will, Argylle.'

'I'm leaving it all to you, Carter. You can buy yourself an ice cream.'

By now he is out of the principality and heading along the coast road.

'Okay, I got you. You're on the Lower Corniche. Hey, you ever see that movie—'

'*To Catch a Thief.* Yeah, I saw it.'

Argylle doesn't tell her he was raised on movies. As a child who didn't go to school, videos had been his playmates. He'd seen every Hitchcock film before he was twelve years old and he knows all about the three famously winding corniche roads, one cut into the very top of the mountains, one halfway down and the other at the bottom, hugging the coastline.

'Okay, the path is coming up, sharp right, just around this bend. You'd better pray you don't run into any night hikers.'

He swings the bike off the road and on to a steep concrete path that zigzags up the first part of the mountain, sheer stone walls on either side. His shoulders sag as he relaxes. This isn't so bad.

'Don't know what the fuss was about, Carter. This is a—'

His words dry up in his mouth as the tarmac suddenly runs out and turns into a narrow, gravelly footpath strewn with loose rocks that cuts through brush and undergrowth and olive trees. He risks a look up the sheer mountainside – and wishes he hadn't.

Seconds later he is scrambling up the rocky path with stones spraying out from under the wheels. The incline is so steep he daren't risk slowing down, so he must keep powering upwards even though the path ahead is in darkness and he can't see the bends until he is almost upon them. His veins burn with a mixture of adrenaline and fear as the beast of a bike thunders and roars, the sound reverberating off the soaring vertical crags of rock that surround the gorge he is climbing. It's not cut out for this type of rough terrain. At a particularly acute turn, the wheels skid and his stomach twists around his throat as he braces himself to be flung off into the trees that cling to both sides of this section of the path. Briefly, he shuts his eyes – *Oh God, oh God, oh God* – before miraculously regaining control.

Finally, he settles into a rhythm. Those jungle climbs on his 150cc Honda have stood him in good stead. He relaxes, almost enjoying it, until he rounds a bend and the front wheel smashes into something solid, rebounding so abruptly he feels his body lifting out of the saddle and he has to clutch on to the handlebars, trying to guide the bike back on to the ground. To his horror he sees that what he has hit is a stone step just under a metre across, set into the dirt and gravel, and that it is the first in a steep flight stretching way up the hillside. There is nothing for it but to go bumping up these stone steps, veering around them on to the sheer gravel path whenever he can but otherwise landing on the flat slabs until he feels as if his internal organs have come loose from their moorings and are jiggling around inside him.

All the time, Carter is in his ear. 'Argylle? What's happening? What in hell was that?'

At the top of the incline the path suddenly flattens and widens out. There are benches. A viewing platform. Argylle feels his heartbeat begin to slow, his breath return to something like normal.

'Everything's fine, Carter. Don't know why you're getting so worked up.'

Outside the entrance to the medieval part of the town there is a commotion. Argylle takes it in: the bus blocking the road further up, the trapped crowds gathered. Carter talks him through the maze of streets to the arched entrance to the Michelin-starred restaurant and hotel, a stone chateau teetering on the edge of the mountainside, where, judging by the matching shiny outfits of the couple standing arguing on the cobbled pathway, some of the guests from the ball have been staying and are none too happy at finding themselves cut off from their intended destination, painfully aware that the ball they've sunk tens of thousands of euros into has started without them.

The hotel itself is like something from out of a dream, landscaped gardens clinging to the hillside, tables set out on a magical terrace looking out at the lights of fishing boats and yachts dancing across the surface of the Mediterranean Sea.

Carter has called ahead to let Josef Koller know the ball's organizers have arranged alternative travel for him, and Argylle finds the world-famous lighting choreographer pacing the hotel's chic stone lobby. In his early fifties, Koller cuts a striking figure with his flowing silver hair and beard. He wears a matching silver tuxedo jacket and carries under his arm a sheaf of papers.

Koller's dubious expression when Argylle introduces himself deepens considerably when he sees the motorbike. 'I do not like zis transport. It is dangerous.'

'Not at all, sir. She's far safer than a car. I've yet to have an accident on her.'

Koller does not look convinced.

'As long as we do not go fast,' he says as Argylle deposits his papers in the trunk and helps him on with his helmet. 'I insist on zis.'

By the time they reach the Lower Corniche that snakes along the coastline from Nice to Menton, seven minutes later, Argylle feels as if he has a metal vice around his torso, so rigidly is Koller gripping on to his waist. He wants to tell him he can let go now, but judges it better to refrain from conversation.

Carter is back, talking urgently in his ear.

'I have the Federov vehicle in my sights. ETA eleven minutes. No time for sightseeing, Argylle. Step on it.'

Koller is now making whimpering sounds through his helmet, which Argylle ignores, going faster and faster, arriving at the checkpoint as Carter announces they have four minutes to spare. Once again, he waves the identification documents in front of the police guard on duty without removing his helmet, but this time his luck runs out.

'*Enlève le casque, s'il vous plaît.*'

'No time. Behind me is the most famous lighting choreographer in the world. He is late. Look!'

He grabs Koller's documents from the trunk and thrusts them in front of the policeman, lifting his passenger's helmet. *Did his skin have that green tinge when I picked him up?*

'Three minutes, Argylle.'

The police guard hesitates and time slows to an agonizing halt, breath freezing in his throat, until finally – *thank God* – he is waved through.

Argylle is half expecting to see the lighting tower surrounded by uniformed officers. But the area is quiet, the crowds concentrated in the gardens, hoping to get the best view of the light show and the fireworks.

'Hurry,' he says as he begins to climb, gesturing to Koller to follow him.

'I vill be making a complaint.' It's the first sentence the man has uttered since getting off the back of the bike, white-lipped and shaky.

'Of course,' replies Argylle. 'But in the meantime, would you mind getting a move on?'

Entering the lighting control room, at first Argylle thinks Wyatt must have left, seeing only Max, the technician, his sweaty-cheese complexion accentuated by his gaudy Hawaiian shirt, but then he notices the big ex-Marine attempting to conceal himself behind a tower of electrical equipment at the side of the room, his gun trained on the man at the controls. Hiding is not in Wyatt's skill set, and if Koller were to take a proper look, he would spot a broad shoulder or a size-fourteen foot protruding from behind the tower. But Koller has eyes for no one.

'I nearly died,' he tells his assistant. Seeing as Max is the one with the gun pointed at his head, this statement commands less sympathy than it might have.

'They're here,' says Carter in Argylle's ear. Argylle meets Wyatt's eye, the two of them aware that everything rests on this moment.

'To work,' says Koller, suddenly all business.

The drawstring across Argylle's chest loosens.

Koller is adjusting the knobs on the control panels in front of him and running his hands through the locks of his luxuriant hair, only marginally flattened by the helmet. Now he flicks a switch to his right and Argylle realizes with a lurch that he is turning on a camera and jumps out of the frame just in time. Again, he and Wyatt exchange a glance, and Wyatt shrugs.

The control room has a large glass window that overlooks the gardens. There's a small television, attached by a bracket to the upper corner of the window, which has just sprung to life, revealing the Laval Ball Orchestra, in position and alert, their instruments poised. The stage on which the orchestra sits is dominated by a huge cinema screen showing a close-up of the lighting choreographer himself. Argylle has no time to reflect on the bizarrely meta set-up because Koller is raising his hands and as he brings them down the orchestra thunders into life. Suddenly, all is a frenzy of activity. Max has sprung into action on the mixing desk and Koller himself is half conducting the orchestra and half playing the lighting controls as sensitively as if he is one of the musicians himself.

Swathes of light all the colours of the rainbow chase around the trees, coming to rest on the buildings that surround the square, where the light collects itself into pictures and words that dissolve as soon as they form, all in time with the music so that it seems as if they are one entity. It is a breathtaking marriage of sound and vision, which momentarily takes Argylle back to the Full Moon parties he attended once or twice on the beaches in southern Thailand.

'The Federovs are walking from the car towards the gardens,' reports Carter. 'Is this going to actually work?'

At this point Argylle has no idea. All he can do is hope that while he was gone everything went to plan – in other words, that Samra figured out a way of turning up the internal oscillator of the strobe lights to trigger Irina Federova's flicker vertigo, and Wyatt 'persuaded' Max to make the adjustments as per Samra's instructions.

Now the screen behind the orchestra has cut away from Koller and is homing in on a quartet of people approaching the entrance to the gardens. In front are two men, Prince Florestan, young and handsome in that fleeting way of well-born males who will grow plump and lose their hair by thirty, and the other aggressively ordinary with his rimless glasses and neutral expression and his dark suit, the one nod to the evening's theme being a tie threaded with gold. Argylle has studied photographs of Federov, but this, his first glimpse of him almost in the flesh, is an anticlimax.

The camera doesn't linger on the pair in front, eager to pan back to the woman walking a few metres behind. In contrast to Federov, Jennifer Martin does not disappoint. She is coated from head to toe in metallic body paint that glistens along the entire length of her six-foot-one frame. Even her famous blonde hair is slicked back with something that glitters in the light. Whatever she is wearing underneath the paint, if indeed she is wearing anything at all, is minimal enough to be utterly invisible.

Next to her, Irina Federova cuts a more conventional figure in a gown of mirrored discs that has to have been sewn on to her, clinging to the bosoms that were implanted by surgeons in Brazil and then removed and replacements reimplanted by surgeons in London after the originals burst. The dress erupts behind her head in a towering collar two feet high and lipped like a wave. Her luscious hair extensions made from virgin human hair that has never been dyed or treated have been teased up into an impressive bouffant in which nestles a multi-tiered diamond tiara. The two make an arresting couple as they progress slowly through the gardens, the lights blazing all around them, towards the table where their husbands are now arriving.

Argylle looks at Wyatt. Surely now . . .

Suddenly Koller, who has been building his orchestra to a crescendo of sound and light, does a slight jump in the air so that the little room trembles on its tower, and as he comes down, silver mane flying behind him, something is triggered and the strobes start.

A hundred metres from the glass box, Irina Federova falls to the ground.

Lost in his performance, Josef Koller hasn't noticed. His full attention is trained on the little television that is showing a close-up of his face, exhausted but triumphant. He runs his fingers down the side of his beard, and smiles a modest, depleted smile, raising his hand in a wave. So intent is he on the image of himself on screen, he doesn't see Wyatt stepping out from behind the lighting tower with his gun raised. Only when the camera switches to the fireworks does he turn around.

'That was great, man. Such a big fan,' says Wyatt, walking towards him brandishing a length of fine electric cable.

Two minutes later, Argylle and Wyatt descend the lighting tower. They can just about hear Max and Koller yelling behind the locked control-tower door, but the sound is masked by the exploding fireworks.

'How much do you guess a lighting choreographer makes?' Wyatt asks.

'Not any old lighting choreographer,' Argylle corrects him.

'Only the most famous lighting choreographer in the world,' they chorus as they hit the ground and break into a run.

21

SPORTING A CLASSIC DINNER JACKET WITH A SUBTLE GOLD POCKET square, Tony Corcoran makes a convincing off-duty physician. Older than the rest of the team, he has a natural gravitas courtesy of the white streak in his hair and his way of pausing before speaking, as if carefully weighing up his words.

At this moment, as Argylle watches from the front of the small gathered crowd, Corcoran is crouched down next to Irina Federova, who is moaning softly and trying to raise her hand to her head. 'I'm a consultant neurologist at Cedars Sinai in California,' he tells the onlookers. 'Stand back, please, and give this woman some space. She's suffered some sort of seizure.'

As the patient tries to protest he puts his fingers into her mouth, 'I'm just checking for obstructions,' he explains.

'Nicely done,' murmurs Carter, listening to everything via radio link, in Argylle's ear. 'He's actually giving her the leftover Rohypnol from our aborted Plan A.'

A man pushes to the front of the crowd.

Sergei Denisov. Argylle has been around some bad people in the last few years. The drug lords in charge of the jungle labs who traded their humanity for profit, seeing anyone who stood in their way as collateral damage. But this man, who was the first commander to authorize rape as a weapon of war in Grozny and who ordered the bombing of a refugee convoy travelling under white flags and the cold-blooded execution of Chechen fighters who surrendered in a so-called amnesty, reportedly scalping one who tried to resist, takes evil to a different level entirely.

'Sir, stand back. Give the lady space,' Corcoran commands him authoritatively.

'Is not problem,' says Denisov. The fact that he speaks English is a surprise. The words commonly used to describe him – beast, monster, psychopath – don't allow for nuance, for the possibility that he might have travelled, might have other interests outside violence and butchery.

'She not have, how you say, epilepsiya. Is only lights.'

On the ground, Irina makes an attempt to sit up, only for Corcoran to gently push her back down.

'Flickering vertigo. Am I right? Normally, as you say, it's nothing serious, but I'm afraid it has triggered something more worrying. Her heart is dangerously arrhythmic. I need to get her to a hospital quickly or we risk cardiac arrest.'

A woman standing close by takes out her phone and Argylle stiffens, but Corcoran has already whipped out his own. 'I have a friend who is a cardiologist at the Princess Grace Hospital just up the road. I'll call him directly and get him to organize a—' He breaks off to talk into his phone. 'François? I need an ambulance and a defib, and get your team ready to receive us when we arrive.'

By now word has reached Federov and he has tracked back, arriving tight-lipped.

'Irina, my love, it's time to get up now.' His face, near hers, gives nothing away.

'Irina.' The voice is soft and low, but to Argylle's ears there is a thread of threat that runs through it like wire, and when Argylle looks closely at Federov's hand on his wife's arm, he sees that his fingers are pressing into her skin so hard their tips have turned completely bloodless.

Irina Federova stirs and this time manages to sit up. 'Woah,' says Wyatt at Argylle's shoulder. Argylle himself can hardly bear to look. If Federov succeeds in getting his wife to go with him, everything is lost.

'Oh my God!' shrieks Jennifer Martin as the Rohypnol kicks in, sending Irina slumping dramatically backwards once more, only Corcoran's quick reflexes cushioning her fall.

In the distance there comes the sound of a siren, and almost simultaneously Carter announces unnecessarily, 'Ambulance on its way.'

As the ambulance pulls up, Argylle recognizes Washington at the wheel and is surprised by the rush of relief that shoots through him. While he knows some of his teammates still distrust him, Washington has been a solid, reassuring presence over the past two months, his dry humour masking a deep well of empathy.

Argylle and Wyatt circle around the knot of bystanders until they are as near to the back of the ambulance as they dare get until Washington jumps out, wearing a dark uniform with a hi-vis vest over the top, and flings open the back doors, providing enough cover for the two of them to dive inside.

Argylle and Wyatt scramble to pull on the uniforms that have been left out for them. It takes seconds, but as Wyatt prepares to exit Argylle yanks him back, shaking his head and pointing down to where the uniform trousers end comically halfway down his calf. For a split second it seems as if Wyatt will protest, but then he nods and clambers into the driving seat.

Argylle joins Washington in carrying the stretcher to the incoherent Irina Federova. 'The bracelet,' says Federov as his wife is loaded on to the ambulance. But Corcoran has a firm hold of her wrist and is taking her pulse as they run right past him to the open doors of the ambulance.

By now Argylle feels the adrenaline in every part of his body – heart hammering, breathing accelerated, sweat trickling between his shoulder blades.

As they strap their patient in, he senses someone behind him and the hairs on his neck prickle as he turns to find Denisov just inches away.

You can't be here, he wants to say, but finds his voice dries up in the yeasty sourness of Denisov's breath. Instead, it is Corcoran who yells, 'Get away, sir! We need space to use the defibrillator.'

Denisov reluctantly retreats. 'I follow behind,' he says. Through the crack of the ambulance door, Argylle sees Denisov shake his bullish head at Federov, and Federov stiffen, although his expression doesn't alter. 'I don't need to tell you how important this is to me,' Federov hisses in Russian, and though Denisov is twice as broad as his boss and looks as if he could rip his head from his body with his bare hands, Argylle sees him flinch.

'I understand, boss,' he says. 'Your wife—'

'My wife? Don't be a fool. It's the bracelet I want back. You bring it to me. Remember Aminoff? Just thirty-three and so handsome – though not by the time his family buried him, of course. It would be a shame if the same thing that happened to your predecessor happened to you or, God forbid, your beautiful daughter. She lives on Romanov Lane, I believe? A fine address. Those corner apartments in the Sheremetev Building are very special, I think.'

All this time, Federov's voice is a monotone, as if he is reading out a coffee order, yet Argylle's skin crawls. As he reaches out to slam shut the ambulance doors, relief ripples through him at the prospect of getting far away from this strange, cold man.

And now the ambulance is racing ahead with the siren blaring. Argylle hears a whoop from Wyatt at the wheel, the tension of the last few minutes bursting as he floors the accelerator. But even a speeding ambulance can't outrun an angry Russian behind the wheel of a Porsche 911 GT2 RS. 'The hospital Corcoran mentioned is around six klicks from here,' says Carter. 'You have about eight minutes to lose our friend.'

Through the ambulance's rear window, Argylle can make out Denisov's pale face, the grim set of his jaw. The original plan had been to deposit Irina Federova by the roadside somewhere and take off, but with Denisov in pursuit they have no choice but to keep heading towards the hospital.

'Carter, there must be something you can do to stop that car. Hack into something or reprogram something. You're the tech person.'

'Hold on,' says Carter.

He hears a dial tone, then the sound of ringing, followed by an ear-splitting shriek.

'Police!' Carter yells. 'This is Julia Roberts. I'm at the Laval Ball.

Someone just stole my car!' Then she adds for good measure: 'With my baby in it!'

'Overkill, Carter,' hisses Argylle. 'Does Julia Roberts even have a baby?'

'My what? Number plate? Yes, sure, it's . . .' Argylle squints through the window. 'N,' he calls out. 'R, S . . . Jesus Christ, Wyatt, what fairground did you learn to drive at?'

The tiny principality of Monaco is crawling with police so the flashing blue lights are behind them in seconds. Argylle lets out the breath he's been holding as the Russian's car is pulled over, the pale disc of Denisov's face growing smaller through the glass.

'Way to go, Carter!' shouts Wyatt from the front. 'Now all we have to do is get off this road and—'

He slams on the brakes. Rounding the corner, they have driven into gridlock, cars queueing in every direction, having been rerouted around the closed-off centre. Even the insistent scream of their ambulance siren can't carve a path through.

The ambulance idles, its siren still screeching uselessly, which seems to rouse Irina Federova. 'Let me up,' she slurs in Russian, attempting to rise. Corcoran gently pushes her back down. 'It's too dangerous to sit up,' he says, taking her arm so that the bracelet slides to her wrist. He takes it off. 'I need to monitor your pulse.' He presses the soft skin of her wrist with his right hand while dropping the bracelet into the bag Argylle has snatched up from a pocket in the back of the passenger seat. 'Sick bag?' Corcoran murmurs. 'Keeping it classy.'

Argylle goes to tie the top of the bag, but Corcoran stops him. 'Wait up,' he says, cradling Irina Federova's head so that he can unclasp the diamond necklace from under her hair and unclip the diamond clusters from her ears, tossing them into the bag to join the bracelet. 'Don't worry,' he reassures his semi-conscious patient. 'We'll keep them safe for you.'

Argylle frowns. They've been told to get the bracelet, that's all. 'Wait. That's not—' he starts, but Corcoran shakes his head and puts a finger to his lips and Argylle reluctantly backs off.

All the time, Wyatt is trying to nudge the ambulance through the stationary traffic. 'Move!' he shouts at a twenty-something man in a white vest driving a hundred thousand euros worth of convertible. The guy raises his hands. Shrugs.

Gradually a path forms as cars reverse a few inches here, move forward a few inches there. Wyatt takes his foot off the brake, allowing Argylle to breathe. But the oxygen dries up in his throat as he glances back to see the Russian's car bearing down on them again.

'Guess it didn't take long to work out there was no baby in the car,' he says to Carter. 'Who could have foreseen that?'

'Creative licence, dude,' mutters Carter.

Now they are through the jam, but the Porsche is back on their tail.

'Don't sweat, Argylle,' mutters Washington, who is strapped into the backward-facing seat behind Wyatt. 'We'll just turn up at the hospital, deposit our patient and vamoose. Our Russian friends will be too busy making sure the boss's wife doesn't die on them to bother about us.'

Unconvinced, Argylle taps his fingers insistently against his thigh.

'Hang a right!' Carter yells, loud enough to reach Wyatt in the front, who swings the wheel around, sending his passengers lurching.

'What is happening?' says Irina Federova, trying again to raise herself up on to her elbows.

This time Argylle addresses her in Russian. 'You just need to be checked out. You'll be fine as long as you lie still. Back with your husband in no time.'

This last line doesn't seem to bring the patient much solace.

The plan is to pull into the ambulance-only section and deposit Mrs Federova in a wheelchair for Denisov and his gang to deal with, claiming to be needed on another emergency. But when they back into the ambulance drop bay ready to make a quick exit, there is already a team of medical staff outside, waiting with a gurney.

'Goddammit, someone must have tipped them off,' says Wyatt. But there is no time to find out more as the rear doors are being thrown open and all is movement and activity. Hands detaching equipment, corners of a sheet being lifted, a body shifted from one site to another, and now the hospital team are back on the ground and Argylle is leaning in to close the doors when he hears Wyatt cry out, 'That asshole!'

Turning to the front, he sees that Denisov and his minions have ignored the restrictions and driven into the ambulance bay, boxing them in. The French hospital staff are not impressed. They want to take their patient for testing, the patient herself wants to get the *fuck* off the gurney, Argylle is trying to explain in French that they have to get to their next call. And now, on top of it all, here comes Denisov, pointing at Irina Federova's wrist, which is being hooked up to a drip, despite her objections. Her skin looks shockingly pale and bare.

Argylle dives into the corner of the ambulance, where his and Wyatt's discarded clothing has been bundled under a pull-down seat.

'What in God's name are you doing, Argylle?' hisses Washington as Argylle rummages around. 'Do not bring out a weapon in a hospital. Are you crazy?'

From the corner of his eye, Argylle sees Denisov staring at him and reaching into his jacket. '*Voilà!*' he shouts, brandishing the fake bracelet he has just liberated from his trouser pocket, where it has been languishing since the earlier plan was aborted. 'We almost went off with Madame's bracelet.' He hands it to Denisov, who has no choice but to abandon whatever he was about to withdraw from his inside pocket and accept the bracelet.

'Now, if you'd please let us get on with our jobs . . .'

Denisov eyes him with suspicion, but when he sees that the hospital team are already wheeling their patient inside, he nods to his wingman, jerking his head towards the car. The man cannot suppress his delight at getting to drive the gleaming Porsche. As he screeches away, Denisov throws one more look in Argylle's direction, his black eyes inventorying every feature of him.

The barbarities those eyes have witnessed.

Then the Russian turns and hurries after the gurney before the doors swing shut.

'Not bad, Argylle,' says Carter. 'Now I suggest you all get the hell out of there.'

As the requisitioned ambulance pulls off, Argylle sinks down on to a seat and leans forward with his head in his hands so no one can see his legs tremble.

22

FRANCES COFFEY KNEW FROM THE OUTSET WHAT SHE WAS GETTING into when she joined the operational side of the CIA. Having started out in the archives, any illusions she might have had of a staff job at the Agency offering a glamorous life full of suave, handsome men and state-of-the-art gadgetry were long gone by the time she had decided to switch channels from research to management.

Even so, the temporary HQ for the team's European mission takes unglamorous to a new level. Under the guise of running a series of international symposiums for managers and staff involved in the field of private waste haulage and logistics, they have taken over a small business unit based in an industrial estate ten kilometres from Charleroi, selected because it has an airport rather than for its other notable claim to fame – that it regularly tops the list of most depressing towns in Belgium.

Here, her office is a carpet-tiled cubicle with a view over the car park towards the estate's two-star hotel, the ill-named Hôtel Beaux Rêves, an anonymous rectangular building with grey rendered walls and three rows of mean windows and a wholly Polish-speaking staff. This is where the attendees plus organizers of the fictional waste haulage convention are being housed.

She is listening to a CD. More specifically, she is listening to a man talking on a CD. He is explaining what happens to her body when she smokes, describing in lurid detail the effects of tar on her lung tissue and the fatty deposits furring up her artery walls.

It is Coffey's husband, Andrew, who is behind this push to stop smoking. He says he is tired of how the house stinks, even though she only smokes outside in the garden. He says he doesn't want to be a carer when she's shuffling around the house with an oxygen canister or confined to an armchair.

What he doesn't say is that he doesn't want her to die. But this is what it is really all about and they both understand that.

Coffey loves her husband, whom she met many years ago at a friend's wedding while still working as an archivist. Andrew was the groom's best man and made a speech that was more sincere than entertaining and that touched the young Frances Coffey, who had been at the CIA for two years by this point and was used to a certain level of grandstanding, to men who preferred to hold the floor than hold a conversation. They have been together thirty-two years. No children – it didn't happen for them – and the widespread assumption that she sacrificed motherhood for her career brings its own special pain. But they have a companionship that suits them. Andrew knows better than to question what she does when she's at work, which takes up almost all her time, and she refrains from asking whether he's truly happy with the little life he has carved out for himself – making beautiful bespoke furniture in the workshop out back in their rural Delaware home, the odd Friday-night beer with a neighbour.

Nor would she ever ask if he's aware that for the past eleven years she's been having an affair with Darius Johnson, head of the Office of Public Affairs, whose job it is to keep her from making an idiot of herself in front of the world's media. Darius has a wife. Two children who are no longer children. A dog with a heart condition. She loves him. And she believes he loves her too. But Coffey has been around long enough and seen enough to know that love isn't everything.

'The team are ready for you in Meeting Room One, ma'am,' says Mike Randall from the doorway of her cubicle.

As she descends the stairs, she sifts through the information in her head. After twelve years in the post she's discovered that the key to her job is knowing what to hold back and what to divulge.

And who to divulge it to.

The squad are arranged around the table, looking markedly different to the immaculately dressed figures from the Laval Ball. Instead, they wear the smart-casual attire attendees of a global symposium on private waste haulage and logistics might choose – white shirts rolled up at the elbows, dark trousers or knee-length skirts. Loosely knotted ties. They sit up straight when she enters.

'First, hats off to the Monaco team,' she says when she walks into Meeting Room One, which is bigger than Meeting Room Two and Three, but otherwise identical, with its U-shaped Formica table, grey padded chairs and the whiteboard at one end. 'I know things didn't go to plan back there, so you all did a helluva job of improvising. I'll pick out a couple of individuals for a special mention. Aubrey – that was some ride you took on that bike. I'm not sure Josef Koller appreciated it quite as much as the rest of us, but you did well.'

Argylle looks down at the table. To the left of him he hears Schneider say, 'Yeah, *Aubrey*,' and someone else snigger, but still a warmth radiates from his stomach at Coffey's words. What is it about her that makes them all so keen to please her?

'And, Tony, I think *ER* is looking for a new cast member. Seriously, I'm sure your Oscar is in the post, and let it be known that if I'm suffering a heart attack, only Dr Corcoran will do. Am I clear? And it's you we have to thank for throwing Federov off the scent. By snatching *all* his wife's jewels, not just the bracelet, you managed to convince him he was the target of a criminal gang. Some strategic tip-offs have led him to Alexandru Skutnik, a rather charmless Romanian gangster we've had our eye on for some time. One of our agents working undercover in Marseilles offered Skutnik the necklace and earrings for a fraction of what they're worth and he was very happy to snap up such a bargain.'

She sees something in Argylle's expression. 'Don't lose any sleep about this guy. Buying and selling stolen jewellery is only a sideline for Skutnik. His real business is people trafficking. Last month the French authorities rescued eleven Romanian women from a prostitution ring he ran on the outskirts of Paris. He'd told them they would be working in bars, promised them a standard of living they could only dream of back home. Then took their passports and forced them to see up to fifteen clients a day to pay back the "debt" for their transportation. The youngest was just seventeen. He's a sleazeball.'

Coffey pauses, gazing out across the car park to where an advertising hoarding shows a smiling woman pressing a household cleaning spray to her cheek as if it were a lover's hand. Though summer is well underway, the Belgian sky is the dirty grey of old dishcloths, and she feels a fine web of melancholy slip over her at the reminder of all the ugliness in the world and the victims she will never be able to help. It's why she does what she does, but the knowledge that their best efforts will only ever be a drop of succour in the ocean of misery that men like Skutnik create sometimes weighs her down.

'I know some of you will be wondering what this mission is about, why I assembled the Agency's best people to carry off what looks on the surface like a commonplace jewellery theft. I'm afraid I can't tell you the details, but please be in no doubt, it has far-reaching ramifications. Trust me, what you are doing will directly affect the stability of the entire world.'

It is the truth. And also only part of the truth.

It's lonely being the only one in full possession of the facts. It means there is no opportunity for Coffey to share the heavy burden of responsibility.

She glances at Argylle – this new Argylle with his short hair and his new-found confidence. The first time they met, he could hardly meet her eyes. Now he sits up tall as if no longer apologizing for taking up space in the world.

Frances Coffey loves all of her young recruits for their commitment and their idealism and their conviction that they can change the world. But there is something about Argylle that tugs at her heart.

'You know that the bracelet you stole belongs to Vasily Federov. What might come as a surprise is that it is worth a million dollars and yet Mr Federov paid five million. Why? It didn't take his experts long to realize that the one Argylle handed over in the ambulance is a fake, and already he's offered another million as a reward for the original's safe return. Again, why? In the meantime, we understand he has assembled – or bought – a crack team of active and former Spetsnaz personnel. We can only assume the two things are linked, though we currently have no idea how. Only that they are both key to Federov's aim of building a united, ultra-right Russian super-state.

'And it's our job to stop him.'

23

Sixteen weeks after Federov's promise to the Russian peo-
ple and two weeks after Monaco

IN THE EIGHT YEARS HE'S BEEN A PRIVATE INVESTIGATOR, MIKHAIL
Poltorak has met clients from every spectrum of society in every type
of venue, from seedy bars to suburban kitchens and flash offices. But
he has never been anywhere quite like Vasily Federov's city residence
in Rublyovka, Moscow's answer to Beverly Hills.

Like a pale pink wedding cake, the enormous pastel-coloured
mansion sits surrounded by landscaped gardens, its manicured lawn
sloping down to the banks of the Moskva River, which runs through
this enclave of Russia's uber rich. There's an extravagant white marble fountain, teeming with fat koi carp, and a neatly cut maze such
as you'd find in the grounds of an English country house. Through
an arched hedge, Poltorak can see the gleaming turquoise tiles of a
swimming pool, and beyond it a teak lounger, padded with a thick,
ivory-coloured cushion. Next to the lounger a tall drink loaded with
ice cubes sits sweating in the sun on a glass-topped table. You never
used to get proper heat in Moscow, but recently things have been
changing. There's something in this global-warming stuff.

From the low-slung white outdoor sofa he was shown to when he
arrived, he casts a longing look towards the open French doors in

the mansion's back elevation. Boy, what he wouldn't give to have a nose around inside. The security guard who came to the gate to meet him told him Mrs Federova wouldn't allow tradesmen into the house. He'd shrugged at Poltorak when he said that in a 'what can you do?' gesture, and they'd each understood, without it needing to be said, that they were both ex-KGB.

When he glances back through the arched hedge, he sees Irina Federova standing in front of the lounger, tying up her expensively highlighted blonde hair in a ponytail over the top of a white visor. Though he's never met her, he recognizes her from hundreds of photographs in magazine society pages – black-tie balls, fundraisers, carefully posed family portraits with her father and sisters. She wears mirrored sunglasses so that when she looks in his direction, he can't tell if she's actually seeing him, and a gold swimsuit cut away in so many unexpected places the thing is more holes than fabric. Her surgically lifted breasts hover in front of her chest like a toddler's strapped-on flotation device.

'Good afternoon, Poltorak. I hope it's not too hot for you.'

Mikhail Poltorak knows he is sweating like a pig, but he hasn't been offered any shade. He wouldn't be surprised if Federov hasn't arranged that deliberately.

Vasily Federov himself looks cool and crisp, approaching from the house in a white linen shirt and bone-coloured trousers. Poltorak has met him once before, when he gave him the commission at his swanky offices in the centre of town, and he is struck by the way the man seems somehow set apart from his surroundings, even here in his own home, just as he was there.

Federov makes a barely perceptible movement with his hand and a uniformed member of the household staff appears to wheel over a vast square umbrella.

'You have something to tell me about my stolen property?'

Federov's delivery is so without nuance it's impossible to distinguish between a question and a statement.

'Yes. I traced Nathalie Chabert's younger daughter, Amélie, like you asked. As you know, there's a long-standing animosity between

Chabert's older two children from her first marriage and the younger one from her second. Amélie hasn't had an easy life. She's an ex-junkie, and it shows in her face, you know?'

Poltorak sucks in his cheeks to demonstrate Amélie Chabert's ravaged appearance.

'Anyway, here's the thing. When Nathalie Chabert died, she left the bracelet that you bought at auction to her elder daughter, Isabelle. But what Isabelle never knew is that she also left a second bracelet, just like it, to her younger daughter.'

Federov sits perfectly still.

'There were two bracelets?'

'That's right. I showed Amélie the photo of your stolen bracelet, and she said, as far as she could remember, it's the same as the one she inherited, or at least very similar.'

'As far as she remembers?'

'Yeah, she sold it soon after her mother died, to get her next fix. A rich Greek tourist bought it, who was on vacation with his wife in the French Riviera.'

'She doesn't know who he was? Or where he was from?'

'No. She couldn't even describe him, although it was decades ago, so it's not surprising.'

Mikhail Poltorak prides himself on having a second sense for what people are thinking, and while Vasily Federov is a closed book, he's pretty sure the guy will be quietly seething. He bought the first bracelet because he was convinced it held the clue to this mythical Amber Room, and now it turns out there's another one just like it. What if he bought the wrong bracelet? Imagine laying out all those millions of dollars on a dud! Not that Federov can't afford it . . . Poltorak's eyes once again rake his surroundings – the lush lawn, lined with sprinklers, with the majestic green river running along the bottom, the manicured hedge with the perfect arch cut into it, through which he can see Irina Federova, now stretched out on the lounger, applying suncream to her gym-honed legs. She looks up, as if she can sense him watching her, just at the moment that Federov turns his head to see what has caught his guest's attention.

Wordlessly, Federov gets to his feet and crosses the black slate terrace to stand framed in the archway, from where he addresses his wife in a voice that is soft but not warm. For a few long moments after he stops speaking the two glare at each other, Federov reflected back to himself in his wife's mirrored shades as the rope of tension tightens between them, dense and fibrous. Finally, Irina Federova gets to her feet and decamps with her drink, presumably to a neighbouring, unseen lounger.

Poltorak looks around at the two sofas and three chairs in the configuration where he is sitting and wonders why Federov didn't just ask him to move seats. But he learned long ago that if you let yourself get sucked into a couple's power games, you will always, always lose.

24

'YOU WRITING YOUR MEMOIRS THERE, ARGYLLE?'

'Just important waste haulage business, Carter.'

Argylle, who is sitting at one of the moulded white plastic tables fixed to the concrete floor in the back of the business centre, closes up his notebook as Carter slides in opposite him. When he first arrived at the Point he'd tried to keep up his journal, but it had made some of the others nervous and in the end Will Hooper had demanded to look through it, Argylle gazing fixedly out of the window while the back of his neck burned. So he'd put his notebook away, but he still felt the loss of it. Only here, posing as a delegate at a convention, had he reasoned he could get away with it. A useful prop.

It's the first break in the weather since they arrived, a tepid sun pooling on the car park of the tiling warehouse next door, and the team are making the most of it. On a nearby table, Lawler is arm-wrestling Reynolds, the college-leaver mounting a surprisingly sparky fight against the battle-scarred former vet. Jim Ryder, the mechanic, has fallen asleep next to them with his head cradled in his arms, his balding scalp already turning pink. Meanwhile, from the table over by the uPVC back door, which has been wedged open by a potted plant, comes the sound of Erin Quinn's laughter as she slaps down a five-card flush and wipes out Wyatt, who has gone all or nothing on the last hand.

'She's out of your league, Argylle.'

He laughs, to cover up the fact that his throat has gone dry. How obvious is it? Who else has noticed?

'You jealous, Carter?'

'Of Quinn? Are you crazy?'

'No, not of Quinn.'

Now it's Carter's turn to look surprised, though she recovers quickly.

'She's not my type.'

'Oh yeah, and what type's that?'

'I prefer edgy. Mean. The kind you look at and kinda know they have strings of meat between their teeth left over from lunchbreak.'

Argylle snorts. Then he becomes serious.

'You know, you shouldn't feel you have to hide who you are, Carter.'

She has been peeling the label off her bottle of Coke and now she scrunches it up and throws it at him.

'Remind me, Argylle. When was it you announced to the group that you were one hundred per cent dick-swinging heterosexual?'

'I never—'

'Exactly. You know, the reason I keep quiet about my private life isn't because I'm ashamed of who I am, it's because I'm so goddam proud of who I am I refuse to share any part of it with the likes of Matt Schneider or Martin Casner so they can bad-mouth me behind my back. I haven't even talked about it with my parents.'

'Don't you think it might improve your relationship if you did?'

'Let me tell you something about immigrants, Argylle. Sure, when they're together, it's all about celebrating their culture and language and traditions, but when it comes to engaging with the wider world, they just want to fit in, not to stand out. And you know why? Because it's safer that way. No danger of being singled out or sent back where they've just escaped from. You know, when I first heard about Steve Jobs, I said to my mom, "I want to be just like him," and she looked at me and she said, "Why you always gotta aim so high? The top of the middle, that's where you want to be." You hearing me, Argylle? My mother doesn't want me aiming higher than top of the middle in

147

case I draw attention to myself. Can you imagine what she'd say if I told her I was queer?'

'So what, you're just never going to be yourself around them?'

'Hasn't anyone ever told you, Argylle, sometimes being yourself is overrated? I mean, why would I be myself when I could be Halle Berry or Ruth Bader Ginsburg?' Then she softens. 'Actually, I've been thinking about telling them for a while. Not coming out, because as far as I'm concerned I've never been in. More like forcing my folks to come out and admit what deep down they already know.'

They lapse into silence. But it's a comfortable one. Carter is the closest thing to a friend Argylle has out here. There's something about her spiky honesty and her wide, lopsided grin that has crawled beneath his defences.

'She likes you, you know,' says Carter now. 'Quinn.'

Argylle's treacherous heart jolts. 'Has she said something?'

'To me? Please. I can just tell. Anyway, it's just a fact – women like you. You wanna know why?'

'Because of my sheer animal magnetism?'

'Because you like women.'

'Come on. All men like women.'

Carter's eyebrows shoot up. 'You know, for a smart-ass, you can be really dumb. Most men either hate women or are scared to death of them. Now, why don't you write that pearl of wisdom down in your little book?'

Having started her working life buried in the CIA archives, the sight of a neatly clipped newspaper cutting can still bring on a warm rush of nostalgia in Frances Coffey, so she's delighted when she opens an envelope from Molly Riggs, her great friend and successor as Director of the Department of Records and Information, and finds a photocopied clipping from the *New York Times*. Molly is one of the very few Agency personnel Coffey trusts absolutely, and her one-time mentee was the only choice when the Monaco mission was being hatched and she needed someone to conduct discreet research into the Bracelet of Fidelity. There's a fluorescent pink Post-it note stuck to the front of the clipping on which is scrawled: 'Isn't this your bracelet?', followed by an arrow pointing towards a photograph in which something has been ringed in black marker pen.

Closer inspection reveals the clipping to be a report on an exhibition being mounted in Saloniki in Greece, showcasing treasures from Mount Athos dating from as far back as a millennium ago. Mount Athos has fascinated Frances Coffey since she was a child and first saw a photograph of a monastery improbably clinging to the top of a sheer rockface. She knows that there are twenty such monasteries on the mountain, which is home to two thousand monks. Entry to the peninsula is restricted to one hundred and ten 'pilgrims' a day, and visas must be applied for long in advance. Most intriguing of all, women are banned, not just from setting foot on the holy mountain, but from coming within five hundred metres of its shoreline.

Over her long career in a traditionally male-dominated institution, Coffey has been surprised how many men in positions of power turn out to be secretly afraid of women, and she has often been tempted to suggest they give Mount Athos a try.

The article dates from some years before and reports on a forthcoming exhibition of some of the priceless artefacts which the monasteries have amassed over the years. These artefacts are mostly religious – icons and manuscripts, chalices and crosses. However, there are also secular items bequeathed over the centuries by wealthy benefactors trying to curry favour with God or else handed over by novice monks in the process of relinquishing their worldly goods.

Coffey studies the picture. Then she picks up the phone.

25

UNABLE TO BEAR THE PROSPECT OF ANOTHER EVENING AT THE HÔTEL
Beaux Rêves, a handful of team members venture out of the industrial estate looking for a bar, as delegates of a global private waste
hauliers' convention might. It is a more difficult task than it first
seems. This is a neighbourhood of endless flat, wide roads lined with
houses, but actual shops, bars and restaurants are thin on the ground.
The grey summer sky over the grey-stone buildings makes Argylle
ache for the luscious green banana plants that overhung the terrace
of his little hut back in Thailand.

Eventually they come across a small concentration of busi-
nesses. There is a betting store and a veterinary surgery, three
goodwill stores, two pharmacies, a dusty furniture store promising *Moins Cher Impossible*, a Chinese restaurant and a Stella
Artois sign. *Café du Parc* reads the name on the establishment to
which the sign is attached. Argylle searches for anything resem-
bling a park.

There is none.

Inside, a middle-aged couple sit sipping Pernod with a small dog
lying at their feet on the scuffed chequerboard floor, while at
another table four men play cards around a collection of empty
beer bottles. The whole place falls silent when they walk in. Argylle
stiffens as the card-players eye up Washington, can see how he
might present a challenge just in being who he is and how he is. He

wonders how it feels to walk around in the world that way. So visible.

'I still don't get it,' Argylle says sometime later, nursing a beer so weak it might just as well be flavoured water. 'Why are we going to all this trouble just to rob some old jewellery Federov wants? I mean, sure he's a dangerous man, but stopping him getting his hands on some nice, shiny, expensive things he's set his heart on isn't going to make the world a more stable place.'

'It's just the way it is, Argylle,' says Quinn. 'You'll soon learn that one of the great paradoxes of the organization you currently work for is that it deliberately recruits people who think outside the box, but when it comes to obeying instructions you're expected to stay so far inside the box you'd need to be Houdini to get out again.'

Quinn is wearing a white sleeveless top which shows off the fine gold chain she wears around her neck. She smells of sunscreen and sweat and the harsh lemon shampoo the hotel supplies.

'What I don't understand is why he wants another one of those ugly-ass bracelets so badly?' muses Washington. 'Don't get me wrong, I'm partial to a little bling myself, but if you ask me, whoever designed that thing had no flair. You seen those random scratches on the side? I mean, have they not heard of inspirational quotes?'

After the jewel heist in Monaco, the team had been hoping for something meatier for their second assignment, so finding out they are to steal a second bracelet, near identical to the first, has not gone down well.

'How do we even know this thing exists?' Wyatt had asked Coffey after she broke the news that afternoon.

'Because it was displayed in an exhibition of priceless objects and antiquities belonging to the monasteries. They usually keep them locked away in their treasure rooms, but every now and then they loan a select few to a gallery or museum to be exhibited to the public. It just so happens that this particular exhibition also featured an artefact that was stolen from a private collection in Washington fourteen years ago, so the Agency had an interest in it and ordered in all the research – which is where Molly Riggs spotted it. According-ing to the scant details that we could find, this was the first and only time the bracelet had been shown. And listen to this, it's listed in the newspaper as the Bracelet of Piety, not Fidelity.'

But while Coffey seems fired up, for the rest of them the details of their second mission haven't exactly lit a fire in their bellies.

'On the plus side, I suppose we get to visit Greece,' says Argylle.

'And scale tall buildings on ropes,' adds Wyatt.

Though the mission will be carried out in darkness, Quinn and Mia Matsyuk have been instructed to sit this one out. Because women are banned on the peninsula, they're to keep Carter company on the fishing boat that will be taking the rest of the team home.

'At least you have a role,' Quinn complains to Carter. 'Twiddling knobs and doing whatever other voodoo shit you do on the computer. I don't even get to steer the boat.'

Eight of them will be going on the Mount Athos mission. Joining Argylle and Wyatt will be Washington, Schneider, Corcoran and Martin Casner. Argylle doesn't know what to make of Casner, who still seems to view him with suspicion. Not that he's exactly unfriendly, but he has so many barriers up that Argylle's few attempts to engage him in conversation have been like hitting tennis balls against a wall. Asif Samra, the softly spoken engineer, is also coming, as the mission requires someone with knowledge of both machinery and buildings, as well as Alex Kellerman, the explosives expert.

The holy mountain is notoriously hard to access. Visitors require a visa that has to be applied for months in advance. The only people allowed within five hundred metres of the shore are the pilgrims – every day a hundred Orthodox visitors plus ten non-Orthodox are granted permission to remain on the peninsula, living among the monks for a maximum of four days. Their paperwork is thoroughly scrutinized before entry.

The borders – coastal and land – are heavily guarded by armed Greek police with dogs. A high fence divides the peninsula from the mainland and the terrain inland is all but impassable, marked by densely forested hillsides and steep ravines. The only vehicles on the peninsula belong to the police, or are the few official taxis.

It doesn't help that the team's target – the monastery of St Benedict – is one of the least accessible monasteries on the peninsula, a soaring beast of a building constructed nearly a thousand years ago on the very top of a single towering rock, a seemingly impossible feat of perseverance and engineering.

So they will be parachuting in, under cover of darkness, landing on the hillside immediately behind, from which a steep path with seven hundred and forty-two steps leads up the back of the mountain on which the monastery stands. Corcoran and Schneider, not only the most experienced parachutists among them, but also – with the exception of Samra – the lightest among the men, will be landing on the roof of the monastery, some two hundred and thirty metres above sea level, laden with anchors and climbing ropes, which they will let down ready for their team members once they've made it up the steps.

Then they have precisely forty-seven minutes to carry out the mission. That's the length of the annual saint's day service, one of the most important dates in the monks' calendars, when the entire population of the monastery will congregate in the chapel to view the monastery's most sacred treasure – a fragment of St Benedict's jawbone, normally kept under lock and key in the treasure room.

During this forty-seven-minute period while the monks are otherwise engaged, the team must scale the facade of the monastery and mount a raid on the heavily fortified and alarmed treasure room, which also houses the bracelet they're after. Then it's just a question of travelling the nine kilometres to the shoreline, where a dinghy will be waiting to pick them up and take them to Carter's boat.

What could possibly go wrong?

'Please don't make the mistake of assuming that because these guys are monks, they are all smiles and benign intentions,' Coffey had warned them. 'Like many of the monasteries, St Benedict's has a priceless collection of religious iconography, rare illustrated manuscripts, sculptures and sacred ancient relics, as well as gifts bestowed by wealthy benefactors over the years, such as the Bracelet of Piety, which is what we want. And these things aren't just lying around. They're stored in a secure, climate-controlled chamber protected by an armoured door with an ancient lock that requires four different keys kept by four separate monks to ensure against one rogue monk helping himself.

'Over the centuries there have been many attempts to pillage the treasures of the monasteries. Hitler himself sent experts into the monasteries to take inventories with the intention of shipping the choicest items back to Germany. Luckily, the monks were smart and appealed to his vanity by inviting him to become the peninsula's personal protector, so the plan stalled.

'What I'm saying is that the monasteries know the value of their collections. That's why they have sophisticated alarms and armed security. Have no doubt, if you are discovered, you will be in very serious danger.'

Argylle is trying not to think about all the different steps in this operation, all the different points at which things could go catastrophically wrong. And definitely trying not to question whether any bracelet is worth the risks they will all be taking.

By now they are on their third or fourth round in the Café du Parc and, while the others have stuck to the small, watery beers, Wyatt has branched into bourbon and is growing exponentially more morose as the empty glasses line up. The talk has turned back to the previous mission in Iran – the one that was aborted with severe losses after the Russian-backed Iranians were tipped off.

'I just can't believe I got Dabrowski so wrong,' Wyatt is saying, and it's the first time Argylle has heard that note of doubt in the big man's voice. 'I *liked* him. Loved him, even. I woulda trusted him with my life. And if I got him wrong, what's to say I won't make that mistake again?'

'Don't you go thinking you're so special, Wyatt,' says Washington. 'We all misjudged Dabrowski. Guess that's what made him so good at what he did.'

Argylle, meanwhile, is shifting in his seat. He feels uncomfortable whenever Dabrowski's name comes up and wishes there'd been some other reason a vacancy had opened up rather than someone selling his team down the river and ending up behind bars.

'Yeah, well, if Dabrowski was here, I'd make him wish he wasn't,' says Schneider, who seems to grow less mellow with drink, if that were possible. 'That bastard got Fisher killed, and Levy.'

'I don't remember you and Levy getting matching tattoos or anything,' says Washington.

'I never said I liked the guy, but I didn't want the fucker dead. I don't much like you, Washington, but I don't want you dead either.'

'Enough with the schmaltz, you're making me cry.'

26

Seventeen weeks after Federov's promise to the Russian people and three weeks after Monaco

ANDREI BELINSKY HAS NEVER BEEN ANYWHERE QUITE LIKE THE enormous palace on a promontory somewhere on the Black Sea coast where he now finds himself.

He has been brought in by helicopter with the window blacked out so he has no idea of the specific location. On the way from the helipad to the side door of the palace where they entered after being frisked by security, he catches sight of a swimming pool and tennis courts, a golden church and a vast greenhouse, bigger than the apartment block where he now lives.

Once inside, they walk along lofty marble corridors, ceilings winking with the red lights of alarms. Through a distant doorway he glimpses a theatre, complete with a curtained-off stage and wide, sofa-lined booths. Another doorway reveals what looks to be a hookah bar.

He is shown into a room where the floor is intricately patterned with delicate inlays of wood and ivory. Tall marble pillars line the room, each topped with an ornate gold fleur-de-lis moulding, while the grand double doors are flanked by white marble plinths on which stand elaborate porcelain vases, as tall as Andrei's waist.

Two high-backed cream brocade sofas face each other across a vast Chinese silk rug, each the length of Andrei's sitting room at home, their arms and legs carved in gold, their backs curved, the two sides meeting in a golden crest in the centre. There is a low table in the centre of the rug, with gold legs to match the rest of the furniture, and the day's newspapers – so smooth they must have been ironed – are laid out in such immaculate formation it would take a brave person to pick one up and start browsing. Completing the square are four matching cream armchairs with similar Italianate gold legs and crests.

It is on one of those chairs that Andrei Belinksy perches, clutching his cheap nylon backpack to him as if his life depended on it.

Now the double doors are thrown open and the housekeeper appears.

'Mr Federov will be with you shortly. I should advise you that Mr Federov does not shake hands, nor does he permit anyone to come within two metres of him or to look him directly in the eyes. Did you touch the newspapers?'

'No.'

'Only, if you did, they would need to be replaced. We have CCTV, of course.'

'I didn't touch the papers.'

The housekeeper, lips pressed closed, looks him up and down, making her thoughts clear on the matter, before withdrawing.

And then the doors are opening once more and Federov enters, accompanied by a security guard. Belinsky has seen him on the television, of course, but even if he hadn't he would have known instantly that here was someone of consequence. Rich people have a complexion that is all their own.

Federov sits in the chair opposite Belinsky, across that vast swathe of rug.

'I hear you have information for me. About my missing bracelet.'

'I read your advertisement. Of course, I didn't know it was you. The post-office box—'

'What do you have to tell me?'

Belinsky's palms are damp against the nylon bag.

'The advertisement mentioned a reward? A million dollars?'

'For useful information, yes.'

Federov's eyes behind his rimless glasses are pale, almost colourless, and Belinsky feels an icy fingertip trace the ridge of his spine.

'Do you know where my bracelet is, Mr . . . ?'

'Belinsky. No, not exactly.' Belinsky starts to panic as he sees a shadow pass over Federov's flat, expressionless face. 'But I have seen another bracelet exactly like it.'

He was expecting some sort of reaction, but there is none.

'My bracelet was unlike anything else. A completely unique piece.'

'And yet, allow me . . .' Belinsky unzips his bag and the security guard steps forward, his hand already on his gun underneath his jacket, even though the bag has already been thoroughly checked by the security detail on the front door.

'Here.' Belinsky removes a photograph and rushes forward to show it, stopping short when Federov holds up his hand.

'On the table,' he says.

Belinsky lays the photograph on the table as instructed and returns to his seat, while Federov inspects it, without picking it up.

'Where did you get this?'

'I used to be an Orthodox monk – until I had a crisis of faith. I spent twelve years in the Russian Orthodox monastery on Mount Athos – it is a holy site in Greece with twenty monasteries. And because of my civilian occupation as a dealer in antiquities—'

'Please do not elevate yourself, Mr Belinsky. I had you checked out. You were a pawnbroker.'

Belinsky feels the blood rush to his cheeks.

'However you describe it, in Mount Athos my job was to safeguard and curate the monastery's treasure room.'

'Treasure room?'

'Those monasteries on Mount Athos have been there for centuries. They have in their possession priceless religious artefacts either donated or salvaged from churches or cathedrals or from private estates at risk of falling into enemy hands or being ransacked. In my own monastery there was an altarpiece taken from—'

'I'm a busy man. I have no interest in religious art.'

'Very well. The monasteries also possess other valuable items either brought in by the monks themselves when they turn over all their worldly goods or bequeathed in wills by wealthy benefactors wanting to buy their way into heaven.'

'And this bracelet' – Federov gestures towards the photograph – 'was in your monastery's treasure room?'

Is he interested? It's hard to judge, and Belinsky shifts uncomfortably in his seat.

'Not my monastery, but a neighbouring one. I knew the custodian there and we occasionally consulted one another on questions of restoration or storage or insurance. The bracelet was there.'

Federov's eyes go back to the photograph.

'And what makes you think this isn't the very bracelet that was stolen from me? Perhaps it came from the monastery before I bought it at auction.'

'I believe the bracelet you lost had the word "Fidelis" engraved on it? This one was engraved with a different word: "Pietas".'

Vasily Federov's unnerving eyes flicker momentarily behind his glasses, before they become flat and dead again, as if that flicker of life has been instantly sucked out.

'What is the name of this monastery?'

Belinsky clears his throat. Glances at the security guard.

'About the reward . . .'

For a few moments after Andrei Belinsky leaves, clutching a cheque and blissfully unaware he has only twenty-seven minutes to live, Federov remains in that mausoleum of a room, gazing into the middle distance. Then he gets to his feet and calls to the housekeeper, telling her to throw out the newspapers. He doesn't wish to take any chances.

He heads out into a wide, high corridor, decorated in shades of rich cream and lined with paintings in ornate gilt frames. He tries to buy Russian artists wherever possible, but the truth is they mostly leave him cold. Still. Optics matter. A second corridor – this one narrower and painted a deep red, so that walking down it feels like being inside a vein or an artery – brings him to a lift shaft. He presses his finger to the smooth metal plate on the left and the lift doors slide soundlessly open.

Inside there are no floor numbers. This lift has only one destination.

After descending just one storey, Vasily Federov steps out into an environment so different from the one he has just left it might as well be another planet. Here there are no elegant drapes, no crystal chandeliers. Instead, there is a dank, chilly chamber, lit by bare bulbs that cast a sickly greenish light over the stone walls. At the far end is a steel, handleless door. Again, he presses his fingertip to the metal plate on the wall, and again the door slides open.

Now he is in a second, smaller chamber, where the ceiling is at least two feet lower. He wrinkles his nose in distaste as the foetid air hits his nostrils, musty and damp, unpleasantly clammy but with a chill edge that seeps into the marrow of his bones. There's a sour smell in here, and the bite of bleach fumes doesn't cover the tang of sweat and vomit and shit.

There are two figures in this hellish place. One seated and the other standing over him. The more upright of the two is Sergei Denisov, his thick neck corded with veins as if he has been exerting himself. He holds a heavy, wooden-handled hammer. The claw end of the hammer is red and sticky, with a clump of hair matted to it. When he sees Federov, he nods, and the two exchange a few words, Federov seeming none too happy about what he hears. Then Federov positions himself in front of the second man, who is strapped by his wrists and his ankles to a heavy metal chair, which is itself fixed to the stone floor with iron rings embedded in concrete.

The man's head is hanging down and blood drips from a gash in his dark hair on to the bare skin of his thighs. Federov daintily hitches up the trousers of his Tom Ford suit and crouches down so that he is on a level with the slumped figure.

'Do you know how many bones there are in the human foot?' he asks. He speaks in English and, while his tone is conversational, it contains no warmth or lightness. It is a voice with all the life wrung out of it.

When there is no response, he answers his own question. 'Twenty-six. That's how many. And the last fellow who sat where you are sitting had every last one of them broken by Mr Denisov here. And when he'd finished with his foot, he worked his way up to his ankle, and then his fibula and tibia and knee and femur. I don't need to tell you what he arrived at next. It's quite sad, because he was newly married, and now, of course, there can be no question of children . . .'

The man in the chair raises his head finally. His face is grotesquely swollen, one of his eyes sealed tightly shut and the other a demonic red where the blood vessels have burst.

Federov surveys him impassively, as if he is taking an inventory. Then he stands, frowning as he spots a speck of dirt on his jacket then flicks it away.

'Anyway, enough small talk. It's time to get you cleaned up a little bit.' Federov stretches his mouth into a tight line that might have been a smile, or perhaps a grimace.

'You're about to make a video.'

27

THE FIRST COCK-UP OF THE MISSION COMES EARLY.

'Where's Corcoran?' Coffey is pacing the grey-carpet-tiled lobby of the Hôtel Beaux Rêves, backwards and forwards in front of the cramped and currently unmanned reception area, from the vending machine to the emergency exit and back.

'Carter is checking up on him,' says Samra, who, alongside Quinn, is sitting on one of the lobby's plastic seats. Though the unassuming engineer is not the most physically able, they will need his logistical brain. 'Here she comes.'

But the news from Room 141 is not good.

'What the hell did he eat?' Coffey demands.

'I think it must be the shrimp croquettes,' says Wyatt, who had accompanied Corcoran to lunch at the Café du Parc. 'I had the chicken stew. Can't go wrong with a chicken stew.'

'He tried to come down with me, insisted he was okay, but we didn't even make it as far as the stairs before he had to . . . you know,' Carter informs them, her mouth twisting in distaste.

'I'll do it.' Wyatt is already on his feet.

'Forget it,' says Coffey. 'You're too heavy, Woody. No offence. There's just too much equipment to carry. The chute won't take it.'

'Especially since you'll be landing on a roof the size of my pinkie,' says Washington, helpfully.

'How about Samra?' suggests Schneider, much to the engineer's visible horror.

'Again, no offence, but Asif, I'm not sure your 'chuting skills are up to it. Quinn, go get ready to leave.'

'Wait . . . What? But she's a woman,' says Kellerman, the heavy-set Canadian with sad eyes.

'Thanks for pointing that out, Alex,' says Coffey. 'There's no alternative. Quinn is the only one with the parachuting experience to land on that roof who isn't going to drop to the ground like a sack of potatoes once we load her up with equipment. It's not ideal, but—'

Quinn doesn't even stop to hear the end of the sentence. She is out of the door, heading for the stairs.

From two thousand metres in the air, as the low sun sets, bleeding orange and pink across the western horizon, the Aegean Sea is a vast swathe of inky velvet studded with diamond crystals that are the lights from the fishing boats and the pleasure cruisers and the sleek yachts. Over Mount Athos, the landscape changes, the dark crags of the one-hundred-and-thirty-square-metre mountainous peninsula below broken up every now and then by the subdued lights of the monasteries, the sheer majesty of the geological formations standing just as they have done for millions of years.

This really is a world that time forgot. The roads are unmade and rough and there are few cars, only the odd official taxi, which is more like a four-by-four minibus, to ferry pilgrims from one monastery to another. The twenty monasteries are spaced well apart. Argylle knows from his research that each has its own architecture and traditions, and many were built at great altitudes on top of rocky outcrops or cliffs, taking the monks nearer to God . . . and further from the temptations and distractions of other people.

Those monks who cannot deal even with the society of their brethren can choose to live a life of complete isolation in *sketes* – tiny cells up in the highest part of the mountain – which they access by lowering themselves in baskets over the side of the sheer cliff face using a system of ropes and pulleys.

The plane circles wide and high to avoid both the hillside town of

Karyes in the centre of the peninsula, where a police station stands on a cobbled street alongside a post office, and also the heavily guarded port of Dafni to the west, where the official ferries from the mainland pull up.

Normally, Argylle would be relishing being in a small plane once again for the first time since his father died, but instead his heart is racing.

Parachuting.

Though he passed the training with ease, he still doesn't trust the mechanics of it. When his life is in his own hands, that's one thing, but when it rests on a piece of equipment with different components, any of which could go wrong at any time, well, that's quite another. And when you add the gathering darkness into the mix . . .

Erin Quinn, however, shows no such compunction. Instead, she is hyper-excited, her foot tapping on the floor of the Cessna 208 so that he can feel the vibrations through the sole of his own shoes. He reminds himself that the Agency runs through her veins like blood, that she grew up in a CIA Petri dish, steeped in its culture, its norms, its risks and its rewards. No wonder she's more confident than he is. This is her happy place.

The plan is for the plane to fly over once to drop off the two who will be landing on the monastery roof, and then a second time to drop off the others. Approaching from the back of the peninsula and shielded from view by the vertiginous crag that looms up behind the rock on which the monastery is built, they will, with luck, avoid detection.

The advance pair will set up the ropes and pulleys on the roof, ready for the others to scale the front of the monastery, carrying with them the various parts of the motorized winch they'll need in phase two of the mission.

Now the door of the plane is opening, and Quinn and Schneider are perched on the edge of the fuselage, gazing down into the abyss, and they look so damn chilled out about it, like they are sitting side by side on a park bench. Argylle wants to say something to Quinn before she jumps, but it's so noisy up there in the plane with the engine roaring and the wind whooshing past the open door, and besides, what would he say?

Will Hooper stands up. 'Remember, you're against the clock here. In seven minutes, the monks will be heading to the chapel, and then you have just forty-seven minutes to do what you have to do and get the hell out of there before the monks process up from the chapel to return the relic to the treasure room. Or God help you.'

He counts them out. First Schneider, then Quinn. One minute they are there and the next gone, falling through the vast, empty midnight-blue sky. Now, as the tiny plane arcs around, the rest of them must prepare to jump. They have already worked out the order, Wyatt first and Argylle bringing up the rear. It means he must watch, his insides stitched up tightly, as the others drop off one after the other – Wyatt, Kellerman, Samra, Washington – each of them carrying not just the chute on their back but also a piece of the dismantled mechanical winch. Argylle himself has the battery in a pack strapped across his body. It feels stupidly heavy. And now Hooper's arm comes down and he is falling through space, just as the final halo of pink and orange fades from the horizon and the stars prick the sky above him like lights through a pinhole camera.

He can just make out the dark shapes of the other four beneath him, but he focuses on calming himself. There is nothing he can do now, free-falling through a balmy Greek night, so why not enjoy this moment suspended between the stars and the Earth? Thus, through desperation rather than design, he finally clears his racing mind so that when it is time to pull the cord for the chute, his heart is no longer beating in his chest as if it will burst straight out, and when the ground rises up to meet him he is ready, landing on his feet in the undergrowth of the valley behind the monastery.

From here he can see the rock looming up in front, blocking out the sky, with the monastery teetering impossibly on the summit.

The walkie-talkie clipped to the strap across his chest crackles into life. Quinn's amused voice in his ear. 'The eagle has landed. Both eagles. Over.'

With no cellphone coverage on the peninsula, they are having to go old school with walkie-talkies set to an encrypted frequency.

'Roger that,' he replies, and then bursts out laughing from the sheer relief of having made it this far.

But there is no time to say more because the clock is already ticking. Even now the monks will be making their way to the chapel for the start of the vigil for St Benedict, the one time of the year when the most precious of the treasures they keep inside their fortified treasure chamber – the piece of their patron saint's jawbone, nestling on a velvet cushion in an ornately decorated gilded box – is carefully removed from its glass case and taken to the chapel to be carried up and down the rows of kneeling monks, allowing each to gaze upon it for just a few seconds.

The ceremony is considered so sacred that the great arched doors of the chapel are locked so that nothing can disturb the monks' holy contemplation. But such is the level of anxiety about protecting the relic that it is permitted only forty minutes out of its climate-controlled storage case before the monks will walk in slow procession through the monastery to the treasure chamber to return it, a journey of exactly seven minutes, at which time the theft of the bracelet will be discovered and, as Coffey put it, 'All hell will break lose.'

The first test is to climb the seven hundred-plus steep, narrow steps up the side of the rockface to reach the base of the monastery. The team are fit after their training but, even so, by the time they are only halfway up Argylle's muscles are straining and his lungs on fire, and when they arrive at the top he has to lean over with his hands on his knees, trying not to throw up.

'Too much for you, Argylle?' mocks Wyatt, who seems barely out of breath. 'Maybe you should have done the full training instead of the taster course.'

They have arrived at a strip of land that skirts the base of the monastery, separated from the sheer drop beyond by a rudimentary wooden fence. Up here, the air is fresh and scented with pine and laurel. To the side of the monastery, where the land widens, an unmade track zigzags down the mountainside towards the sea, while several narrow paths plunge directly down the steeper slopes. In the foreground, a vegetable garden has been carefully planted with tomatoes and green beans snaking up wooden stakes. By the light of the hooded torch that clips to his belt, Argylle sees a cluster of fruit trees at the end. Walking around it to the long, narrow cobbled terrace at the front – flanked by a low stretch of outbuildings clinging to the precipice, which, judging by the smell, houses the monastery's livestock – Argylle risks a glance up the towering facade. The roof where they'll be climbing is so high it seems to be part of the sky itself.

The monastery's chapel is at the far end of the building from where they arrived – a bell tower that soars above the main roof, studded with stained-glass windows lit up by the flickering light of thousands of candles. From the nave comes the sound of hundreds of male voices chanting. The ceremony is getting underway.

Someone's walkie-talkie sounds. Schneider telling them the first ropes are ready, and can they fricking well hurry up. And now, despite the still-aching and protesting limbs, they must again start climbing, unclipping their harnesses from around their waists, feeling once more the heft of the machinery they are each carrying.

Argylle is the first to go. He is at home here on the ropes, having led tour groups up the sides of waterfalls and gorges. When he was in his early teens, his parents rented an apartment on the fourth floor of a swanky apartment building in The Peak on Hong Kong Island with panoramic views from every window. Argylle was in a rebellious phase and saw curfews as a violation of his rights, so he used to climb down the side of the building from balcony to balcony, and then back again in the early hours when dawn was breaking over Victoria Harbour.

But now there is no soft dawn light tearing a hole through the darkness, no easy footholds on balcony railings and feature steel window frames. There is only the soaring stone wall, hostile and crumbling, and the awareness of the seconds ticking away as he hoists himself up in the harness, bracing his feet to the walls where centuries of masonry crumble under the soles of his size-eleven boots. He passes an open window through which he can see a spartan room, furnished only with a single bed, the sheet stretched neatly across the thin mattress, and a wooden desk, its surface bare apart from a leather-bound Bible.

In one room he spies a pair of spectacles on a bedside table, in another a cushion on the floor to make praying easier on elderly or infirm knees. Argylle glances down and sees the dark shapes of his teammates below him, and beneath them the sheer rockface falling away into a black lake of nothingness.

When he reaches the roof, Quinn and Schneider are there to pull him up. 'Welcome to our humble abode,' says Quinn as he straightens up and sees he is on a narrow, flat, castellated ridge of roof, not quite two metres across. 'It's not much, but we like it.'

Now come the others – one, two, three, four – all needing to be helped up, harnesses unclipped, precious seconds ticking past. Wyatt is the last. Fit but bulky with muscle, he hauls himself over the parapet and lands on his left knee. There's an ominous squishing sound.

'What the—' Wyatt's torch reveals that he is kneeling in the remains of a dead pigeon.

'God is testing you, my son,' smirks Schneider.

The chimney they need to find is halfway along the roof. As they approach the looming bell tower, the chanting that has been growing steadily louder suddenly stops, the abrupt silence leaving them feeling exposed.

'Twenty-two minutes,' announces Carter over the walkie-talkie from the fishing boat.

They are already a minute behind schedule.

The plan had seemed achievable when Coffey had broken it down into steps on the whiteboard. The Bracelet of Piety had been bequeathed to St Benedict's alongside a raft of other valuables – paintings and rare books as well as jewels – by a wealthy benefactor who'd led a debauched life and was trying to make last-minute restitution. It is being stored, with the other priceless treasure the monastery has accumulated over the centuries, in a secret chamber deep in the bowels of the building.

While the chamber itself is alarmed and fortified, its door protected by the four individual locks, their keys entrusted to four monks, the plans Carter managed to retrieve from the monastery's own hard drive revealed an antechamber attached to the far side of it, accessible only through an archway from the chamber itself. This antechamber was once at the heart of the monastery, with a roaring fireplace to insulate the building from the freezing-cold winters at this altitude. When the monks established the secret treasure chamber, they bricked up the fireplace to make sure the temperature inside could be properly controlled. Only the chimney now remains, its empty flue leading down to the bricked-up grate.

The plan is to send a rope down the flue packed with just enough charge to blow a hole in the fireplace. It's a delicate operation. Kellerman must use sufficient explosive to make an opening that Argylle and Wyatt can get through, but not so much that it will trigger the smoke alarm or cause the rest of the chimney to collapse.

Argylle hadn't been expecting the sheer scale of the chimney. It stands shoulder height on him and, when he peers over the top, there is just blackness inside.

They all unbuckle their packs and hand over to Samra the various components of the mechanical winch, which he then fits together. They've timed this over and over, but it's one thing putting something together on the carpeted floor of Meeting Room Three in the Hôtel Beaux Rêves, and quite another three hundred metres up, while the clock is ticking and the only light comes from their torches.

Meanwhile, Kellerman is working on the explosives, measuring out what he believes to be the right amount and leaving the rest. There will be no second chances.

They set the timer and send down the rope. Washington is muttering under his breath.

'Dude, are you praying?' Wyatt asks.

'When in Rome,' says Washington.

The explosion, when it comes, sounds deafening in the still, clear night, the roof vibrating underneath their feet. A plume of smoke emerges from the chimney. They all freeze, waiting to hear the wail of an alarm. Instead, the silence that follows the explosion is broken by a sound coming from the nave – a man's amplified singsong voice intoning the prayers, interrupted at intervals by a chorus of chanting monks.

Argylle closes his eyes as Quinn helps attach his harness to the winch.

'Go,' says Schneider as Argylle perches on the lip of the chimney, P95 air mask and goggles securely strapped on.

'There's still too much smoke,' says Argylle.

'*Now*. We're losing time.'

There's a hand on his back and now he is falling down inside the smoke-filled chimney with his eyes shut and his breath held.

28

THE PAIN IN HIS LUNGS WHEN HE TAKES HIS FIRST GULP OF SMOKE-gritted air is agonizing, stripping the skin from the back of his throat. His feet hit the floor at the bottom of the chimney stack and he opens his eyes. At first, everything is just a dense black fog, but as his eyes acclimatize he sees a faint grey light at ground level. Crouching down, he crawls towards it, knocking his head as he does so on a brick overhanging the jagged aperture the explosion has created.

Inside the antechamber, although the air is thick with disturbed dust, the smoke isn't so bad. Which allows him to see . . .

'Guys, we have a problem.' The lack of static on the walkie-talkie tells him there is no signal.

Dammit.

He sticks his head back inside the newly opened hole and tries again, his already sore throat protesting as he gulps in more smoke. This time the connection works.

'The archway to the treasure chamber isn't an arch. It's a door.'

By this time Wyatt is on his way down, arriving seconds later, gasping for breath. While he recovers, Argylle tries the door. Locked fast, as he'd suspected.

When they go back to the chimney, Kellerman announces he is sending down the rest of the charge so that they can blow the lock. Wyatt and Argylle exchange a worried look.

'They won't have bothered to alarm it if it only leads to this dead-end room,' says Wyatt. 'Am I right?'

There's only a small amount of charge left and Wyatt packs most of it around the solid iron lock.

'Actually, I think—' Argylle begins.

'Don't worry, man, I got this. I dealt with explosives all the time in the SEALs.'

'But the hinges—'

Too late. Wyatt pulls Argylle back, just as the charge detonates, causing a cloud of smoke that clears to show a hole where the lock was.

'What did I tell you? Still got the touch,' says Wyatt, but he's not so smug when they try to pull the door to find it still locked fast.

'We'll have to do it again.'

'Try the hinges, Wyatt.'

'Dude, I already told you, I got this. Hey, what you doing?'

But Argylle has already seized hold of the remaining charge and, splitting it into two equal amounts, applies what little is left to the hinges of the great door, on the opposite side to the lock.

'This is on you, man,' says Wyatt, stepping back with his hands raised as if surrendering all responsibility.

This time, when the smoke clears there are two more craters. But the door is still in place.

'And now we've used up all the—'

Wyatt's words are lost in a loud, ominous creak. As they watch, the door drops two inches on the side where the hinges once were.

Relief tastes sweet in Argylle's mouth.

'How did you—'

But there's no time for discussion. They have lost valuable minutes. They cautiously push the side of the door that is now free. There's another ominous creaking sound and for a moment Argylle thinks the fortified oak slab will break free of its lock and crash to the floor, but though it twists, it holds up enough for them to squeeze through.

Now it is clear why the first attempt failed. On the other side of the door to the ancient iron lock they'd tried to blow up is a modern monstrosity made from a solid block of stainless steel, over half a metre high, with its own multi-point locking device.

'Unbelievable,' Wyatt mutters under his breath as he follows Argylle into the chamber.

The first thing Argylle notices is the change in temperature. Back there in the antechamber it had been uncomfortably warm. Years of stagnation had made the air thick and dirty with heat. But here it is cool. Cold even. Argylle had imagined something like Ali Baba's cave – piles of gold treasures in every corner. Instead, the room is like a contemporary art gallery, a low, vaulted sandstone brick ceiling set with downlighters that tastefully illuminate a religious arched trip-tych mounted on a wall, no doubt liberated from a grand cathedral. In the centre of the room are two glass display cabinets, one of which is empty, its doors hanging open, suggesting it might normally house the relic currently being worshipped in the chapel. The second has, displayed on a purple silk cushion, a chalice with golden dragon handles sitting on a base in the shape of a golden flower, the cup inlaid with turquoise and precious stones. There is an alarm sensor winking red from the ceiling.

'The Jasper Chalice,' says Argylle, momentarily lost in wonder. 'The cup is formed from a single piece of jasper and is supposed to have been used by Jesus at the Last Supper.'

'Fascinating, I'm sure, but how about you hold the history lesson until we're outta here?'

The only other thing in the chamber is a marble slab on a low plinth on one side of the chamber with several names carved into it.

The vaulted chamber is the nucleus from which five short corri-dors radiate. Wyatt dives into the corridor nearest to him, which is lined on both sides with tall, narrow doors. He pulls a door handle at random, surprised to find it slides out towards him, revealing four paintings displayed on rigid panels hanging from the runners. Mov-ing on, he hurries down the corridor pulling out one door after another, revealing icons, scrolls, tapestries.

Meanwhile, Argylle is in a different corridor, this one lined with wide, shallow, glass-lidded drawers. The first one he opens contains bones – the nub of a thigh bone, a whole skeleton hand – all displayed individually and catalogued with neatly typed cards in Greek. He tries a second. More bones. He turns and tries a drawer on the other side. This one reveals beautifully illustrated manuscripts, their pages glittering with gold.

'You got anything?' Wyatt calls, and there's no mistaking the urgency in his voice. Argylle checks his watch. They have nine minutes before the procession will be arriving back at the chamber, the monks looking on while the four monks in possession of the keys take it in turns to turn the locks before ceremoniously returning the relic to its display case.

Invisible needles prick at his chest and stomach and his mouth is as dry as the bones in the drawers.

He slides open a tall, thin cupboard that turns out to be a glass display case containing a carefully pinned monk's habit. The label on the bottom reads *Agios Alypius*. A second identical case, with a slightly different habit, is labelled *Agios Nicholas*. From the reverential way in which the vestments are displayed Argylle guesses these habits were once worn by monks who went on to become saints.

The next corridor is more promising – non-religious items. Gold ingots, ancient Roman and Greek coins, maps, embroidery, ceramics. The kinds of valuables a monastery might have been donated or left in wills. He whirls around to pull out the drawers from the other side. Bingo. Jewel-encrusted pendants on thick gold chains, diamond rings, strings of pearls as big as Argylle's thumbnail, a silver dagger inset with rubies. 'I think I've—' he says, just as Wyatt, whose motto has always been 'Act first, panic after' yanks down on a woodenhandled lever he's just spotted set into a wall.

There is an ominous rumbling, followed by a loud groan from the ground as if a long-buried creature is waking up after a long sleep.

'What the hell did you do?'

'I just—'

Wyatt's excuses are drowned out by a loud creaking that sends both of them running back to the main chamber in time to see the marble slab on its low plinth slide slowly open.

172

'Holy *crap*!' Wyatt is standing on the edge peering in. 'Are those bones down there?'

'It's a crypt,' says Argylle, joining him. He hopes Wyatt can't sense the shudder that passes through him as he peers down into the grave-sized vault at the two skeletons lying side by side, each with a large, ornate crucifix nestling in the bones of their hands. 'No time for gawking, Wyatt. Get that thing closed up. I think I'm close.'

As he returns to the corridor he's just come from, Argylle can hear that the chanting is louder. The monks are on the move.

'Oh, Christ. Come on, Argylle, we have to abort.'

'Not yet. I know it's here somewhere.'

'Argylle, *abort*!'

Wyatt, usually so laid-back, is rigid with tension standing in the mouth of the corridor. Even if the monks have only just left the chapel, how long before they arrive?

'One more,' says Argylle, flinging open the bottom drawer.

There. In the centre. In a glass case lined with bottle-green silk. His breath catches in his throat. The Bracelet of Piety.

'*Now*, Argylle.'

Snatching up the case, Argylle sprints towards the heavy fortified door that leads to the antechamber and the fireplace and freedom.

'Shit.'

'Wanna hurry it up, Argylle?'

Outside, they can hear the echoing sound of the procession approaching, hundreds of chanting voices reverberating off the monastery's stone walls.

'It's jammed.'

'Move over and let a real man take over.'

Wyatt shoves him aside and puts one of his meaty shoulders to the door, his face puce as he grunts and heaves. Nothing. The door that had been opened enough for them to slip through on the way in has twisted inwards, become wedged in the door frame and is blocking their exit.

'This is on you, man. If you hadn't blown the hinges—'

'Then we'd never have got the bracelet.'

'Hope they let you wear it in your Greek jail cell.'

Outside, the voices of the monks are noticeably louder. Wyatt gives one final heave and gives up. 'Plan B – we arm ourselves. There's a case back there with a weird silver dagger.'

'So the two of us against several hundred men.'

'They're monks, dude, what are they gonna do? Pray us to death? You got a better plan?'

29

THE PROCESSION OF MONKS, SOME HOLDING FLAMING TORCHES, others candles or rosaries or tiny pots of smoking incense, has reached the end of the long stone corridor, stopping outside the vast wooden door that leads to the treasure chamber. Most of them only come to this part of the monastery once a year and there's a buzz of anticipation as four of their number step forward, all wearing the long black robes and distinctive high, round, black rimless hat topped with black, flowing head-covering that characterize the brethren of the Greek Orthodox Church.

From the folds of their gowns, the four monks each produce a heavy iron key, six inches long, and one by one the keys are inserted into the four locks that descend the door one beneath the other. The chanting grows louder and more fervent as the abbot himself, the head of the monastery, turns the handle and the great door creaks open.

The cool air from the climate-control device comes as a surprise and as they progress through the chamber, following the relic in its box, the monks steal furtive, awed looks at the glass display cabinets and the vividly realized religious iconography on the walls. There's a sense of building emotion as they prepare to transfer the sacred fragment of bone from its metal box back to its glass display cabinet, where it will be locked away for another year.

But as they approach the open cabinet, a low muttering begins from the back fringe of the group, voices gradually rising. The abbot stops intoning as a monk whispers in his ear. His expression hardens as he pushes through the throng that parts in his path until he arrives at the mouth of one of the arched spurs that fan out from the main chamber, where he stops abruptly, taking in the carelessly open drawers and cabinets, evidence of an intruder.

He turns to his congregation, nostrils flaring, and shouts out one word. You wouldn't need to know Greek to understand what he's saying.

Theft.

'I think they're on to us,' Wyatt whispers, registering the sudden change of tone in the monks' muffled voices.

'Relax. They'll assume we escaped before they got here.'

'Right, so we just hold fire until they go after us and then get the hell outta here?'

'Exactly.'

'Cool. And how exactly do we do that? I mean, I know you wouldn't be dumb enough to pull the lever and have us dive down here into this pit of bones as the slab slides shut on top of us without knowing there's a way out, right?'

Argylle doesn't reply and Wyatt shifts around until he is turned towards him, switching on his flashlight so that his companion's face is illuminated.

'Right?'

Argylle tries not to look at him, but seeing as the two men are lying wedged side by side in the grave-sized crypt like a pair of sardines in a can, it's almost impossible.

'There wasn't time to check,' Argylle hisses. 'They were through the door. We had to do something. But there's got to be a button or lever somewhere down here. How else would people get out?'

Wyatt shines his flashlight around the cramped space, lingering on the two full-sized skeletons who are wedged in there with them.

'Er, I'm not sure that's really an issue for them.'

'Trust me. There'll be something.'

Argylle hopes he sounds more convinced than he feels.

*

In the treasure chamber, all is chaos, the monks murmuring to one another, passing up and down the spurs to report back on anything that seems to be amiss. Someone has spotted two illuminated manuscripts in the wrong cases; someone else reports a chalice knocked on to its side.

'But what has been taken?' the abbot wants to know.

So now they must scour the display cases once more. A young monk becomes excited when he spots an empty cushion – until the case next to it is revealed to contain two jewelled chalices instead of one. Finally, a cry goes up. 'Here!' A priest is dispatched to check and returns to the abbot, looking grave.

'It's the Bracelet of Piety, Reverend Father. It's missing.'

The abbot needs to act. The monks – unused to so much deviation from the rigid routines of their lives, first the procession and now the robbery – are growing overexcited, their normally calm voices rising in volume. He must restore order.

'Thank you, brothers,' he says. 'Now we must clear the treasure chamber and leave everything for the police to conduct their investigations. Please return to your cells to pray for the bracelet's safe return.'

The monk closest to him, a rotund fellow with a round baby-face, looks disappointed, but like the others he bows in acquiescence. 'Of course, Father.'

Within minutes the chamber is empty. The abbot takes one more look around before exiting. The four key-carrying monks have dispersed with the rest of the monks and he doesn't bother summoning them back. The police will be here in minutes. Instead, he positions Brother Tobias, one of the longest-serving monks on the door, to make sure no one goes in. Then he hurries off down the corridor towards his office, which houses the monastery's sole telephone. The abbot can't remember the last time he used it. He's quite looking forward to it.

'What do you mean, you can't find it? Oh Jesus, there's no oxygen in here.'

Argylle tries to block out Wyatt's laboured breathing and focus on his surroundings. Since the monks' voices stopped, he and Wyatt have done a fingertip search of every inch of their new home, trying to find the button that will cause the slab to miraculously slide back open and let them out the way they came, but while they've found candles and rosaries, plus the two ostentatious golden crucifixes, an escape route has proved frustratingly elusive.

'I can't breathe. Can you breathe?'

Wyatt shifts his weight in an attempt to turn to Argylle and there's an ominous cracking sound.

'Oh shit. Tell me I didn't just crush that skull? Isn't that bad luck?'

Argylle doesn't bother asking him how much worse his luck could get than being trapped in an airless hole in the ground with a couple of skeletons for company.

'We can leg-press it,' he says.

The two of them lie on their backs with their knees bent above them, feet resting on the marble.

'On the count of three . . .'

For a brief, wonderful moment as they both grunt and groan in unison, it seems as if it might work, the slab lifting infinitesimally, only to come slamming back down again. A second attempt also ends in failure.

'You're not even trying, dude. I'm carrying this whole thing here.'

'Oh yeah, so you do it on your own, then.'

Wyatt obligingly takes over, bracing his feet against the marble above him and straining his thighs and calves, managing to raise the marble just a few millimetres. But it's enough to give Argylle an idea.

He shuffles down the crypt on his back until he has hold of the two crucifixes, each formed of two cylindrical gold bars, one vertical, the other horizontal, fused at the meeting point with a cluster of rubies.

'When I say go, give it all you have,' he instructs Wyatt, transferring a crucifix so that he holds one in each hand.

Wyatt's first lift is a write-off, but the second raises the slab just enough for Argylle to slide the long ends of the crucifixes underneath it, one on each side, with the fused cross-bars protruding into the space above their heads.

Wyatt stares at them.

'And this helps us how?'

'Ever wondered how the Egyptians dragged those enormous stone slabs across the desert to build the Pyramids, Wyatt?'

'Can't say I—'

'So one theory is that they put them on giant logs which they used as rollers, with teams of poor schmucks at each end turning them by hand to shift them across the sand.'

Wyatt blinks.

'So you're saying we turn the crucifixes like handles and the slab will just magically roll off?'

'You got a better idea?'

The first attempt is a disaster. Their hands, clammy with sweat, simply can't get a purchase on the slippery metal crucifixes.

'What do you rub into your hands at the gym when you're lifting, Wyatt?'

'You seriously don't know? Have you never—'

'Just answer the question.'

'Chalk. Everyone knows you use chalk powder, to absorb the sweat and create more friction. Hey, what are you doing, man? Don't do that. Ew, that's gross. Show some respect.'

Argylle has dipped his hands into the pile of crumbled bone created when Wyatt accidentally rolled on the skull a few moments before and is rubbing the powdery residue liberally into his palms.

'Our need is greater than his at this point, Wyatt. Unless you want to stay down here and slowly suffocate to death?'

Wyatt takes a deep breath and mumbles an apology under his breath before following suit.

This time, when they grip the crucifixes, which Argylle has deliberately positioned diagonally across from one another so that his is towards the foot of the vault and Wyatt's towards the head, they manage to turn them.

'No way!' mutters Wyatt, as, above their heads, the marble slab slowly starts to move.

When they emerge into the empty treasure chamber, Wyatt gulping down the cool, climate-controlled air, their euphoria at being free is short-lived. What now? They can't go back the way they came. Even if they could get past the wedged antechamber door, the others will be long gone, bailing out as soon as the alarm went up. The only other option is to go through the main door into the corridor and escape through the monastery itself.

Which is in a state of high alert.

The two men look at each other, each thinking how badly the other would stand out among the sombrely clad monks.

'I have another idea,' says Argylle, swinging his gaze towards the corridor where he'd seen the sanctified monks' outfits.

'Oh, sweet Jesus, no.'

Minutes later, Brother Tobias is in position outside the treasure chamber, deep in prayer, when, to his immense surprise, the door swings open and two monks emerge, their black headdresses obscuring their faces.

His immediate thought is that they must have been left behind in the chaos of the discovery of the robbery.

'Forgive us, brother,' says the broader one, though as he's talking English, his apology is lost on the older monk, who is taken by surprise a second time at finding himself being lifted bodily through the air, through the cool treasure chamber and deposited inside the open crypt. The last thing he hears as the marble slab slides over his head is the American promising to leave a note. Though, unfortunately, he doesn't understand a word of it.

Now Argylle and Wyatt are progressing along the dimly lit corridor. Wyatt has a rosary in his hands over which he bends his head so that his face is hidden, while Argylle holds in front of him a small golden tray suspended from his hands by gold chains on which he burns frankincense, swinging it from side to side so the smoke creates a screen in front of them as they make their way down the stone staircase.

Nearing the bottom of the stairs, they see a set of arched doors ahead and Argylle's spirits lift as he thinks of the outside and freedom. Even without being the object of a manhunt, he would find the monastery oppressive. The dead weight of history and of religious conviction.

Just then, one of the doors opens and a monk comes in, looking surprised to see them there. He intones something in Greek and Argylle swings the frankincense in front of them as he mumbles something unintelligible in reply. The monk looks confused, but they push past him, emerging on to the narrow cobbled terrace that runs the length of the front of the monastery, lined on one side with outhouses and beyond which lies the sheer drop to the bottom of the mammoth rock on which the monastery is built. The only way down off the plateau where they are now is via that steep path accessed to the side that zigzags down the mountain towards the distant sea.

Risking a glance up towards the roof of the monastery, Argylle sees that is it swarming with monks.

'Crap,' says Wyatt, emerging from the folds of his headdress. 'Hope the others got away okay.'

Up ahead, they spot two robed figures rounding the corner of the monastery and dive through the nearest outhouse door.

'What the hell?' Wyatt's voice is lost in loud squawking and flapping and Argylle feels beneath his vestments for his flashlight as ominous dark shapes loom out of the shadows.

'Chickens,' he says, relieved, shining his beam around.

They pick their way through the strutting birds to a doorway at the end that leads into a second outhouse.

'Oh Jesus. Please, what is that?'

The smell of warm shit mixed with rotting veg is overpowering.

'It's pigs, Wyatt. Nice, friendly, cuddly pigs.'

The pigs – enormous black creatures – seem neither friendly nor cuddly, and both Wyatt and Argylle are relieved to pass through to a third, straw-strewn building in which two mellow goats share a space with a handful of sheep.

'See, these here I can get on board with. Nice, cute fellows minding their own . . . *Jesus Christ, what is that?*'

A huge shadow has come looming out of the darkness behind Wyatt. Argylle's pulse quickens, his breath stops, until his flashlight reveals a donkey, its big, wet nose nuzzling Wyatt's thick neck.

Another donkey ambles over.

'Don't think much of yours, Argylle,' says Wyatt, as the new arrival nudges Argylle's arm, as if wanting to get closer to him.

'Yeah, funny guy. Come on, we've got to catch up with the others.'

But when they emerge through the door at the far end back on to the cobbled terrace and make their way to where the zigzag track begins, they can see no sign of the taxi-bus that should have been waiting at the bottom of the rock to take them down the mountainside to the port, its driver willing to take the risk of helping what he has been told is a group of pilgrims keen to venture off the official track, in return for a generous bribe to prop up the meagre stipend he receives from the authorities. The others must have left, which is not surprising, given that there are monks milling around everywhere. There's no way they can catch them up. But with the authorities almost certainly on their way, staying where they are is out of the question.

'We're screwed,' says Wyatt.

Argylle weighs up the scenery. The zigzag track that meanders down the gentlest gradient of the mountain towards the sea nine miles away, and then the other single-file paths that veer off steeply down the sheerer face, disappearing into the shadows of the mountainside out of view.

'How are you at riding?'

'When you said riding, I was imagining bikes.'

'Aw, and you look so manly on a mule, Wyatt.'

'Yeah, very—'

Something shoots across the path, a fox or a boar, spooking Argylle's donkey, which sets off at a gallop through the undergrowth to the side of the path, swerving around an olive tree, so that the lowest branch knocks Argylle off the creature's back. He feels himself flying through the air, a sense of dread building as the ground comes up to meet him. And now he is rolling, feeling a sharp pain in his shoulder where he landed. Down below him, he can just about make out a sheer drop, but the ground beneath him is gravel and dirt and he can't seem to stop his momentum. The chasm is getting closer and closer, Argylle trying to grab on to roots to stop his fall, but nothing holds. He closes his eyes as the earth beneath him falls away . . .

But the anticipated crash never comes. Instead, when he opens them again, he finds that Wyatt has somehow managed to manoeuvre his donkey close enough to him to scoop him up from the edge of the precipice and is now depositing him gently on the ground. He sits still, clutching his shoulder, waiting for his heartbeat to slow. Then he glances up to where he can just about make out Wyatt looking down at him with a smile that evaporates when Argylle says:

'Scoot up, then.'

Because the steep donkey path is so much more direct than the zig-zag track, they manage to intercept the rest of the team two thirds of the way down the mountain, blocking the bumpy, unmade road so the taxi has no choice but to stop.

'Don't even . . .' Wyatt snarls at the openly smirking Schneider as he dismounts the donkey.

Inside the minivan, the atmosphere is tense. The driver – a small man with black whiskers poking through his weathered skin like nylon stitches – is obviously none too happy at picking up these two imposters who have just ridden a donkey directly into his path. He is driving with only his side lights on because the monasteries close at sundown so there's no reason why a vehicle should be out.

Argylle is squeezed into the back seat next to Erin Quinn. She keeps her face turned away from the driver's rear-view mirror, but her hand rests on the seat between them, and when the van makes sudden lurching turns around the bends in the path that come up fast and unexpected, her fingers brush his. *No*, warns the small part of Argylle that isn't drowning in adrenaline. For the past five years he has kept his emotions as effectively stored away as the treasures back there in the hidden chamber. If he opens up a door, even a crack, what else might come flooding out?

There's not a single other vehicle around. That should be comforting, but with the night air so still and dead, Argylle wonders how far the sound of the engine will carry and how high those police posts are, how much of a vantage point they give.

From the front passenger seat comes the sound of Schneider's walkie-talkie crackling, and the taxi driver's eyes widen as Hooper's voice booms out, shockingly loud in the confined space. 'We just did another flyover. You guys have company. Two Yastreb speedboats have just pulled up to the police post in Dafni. There's quite a ruckus going on over there.'

Argylle pulls out his own walkie-talkie. 'Carter, can you hack into the police frequency?'

'Demanding? Much? Hold on . . .'

There's the sound of static and a whistle that sets Argylle's teeth on edge. In front, the driver mutters, clearly nervous.

Carter is back. 'The good news is I'm in. The bad news is I can't make out a goddam word of it. It literally is all Greek to me.'

'Patch it through.'

'What? You speak Greek now as well?'

'Just a few words. It's worth a try.'

More crackling. Then the sound of a man's voice, answered by a second man.

The taxi driver turns around. Shouts something.

'Well? You get any of that?'

'Sure. Everything. Because it's not Greek. It's Russian.'

'The Greek police are talking Russian?' Carter sounds incredulous.

'There's someone talking Russian and another person interpreting in Greek.'

Now everyone in the car is on alert, the tension thick enough to suffocate anyone who breathes too deeply. There is no reason why there should be someone speaking Russian in the Greek police station, unless . . .

'What are they saying?' Samra is normally measured and controlled, so the anxiety in his voice does little to assuage the others' nerves.

'They're claiming to be Russian officers working for Interpol.' Argylle frowns, concentrating. 'They're reporting a robbery.'

30

THE TAXI CRESTS A CRAG AND NOW ARGYLLE CAN MAKE OUT THE inky sea lapping around the base of the cliffs ahead. But there is still a long way to go as the path zigs and zags, avoiding olive trees and sheer, vertiginous drops, down to the coast. As they descend towards the tiny port, protected by rocks on three sides, where the dinghy awaits with Martin Casner at the helm, there comes the wail of sirens and Argylle spots the glow of lights approaching in the distance, skirting the base of the mountain off to the right.

There's silence while they all perform the same calculation, realizing they can just make it.

A screech of brakes. The driver, who has been glancing nervously in the rear-view mirror this whole time, has come to an abrupt halt and is gesturing wildly behind him. Glancing over, Argylle sees that the peak of Erin Quinn's cap has been knocked askew and a tendril of long hair has come loose. Argylle has no idea how much time has passed since the man last saw a woman, but the expression of abject horror on his face suggests it's not inconsiderable. He starts shouting at them and gesturing at them to get out. Argylle understands only snatches of what he's saying, but it's not hard to guess. Taking a bribe to help out some rule-breaking pilgrims is one thing, but betraying a thousand-year tradition and one of the Mount's most fundamental and deeply held beliefs is something else entirely.

Instant loss of livelihood, perhaps trouble with the police. And that's without factoring in the wrath of God.

Wyatt flings open his door. Before the driver has a chance to react he has been dragged from the car and Wyatt has taken his place. He reaches for the ignition.

'Dammit. That asshole has the keys.'

'No time,' says Argylle, reaching over Quinn to throw open the back door. 'We have to make a run for it.'

And now they are all out of the van and scrambling down the hillside, through dense, prickly scrubland and thick bushes, thrusting aside the branches of the trees. They can see the lights from the vehicles approaching down the hill. Two long white SUVs with police insignia and sirens on the top are already bumping mercilessly along the twisting road.

Argylle's eyes rake the shoreline as he makes his descent, half running, half tumbling. Three times a week a speedboat belonging to the Mount Athos authorities calls in to this secluded port, dropping off adventurous pilgrims heading for the remote Katunakia monastery, but at night it is deathly quiet. He can hear an owl calling in a nearby tree. But mostly what he can hear is the sirens getting closer.

Ahead, Wyatt stops.

'You gotta flash your light, Casner,' he says into the walkie-talkie.

'Are you crazy?' comes Casner's answer. 'They'll see me.'

'They already know where we're heading. You gotta let us see where you are.'

There is an audible sigh. And then . . .

'There.' An unmistakable flash of yellow in the black treacle sea.

Again they are on the move. Quinn is first, light and nimble, Wyatt crashing behind her, followed by Washington, Schneider, Kellerman and Argylle. Samra, to the rear, picks his way down.

As they arrive at the port, which is nothing more than a concrete jetty, Argylle's breath is tearing from him in ragged strips, yet at the same time he feels elation bubbling up in him. They're going to make it. The cars are still way up there on the cliffs.

But as the first team members cross the small stony beach to the jetty, his relief evaporates at the sound of gunfire.

Looking up, he sees that the police vehicles have pulled up on the bluff overlooking the port and there is a cluster of men standing on the edge of the cliff. He can just about make out three figures in police uniform, but they are comprehensively outnumbered by what he guesses to be Russians in plain clothes with their weapons drawn. The police seem to be arguing and gesticulating but unwilling to escalate a fight they would almost certainly lose. In the moonlight Argylle makes out a silhouette he recognizes. Denisov, with his distinctively spiked hair, standing still with a revolver resting in the crook of his left arm.

'Over here!' shouts Quinn, diving over to the far side of the concrete jetty, followed by Wyatt, Washington and Schneider. Argylle is about to cross the beach to join them when he hears a cry behind him. Kellerman has gone down on his ankle.

'Can you walk?'

He and Samra have gone back to help him up. But as he stands, his leg buckles under him and he cries out again.

'Here,' says Argylle, hoisting Kellerman's arm over his shoulder. With Argylle taking most of Kellerman's weight they're able to make their way down to the undergrowth just behind the beach.

'Argylle, get your ass in gear.' There's been a break in the gunfire and Wyatt's voice, on the walkie-talkie, fills the air. 'Casner is bringing the dinghy in behind us in one minute. We have to be in position.'

'Go. I'll cover you,' Samra tells him.

Argylle takes a deep breath. 'Ready?' he asks Kellerman.

It's only a few metres to cross the beach to the relative shelter of the concrete jetty, but every single one seems to take hours as Argylle and Kellerman stumble across the uneven pebbles. Argylle is aware of Samra shooting from the undergrowth behind and answering shots from up on the clifftop. He reaches the jetty just as Casner steers the dinghy in as close to the shoreline as he can get while remaining out of firing range from the clifftop.

'Here,' says Wyatt, standing up to relieve Argylle of his burden. '*Vámonos!*'

The team members who have been shielding behind the concrete jetty make a break for the dinghy, splashing through the surf behind Wyatt and Kellerman. Argylle is about to do likewise when a hail of gunfire explodes around him. Glancing around, he sees that Samra has broken cover to make his run.

Now everything is in chaos. The once-balmy night air crackles with tension and bullets.

Argylle is in the water, wading towards the boat. So close to safety he can taste it.

He glances again over his shoulder. Sees that Samra, twisting to fire off another round at the figures on the clifftop, has almost reached the jetty. Looks forward again, but something catches in his mind, something about the angle of Samra's trajectory. He turns back. But where there should be the upright figure of a man, there is only empty space. Samra is down.

'Hold up!' he shouts at the others. But the noise of the gunfire back and forth and the crashing of the waves drown out his voice.

He crouches when he reaches the cover of the jetty, his eyes fixed on the dark shape on the beach. Up on the cliff, the Russians have piled into the police vehicles, leaving the Greek police stranded, and are already bumping down the hill towards the beach.

Argylle takes advantage of the lull in gunfire and drops to Samra's side.

'Are you hit? Come on, let's get you up. Lean on me.'

The moon picks out the delicate angles of Samra's face and his puzzled expression. He is panting softly but he doesn't speak, just gestures towards his chest. Argylle, misunderstanding, thinks this must be the site of his injury and gently probes where Samra is pointing, but instead of a wound his fingers find in Samra's breast pocket a thick, squarish object. Samra nods, and Argylle pulls it out, conscious the whole time of the headlights zigzagging down from the clifftop and the shouts of the others in the boat behind him.

'Please, man, we have to go.' He tries to pull Samra up, but he whispers, 'No,' so softly it might even be the sea breeze moving through the air.

Argylle examines the object again, recognizing from its well-worn leather cover that it must be a Quran. He tries to hand it to Samra, but the injured man shakes his head, and Argylle realizes there is a folded card tucked in between the pages.

Opening the card, he can just about make out that it is a photo of Samra's striking lawyer wife with her arms around two little girls, their dark hair in pigtails and their smiles wide, the youngest missing her front teeth. He holds the photograph up to Samra's eyeline, watching as the man drinks in his little family. Then he wraps Samra's fingers around it while he searches in vain for the wound.

'I can't see anything. I think you're going to be—'

Argylle looks up and stops abruptly.

Samra's panting breaths have stilled. His eyes are shut. The photograph clasped to his chest.

'Argylle. Get over here. We have to leave. Now.'

Argylle is too numb to work out if Casner's voice is coming through the walkie-talkie or from the dinghy. Up ahead he sees the lights of the police car rounding the last bend.

Jolting himself into action, he tries to pick up Samra, but his shoulder is still in pain from his earlier fall and he can't find the strength.

'Samra is gone,' he says out loud. 'Requesting help to bring him in.'

A sharp intake of breath. The lights are coming directly towards him.

'There's no time, Argylle. Leave him and come now.' This is Schneider, the appointed leader of this leg of the mission. 'That's an order.'

Argylle hesitates. Then scrambles to his feet. And then he's running, hearing the roar of an engine behind him. Car doors slamming. And now comes the gunfire, strafing the air around him. He is in the water, his heart jumping into his throat as bullets miss him by inches.

And now the throttle of the dinghy bursts into life, and arms are reaching for him, and before he is even properly inside they are away and skimming over the surface of the water. Behind him, the silhouettes of the Russians at the shoreline grow smaller, the sound of their now-futile gunfire more muffled.

No one speaks as the gunfire stops and they bounce through the spray with the clear, navy-blue night all around them, its beauty an affront to what has just happened.

When they climb the ladder into the fishing boat, Carter breaks the silence.

'The police speedboat they dispatched from Dafni will be here in three minutes. We have to go now.'

The others stare dully at her, made mute by the horror of going home a man down, without even a body to take back to his family.

As the boat pulls away, Quinn, who has sat with her head in her hands since they left the shore, gets to her feet and heads down the stairs to the cabin below.

'This will hit her hard,' says Wyatt flatly. 'After what happened to her dad.'

'What happened?' asks Carter. 'I mean, I know he was CIA royalty or something . . .'

'He was killed out in Iraq. IED. Blew him to pieces.'

No need to ask what that means. No body to view.

'Those poor kids,' says Kellerman softly.

'And all for what?' says Wyatt, reaching into his jacket for the bracelet. 'For this piece of junk? Samra was a good guy. Never made any fuss. Just wanted to get the job done and get home to his family. Was this thing worth his life? Would a hundred of these be worth his life? A thousand?'

Argylle, sitting apart from the group, plunges his shaking hands into his pockets and is surprised to pull out Samra's Quran. He must have picked it up without thinking. But when he turns the little book over he finds something astonishing.

There is a hole burned clear through the back cover of the book. And when he opens it up, he finds a bullet embedded in the pages. Shaking it into the palm of his hand, he recoils when he discovers it is slick with blood, realizing it must have passed through Samra before its trajectory was stopped by the wad of paper.

He is about to let the others know what he's found when something stops him. He pauses, deep in thought, turning the bullet over between his thumb and forefinger before slipping it back into his pocket.

As the boat picks up speed, his thoughts are as dark as the Aegean Sea.

31

HE IS WALKING ALONG A DARK ROAD. A CAR PULLS UP. HE CARRIES on walking, but he knows that the people in the car want to do him harm. His mouth is dry, his palms slick with sweat. The back door of the car opens and a man gets out and opens the trunk. He knows they plan to put him in the trunk and then they will kill him. He tries to cry out, but there is no sound. He tries again, but still only thin air escapes. Now the man's hands are around his neck, pushing him down, and he feels the panic welling up inside him. He opens his mouth and tries to force a sound out. Again and again he tries, each time a little louder, but now he is folded into the trunk of the car and the door is closing, and by the time he finally finds his voice everything goes black.

Argylle wakes himself up yelling in his beige room in the Hôtel Beaux Rêves. Covered in sweat. His heart thumping as if it has come loose and is bouncing around in his chest like a rubber ball. He lies on his back without moving until his breathing comes under control.

Always the same dream. The scream that won't come until it's too late. The situations might change but the dream is the same.

It started after his parents died, intensifying once he found out who they'd really been and the kind of people they might have upset, the horrors they might have experienced during their last minutes on Earth. Over the last couple of years the dreams have got fewer and further apart until he thought he was finally rid of them. Until now.

'You don't need to be a shrink to work out what that's all about, Argylle,' says Carter when he describes it to her over breakfast, two mornings after the Mount Athos mission. Well, right after she told him that there's nothing more boring than other people's dreams. He'd almost clammed up then, but was still so shaken he'd found himself himself blurting it out anyway.

'Oh yeah, well, do share your professional opinion, Dr Carter.'

'It's obvious. You feel like you have no voice. You feel powerless. That'll be a hundred and fifty dollars, please.'

Argylle tears off a strip of the chewy croissants the hotel specializes in, rolls it up and throws it at her.

'Shows what you know. Everyone knows the real answer is that I'm in love with my mother.'

But later on, as he lies on his bed, he finds himself wondering if she might not have a point.

Argylle is not the only member of the team struggling. All of those who'd been to Greece are subdued, preferring to keep to their own rooms rather than face reminders of what they just went through. The previous day they'd gone for walks alone or in pairs, or sat watching TV on their beds, bringing in food from the vending machine or from the supermarket on the other side of the industrial estate. The weather obligingly matched itself to the sombre mood, coating the world in a film of grey. Today they are starting to emerge again, but still no one wants to talk about what happened, and no one goes near Samra's empty room.

On the evening of the second day the word goes around that Frances Coffey wants to see them all in Meeting Room One for a debrief.

They don't want to discuss what happened. And they don't want to face Coffey in case their anger shows. For the sake of a bracelet, two little girls will grow up without a father.

So there is a sour taste in the air when they finally assemble at six thirty, while the grey day bleeds into a grey evening. No one looks at anyone else as they take their seats around the U-shaped table. Instead, they pick at their plastic coffee cups or stare at their phones or gaze moodily out of the window.

Never have a team felt less like a team.

Into this terse atmosphere steps Frances Coffey. If you were to get closer to her, you would get a faint whiff of the mints with which she has tried to disguise the even fainter whiff of cigarette smoke. She has fallen off the wagon, and she currently despises herself for it. Back to square one. But thinking this just makes her despise herself more, because she is well aware that Asif Samra doesn't have the luxury of beating himself up about having one cigarette. This is the very worst part of her job, the thing that has her questioning whether she shouldn't just step back and retire. Grow vegetables. Eat lunch every day with her husband, Andrew, in companionable silence. Anything that doesn't involve sending men and women who she has helped recruit out on missions from which they might never return.

Coffey makes the calls herself. Would never delegate the very worst of all tasks. But the fact that it's her responsibility doesn't make it any easier. 'I'm so sorry to have to tell you . . .' 'Died so bravely . . .' 'You should be very proud . . .' Words and phrases as inadequate as sticking plasters over gaping wounds.

She opens the debrief with a tribute to Samra. 'The very best of us. The highest integrity. Quietly efficient. Resolute. Kind.

'I know you are all suffering,' she continues. 'I know you have lost a comrade and a friend. And you deserve to know why.

'I told you before that Vasily Federov is easily the greatest threat to world stability at this present moment in time, as Mia here knows only too well.' She indicates slender Mia Matsyuk, and Argylle remembers that his teammate lived for seven years in Russia. 'Federov is riding a wave of populist momentum and bringing vast swathes of the disaffected Russian electorate with him. We believe that if he wins the presidential election in Russia, he has the power to unite the most dangerous extremist elements in Europe behind him in a cross-country ultra-right-wing alliance funded by shady billionaires who have grown rich from spreading misinformation online. We know he wants to rebuild the shattered Soviet Union under this new extremist flag.

'I told you also that we went after the first bracelet because

Federov wanted it enough to pay way over the odds for it. And the second because we knew Federov would have his sights set on that one too. What I haven't told you is that we believe this is all part of his quest to find the Amber Room.'

Thirteen pairs of eyes are fixed intently on her.

'Let me explain. The Amber Room was a priceless treasure of unrivalled opulence, once considered to be an eighth wonder of the world. A magnificent chamber made entirely from sheets of amber which were themselves made up of hundreds of thousands of individual mosaics. You probably all know that amber is fossilized tree resin, but you might not be aware that in the eighteenth century it was also known also as the "gold of the north". The great German sculptor Andreas Schlüter had an idea to decorate the walls of a grand room in the Berlin City Palace entirely in amber. This work took decades. When Peter the Great saw how beautiful it was, he fell in love with it and was promptly given it as a gift, taking it to St Petersburg in large boxes, where it eventually hung in the Catherine Palace. All fifty-five square metres of it. Six tonnes of amber, augmented by gold and mirrors and candelabra. It was said to glow from within. To stand inside it was by all accounts to be utterly dazzled.

'During the Second World War the Russians tried to protect their unique treasure by pasting wallpaper over it, but it was discovered and dismantled by the Nazis and taken to the city of Kaliningrad, at that time known as Königsberg. This used to be part of Germany until it was annexed by Russia after the war. There the legendary Amber Room was put on display for two years before it was dismantled again in late 1943 or early 1944 and stored in stamped, numbered crates in the basement of Königsberg Castle, waiting to be shipped out on Hitler's orders.

'And that's the last concrete information we have. As you might know, Königsberg came under heavy attack both by the Allies in '44 and by the advancing Red Army in '45, leaving it in ruins, and by the time the dust of war had settled, the Amber Room had vanished without trace.

'Most experts believe it was most likely destroyed by Allied bombs, but over the years there have been various reports that it survived and is either at the bottom of the sea, having been packed off on a ship that was then torpedoed, or else buried deep in a vault under some other castle. The most pervasive myth is that it was loaded, along with other stolen loot, on to a Nazi train which then disappeared somewhere in the mountains of south-western Poland.'

What Frances Coffey judges it best not to share with the team for now is the so-called Curse of the Amber Room. So many people closely linked to the treasure have met untimely ends. Alfred Rohde, director of the Königsberg Castle Museum, who became obsessed with the room, only to die of typhoid fever, along with his wife, just before they were due to be interrogated about its fate by the KGB. A high-ranking Russian officer called General Gusev who died in a car crash after helping a journalist investigating the Amber Room. And Georg Stein, Amber Room hunter extraordinaire, who was found naked in a Bavarian forest with his stomach slit open.

'Federov has been offering huge rewards for new information that might lead to the Amber Room,' she continues. 'He has a private investigator working on it round the clock. And don't forget, his father-in-law controls Russia's intelligence service. We now believe he has a concrete lead on the room's whereabouts, which is what led him to promise the Russian people live on air that he will track it down and present it to the nation as a gift. You have to understand how important this artefact is to the Russians. If he fails, having publicly staked his reputation on this hugely symbolic gesture, his standing both in Russia and abroad will be badly – maybe even fatally – damaged.'

'And if he succeeds?' asks Quinn.

Coffey sighs. 'If he manages to succeed where generations of politicians and bounty hunters have failed, it will cement the legend he has been carefully curating around himself.'

'And then?' asks Quinn.

'Then God help us all.'

Woody Wyatt has been leaning back perilously on the back legs of his chair, which does not look as if it was built to withstand his kind of bulk. But now he brings the front legs crashing down.

'So you're saying it was just a coincidence that the Russians turned up at Mount Athos at the same time we did, because we're all following the same intel?'

Coffey nods.

'The location of the bracelet wasn't any kind of secret, for sure. The Russians must have turned up at St Benedict's just after us, found that it had been stolen and gone straight to the police. They might have had an easier time gaining access. Russia has close links to the peninsula. In fact, one of the monasteries – St Panteleimon – is owned and operated by the Russian Orthodox Church.'

'Is that why the Greek police seemed so friendly with our Russian buddy?' asks Wyatt. 'Or is that just down to Denisov's natural charisma and charm?'

Coffey shrugs. 'Denisov is in the Russian international secret service. He claimed to be working with Interpol. That would have given him a certain amount of clout on Mount Athos, I would imagine, though the Greeks have since launched an official inquiry into the Russian use of force.'

'So what about the bracelets?' asks Quinn. 'I still don't get what they have to do with this Amber Room Federov is so set on finding.'

Coffey has Mike Randall bring in the bracelets, which are being kept in an armoured box in the hotel safe. Though he has handled both bracelets by this point, not to mention the fake bracelet in Monaco, it's the first time Argylle has been able to study them properly.

The room falls silent as the team take in the two weighty and yet delicately wrought gold bangles, inset with clusters of tiny diamonds which cover the bulk of the bracelets' surface, the rest being adorned with an intricate but irregular design made up of scratches and dots. On the rim of both bracelets are two tiny, almost invisible, slots that Argylle had missed first time around, while one also features two tiny raised golden discs, each with a deep groove running horizontally through.

'As you can see, the design on the two bracelets is not identical,' says Coffey, holding them both up so they can see how the strange patterns of engravings differ from one to the other.

'What does the engraving say on the inside?' asks Quinn.

Coffey holds up the first bracelet. 'Both are engraved with the jeweller's name, Mellerio. This one also has the Latin word *fidelis*, which means loyalty or faithfulness, and the digits 15.X. It also bears the initials *NC*, although we believe these were added at a different date.'

Now she picks up bracelet number two.

'Here we have Mellerio again, and the word *pietas*, which means piety, with the number 1867.'

'So why don't you just contact this Mellerio and find out what it's all about?' asks Schneider, who doesn't bother hiding his impatience.

Coffey beams at him, and Argylle finds himself admiring her refusal to get riled, her dedication to treating them all the same.

'Excellent point, Matt. Which is why I called their headquarters in Paris yesterday and spoke to a very helpful gentleman called Monsieur Fouquet, who obligingly buried himself in the company archives for an afternoon to see what he could find out. What he discovered is that the bracelets were commissioned in the 1860s by Napoleon III for his wife, the Empress Eugénie. As you might know, Napoleon III was a connoisseur of art and a patron of artists and designers. We believe the bracelets were created as some sort of playful secret message from husband to wife. After Eugénie's death, the bracelets had several owners before ending up in the hands of a very beautiful French screen actress called Nathalie Chabert. Mike Randall has done some digging and discovered that when she died, she left a bracelet to each of her two daughters. One was sold almost immediately to a wealthy Greek tourist who left it to St Benedict's in Mount Athos when he died, and the other was recently bought at auction by Vasily Federov. And there's actually something very neat and unique about these two bracelets. Wait till I show you. Don't suppose anyone has a screwdriver with them? Or, failing that, the end of a knife will do. Scissors?'

It is Wyatt who unaccountably produces from his pocket a nail file. 'Don't judge me, okay? My mom is big on hand hygiene.'

Coffey inserts the metal tip of the file into the horizontal slot in one of the tiny raised discs on the Bracelet of Fidelity and twists, causing it to turn ninety degrees. She does the same to the other one. She holds it up, and Argylle's pulse quickens as he notices that two delicate gold prongs have now popped up from the slots in the rim.

Frances Coffey is smiling as she introduces the newly visible prongs on the Bracelet of Fidelity into the two empty slots in the rim of the Bracelet of Piety. There's a click as they lock into place.

'*Voilà*, ladies and gentlemen. I give you the Bracelet of Concordia, otherwise known as the Bracelet of Harmony.'

Separate, the bracelets were impressive, but together they are awe-inspiring, the gold-and-diamond surfaces seeming to melt into each other, becoming one perfect, dazzling, gleaming band.

Coffey's beam broadens as she takes in their open-mouthed expressions.

'And now, when you look at the engraving on the inside, the two numbers have lined up to form a date: 15.X.1867 – historically, the French would often use roman numerals to represent the month. Monsieur Fouquet believes it commemorates the date the bracelet was commissioned—'

'And did he tell you what those lines and dots mean?' interrupts Schneider.

'Sadly not. As the commission came from the emperor himself, the designs were kept in a special safe, the contents of which were destroyed when the Nazis invaded Paris. You'd be amazed how many important documents mysteriously perished in fires or floods, just before the Germans could get to them.'

Argylle feels his spirits drop.

'So, basically, we're nowhere nearer finding out how this bracelet is connected to the Amber Room – *if* it's connected?' he says, slumping back in his chair.

He had thought for a moment that they were getting somewhere, but instead it seems they are no closer to the truth than before. He feels himself deflating, staring at the bracelet, this shiny thing that has robbed two little girls of their daddy. He puts his hand in his pocket until his fingers close around the cool, hard surface of the bullet, and all of a sudden it is all too much.

'So we come home with this pretty bangle that has some link with the famous Amber Room, though we have no idea what, but without a body for Samra's family to bury. Seems fair.'

He isn't usually so sardonic, and the shadow that passes over Frances Coffey's face doesn't make him feel good. He doesn't look at Matt Schneider, but the animosity flows between them like a river.

'There was no time,' snaps Schneider. 'We would all have been—'

'I gave the order, Aubrey,' Coffey cuts in quietly. 'I made that call, and I would do it again in the same circumstances.'

Argylle bites the inside of his cheek until it bleeds. Turns the bullet over in his hand. Says nothing.

After they have left the room Frances Coffey stays behind. Glancing at her phone, she sees missed calls from both her husband, Andrew, and Darius, her lover. She turns her phone face down. Standing up, she walks to the window and watches the members of the team drift across the car park in twos and threes, heading for the supermarket or the strip of shops that passes for a town.

Coffey runs her finger along the reassuring sharp edge of the cigarette packet in her pocket and feels like the most friendless person on Earth.

32

THE FOLLOWING MORNING, THEY ASSEMBLE AGAIN. IN MEETING Room Three this time. Perhaps Frances Coffey is hoping to leave the heavy atmosphere of the preceding day behind in Meeting Room One.

'Right. Moving forwards,' says Coffey firmly.

She outlines the steps they might take next to try to better understand the nature of the bracelets and why Federov is so desperate to get hold of them, what links them to his search for the Amber Room. There are meetings to be had with jewellers, with historians, with Nathalie Chabert's descendants.

Wyatt, who has been listening with his eyebrows knitted into a tight, dark knot, puts up his hand.

'Okay, I know I'm not the smartest person in the room.' He pauses, looking around. 'Feel free to contradict me, guys. Whatever. Trying to wrap my head around these bracelets is seriously frying my brain. First there's one of them, then there are two, then one again when they both join up. First Napoleon has it, then some French broad, then the French broad's daughters, then some old Greek guy, then Federov. Can someone just talk me through it real quick?'

Schneider snorts. 'You want us to draw it in pictures, Wyatt? Make it easier for you?'

Coffey ignores him. 'I'm not surprised you're confused, Woody. In fact, we're all in the dark still about a lot of it – what do the bracelets have to do with the Amber Room? Why is Federov so desperate to get hold of them? All we do know for sure is this:

'About fifteen months ago, right around the time Federov's birth father died, he started trying to track down a bracelet belonging to Nathalie Chabert, an obscure French movie star from the forties and fifties. When Chabert's older daughter, Isabelle, sent just such a bracelet to auction in Hong Kong last year, Federov attended in person – which is quite unusual – and paid over the odds. Very soon after, he promised, on live television, to return the stolen Amber Room to the Russian people. This turned out to be a rallying call for populists and extremists and the disaffected all across Eastern Europe.

'After this he started amassing his own militia. Both of these things made him a very dangerous individual indeed and someone of great interest to us. And naturally his preoccupations also became of great interest to us. So when he started doubling down on his efforts to trace the history of Chabert's bracelet, which was now in his possession, we wanted to know why.'

'So we stole it from him?'

'Exactly, Woody. And he immediately offered a million-dollar reward, which of course made us even more keen to find out the significance of the bracelet. But while we were searching for that, two things happened, almost simultaneously. First Federov got a tip-off about the existence of a second, identical bracelet in Mount Athos from someone who then tried to claim the reward and was found floating in the Black Sea for his trouble, according to his angry widow. But well before that, we'd independently found out about the second bracelet via the head of our archives division, one of the few other people who know about our mission, who spotted it in a news article about an exhibition of artefacts from the monasteries in—'

'—Mount Athos,' Wyatt cuts in.

'Right again. It turns out Nathalie Chabert had two bracelets and, when she died in the seventies, she gave one to each daughter, only the younger one sold hers almost immediately to a wealthy Greek tourist, who later left it in his will to St Benedict's monastery on Mount Athos.

'Having failed to find the link he was after with the first bracelet,

Federov decided he must have had the wrong bracelet, and went after the second one.'

'Except we got there first.'

All this time, Argylle is staring at the bracelets clipped seamlessly together as if they'd never been apart, nestled on green silk cushions in an open-lidded fortified case. The whole of the preceding evening a memory nagged at the blurred edges of his mind. Throughout the night, he had woken up at intervals, sure he had it, but by the time his brain kicked into gear it was gone again.

Now, as he stares at the random pattern engraved into the bracelet's gold surface, something comes back to him, shimmering through time like a heat haze.

'May I?' he says, interrupting Coffey to lean forward, gesturing towards the metal box.

Coffey frowns, but hands the case down the table to Argylle.

He gingerly lifts the bracelet out. Though he'd handled the second one so casually when they liberated it from the monastery, now that he knows its true value he feels the full weight of responsibility. He holds the exquisite double-bracelet to the light, lost in thought.

'Well?' asks Coffey gently.

'When I was younger we spent some time travelling in Mongolia.' He feels the blood come to his cheeks, knowing that both Coffey and Wyatt will jump to conclusions about what exactly brought his parents to that particular region. 'Anyhow, we were in the Gobi Desert and our guide used to sit with me in the evenings and look at the stars – it's one of the best places in the world for stargazing, as there's no light pollution and . . .' He feels self-conscious, the eyes of the team all on him, Lawler and Ryder openly mocking. 'Well, don't you think this little zigzag here looks a bit like Cassiopeia?'

Schneider snorts. 'Sure, and those two little dots are the man in the moon.'

But Quinn is on her feet to get a closer look. 'My dad and I used to drag our sleeping bags outside all the time back home in Colorado, and he'd tell me the names of all the things we could see in the sky.' She points to another tiny cluster of dots on the bracelet. 'I think that could be Ursa Major, the Great Bear.'

'Yes,' says Argylle excitedly. 'So I think this could be—'

'A star map,' says Coffey, who has been standing stock-still until now, her lips pressed together in thought. 'You might have something here, Aubrey.'

'What the hell is a star map?' Schneider asks.

'Aubrey? You want to explain?' Coffey's demeanour has entirely altered. The sloping shoulders that seemed to be carrying the world upon them just a few moments before have given way to a straight-backed alertness as she leans forward to catch his reply.

Argylle clears his throat, ignoring Schneider's predictable smirk at the mention of his name. 'Basically, it's a map that charts the positions of the stars and constellations in the night sky at a particular date and location.'

'So with the map plus the date engraved on the inside, you should be able to get a location?' says Quinn. 'That's pretty cool.'

'Let me get this straight,' says Casner. 'This Napoleon has a bracelet made for his wife with a map of the night sky that could only have been made at that particular time in that particular location?'

'Exactly,' beams Coffey. 'And he has the bracelet made in two halves so that no one else would know what it meant. Like a secret code between the two of them.'

'Well, I think that's just *fascinating*,' drawls Washington. 'From now on, I am going to send all my *billets doux* via the medium of star maps. The only thing I'm not getting, though, is what some old emperor's nineteenth-century bracelet has to do with the Amber Room, which didn't go missing until the mid-1940s?'

All eyes swing expectantly to Frances Coffey, who is fidgeting with something in her jacket pocket.

'That remains a mystery, Noah, I'm afraid. But now at least we have a line of enquiry. We find out where the star map points to, and then, once we have that information, we dig around to see how we can connect it to the Amber Room. It's the only thing Federov is interested in. He must know something we don't. There has to be a link.'

She tries to make it sound straightforward and hopes they can't guess how much it feels as if she is grasping at straws.

*

As the others file out, Coffey asks Argylle to hang back.

'How are you getting on, Aubrey?'

'Okay, I think.'

'That was a real stroke of inspiration there about the star map.'

'Got to be some compensation for growing up with parents who are international drug dealers. Right?'

Argylle is trying to sound jokey, but he hears the false note in his own voice and wishes he hadn't said it. Frances Coffey has a way of looking at you as if she already knows everything in your head and your heart, so what point is there in pretending it's not painful?

'And the others have eased up on you?'

'More or less. I mean, Dabrowski is banged up in Super Max, so it's not as if I've pushed him out. But I'm not going to lie, he's a hard act to follow.'

'You're doing great. And are you sure there's nothing bothering you? Nothing on your mind?'

He looks up, startled, his fingers automatically going to the bullet in his pocket. For a moment he wavers, imagining the relief of being able to share the worst of his thoughts. But then his father's voice comes back to him from the past that will not stay buried. 'Family business stays in the family.'

And if you have no family, the only one you can trust is yourself.

'No,' he says. Then: 'There is one thing.'

Coffey is instantly alert.

'I'd like to talk to Mrs Samra.'

She hadn't been expecting this. Doesn't know what to make of it.

'Why's that? Did Asif give you a message to pass on?'

He shakes his head and out of habit goes to run his fingers through his hair before remembering he had all that cut off before Monaco.

'I was the last person to see and talk to her husband. I know the things he said and did just before he died. At first, I wasn't sure she'd want to think about those final moments, but then I thought that if I was her I'd want to know that he died holding a picture of his family.

'I don't want her to be left with questions, boss. It's the questions that kill you in the end.'

*

Argylle and Carter sit opposite each other at a table flanked by a wall of plastic plants in the coffee bar on the main concourse of the supermarket on the other side of the industrial estate. The air-conditioning is on so high the fine hairs on Argylle's arms stand up.

Carter is sucking a syrupy pink milkshake through a plastic straw, with a gurgling noise that sets Argylle's teeth on edge.

'How can you drink that shit?'

'Nectar of the gods, Argylle.'

He shakes his head, sipping at his mineral water, then lapses into silence.

'Good job you're pretty, because your conversation skills need work,' Carter says at last.

Argylle responds by lifting his glass to his lips again, this time with his middle finger raised.

'Okay, you want to talk, tell me if you've written to your parents yet.'

Carter makes a face and has an extra-loud slurp of her drink.

'You wanna know if I've *shared my truth*?' She puts on a Californian drawl. 'Well, it might surprise you to know that I have. What happened to Samra . . . it made me think that I don't want to die without at least trying to get everything out into the open. If they're gonna bury me, let them bury the *real* me, not the one they've invented to fit their own pretty narrative. I wrote them yesterday.'

'What, an actual letter? I don't know how to break this to you, Carter, but there's this thing called email . . .'

'Haha. Hilarious, Argylle. My folks don't really do email. Least, not for important stuff. Births, deaths, sexual proclivities – it's snail mail all the way.'

'Well, *mazel tov*,' he says, raising his water to her. 'I mean, what's the worst that can happen – apart from you lose your entire family and live a sad, lonely life and end up buried in an unmarked grave?'

'Gee, thanks, Argylle. I had no idea you were such a softie.'

'Don't you think,' Argylle says after another silence, 'there's something else going on? That we're not being given the full picture about this mission?'

'Well, duh. What did you think when you joined the CIA? That you'd be copied in on every bit of background information? What part of "secret service" did you not understand? Anyway, it sounds reasonable enough to me. This Federov may be bad news, but he ain't dumb. So if he's putting his reputation on the line for what amounts to a treasure hunt, then there's gotta be something in it. Anything we can do to beat him to it has got to be a good thing.'

'Sure.'

'You'd better spit that "but" out before it chokes you, Argylle.'

'But don't you think there's something more that Coffey isn't telling us?'

He thinks about the bullet in his pocket and the desecrated Quran back in his room. Glances over at Carter, her dark, probing eyes, her expression so serious until a wide, wonky smile cracks it in two. Opens his mouth to blurt out what's been churning through his head at night, making it impossible to sleep, just as Carter shrugs and says:

'Ours is not to reason why, Argylle. Instead, tell me where we are on the Quinn-ometer. Hot? Very hot? Scorching?'

And just like that the moment is lost.

33

THERE ARE DEFINITE ADVANTAGES TO BEING A MIDDLE-AGED woman, society's least visible demographic, at the top of the foremost secret service in the world. If no one even sees you, how could they ever suspect you of holding one of the most powerful positions on the planet?

On the flip side, you have to get used to people's eyes sliding off you, searching for your boss, who they feel sure must be right behind you, to having rules painstakingly explained to you that you yourself came up with.

Right now, Frances Coffey is strapped into a twelve-seater Gulfstream out of Denver, usually used by CIA bigwigs and VIP guests, while a young steward, clearly under the impression she is a high-ranking officer's mother or wife being treated to a special trip, fusses around her, making sure she has everything she needs and doesn't feel nervous. 'I couldn't stop praying the whole journey the first time I went up in one of these,' he tells her, comfortingly. 'But you get used to it.'

His name is Jerome, and Coffey already knows he is new this week because she's done this trip many times before and knows all the flight staff.

Somewhere over Wyoming, Jerome starts to look uneasy. 'Between you and me, I think there's something going down,' he tells Coffey in hushed tones. 'It's nothing for you to worry about, but it sometimes happens in, you know, the Agency.' He mouths the last two words without making a sound. 'You're told one thing, but it's not exactly the truth. For example, you might have been told we're heading to Nebraska, but I'm pretty sure we are actually going due north, that would be into South Dakota. Montana even.'

'Wherever we're going, it's probably best you forget about it,' says Coffey, smiling.

Jerome's own ultra-white smile falters as, for the first time, it occurs to him that the five-foot-four quietly spoken passenger in seat four might actually be someone of note in her own right.

An uneasy silence descends as the plane passes over green forested mountains into a landscape that turns increasingly rural – small clusters of farm buildings surrounded by mile upon mile of wheat fields and wide river deltas.

They land on a single airstrip apparently in the middle of nowhere. Just flat, open space, ringed by distant mountains.

'Thank you, Jerome,' says Coffey as she gets her things together to leave. 'Don't forget, you were never really here.'

Out on the tarmac, a lone figure, she stops to take a deep breath in.

Far in the distance, just before the smudge of a mountain range rises up into the vast sky, there's a gas station and a Dunkin' Donuts sign and a store that sells farmyard machinery, while a railway draws a straight black line across a swathe of grassland. The sun is setting, pouring liquid gold over the fields and the trees and the gleaming metal roof of the tall grain silo.

Coffey climbs into a waiting jeep. 'They don't call it Big Sky Country for nothing,' she says to the driver, a big, broad man with raw, reddened cheeks and pale, watery eyes. 'Good to see you, Jeff.'

'And you, boss.'

'Can we just sit for a minute and watch the sun go down?'

Side by side they gaze out through the window as the sinking sun sends ribbons of orange and then pink streaking across the horizon until the world is ablaze around them.

'I still can't believe that just over there . . .'

'Yeah, I know.' Jeff's wide, flattened face glows soft and rose-gold in the reflection of the sun. 'General Custer yada yada yada.'

It's a running joke between them, Coffey's fixation on the bloody battle between the US cavalry and the Native Americans that saw the cavalry woefully outnumbered and culminated in the death of General George Armstrong Custer during the Battle of the Little Bighorn, otherwise known as Custer's Last Stand.

'You can laugh, but however wrong his cause, the man died fighting for this land of yours.'

'Yeah?' says Jeff, casting his gaze around the empty, desolate landscape. 'Well, he's welcome to it.'

They drive along empty roads for twenty minutes or so until they arrive at an isolated farmhouse where only a single yellow light in one of the downstairs rooms hints at any sign of life.

Coffey stifles a sigh. She has been in the Agency for decades, accepts everything that is demanded of its officers, everything she now has to demand from them as its operational head. But sometimes their sacrifices catch like a fish bone in her throat.

'Thanks, Jeff,' she says, climbing out of the car.

'No problem. See you in a coupla hours.'

Coffey hoists her tote bag over her shoulder and pushes open the wooden three-bar gate, which creaks on its hinges. The front door is open even before she is halfway down the path. A car engine is a big deal in these parts.

The man in the doorway has the light behind him so that he is completely in shadow.

'Hello, stranger,' he says gruffly.

'Hello, Glenn. It's good to see you.'

Glenn Dabrowski hasn't put much of a stamp on the house that has been his home for the last seven months. The walls still have the generic framed prints they sported when he arrived – Monet's lilies in the front room, Van Gogh's sunflowers in the back. Only the kitchen bears any evidence of personality, a photograph pinned to the fridge by a magnet in the shape of a pineapple. It shows a family group on the deck of a speedboat – Dabrowski himself, with one arm around a laughing woman whose blonde hair is flying out behind her and the other around a boy of eight or nine who has his head turned to the side and his tongue out.

'I like what you've done with the place,' says Coffey, glancing around at the bare shelves, the one solitary tea towel draped over the back of a chair bearing a logo for the Peking Palace, South Montana.

'Yeah, well, I didn't expect to be here quite so long or I'd have got my interior designer in.'

'I'm so sorry.'

Dabrowski shrugs and looks away, knowing that if he sees the pity in Coffey's soft grey eyes, he will go to pieces. It happened once before.

'Shall we?' Coffey asks, after Dabrowski has made a pretence of offering tea or coffee before cracking open two beers from the fridge. Coffey's heart tears a little at the fridge's contents – a few more beers, a small carton of milk and an open can of spaghetti and meatballs with a spoon still in it.

Glenn Dabrowski leads the way through the dark hallway, where one solitary jacket hangs on the row of pegs and one pair of boots is lined up by the door, to a small, airless study tucked in behind the stairs. He has always been skinny, but these last months have whittled him down further. His narrow shoulders slope down towards the wooden laminate flooring and his dirty blond hair falls unkempt to his shoulders.

Inside the study is a different world. Walls lined with charts and spreadsheets, piles of cardboard folders and a desk which houses a bank of monitors on which various footage is unrolling. On the nearest, Coffey watches a woman in an overall wheeling a cart of cleaning materials along the first-floor corridor of the Hôtel Beaux Rêves on the outskirts of Charleroi in central Belgium.

'At least you know you're not missing anything,' says Coffey, as the next monitor shows the view from the hotel lobby across the car park of the industrial estate, eerie in the post-dawn light.

'I'd happily swap.' Dabrowski is looking at a photograph pinned to the study wall showing a younger, healthier version of him, hair neatly cut, posing with a bunch of recruits in the grounds of The Farm. Woody Wyatt is there, and Tony Corcoran. Coffey's stomach muscles constrict when she sees Asif Samra's steady brown eyes looking out from the back row.

'He was one of the good ones,' says Dabrowski softly, following her gaze.

'I know.'

'Did Argylle tell you what he took from him?'

Coffey shakes her head. 'Can you play the footage again, Glenn?'

Dabrowski obligingly goes to the computer at the far end of the desk, punching a few keys. The hacks at the CCIE – the Agency's Europe-based hacking division, working out of the US consulate in Frankfurt, most of whom look in their file photos to be little older than his own son – have excelled themselves in getting him hooked up to the various computer-operating systems over in Europe. Dabrowski, who grew up in the days when the cordless telephone was the height of technical innovation, marvels at the next generation's innate understanding of it all.

'We should thank those monks for being so paranoid. CCTV footage in even that tiny port. Not that it's a whole lot of use to them without any internet.'

'At least they'd have a record, I guess,' says Coffey. 'Maybe they play all the footage back at the main police HQ. Make sure no rogue females have infiltrated the holy land!'

An image loads on the computer monitor, and now they are watching grainy footage that at first appears to be just dark shapes moving around, but as her eyes accustom to the gloom, Coffey is able to pick out shadowy figures moving across a beach towards a dark shape in the water. There's a volley of flashes from high up and then the figure at the rear of the group falls to the ground. Now there are flashes coming from the group in the water as well, as a second figure doubles back to bend down near the first. Dabrowski presses a key to focus in on the man on the ground and, though the figures are now pixelated and blurry, it's possible to see the figure crouching over him shove something into his jacket pocket before running to join the others in the water.

Dabrowski cuts the footage off.

'Any guesses what he took, Glenn?'

'Whatever it was it came from somewhere near Samra's chest region. Now, I worked closely with Asif Samra for nearly two years.

211

I know he carried a copy of the Quran with him wherever he went, usually in his breast pocket.'

'If that's what it was, why keep it a secret?'

Dabrowski hesitates. 'I studied the footage of when Samra was hit, one frame at a time, how he fell. I think he was shot through the back.'

Coffey is silent, working through what this means.

'You think the bullet might have passed through him and embedded itself in the Quran?'

'It's not impossible.'

For a few moments, the two of them don't speak. Then:

'You know, I'm kinda glad he didn't say anything to me,' Coffey says. 'He's still finding his feet. He doesn't know who he can trust and who he can't. If he has kept hold of the bullet that killed Asif – and we have no idea if he has – he's right to keep it to himself, for now. It's what you would have done.'

'I guess. Except—'

'I know. If he's picked up on something, it makes him a target.'

'I just hope he knows what he's getting himself into.'

'What else have you found, Glenn?'

'Not much. I've been through all the files with a fine-toothed comb. Not much else to do around these parts.'

Coffey knows what he would have found in the files, because she herself spent six weeks with them after the botched mission to Isfahan, hidden away on her own in a different safe house to this one, forensically going through every last record, looking for the weak link she knows is there.

The traitor in the team who tipped off the Russian-backed Iranian troops.

She'd pulled out the files on each of them, going through their backgrounds, their phone logs, comments from their mentors and training commanders, any files they'd requested from the archives, any books they'd withdrawn from the library. And when that didn't throw up anything, she'd gone through all the missions each member had been involved in, cross-referencing them with other missions. She'd been looking for a pattern. A commonality. Missions that had gone unexpectedly wrong. Instances where they'd expected an event to be straightforward and it hadn't turned out that way.

All the time, she'd been thinking about Philby, Maclean, Blunt, Burgess and Cairncross. Five individuals who brought the mighty British intelligence service to its knees.

In the end she'd only been certain of one thing: the person they were looking for was not Glenn Dabrowski. Frances Coffey knows by now you can never completely trust anyone, and yet paradoxically she also knows you have to trust *someone* or risk going insane, and Dabrowski is the straightest recruit she's ever known. If she has to pick a hill to die on, he would be it.

'I think Denisov took a hit,' Dabrowski says, scrolling through footage on his monitor until he finds the picture he wants. Zooming. Zooming . . . until they are looking at the grainy figures of the Russians on the clifftop as Argylle is running from the beach to the boat. It's impossible to make out individual faces or features, but Denisov has a distinctive build, broad across the shoulders, and a way of holding himself so that he seems to expand to fill the space around him, that strange hair. *There.* One moment upright, the next down on his knees, clutching his hands over the right side of his face.

'Was it his eye?'

'Impossible to say. He's not dead though, or we would have heard by now.'

'More's the pity.' Coffey spares no sympathy for Sergei Denisov. She has seen pictures of the carnage he has left in his wake.

'And how are you doing in yourself, Glenn?'

'Oh, you know, keeping busy. I'm teaching myself French. I can say "I work in the bank and go fishing at the weekends."'

'And how are you really?'

Glenn Dabrowski has a narrow face with hollow cheeks, a prominent nose and fine, expressive green eyes that he keeps averted as he asks: 'How much longer, boss? It's killing me. It's not so much being away from them as knowing they believe I did what I'm supposed to have done and that I'm now rotting in that hellhole. The last image they have of me is in that place. It must be eating them up.'

'I'm sorry, Glenn. You know it was necessary.'

Dabrowski nods. Swallows. 'Yeah, I know.'

Coffey can only imagine what it must have been like. Publicly branded a traitor who gave away classified information to an enemy power, family convinced he was doing serious time in a Super Max facility in Colorado. They'd set it up meticulously. First off the official story that he'd been unexpectedly reassigned, and at the same time the staged 'covert' arrest, deliberately employing the loosest-mouthed officer to drag him from his bed at dawn. Knowing that the rumours would soon reach the team he'd so recently been part of. Arranging for his family to visit him in the facility following the supposed kangaroo-court trial, knowing that convincing them was the only way to convince the wider world. Hoping that all of this might just be enough to tease out the real traitor, but aware all the time there was a chance it was all for nothing. His sacrifice. His family's grief.

Even so, he feels duty-bound to ask: 'Boss, aren't we taking a major risk by letting the compromised team carry on when there's so much at stake? Shouldn't you put together a whole fresh group of personnel?'

'I agree that would be the safer option, Glenn. But this team are the finest we have. And keeping them together is our best shot at outing the traitor. I take every precaution I can to limit the damage – I only give out mission details at the last minute and on a need-to-know basis, and obviously we're thoroughly monitoring every aspect of the team's communications. But believe me, this is the quickest way of returning you to the people who love you. Or rather, who love you even more than we do.'

'Yes, ma'am.'

Dabrowski takes out a sheaf of papers and, heads bent, they begin the process of sifting through what he has found.

It is late when Coffey climbs back into the jeep, and the darkness in this empty land is absolute. A metal band tightens around her chest at the sight of Glenn Dabrowski framed in the doorway of his cheerless house, his slight figure growing smaller in the wing mirror.

Frances Coffey has a theory that to do her job you either have to be a psychopath who feels nothing for the staff of whom you ask so much, or an empath who feels everything, so your staff implicitly know you understand the depth of the pain they endure at your command.

When she took on the role she knew she would have to demand a great deal of the people who worked under her, but she hadn't reckoned on the collateral damage – the children, the partners, the ones who never signed up for this.

'You flying straight back to wherever it is you came from?' asks Jeff, who knows more than to press for details.

'I have a twenty-four-hour layover.' She checks her watch. 'Twenty-two hours.'

Tomorrow evening she will get the red-eye back to Belgium. But in the meantime she feels weary and heartsore and in need of comfort.

She thinks of her husband in their farmhouse in Delaware with the patchwork quilt on the bed and the beautiful hand-carved rocking chair that he made her for her fortieth birthday, his big, calloused hand resting on the top of her head as she gently rocks. And she thinks of Darius Johnson in the hotel in Manhattan where they always meet, checking in under the name Mr and Mrs Truman, because it tickles them. She thinks of his arms encircling her, the smell of him – leather and musk and, best of all, tobacco. His forehead pressed to hers. Losing themselves in each other so that, for this moment out of time, she is just a woman, and not a woman who has mandated that a man surrender his reputation, his family, his whole life and that a little boy cry himself to sleep missing his dad.

'Nice night for it,' comments Jeff.

Frances Coffey nods and watches as, outside her window, a shooting star burns a trail across the vast Montana sky.

34

THE ROYAL OBSERVATORY STANDS ON A HILL IN GREENWICH PARK IN south-east London overlooking the River Thames. A distinctive red-brick building with a time ball balanced on its eastern turret that drops dramatically at 1 p.m. each day to advertise the time to passing ships, it was commissioned in 1675 by King Charles II and was for centuries at the very epicentre of international astronomical and navigational research. What isn't so well known is that in 1851 it had an impressive transit circle instrument installed which also placed it at the cutting edge of positional astronomy – the science by which astronomical objects are positioned in the celestial sphere as pinpointed on a particular date and time and at a particular location on Earth. In other words, it became one of the leading world centres for star charts.

Now used more as a museum and educational facility, it is nevertheless home to one of the world's most powerful telescopes and is still at the forefront of certain types of astronomical research. It is here that Erin Quinn and Aubrey Argylle have arranged to meet Sir Simon Hennessy, Fellow of the Royal Astronomical Society and old colleague of Frances Coffey's.

'He owes me a favour,' she'd told them, enigmatically. 'That's why he's agreed to see you.'

Sir Simon's office is a high-ceilinged wood-panelled room with tall windows looking out on to a sloping lawn. The walls are crowded with gilt-framed oil paintings while faded Persian carpets break up the polished wooden parquet.

Sir Simon himself turns out to be one of those Englishmen of indeterminate middle age, anywhere from forty-five to sixty-five. He wears a neatly tailored navy suit with a lavender silk pocket square which Argylle, who has come in one of the Nehru jackets he has adopted since the Monaco ball, eyes with approval.

'You're friends of Frances Coffey, I understand,' says Sir Simon as they sink into antique leather chairs in front of his neat mahogany desk. 'I met her years ago when I was studying at Harvard and took a part-time job in the library where she worked to help pay my fees. Extraordinary woman.' He is staring down at some papers when he says this, but when Quinn nudges him, Argylle sees that a deep red flush is working its way up Sir Simon's neck.

Argylle and Quinn know that Sir Simon hasn't seen their boss for decades and aren't entirely sure how much he knows about her actual job so they have come prepared with a backstory.

'My fiancée here is writing a family memoir and she needs to find out the location where her great-grandmother had a very important, um, liaison,' Argylle begins.

'Don't be so coy, darling,' says Quinn, slipping her arm through his. 'What Brad means is that Great-Grandma had a dirty weekend three quarters of a century ago and her mystery lover had this star chart drawn up to commemorate the place they did the deed, and we just want to find out where it was. The memoir is going to be a present to my grandmother, who is in the first stages of dementia. It'll mean so much to her.'

She lays the star chart, reproduced from the bracelet on to paper, down on the desk.

If Sir Simon finds this an unusual, even demeaning, request for someone of his reputation and position, he does not let on.

'I'll get on to it right away, though I must remind you I am not doing this in my official capacity as Fellow of the Observatory. I'll be conducting the research from my university lab in Warren Street, though I should tell you I'm not doing this in my official capacity as honorary professor either. This is simply a favour for an old colleague.' He ushers them out with instructions to meet him there at four o'clock.

Outside, it is that rarest of things in London, a perfect summer day, and the hillside directly in front of them falls away like a giant roll of green silk, past the Naval College towards the river, while in the distance the thrusting skyscrapers of Canary Wharf glitter in the sunlight.

'What now?' says Quinn at the same time as Argylle says, 'Brad? You think of me as a Brad?'

She smiles. 'It was the first name that came to me.'

They head off, feeling like kids bunking off school for the day.

Argylle can't remember the last time he felt this giddy and care-free. Or indeed the last time he properly 'felt' anything at all. As they approach the river, they find themselves staring at the most beautiful boat he has ever seen. An elegant schooner with three towering masts and a long prow that pierces the blue sky, the *Cutty Sark* seems like an unexpected gift.

To his surprise, Argylle finds himself talking about his parents.

'They turned out not to be who I thought they were, but I miss them. You know?'

'Have you forgiven them?'

Argylle is so surprised he stops in his tracks.

'You misunderstand me. I really loved them.'

'That's not what I'm asking, Argylle. Loving is easy. It's forgiveness that's the hard thing.'

They are descending a seemingly endless flight of spiral steps that wind around a central steel lift shaft to the Greenwich Foot Tunnel, which crosses underneath the Thames. The temperature down here comes as a shock after the warm summer's day they have left behind, and Argylle shivers in his T-shirt. Next to him, Erin Quinn's shoulders have come up in goosebumps in her yellow, strappy summer dress.

The staircase brings them into a long, narrow tunnel, tiled on the walls and concrete underfoot, lit by fluorescent overhead panels that create an eerie, sickly light. There's a man way up ahead whose heels make a sound that ricochets off the walls, but apart from that they are completely alone.

'I'm not bothered in the *slightest* that there's approximately a gazillion tons of water over our heads right now,' says Quinn, and her voice is startlingly loud, bouncing off the hard surfaces of the tunnel.

'Have *you* forgiven your dad for dying?' Argylle asks her when they are halfway along.

For a moment he thinks he has said the wrong thing as he senses her body tensing next to his, sees the way she is pressing her top lip down on the bottom one. Then she sighs.

'Of course I've forgiven him. It wasn't his fault.'

'He was killed in Iraq, wasn't he?'

She nods.

'Sorry. Tell me to butt out.'

'It's okay. It's painful, that's all.'

Her voice sounds different, thin and tight.

'His . . . death . . . it changed everything. Changed my family. Changed me. Changed the way I look at the world.'

'I get that.'

They walk on in silence, their footsteps reverberating in the space behind them.

She stops suddenly. Turns to him. Her face in the unforgiving fluorescent light is pale, her eyes huge. 'God, Argylle, I'm so freaking cold.'

He steps forward. Puts his arms around her and feels how her whole body is shaking.

'I've got you,' he whispers, stroking her hair. 'I've got you.'

Then she turns her face towards him and, when they kiss, her lips feel cold but her mouth is warm and he feels as if he has been hibernating and has just woken up.

Argylle has visited London several times. But this is the first time he can recall being here when there is heat hanging solid in the thick fumes around Piccadilly Circus and barefoot children paddling in the fountains in Trafalgar Square.

Walking through the transformed city holding Erin Quinn's hand, he sees it through fresh eyes. For four glorious hours they are just another young couple, strolling through the steaming streets, stopping to peer into shop windows or to eat ice cream in a tiny lawned churchyard, enthralled to find themselves here in this place at this time with this person.

They haven't discussed it, but Argylle instinctively understands that this is a day out of time. Relationships between team members are strictly prohibited, as they compromise both the couple them-selves and their teammates. He knows that. Erin Quinn, steeped in CIA culture from birth, most certainly knows that. Yet for this one unexpected gift of a day they can pretend to be normal, just two people who have been laid low by grief finding comfort in each other and in being young in the anonymity of a big city in the summertime.

So it is with a certain reluctance that he enters an unprepossessing, scaffold-covered building at the back of the Euston Road that houses the University of London's astrophysics department, where honorary professor Sir Simon has his lab.

The cramped office here, with its white plywood desk and bulky computer monitor, is worlds away from the lofty room in the obser-vatory they'd visited that morning. And they find Sir Simon himself altered, as if he has adapted himself to his surroundings, more busi-nesslike and practical.

'I think I can help you with your book, Miss . . . Clayton.' He emphasizes the pseudonym Quinn has chosen as if he is perfectly well aware it is not her real name.

'Oh, you can? That's *wonderful*. My dear Gramma will be so thrilled.'

Quinn smiles and Argylle sees the effect it has on the older man, his English stiffness visibly softening.

'I should think so, because your great-grandmother – your great-*gramma*, should I say – must have had quite the past.'

He turns to the monitor and presses some keys, his face just inches from the screen. From his pocket he withdraws the folded paper on which they projected the star chart taken from the bracelet and smooths it out on the desk next to him. Then he calls up on screen a page into which the same chart has been scanned and swivels the screen round so they can see it.

'You'll know that the positions of stars relative to each other and our solar system change grindingly slowly. However, the stars that are above us each night do change according to the night, season and year, because the Earth is continually rotating and tilting and, as it does, the view of the sky we can see above us also changes. Over the centuries, astronomers have studied and measured and charted the positions of the sun at every stage of the Earth's yearly orbit around the sun, so that it's now possible to compute what stars are above any point on Earth at any time. And as the yearly cycle follows exactly the same pattern, the stars you see on a particular date will be the same on that date in ten years' time, or twenty, or a hundred. So really, an accurate star map together with a date, as you have given me, can be an excellent way of pinpointing a location, as long as you know how to read it.'

Sir Simon is looking at them with approval, as if they themselves are responsible for drawing up the map copied from the bracelet. Now he leans forward, using his pen to point to things on the monitor, which he then magnifies.

'Now, you'll know that these dots are stars, and the larger the dot, the brighter the star, and that the brightest stars can be joined with a line to make a constellation. Sometimes the stars are really close together so one dot is put over the other with a white border around the smaller one, or when there are multiple stars too close together to differentiate, a line is put through the dot. And then you get the stars that vary in brightness, so that might be a dot inside a circle. Are you with me?'

Sir Simon looks from one to the other, and Argylle nods. He learned some of this out there in the Gobi Desert with the guide drawing the dots and dashes in the sand with a stick.

'Excellent. You'll see that some of the brightest stars are linked by lines forming a constellation, or an asterism – the Summer Triangle, the Big Dipper, and so on. And we also have coordinate lines marked on the map – similar to our latitude and longitude, which help to navigate the stars – and these plot the position of the star against two fixed points: the celestial equator, which is roughly over our own equator here on Earth, and the First Point of Aires, which is found in the Pisces constellation. And then, very importantly, we also have the angles between the individual stars and the moon, the lunar distance. Do you see?'

Normally, Argylle is good at this sort of stuff. It interests him, how the world works, and the way the worlds of science and philosophy so frequently converge in the biggest questions that confront us all. But today he is so conscious of the woman sitting just inches away that his brain feels like it has been hollowed out and he can't seem to make sense of what the professor is saying. And judging by the kick Erin Quinn just aimed at his calf, neither can she.

'But there aren't any numbers on the brace—sorry, on the chart.'

'No, there aren't, which is a shame. But by inputting the data you gave me into a software program that superimposes your map over the millions of satellite-generated maps we now have at our disposal – thank the Lord we've moved on from the Astronomical Almanac – I've been able to find an answer for you. And for your dear great-grandmother.

'And let me assure you, your great-grandmother's illicit liaison did *not* take place in the Premier Inn in King's Cross. It was far more glamorous than that.'

'So where?' Quinn has her hands pressed together in excitement, and Argylle feels how the air is charged with energy.

'Whoever your great-grandmother was meeting for her secret rendezvous, he must have been very grand, because it happened at the Château de Fontainebleau, one of the grandest palaces in the world.'

35

QUINN AND ARGYLLE ARRIVE IN BRUSSELS AT SEVEN THIRTY IN THE evening, less than two hours after stepping on to the Eurostar in London. Entering the Hôtel Beaux Rêves an hour after that, they are called directly to Will Hooper's room for a Bright Eyes call with Frances Coffey, who is still in the US. When she appears on the screen, she is in a hotel room with bottle-green walls and a neatly made bed with a matching bottle-green coverlet.

She wants to know about their trip to London, and Argylle finds himself unable to meet her eyes, even long distance, in case she might read in them something of what happened today between him and Erin Quinn. Although the more time passes, the more he wonders what exactly *did* happen. The whole day has taken on the essence of a dream.

Luckily, Quinn seems more relaxed and relates to the boss everything they've managed to find out about Fontainebleau so far. 'It's a royal French palace, sixty or so kilometres from Paris and the size of a small village,' she says.

Coffey smiles, warmly. 'I know, I've been there. Many years ago. It's a magnificent building. So much important art and architecture housed there. And so much glorious history. It gives Versailles a run for its money. In fact' – and her voice grows excited – 'if I'm not mistaken, Napoleon III and his wife, Eugénie, spent a fair bit of time there and he had it fairly extensively remodelled.'

Sometimes it seems to Argylle as if Coffey knows everything, as if she might have absorbed by osmosis all the knowledge and information from those dusty CIA archives over the years she spent down there.

'I still don't understand how we're any further along though, boss,' says Argylle. 'So Napoleon had the bracelet made to remind his wife of Fontainebleau, but we're still nowhere nearer discovering how it's connected to the Amber Room. Unless you think the Amber Room might be hidden there?'

Coffey shakes her head. 'Sadly not. Fontainebleau is one of the best-known buildings in the world. Every inch of it has been picked over by historians and custodians and the public. And besides, at the time of the last-recorded mention of the Amber Room, when it was crated up and stored in the basement of Königsberg Castle, the war had already turned against the Germans. There's no way they would have risked bringing a prize treasure like the Amber Room to France then.'

'So, what do we do now?'

'We carry on looking for the missing link. It's out there somewhere, we just have to work out where.

'Oh, and Aubrey,' says Coffey, just as they are about to hang up, 'I have that number for you, for Melinda Samra. You can call her from your room.'

In Room 315 of the Hôtel Beaux Rêves, Argylle keys the number Coffey just gave him into his phone. His finger hovers over the green connect key. He wants to give Melinda Samra answers if he can, because he knows what it's like to be left with a head full of questions that swirl round and round with no way of escape. But what if she doesn't actually want to know?

Argylle is all too aware that there are as many ways of grieving as there are bereaved people.

He hasn't yet decided what to do with Asif Samra's Quran. He realizes it probably has huge sentimental and religious significance to his family, but it is also stained with Melinda's husband's blood and imprinted with the shape of the bullet that killed him. The bullet Argylle has been carrying with him.

He wishes he could ask Coffey's advice, but that would mean telling her what he knows, and how does he know he can trust her? He presses the key. There's silence and then the international dialling tone. Once, twice, three times. Then Melinda Samra picks up, and in the split second before she says a tremulous 'Hello' there's a click on the line – faint but unmistakable.

Interesting, thinks Argylle.

'Thank you for calling me. I know it can't be easy.'

Melinda Samra's voice is calm and steady, but Argylle hears the tightness in it, as if there is a wire threaded through it holding it in place.

'Your husband was a very good man. A man of integrity, which is a rare thing. I was with him when he died.'

'Did he suffer? Please don't sugar-coat, Mr Argylle. I prefer the truth.'

Argylle is surprised by the widow's directness until he remembers that Melinda Samra is a lawyer by profession. He thinks back to that terrible moment on the tiny port beach at Mount Athos, to Asif Samra's puzzled expression.

'No,' he answers honestly. 'He didn't suffer. He asked for the photograph of you and your daughters that he carried everywhere. Yours were the last faces he saw. His final thoughts were of you.'

There is a beat of silence then, a soft intake of breath that carries down the phone line, arriving in Argylle's ear like a sigh.

'Thank you,' she whispers. 'That's all I needed to know.'

After the call is ended, Argylle stands at the window of his room, looking out across the deserted car park as the last of the sun bleeds out across the inky-blue sky, and he thinks about his parents and what they might have gone through before they died and how it would feel to hear they weren't alone or afraid.

He is still there when the sky turns black.

36

RURAL FRANCE IS FULL OF UNWRITTEN RULES – EXACTLY HOW MANY inches your lawn is permitted to grow, whether you're allowed to mow it on a Sunday, the exact cut-off time for ordering food in the local bar. Those rules are part of the reason the villages here in Provence are so uniformly pretty. But, as Frances Coffey swings the hire car she picked up at Charles de Gaulle airport in through the broken rusty gates, one hanging off its hinge, and bumps along the pot-holed driveway where clumps of weeds grow wild on each side, she decides that Amélie Chabert definitely did not get the memo.

The house she pulls up in front of is small and shabby, though the shutters are painted sunshine yellow and there are hand-decorated flowerpots flanking the door. As Coffey crosses the small yard, she's startled by two chickens that come flapping out of a bush at the side, one of them hopping up on to the seat of an old sofa with a spring poking through the upholstery.

Coffey is expecting the owner of the house to be as unkempt as its exterior, but the woman who comes to the door is neatly dressed in jeans and a patterned floral top, her curly salt-and-pepper hair held back by a bandana. Only her face betrays the fact that her life has not been easy – her cheeks unusually hollow, the skin lined and papery.

'I'm afraid it can be hard to find me,' she says in faultless English, showing Coffey into a small sitting room where every item – sofa, lamp, table – has been covered by a throw or a scarf. 'City life is toxic for me, so I have to hide myself here. Far from temptation.'

Though she does not let on, Coffey has already called in to see Isabelle Chabert, Amélie Chabert's estranged half-sister from her mother's first marriage, drinking tea from delicate bone-china cups in her pristine apartment in Paris, and she can see a family resemblance in the greeny-grey eyes. But while Isabelle was easily the better preserved and groomed, her younger half-sister has a warmth the older woman lacked. That earlier meeting had been short and unproductive, with Isabelle unable – or unwilling – to add to the information they already have, only agreeing to the interview, it turned out, to try to find out more about the second bracelet she hadn't known existed. 'Was it as nice as mine?' she wanted to know. 'How much did *that woman* get for hers?'

'I regret you have had a wasted journey,' Amélie tells Coffey, looking genuinely sorry. 'I already told everything I know, first to the Russian guy and then to your colleague.' She means Mike Randall, who initially quizzed Nathalie Chabert's daughters over the phone and reported back to Coffey that Federov had sent a private investigator to talk to Amélie, which solved the mystery of how the Russian billionaire had found out about the second bracelet. Unfortunately, it was the only useful piece of information Randall had been able to unearth.

Coffey smiles. 'Not at all. To tell you the truth, it's a lovely change for me to get away from the office.'

Both Chabert sisters, on being told Coffey and Randall work for the US government, made the assumption that they are with Interpol, investigating a ring of international jewellery thieves. Coffey hasn't seen the need to correct them.

They begin chatting and, unlike with the prickly Isabelle, the conversation flows. Amélie admits that her relationship with her movie-star mother was difficult, that she was a complicated woman. 'But that isn't why I became an addict, if that's what you're thinking. I believe we make our own choices in life. Mama tried her best in her way.'

Coffey asks if her mother ever mentioned going to Fontainebleau. Mike Randall has already been told no, but still it's worth asking again. She knows she's sometimes able to get things out of interviewees that her less experienced – and less intuitive – staff can't, and she knows also that nuances can be missed on the phone. Like the fractional hesitation before Amélie shakes her head.

'Are you sure?' she probes gently, keeping her eyes fixed on her host's.

The Frenchwoman sighs.

'She told me in secret. She didn't want anyone to know. You can't imagine the shame.'

Excitement pulses in Frances Coffey's throat, but she keeps her voice steady.

'What was she ashamed of?'

Amélie Chabert runs her hands through her thick hair and glances towards a framed photograph, the type that studios used to use for publicity, showing a stunningly beautiful young woman with thick black wavy hair and perfect Cupid's bow lips.

'You have to understand that she was very young during the war. Still naïve. He pursued her. Men did that.'

'I can see why. She's extremely lovely. But who pursued her, Amélie?'

Again that glance towards the photograph, as if apologizing for breaking a confidence.

'Rudolf Naumann.'

'The Nazi art historian?'

Amélie Chabert presses her lips together and nods.

The cogs are whirring in Coffey's archivist brain. She's heard of Naumann, of course, knows that he was a leading art expert in the 1930s, and as an SS officer during the war oversaw the department which processed the paintings and sculptures and artefacts the Nazis looted from the stately homes and palaces they occupied, crisscrossing Europe to evaluate and assess. She even knows about the time he spent at Fontainebleau, which the Nazis had once intended to make their Western centre of operations, spurning the better-known Versailles, where Germany had been forced to sign the humiliating treaty following their defeat in the First World War. Because of that, Hitler had ordered several priceless stolen artworks to be transported to France and installed in the Fontainebleau palace under Naumann's supervision.

But though she was quite certain Naumann would have made sure he personally oversaw the dismantling of the prized Amber Room from the Catherine Palace and its subsequent reassembly in Königsberg Castle, there was no way he would have brought it to Fontainebleau.

Desperate as she is to find the link between the Amber Room and the French palace, she knows that the Nazis were meticulous record-takers, Naumann more than most. And Fontainebleau is so large, with people coming and going all the time – not only the German occupiers, but the teams of domestic staff it takes to maintain a place like that – word would have got out if it was ever there.

'What happened between your mother and Naumann?'

'They met at a premiere and, afterwards, like I say, he pursued her relentlessly. At first I think she was a little flattered. She was young and he knew how to say the right things. She ended up going there, to Fontainebleau, to meet him, and he led her into this amazing golden room, and gave her champagne until she didn't know what was happening. Today you might call it assault or at least *la coerci-tion*. Sorry – I don't know the word in English. But back then it was just how things were. Powerful men got what they wanted. That's why she never wore the bracelet I sold to that Greek guy all those years ago, even though it turns out it was worth a fortune. Because *he* gave it to her and she didn't want to be reminded of it. That wasn't the only thing he gave her either. The bastard also gave her a disease, if you know what I mean, though she managed to get rid of that eventually, thank God.'

All this time, Coffey is staring at the distinctive ring Amélie wears on her middle finger. A square, flat, yellow stone mounted on a gold band. 'Did you get that ring from your mom also?'

'Yes. She didn't wear this either. In fact, I found it hidden among her things years after she died – which is probably a good thing or I'd have sold this as well. I don't think it's worth much, but I like it.'

'It's amber, isn't it?'

'Yeah. It was in a box with a note wrapped around it that said "A memory of our night together". I guess it probably came from the same Nazi guy who gave her the bracelets. This Rudolf Naumann. She wouldn't have wanted anyone to see it. You have to remember that, after the war, women who went with the Germans were treated very roughly.'

Coffey nods, thinking of the footage she's seen of women being stripped naked and their heads shaved in front of a jeering mob before being covered in a mixture of tar and feathers and paraded through the streets.

'There was so much shame and blame at that time,' says Amélie sadly, twisting the ring around her finger.

'May I?' asks Coffey, reaching out for it.

Up close, her pulse quickens as she realizes that what she'd taken to be a stone appears more like a fragment of mosaic. An amber mosaic.

'Did she tell you anything more about that night?' she presses Amélie Chabert. 'Anything that might pinpoint whereabouts in the palace this golden room might have been?'

'Oh, she wasn't in the actual palace. Sorry, I should have said. She was in a weird building all alone in the forest. Creepy, she said. Lots of mirrors.'

It's not until the following day that Coffey calls the team together in the Hôtel Beaux Rêves to tell them what she's discovered.

'After I spoke to Amélie Chabert I did some research into Rudolf Naumann. I knew about his reputation, of course, as one of the world's foremost art historians. It was he who oversaw the plundering of some of the world's rarest and most important artworks. He decided which would go to Hitler or Goering's private collections, or be earmarked for the Führermuseum, which, as you probably know, never actually came to fruition, and which works would be labelled degenerate and destroyed.

'What I didn't know is that Naumann suffered from syphilis, which he caught before the war, when there was no treatment. In its later stages, untreated syphilis can lead to a range of symptoms, including brain damage, which can result in erratic behaviour and personality changes. I think he was already showing signs of such behaviour when he was appointed to his role. By all accounts he had long nurtured a fascination with the legendary Amber Room, and my theory is that when it came under his jurisdiction at Königsberg, that fascination turned into obsession.

'When it was decided that Fontainebleau would become Hitler's Western headquarters, Naumann was dispatched there to inventory the existing artworks, including the furnishings and the ornaments, and decide which of the treasures the Nazis had confiscated elsewhere should be brought there to establish it as a palace fit for the conqueror of Europe. Naturally, his first thought would have been to install his beloved Amber Room there in pride of place, but he was prevented by two things – Hitler's insistence that the priceless treasure should remain in Germany, and also the fact that by the time Naumann had finished inventorying, the tide of war had already turned against the Nazis, making the idea of a Paris headquarters untenable. Naumann was summoned back to Königsberg to supervise the Amber Room being dismantled and packed up into crates, ready to be shipped elsewhere for safekeeping.'

Martin Casner has been listening impatiently. Argylle has noticed that he has a very short concentration span, and always wants to be jumping straight to the point without listening to any preamble or the context.

'So how is he connected to Nathalie Chabert, if he was back in Germany?'

'Because he then returned to Fontainebleau, claiming he still had to tie up operations there. But really, by this stage, he had already met Nathalie, at the premiere of her latest film, and fallen madly in love.'

'Love or lust?' asks Quinn wryly.

'Perhaps both. Remember, Naumann was a connoisseur of beautiful objects. I imagine he saw Chabert as just another one. Naumann was married, of course, but that didn't stop him pursuing her. With his mind becoming increasingly unhinged, I believe the two objects of his obsession became inextricably linked and he became fixated on the idea of bringing the Amber Room to Fontainebleau as the backdrop to his seduction of Chabert.'

'Just to be clear, boss,' says Carter, 'is this fact or just theory?'

'Again, a bit of both. I guess you could call it an educated guess. Amélie Chabert told me her mother had talked about an incredible golden room. She was wearing a ring I believe her mother was given by Naumann as a reminder of their night together, which is currently being examined by our experts but I believe will turn out to be a fragment of amber mosaic. We know that the Amber Room was made up of over a hundred thousand pieces of amber mosaic – some carved or engraved with images, others plain like this one – seamlessly joined together to form panels.'

'So he gave her the ring and the bracelet? Not bad for one night of putting out.'

Coffey's expression is unreadable when she turns to Schneider.

'True, but she never wore either of them, and he also gave her syphilis, so on balance she might not have considered it such a good deal.'

'So how come there's no record of the Amber Room ever being in France?' asks Carter.

'Again, this is conjecture, but I believe Naumann had it shipped across in secret. He was in overall charge of the museum storage facility at Königsberg and he had the authority and the logistical expertise to move valuable objects around Europe discreetly.'

'Even so, someone in Fontainebleau would have reported it,' Carter argues. 'Surely it wouldn't have been possible to hide an entire room in a busy palace like that where there would have been people coming and going all the time. What about the servants, or the people who took it out of the boxes and put it together?'

'Except it was never in the palace. Amélie Chabert talked of a building in a forest with creepy mirrors. Not many people know this, but there is a building called the Maison du Plaisir in the middle of the Fôret de Fontainebleau, some distance apart from the palace itself. It's a folly that was commissioned by the Empress Eugénie, wife of Napoleon III, as a gift to her husband to commemorate his many reforms of the main palace. She had a carousel installed there and a Salle de Miroirs – a room of mirrors. And as a thank-you, he gave her the Bracelet of Concordia, with its secret star map.'

'It still leaves the question of the installation.' Carter is not letting this one go. 'It must have taken a whole team of people to do that. Why did no one ever talk of it?'

Coffey nods. 'Good question. And again I can give you only a theory in response. Because of its structure and its remoteness, the Maison du Plaisir was used throughout the war to house prisoners of war – French resistance fighters, captured British soldiers, the many men who came from France's colonies to fight alongside the French.'

'So Naumann got these poor prisoners to set up the Amber Room, and then made them conveniently disappear so they couldn't tell anyone?' asks Schneider, making a gun with his fingers and miming putting it to his head.

'It's a possibility.'

Argylle is following the theory to its logical conclusion.

'And you think the Amber Room might be hidden in this folly?' He can't keep the excitement from his voice, but Coffey shakes her head.

'That would be convenient, but sadly I don't think there's any hope of that. Though that particular building is currently closed, it was open to the public for decades after the war ended. It's quite small. There aren't any hiding places. And it's surrounded by dense forest, so any large-scale excavation would have been noticed. Besides, Naumann would never have allowed the Amber Room to remain in France after he was recalled to Germany. He would have made sure it was taken somewhere where it would be well hidden, along with all the other irreplaceable treasures that went missing after the war. But if I'm right about all this, the key thing is he removed it from Königsberg.'

'So it couldn't have been destroyed when the Allies bombed Königsberg Castle,' says Carter.

'Precisely.'

'You say it's not at Fontainebleau, and yet Vasily Federov paid five million dollars for a bracelet he thought would lead him to the Amber Room, but instead leads to this Maison du Plaisir. There has to be a link,' Carter presses on. 'Something there that will give us some clue where the Amber Room went.'

'I agree, which is why, tomorrow morning, two of you will be heading to a historical archive in western Germany. It's run by a great friend of mine, and I know they have comprehensive records from the various French chateaux and palaces that were requisitioned by the Nazis during the occupation. The Maison du Plaisir is a relatively small building and we're only interested in the period between the end of 1943, when the Amber Room was dismantled in Königsberg Castle, and mid-1944, when the Germans withdrew from France, so maybe you'll be able to turn up something in the archives to tell us where the Amber Room went from there, if indeed it was ever there at all. A note in a ledger, perhaps. Some kind of record.

'Aubrey, as you speak German, perhaps you'd like a road trip. And to keep you company, how about . . . Woody?'

Argylle had thought for a minute she would say Erin Quinn and his heart sags with disappointment, even though he knows it's for the best. There is nowhere for this relationship to go. And he doesn't feel he has anything to offer. Trauma still has him pinned to a point in time five years ago. It's not what Quinn needs. It's not what anyone needs.

Still, he's not exactly thrilled at the prospect of spending a day in the company of Woody Wyatt. He has a horrible feeling Coffey has dreamt the whole thing up as some sort of bonding exercise.

And when he steals a glance at Wyatt, he can tell by his stony expression that he's thinking exactly the same thing.

Will Hooper stays behind after the team have filed out. 'You not tempted to go yourself, boss? If there's something there in those archives, you're the one to find it.'

'Thanks for the vote of confidence, Will, but you know I think those two will do a fine job.'

'And?'

Coffey smiles. 'Quite right. *And* I want to see how they get along away from the distractions of the group. I have a hunch these two could end up being quite special together.'

Hooper raises his eyebrows.

'Provided they don't kill each other first.'

37

TWO DAYS AFTER THE TRIP TO ENGLAND, ARGYLLE IS AGAIN ON THE move. This time he is pulling into the Hôtel Beaux Rêves car park in a VW Golf hire car to pick up Wyatt, who appears none too happy about it.

'Really, Argylle? A Rabbit?'

'We're waste hauliers, Wyatt. We don't drive Porsches.'

'How come you get to take tea at the Ritz in London with Erin Quinn and I gotta wedge myself into this tin can on my way to some German backwater to eat sauerkraut with you? No offence. Actually, scratch that, take all the goddam offence you want.'

In truth, Woody Wyatt cuts a sorry sight as he attempts to settle into the front seat. Though he pushes it back as far as it will go, his knees are bent at an awkward angle and the seatbelt strains across his chest.

'Wait up!'

Argylle is surprised to see Keira Carter hurrying across the forecourt towards them. 'Change of plan. I'm coming with you. Coffey's instructions. It's your lucky day, dudes.'

'Why'd she send you?' asks Wyatt. 'She doesn't trust us on our own or something?'

Carter shrugs. 'I guess she wanted to up the IQ quota of the mission . . . although that would kinda imply there was one to start with.'

But the subject clearly bothers Carter because about half an hour into the journey, she brings it up again.

'To be honest I just don't get what we're all doing here. I mean, why send the three of us to an archive instead of the army of properly trained researchers and librarians she could have sent in our plac? Argylle I can just about understand. You speak German. You're kinda smart – in a dumb sort of way. But Wyatt . . . ?'

'Hey, what are you implying?' Wyatt attempts to twist around to look at her, but the combination of his thick neck and the cramped seat means he barely gets halfway.

'Maybe she just couldn't risk word getting out about what we're looking for,' suggests Argylle. 'Or . . .'

'. . . Or she's testing us out,' says Carter, grimly.

Wyatt glares at Argylle. 'What are you on about, man? Testing us out for what?'

Argylle catches Carter's eye in the mirror. 'You going to tell him or shall I?'

Carter sighs. 'As you know, Wyatt, Frances Coffey is a spymaster and part of her job is figuring out which combinations of personnel work best together.'

'Yeah, I know all that,' says Wyatt, impatiently. 'Microteams. I was in one with Dabrow— Oh shit.' His eyes widen in alarm as Carter's meaning sinks in. 'What, you and me and Escobar here? You gotta be kidding me.'

They sink into silence, Argylle brooding about the idea of being buddied up with Wyatt. Surely Coffey must have realized by now the two of them should be kept as far apart as possible? Carter puts her headphones on and is soon lost in whatever music she's playing. Meanwhile Wyatt's mood darkens, and, given the scale of the man, when Wyatt is in a bad mood it lies across the Earth's atmosphere like smog.

'Hey. Did anything . . . *happen* between you and Quinn yesterday?' Wyatt asks as they coast down the E42 heading for Koblenz in western Germany, checking behind to make sure Carter isn't listening.

'A gentleman never tells,' says Argylle.

It's not Argylle's intention to provoke Wyatt. Well, maybe a little, but not entirely. He just doesn't know how to answer without giving himself away. And what *did* happen, in the end? The bubble surrounding his day with Quinn in London has now burst and it's like when the lights come up in a nightclub at the end of a long evening and you see the sticky floor, the discarded glasses and the mould in the corner. Reality has a terrible habit of souring things.

'Yeah, well, I know nothing happened. For one, Quinn grew up in the CIA. She knows better than to queer her own pitch, and for two, you're an asshole.'

It's a generally uninspiring journey past fields and farmland and sprawling towns, interchangeable with their McDonald's and Lidls. Argylle is still brooding about the click on the line when he'd called Melinda Samra the night before and what it means that Coffey is bugging his phone.

'You drive like an old woman,' Wyatt complains. 'Why can't I drive?'

'Because you're not on the documents. I told you.'

'Are you actually for real? We're the frigging CIA. We don't need documents.'

'Actually,' interrupts Carter, who has taken the headphones off. 'We in the Association of Private Waste Hauliers are big on documents.'

Some three hours after setting off – with only a small detour when Wyatt spots a Kentucky Fried Chicken sign off the highway – they arrive at Koblenz and pull into the car park of an expansive six-storey concrete building that might pass for a conference centre or a particularly unlovely hotel.

'You got ketchup on the seat,' complains Argylle when Wyatt steps out of the car. The big man says nothing, just shakes his head and slams the door shut.

As they make their way in, Carter quizzes Argylle about the mission.

'So this head honcho guy is an old buddy of Coffey's?'

'Yeah, I think they go way back, to when Coffey was working in the CIA archives. He's not Agency, but he has official clearance. He's helped her out before.'

'Probably went to archive school together,' says Wyatt, cheering up suddenly. 'Say, Carter, do you suppose they have conventions, just like us waste hauliers do, where they get together and talk about, I dunno, shelf labels or something?'

In contrast to its utilitarian, oppressive exterior, the lobby of the archive building is lofty and grand, with a central staircase that curves around the space before dividing to join both sides of a galleried landing. There are soaring pillars and skylights and leather seats on which they wait for Friedrich Wolff, president of the federal archives.

Argylle is not prepared for the scale of the place, and it moves him that this enormous building is devoted to recording history so that future generations can learn how the world was then, in order to better understand how the world is now. Not so Wyatt, who is gazing around him incredulously. 'You mean to say this whole, enormous space is filled with old papers and books? Oh, man.'

'Not just papers and books, but also film reels, maps, photographs, posters. Anything that brings the past to life.'

The speaker is small and slight, with a round, guileless face.

'Friedrich Wolff,' he introduces himself, shaking each of their hands in turn and beaming. 'I am so happy to meet you. My dear Frances has told me all about you. Please come this way.'

He leads them into a lift, and when the doors close he leans in towards them conspiratorially.

'Frances tells me you're looking for records on the Château de Fontainebleau. Such a magnificent building. The Nazis were in occupation for two separate periods during the war, and as you know it's one of the largest palaces in the world, so we have quite a lot of material relating to it. It was used as a temporary Nazi headquarters and a billet for officers. The little building you're interested in – the Maison du Plaisir – is particularly fascinating as it's hidden away some distance from the main house, and was still being used by the Germans to house prisoners of war long after the official occupation of Fontainebleau had ended. Oh, I just love this part of my job, that thrill of spending the day with one's nose buried in old documents. Is there anything better?'

He addresses this last question to Wyatt, who looks horrified.

Herr Wolff leads them along a brightly lit corridor lined on each side by a row of sliding doors. 'This is the magazine room,' he says, sliding a door across to reveal shelf upon shelf of neatly filed publications. Next he shows them a warehouse-style space, lined with shelves storing box files. Here he pauses by a desk in front of the space to consult a computerized index system. 'Yes, here we are,' he says, almost to himself. 'This might be a good place to start.'

Minutes later, they are wheeling trolleys loaded with box files to a reading room along the corridor that Wolff assures them will be exclusively theirs for the duration of their visit.

'Any chance I can grab a coffee from the vending machine before we start?' asks Wyatt.

The others stare at him in disbelief.

'These documents are decades old and utterly irreplaceable,' Herr Wolff begins.

'And he doesn't want your cappuccino-with-five-sugars fingers pawing all over them,' Carter adds.

'Three sugars. And I was only asking,' mutters Wyatt.

The files are grouped together under various headings such as personnel, household maintenance, prisoners of war, and within those groups they are arranged chronologically.

'Before you begin, I should warn you that some of the material you will find in these boxes will be of a very distressing nature.' Wolff's baby face now wears a serious expression. 'The Germans knew that they were surrounded by people who hated them and that the resistance movement was very strong, sending messages all the time to the Allies, giving away details of their positions and plotting against them. The officer given overall charge of the Maison du Plaisir during this time was Rudolf Naumann. He was by all accounts a brilliant and cultured historian before the war, but by the time he was sent to Fontainebleau he had acquired a reputation for ruthlessness, made worse by the syphilis that affected his brain and nervous system. So I'm afraid when prisoners were brought here they weren't asked nicely to reveal who they were working with and what they knew. There was torture and appalling cruelty.'

'Dude, we're not a Boy Scout troop,' says Wyatt.

'Quite so. Forgive me.'

They begin sifting through the files, wearing the latex gloves that Wolff has given them. As Argylle speaks both French and German, he is at the far end looking through the written material, while Herr Wolff sits between Wyatt and Carter to talk them through the photographs.

Argylle opens his first file, relating to the running of the household, with a sense of purpose which soon burns itself out as he trawls through piles of dull handwritten ledgers, all in German, recording the requisitioning of farm produce and animals. There's a neat book of recipes and a separate ledger of costings for all the meals.

Next, he moves on to a box marked *Miscellaneous*, becoming briefly excited when he sees it is full of maps, thinking that this could contain a clue to the whereabouts of the missing artefact. 'That's the local area around the Maison du Plaisir,' Wolff tells him, leaning over. 'Naumann had maps drawn up showing where the back roads were, where people might try to avoid a blockade if they were trying to help Allied soldiers evade capture or smuggle black-market goods or weapons to the resistance, as well as the routes an advancing German army might take through the area en route to invade Britain.'

'And these crosses?' Argylle shows him where various buildings in the surrounding farms and villages are marked with the letter X.

Wolff examines it carefully, and the barely legible handwritten note along the side. 'Those show where the informants lived. Some of the French citizens were pragmatists or opportunists who betrayed their resistance neighbours in return for extra provisions or to settle an old score, or because they thought it would help them get ahead. Often these were people they trusted.'

Argylle thinks of the bullet, back in his room, hidden in his torch, and he thinks of that click on the line before he spoke to Melinda Samra. Of trust and betrayal.

For two hours they continue sifting through the files. They find letters written by the wives and families of the German officers. In one, Rudolf Naumann's wife complains bitterly that they have no butter or sugar so the cook's cakes taste like shoe leather. They find inventories of weapons seized and a photograph of guns and grenades laid out on a gleaming wood floor. They find things left behind after the Germans had moved on – a wristwatch with a battered leather strap, woollen socks, false teeth. Then:

'Oh!' Carter's gasp cuts across the desk. When Argylle glances over she has her hand over her mouth. 'It's fine,' she says, collecting herself, embarrassed. 'I'm sorry.'

He sees that she has the contents of a box of photographs spread out on the desk in front of her. He gets up to look and his stomach turns over. The pictures show prisoners – mostly men, although there are women too. Some clothed, many not. In one photograph a group of six men, shackled hand and foot, sit in a row facing a wall, their curved backs striped with raw, bleeding wounds; in another a woman hangs by her handcuffs from a wooden bar while a uniformed German beats her across the back with a club. There is blood running from the woman's wrists and Argylle sees that the handcuffs have spikes on the inside. Another shows a naked man in a bathtub, his legs tied to a wooden bar to which is also attached a chain which the guard is pulling to tip the man under the water. In a fourth a man stares blankly up at the camera next to a heap of dead bodies. Where the man's left eye should be there is only a gaping socket.

Even Wyatt has gone silent.

Friedrich Wolff rests a hand on Wyatt's arm.

'It is good to feel something,' he says softly. 'No amount of training should make you immune from images like this. Otherwise, what would their sacrifice be for? What would we have become? How would we make sure it doesn't happen again?'

'This all happened in the Maison du Plaisir?' Argylle asks.

The veteran archivist nods. 'It was originally conceived as a playhouse. There was a Salle de Miroirs and a funfair and a secret passage that led down to several underground chambers. It was a perfect venue for a torture chamber because very few people knew it existed and it had ready-built dungeons below ground where the sound wouldn't carry. That's why the Gestapo continued to use it right up until the middle of 1944.'

There are more boxes to go through. Inside the first they find more ledgers, except these relate to torture. A list of names and, next to them, the different techniques applied. 'September 5th, nine days without sleep,' one entry reads. Then the next line: 'September 6th, dead.' The third column is for information they have got out of their prisoners. Argylle finds it profoundly moving how little these people give away, despite everything that is done to them.

The second box contains letters and cards and a cheap notebook filled with cramped writing. All of it in French.

'I don't get it,' says Wyatt. 'They torture them and then let them sit down and write love letters to their sweethearts?'

'Not all prisoners were treated equally,' Wolff explains. 'A few were high-ranking officials or enemy officers or people the Germans thought might be useful to them in some way. Or sometimes it was a part of the psychological torture – they would tell the prisoners they were about to be released and they should write to their families to let them know, and the next day they would snatch that away.'

'It's the hope that kills you, am I right?' says Carter.

Argylle, meanwhile, has picked up the notebook and is leafing through. He sees instantly that it's a journal, written entirely in French. Some pages have been left untouched, while others are almost entirely scored through with black marker pen. Towards the end, the writing gets smaller, as if the writer knows he or she has too much still to say for the number of pages that remain.

'Ah, now there's a story behind that,' says Wolff, reaching out one of his small, dainty gloved hands to touch the cover deferentially. 'It came to us as a bequest from a lady in southern France who said it was a journal written by her brother – who'd been a prisoner in the Maison du Plaisir. He wrote the whole thing on the eve of his execution during the very last days of the German occupation – which is probably why it's so hard to decipher. It was sent to her after his death. As you can see, it was quite heavily redacted, but it gives a sense of what his life was like in that place, and a little about his time before he was captured.

'He's a very interesting case, actually. He was known as Henri Dumas, but his real name was Henri d'Avignon. His family were the closest thing France gets these days to aristocracy. He had a very privileged upbringing and could have just taken over the family estate, but instead he went to university to study civil engineering, as he had an enduring fascination with bridges. When his grandfather joined the Vichy government, which as you know collaborated with the Germans, Henri renounced his name and his family and joined the resistance under the adopted name of Dumas, distinguishing himself by repeatedly risking his life carrying arms to stranded Allied soldiers after the disastrous raid on Dieppe.

'He was captured early in 1943 by the Milice, the paramilitary group sent by the Vichy government to help the Gestapo track down the resistance fighters, and was brought to the Maison du Plaisir. Normally, prisoners weren't held long there, but there were some exceptions. It's hard to find accurate records, as the building did not officially exist, but we believe he was there for well over a year. As the journal says, by the end of that time he was convinced he would die there.'

Argylle flicks through the notebook. Though it's such a flimsy thing, he's fully aware of the weight of history it carries. He thinks of the young man who wrote it, all the dreams he must have had for his future, and he thinks of his own journals, currently stored with the rest of his belongings in a corner of his friend Somchai's tiny bedroom.

'So why did he survive so long?' asks Carter.

'Well, that's an interesting question. Certainly, his engineering background seems to have come in useful. Most of that part of the journal is redacted but, cross-referencing it with other records, we believe any prisoners with experience in engineering or construction were sent from the Maison du Plaisir to somewhere in Eastern Europe to labour on a large-scale building project. We don't know what they were building, but it was highly secret. Over a thousand men were rounded up from different prisoner-of-war camps – Poles, Soviets, French. Many of them died from hypothermia or lack of food or extreme physical weakness. Those who survived were forced to march over a hundred kilometres in freezing temperatures, lined up beside a quarry and shot. All except one.'

'Henri Dumas,' murmurs Carter.

Wolff nods. 'We believe that the Nazis discovered who he really was – perhaps his family tracked him down – and they thought he might be useful. So he was sent back. The only prisoner to return to the Maison du Plaisir.

'First Naumann tried a prisoner swap, offering to hand him over to the Allies in exchange for a high-ranking German officer. It's extremely unlikely Naumann would have honoured any such agreement, given what Dumas knew. When that got nowhere he tried to use him as a public relations tool, summoning Dumas's father and grandfather to come to Fontainebleau with the intention of persuading him to reconcile with his family, renounce his past and entreat his resistance comrades to accept defeat. By this stage Dumas weighed forty-two kilos and was suffering from lung damage from working in the quarries and in constant pain from a broken leg that never properly healed. He also experienced hallucinations and depression. They weren't offering him complete freedom. Clearly, whatever project he'd been sent off to work on was too sensitive to allow that. But they guaranteed he'd be housed in comfort and properly fed, and allowed supervised visits from his family. Can you imagine how tempting it would have been for him to give in?'

'But he didn't,' says Argylle softly.

'No. His words are recorded in one of the ledgers that details the prisoners who died in Fontainebleau: "I prefer to die a son of France, than live a son of the traitorous d'Avignons." He was executed the following morning. But not before he'd written the document you have there. It was intended for his younger sister, Marie. The Gestapo must have given him the materials as a concession to his family, so that he could record his goodbyes. As you'll see, it's more like a random collection of thoughts and memories than a proper journal. You can get a sense of how his mind was fragmenting. We've been through it to try to find out more information about the mystery project that cost so many lives, but either he didn't elaborate or it was redacted so heavily there's nothing left.'

Wyatt's voice is leaden with disappointment as he says:

'So if this project Dumas was involved in does turn out to have something to do with the Amber Room, say, digging an underground cavern in a mountainside big enough to hide a train loaded with stolen treasure, we're no nearer finding out where or what it was.'

'I'd still like to go through it,' Argylle says. 'If I may?'

He doesn't know why he is asking permission, except that it seems like a rare privilege.

There's a knot in Argylle's chest as he turns to the first page of the journal and translates the opening lines: 'I am not afraid to die for I have lived already a hundred lifetimes and my soul is weary. I own nothing, and yet I leave behind great riches.'

As Friedrich Wolff said, the journal is disjointed. Some childhood memories. Some philosophical musings about death and life and liberty. Argylle is struck by an excerpt from a T. E. Lawrence poem that his own father used to quote to him: 'I loved you, so I drew these tides of men into my hands and wrote my will across the sky in stars/ To earn you freedom, the seven-pillared worthy house/that your eyes might be shining for me when we came.'

He looks at the next entry, in which Henri talks directly to his sister:

'Our home had fewer than seven pillars and we didn't write our will across the sky in stars but instead, falling through the looking glass, we wrote what we could behind the walls of our lives.'

Falling through the looking glass. The Salle de Miroirs.

'Herr Wolff, is there a room in the Maison du Plaisir that has seven pillars?'

Wolff looks surprised.

'I'm not sure. One of the other prisoners mentions a vaulted ceiling in one of the underground chambers, so that might indicate pillars, but I don't know how many.'

'Might Henri Dumas have been kept there when he was in solitary confinement?'

'It's possible. Why?'

'I think he might have hidden something there. Behind the walls.'

Driving back to Belgium, the mood in the car is sombre. In the back, Carter doesn't bother putting her headphones on.

'I really hope you're right, Argylle,' she says. 'I hope Henri Dumas is the link to the Amber Room and the poor guy's sacrifice can be honoured in some way. It takes a lot of guts to go against your family like that, no matter how much you despise what they stand for.'

Argylle wonders if she is thinking about her own parents. He thinks about saying something, but the presence of Woody Wyatt in the passenger seat stops him. What could Wyatt, with his all-American military background, understand about Carter's immigrant parents and their ambitions for their only daughter?

Instead, they lapse into silence, lost in their own thoughts, until Wyatt, who has been uncharacteristically subdued since they stumbled across that first box of photographs, clears his throat.

'You know, I'm glad in a way Dumas didn't survive the war,' he says gruffly. 'War marks you. After what he saw and went through he wouldn't have been the same.

'My dad was in Vietnam, as a Marine in the Reconnaissance Battalion. He was a scout sniper. It was his job to infiltrate enemy territory and take out whoever he could and then report back to the platoon. He spent days out there on his own, knowing he could be captured or shot at any time. He was awarded the Navy Cross, but when he came home he was a shell. He held it together for a few years, got married, had us kids. But by the time I was four or five, he was a mess, you know. Heavy drinking. Depression. Paranoia. Violence. He'd put on a bulletproof vest just to go to the store and carried two pistols – one in his belt and one in his boot. We were terrified of him. He was just so unpredictable, flying into a rage at the smallest thing. I joined the Marines to make him proud, but also I just needed to get away from him.

'Maybe this *Henry Dumbass* would have ended up the same way. Maybe it was for the best, you know. He might have come out of it a monster.'

Argylle doesn't know what to say. You think you know about a person because you've gleaned a bunch of facts about where they came from or who their family is, but the tissue of a person is made up of so much more than that, all the tiny fibres of our lives that weave themselves into a pattern that is unique. People are complicated. Surely he should have learned that much by now? Even the Woody Wyatts of this world have hidden depths.

Clearly Carter's thoughts are running along the same lines.

'Jeez, Wyatt, don't get all three-dimensional on me now,' she says. 'I might have to start actually *liking* you.'

38

THE CHÂTEAU DE FONTAINEBLEAU STANDS IN A HUNDRED AND thirty hectares of parkland around fifty-five kilometres south-east of Paris. Immediately to the north of it lies the small town of Fontainebleau, while the south and west feature carefully laid-out lakes and formal gardens and a picturesque canal. And, surrounding the whole vast estate, is the dense Forêt de Fontainebleau.

There's been a royal residence at Fontainebleau since the Middle Ages, but it was in the sixteenth century that it was redeveloped by Francis I, becoming the lavish Italianate palace it is today, with magnificent galleries and courtyards and an entirely new square of buildings. Subsequent monarchs – including Napoleon III – added embellishments and outbuildings, pavilions and chapels, new wings and apartments, museums and theatres. The most celebrated artists of the day created new frescoes and sculptures while gardeners and architects landscaped the grounds until it rivalled – and many would say surpassed – Versailles itself.

Over the centuries the fifteen-hundred-room palace has housed kings and queens, entire courts; it has seen cold-blooded murder and war and revolution as well as weddings and feasts and treaties and royal births.

The team – eight of them on this mission – are travelling in a mini-van, with bikes fixed to the back. The forest around Fontainebleau, in which the Maison du Plaisir is located, is a mecca for cyclists and hikers. Increasingly, it has also drawn tour groups of climbing enthu-siasts keen to experience bouldering – climbing small rock formations without ropes or harnesses. Accordingly, the team all wear outdoor gear, shorts or leggings and T-shirts with sneakers to blend in with their surroundings.

'Suits you,' Argylle says to Erin Quinn, indicating her red baseball cap.

'Why thank you. I matched it to my blisters.' She pulls down the back of a sock to reveal angry welts on the back of her heel already made by her new sneakers.

Things have been awkward between them since getting back from London and, apart from the odd wave across the room, or stiff chat in the canteen, they've largely avoided each other. But when she came on board and dropped into the seat next to him, Argylle's spirits lifted and he realizes he's missed speaking to her, missed her company.

'How was Koblenz?' she asks him as they pass signs to Fontaine-bleau. 'You and Wyatt best buddies now?'

'Something like that.' Impossible to put into words the intensity of those hours in the archives sifting through the meticulously kept records of inhuman barbarity. And then the car journey, as intimate as a confessional, Woody Wyatt laying himself bare.

On the seat, her hand briefly finds his and she squeezes. 'I'm glad.'

When she takes her hand away her fingers leave an imprint of heat on his skin.

They are driving around a road that skirts the bottom of the estate. Down a straight, tree-lined avenue off to the side, he catches a glimpse of one of the palace buildings, majestic behind a wrought-iron gate.

Instantly, he is catapulted back through time. 'I came to Paris as a child,' he tells Quinn, without even meaning to. 'For various reasons it must have been really . . . *tricky* for my parents to spend time in Europe, but I never once guessed they were under pressure. It makes me worry how I can trust my own judgement when I had so little clue what was happening around me.'

His younger self had been so full of wonder, walking between his parents, drinking in the sights, enjoying that feeling of being utterly safe. When all the time they must have been waiting for the hand on the shoulder, the *Pardonnez-moi, messieurs*.

He is thinking now of the bullet he found embedded in Samra's Quran. 9mm to fit the Glocks the team have as standard issue. Isn't it possible he is wrong about that too? The Russians might well use identical bullets. And just because the bullet had entered through Samra's back before being embedded in his Quran, it didn't prove a thing. True, the last time he saw Samra he was facing off to the Russians on the clifftop, but it's perfectly possible he turned back while Argylle wasn't looking. Instead of churning it over endlessly in his mind, shouldn't he just share his concerns with Erin Quinn, so that she can dismiss them? The temptation is burning a hole in his gut, to open up and have his fears washed away.

'Quinn—' he starts, at the same moment as she says, 'Argylle.' They both stop. 'You go,' he tells her.

'I was just going to say that adulthood sometimes seems like a long procession of tiny betrayals that make you doubt everyone, but if you reframe it as a process of learning how to trust only yourself, it can be surprisingly liberating.'

They all have earpieces disguised as in-ear headphones and discreet microphones clipped to the straps of their bags. As they pull up to the parking area – a sandy bay amid the trees, Coffey's voice comes booming over the airwaves. 'Okay, team, this should be pretty straightforward. We're about to run a few checks on the building from this end, just to make sure it's safe. Then it's just a case of in and out as quickly and cleanly as possible. In a last-minute change of plan, Argylle will be leading the mission.'

What? Even through his headphones, Argylle hears the chorus of groans pass around the van. He is the most junior team member, still earning his stripes. Why is Coffey putting him in charge?

'But, boss—' Schneider comes over the radio, outrage quivering in his voice.

Coffey cuts him off. 'That was a statement, Matt, not an invitation to discussion.'

As they disembark, wincing as they step from the air-conditioned interior into the fiercely hot day, no one says anything to Argylle, but the resentment hangs like smoke in the hot air.

From here it's a kilometre's cycle through the trees to their destination.

The Maison du Plaisir has been closed to the public for the past two and a half years and fenced off behind slotted plastic panels in a secluded, little-used area of the forest. It is a miniature chateau, built in exquisite detail in the Second Empire style in sand-coloured stone with a mansard roof and a central tower with a clock inset into the front and a porticoed entrance.

They stop beyond the perimeter of the fence and Argylle takes himself off behind the trees to speak to Coffey. 'Boss, we're at the house now.'

'Okay, Aubrey, we've just run a satellite thermal-imaging check and the place is clear. You're good to go.'

'Who did you expect might be there?' Argylle is sure Coffey was checking to make sure the Russians hadn't shown up, just as they did in Mount Athos. What he doesn't know is why she might think that a possibility. There was an explanation for them turning up last time – they'd found out independently that there was a second bracelet at St Benedict's Monastery. But there was no way they could know about the link with Fontainebleau. Unless . . .

'We're just being cautious.'

Argylle doesn't believe her. The cogs are turning in his head: the bullet in Samra's back, the way the Russians happened to turn up at Mount Athos at the same time as them, the feeling he's had this whole time that Coffey is holding something back. Has someone in the team been tipping Federov off? Someone maybe in cahoots with the disgraced Dabrowski? He thinks about that click on the line before he talked to Samra's wife. Is *he* under suspicion? What the hell is going on?

He returns to the others. 'All systems go,' he tells them, giving a thumbs-up, but the back of his neck prickles with unease.

Coffey and the Agency techies have managed to remotely override the Maison du Plaisir's alarm system. Luckily, being so far from the main building, and with little in the way of portable valuables, it is on a different circuit to the rest of the palace, which enjoys state-of-the-art protection. And Carter is on hand to deal with any unexpected security set-ups they might encounter once they get inside. The whole thing ought to be, as Coffey says, straightforward. They go in, they search, they get out.

Simple.

They are inside the fence within seconds. In the garden to the right of the house's ornate front entrance is a structure taller than a man and covered in a tarpaulin. 'That's an automaton,' Coffey tells him through his earpiece, and it still amazes him to know she is watching him through a satellite feed from so far away. 'It's a cage containing mechanical songbirds that the Empress Eugénie had specially made. Automatons were all the rage during that period. People thought they were magic because they could move and even speak independently, though in reality they were operated remotely, through a complex system of rods and levers. You'll find a control device inside the house to operate it, probably somewhere near the closest window.'

Now they have reached the front door, and when Washington makes short work of getting them inside, Argylle allows himself to relax a fraction. Inside, there's a hallway with a staircase rising up straight ahead and, through a set of double doors on the left, an airy room dominated by an ornate turquoise-and-gold carousel from which hang four gaily painted swings. The carousel's central pole descends through the floor to the basement. Argylle guesses a servant would have been down there turning it by hand.

There is a raised stage at one end of the room, made of polished wood, where musicians would have played, and pale blue silk wallpaper with a pattern of tiny yellow birds. On the right wall is a magnificent stained-glass rose window that sends patterns of coloured lights playing across the polished oak floor, while at the far end is another window, no bigger than a slit, and next to it a box-like mechanical contraption that he assumes to be connected to the automaton outside.

The room on the opposite side of the hall is breathtaking. Lofty, with a high vaulted ceiling painted with a fresco of clouds and angels, and lined with arched alcoves. Each of the alcoves is in turn lined with interconnecting panels of mirrors, bevelled so that the light refracts from their angled edges. In the middle of the room, a central pillar is inset with multitudes of ornate mirrored tiles which reflect back the mirrored alcoves. Vast chandeliers hang from the ceilings, reflecting the mirrors in each of their hundreds of crystals. The effect of the whole is to make you feel as if you are trapped in a shimmering optical illusion.

Argylle's eyes sweep the room and he spots the winking eye of a CCTV camera high up in the topmost part of the ceiling at the back of the hall. He raises his eyebrow at Carter in query, but she shakes her head. 'Coffey has it covered, don't sweat,' she says.

They are looking for an entrance to the dungeons, which they know from the Koblenz archives lies beneath this floor. He sends Quinn and Schneider to search the only other room on the ground floor, a kitchen, accessed through a doorway behind the staircase. At first he thinks Schneider might refuse to do as he is asked – he's made no secret of thinking Argylle unfit to lead the team. There is a moment's stand-off, but then Schneider follows Quinn to the door, an expression of contempt flickering across his small, sharp features as he passes Argylle.

'Let's move, buddy,' says Wyatt, chivvying him out.

Wyatt and Argylle will quickly scope out the upstairs rooms, even though Argylle feels sure that what they are looking for will be found below ground rather than above.

Upstairs is an enormous marbled bathroom with an ornate gold ceiling. A plush velvet-covered chaise stands next to a luxurious tub prominently positioned in front of a fireplace. 'I'm guessing there would have been *bow-coop du plaisir* in this place,' grins Wyatt.

Argylle isn't really listening. All he can hear is the drumbeat of disquiet thrumming through his head, making small talk impossible.

In the doorway of the next room, Argylle hesitates.

'Do you think this is where Naumann set up the Amber Room?' he asks, gazing around at the sumptuous bedchamber with its canopied bed. He thinks about young Nathalie Chabert being brought here in the dead of night to this strange building on its own in the middle of a forest. Was she already regretting her decision to come, even as she stood in this same doorway? He thinks about Rudolf Naumann, already losing his grip on reality, risking everything to possess her against the backdrop of one of the great treasures of the world, the art connoisseur nailing down her beauty to the Amber Room's dazzling surface like a butterfly on a pin.

They bump into Schneider and Quinn in the downstairs hallway. 'There's a back door to the outside, but it's sealed up behind a metal grate,' says Quinn. 'No entrance to a basement.' They rejoin the others, who have been searching the Salle de Miroirs for a hidden doorway.

'Nothing,' Corcoran calls out. Argylle thinks of Henri Dumas's journal. *Falling through the looking glass*, Dumas had written to his sister. Instinctively, he knows what they are looking for lies in this room. 'Look harder,' he says. 'Knock on the walls, listen for anything that sounds hollow.' He is aware of time passing. He doesn't know how long they have until someone notices the security system is down.

'Try the alcove at the end of the room, the one where the mirror is slightly discoloured down one side.' Coffey's voice in his earpiece takes him by surprise.

'But how—' He stops, realizing she must be monitoring them through the CCTV camera.

'Here!' The shout comes from Corcoran, who has gone to investigate. Jogging over, Argylle sees that a large mirrored panel has swung open in the centre of the alcove wall, revealing a small doorway through which even Carter has to duck to enter. He switches on his flashlight, calling to the broad figure at the back of the group.

'Casner, you stay up here to keep watch. The rest of you, follow me.'

Then he is gone, leaving Martin Casner alone, but for the hundreds of versions of himself reflected back at him from every surface of the room.

39

THE PASSAGEWAY THEY ARE IN IS NARROW AND DAMP. ARGYLLE'S head brushes the ceiling and a chill spreads across his skin as he imagines the prisoners who must have walked this same cheerless corridor, the fear in their hearts, the way their breath must have echoed off the clammy stone walls. He wonders what Henri Dumas thought, brought here for the second time. Did he realize he would never leave? Or did he imagine his luck would hold?

The basement level turns out to be a warren of rooms. In one, Argylle sees the lower end of the central pole from the carousel in the room above descending through the ceiling with a wooden handle near the bottom to make the carousel revolve. But most of the rooms are small, damp, windowless spaces where a prisoner might have been held in solitary confinement with only the rats to hear their screams.

They arrive at a larger chamber and Argylle shudders, seeing two giant iron hooks in the ceiling and, at ankle level, a heavy chain coiled in the corner and attached to the wall at one end by a metal ring. The next chamber is the same size, only it features in the centre of the room a cast-iron bathtub. A wooden bar runs above it for the width of the room.

He backs out, closing the door fast, remembering the photograph in the archives of the naked prisoner with his legs chained to the ceiling, his head tipped back under the bathwater. Neither he nor Wyatt speaks.

He has divided the team into pairs, each pair taking a different section and shouting 'No!' each time a room is ruled out. Argylle and Wyatt are part way down the corridor when they hear Quinn yell, 'Here!'

When they reach her, she is in a room around three metres square, the walls bare brick, the low ceiling vaulted. The vaulting creates arched alcoves along the walls, each one supported on each side by a brick pillar. He counts them. Six.

It will do.

There is a wooden ledge running across the largest alcove, long enough to allow a man to lie down. But not wide enough, surely? Then Argylle thinks about what Henri Dumas would have been through in the years leading up to his incarceration in this room. The starvation. The forced labour. The diseases that would have laid waste to his body. He reappraises.

Wide enough, maybe.

On one side of the room a heavy metal shackle is fixed to the wall, but he can see no other evidence of ill treatment. Yet he is sure this is where Henri Dumas was kept after he was unmasked as a d'Avignon. It's also where he would have spent his final night after refusing to reconcile with his family and betray his beliefs, scribbling furiously in the notebook that Argylle had held in his gloved hands in the archives in Koblenz.

We wrote what we could behind the walls of our lives. Dumas's words are engraved across Argylle's mind, but the walls here are all exposed brick. There are no hiding places. Still, he instructs the team to do a fingertip search, running their hands over the bricks to see if there's a place where the mortar is loose and something might have been tucked in behind.

Nothing.

Disappointment leaks through him. He'd been so sure they were on to something. And here they are, at another dead end.

'Anyone else come across anything?' The others shake their heads. Someone has found a room full of old paint, someone else a stack of rotting fencing.

'Looks like the end of the line, huh, *Aubrey*?' says Schneider, hardly bothering to hide his smirk.

Argylle taps his fingers on his thigh, trying to hold back the swell of anger he can feel building up.

As if she can sense his mood, Quinn steps in between the two.

'It could still turn out to be the right place. I mean, decades have passed since Dumas was here. Who knows what changes might have been made to this room in the meantime?'

'So all we need is a time machine,' says Schneider. 'Brilliant!'

'There'll be someone out there who knows about this place,' says Carter. 'An old caretaker or a historian who'll be able to tell us what's changed since the war. I got my gear in my pack. Want me to hack into the Fontainebleau database and see if I can dredge up a number?'

'Sure, just tell them we're in the middle of breaking into one of the palace buildings and we're having trouble finding what we're looking for.'

'Shut up, Schneider. I'll pretend to be a student, working on a dissertation or something. Experts love the chance to prove why they're the experts!'

'Great idea, Carter. Go upstairs, where there's a signal, and we'll carry on searching down here.'

Argylle holds out little hope that Carter will succeed, but he can't think of a better idea, and he wants to at least be able to tell Coffey that he tried everything.

He sends the teams to search again, hoping against hope they might find something they missed the first time.

Fifteen fruitless minutes later, Carter comes to find him in the vaulted room, looking sombre.

'I found an academic paper published by Oxford University Press about French chateaux that were used as Nazi prisons and torture chambers during the Second World War. The Maison du Plaisir featured quite prominently. It was written by a professor at the university, and I managed to get hold of him from the online staff directory. He said he was here in the nineties and he remembered this room. He said it had once been a wine cellar, but all the shelving had gone and by the time he saw it only the insulation remained.'

'Insulation?'

Carter nods, grim-faced. 'The walls were panelled, Argylle.'

Argylle feels sick. Now that Carter has said it, he can see – in one corner where a pillar intersects with the recessed wall of an alcove – a short strut of wood with holes in it, as if something had once been nailed in place there.

Behind the walls of our lives. If a clue to the whereabouts of the Amber Room had been hidden behind the panelling in the walls, it is clearly long gone now.

'Wait a minute,' says Washington, who has been sitting on the bench to avoid having to fold his six-feet-seven frame in half under the low ceiling. 'When we were searching down here in pairs earlier, Schneider said he found a room full of wood.'

Matt Schneider looks up from the wall against which he is leaning, his expression bored.

'Not wood, just a broken-down old fence.'

'Show me.'

'Relax, Argylle, I told you it's not what you're looking for.'

'Show me.'

Schneider pushes himself away from the wall as if what he's being asked to do is beneath him, and leads the way into the corridor. They turn one corner, then the next, and come to a dead end.

'What the—' Schneider mutters.

'Through here,' calls Washington, from behind them. 'This is where we were before.'

They follow him to a smaller corridor off the main one where there are just two doors. 'That's the one Schneider was in earlier.'

Argylle pushes open the door. Inside is a narrow, shelf-lined room that would have been used as a storeroom. The shelves are mostly bare, only a few rusty tins and bottles of cleaning product, the labels faded to nothing. Leaning against the far wall are two stacks of what does indeed seem at first glance to be old, broken fencing but they reveal themselves, as Argylle approaches, to be ripped-out wood panels. The wood is thin and clearly very old, although nothing like as old as the house itself. He'd guess it might come from the early part of the last century. Certainly before the Second World War.

He summons Carter and Washington. There isn't room for more bodies in here.

'What are we looking for?' Carter asks.

Argylle shrugs. 'Something that's been attached to the panels, maybe?'

But even as the words come out he hears how futile they sound. The panels are split and brittle as if they've been stored here for years. If they did indeed come from Dumas's cell and he'd been able to find a way of fixing a map or directions to the back of one of them, the chances of it having stayed undetected through all that time are slim to non-existent.

The three of them begin sorting through the stacks. The panels are in poor condition on the whole. One drives a splinter deep into Argylle's hand when he grabs it. Still, he takes his time, pulling them carefully apart one by one, examining both sides.

'Schneider, bring your flashlight over here. It's too damn dark.'

Schneider rolls his eyes before sauntering in to stand with his light dangling from his hand.

'It's a waste of—'

'Higher.'

He continues going through the panels. Then:

'Bring the light closer.'

The others stop what they're doing, alerted by something in his voice. Even Schneider forgets his studied disdain as Argylle lays the panel he's been examining flat on the ground, varnished side down, so that the rusty nail that once helped hold it in place is sticking straight up in the air.

The four of them inspect it in the yellow light.

'Oh my!' breathes Washington.

There, scratched into the underside of the panel, intact apart from a single chip in the wood, is what looks very much like a map.

40

IN THE CIA HQ BENEATH THE AGRICULTURAL CHEMICALS PLANT IN rural Delaware, where, less than six months before, a very different Aubrey Argylle first came to the attention of the Agency, Joe Quintano scans his eyes across a bank of monitors in front of him. Something on the furthest screen snags his attention and he leans in closer. *Holy moley.*

He picks up a phone on his desk. 'Boss, you gotta come in here.'

Seconds later, Frances Coffey is standing behind his desk, preceded by a waft of tobacco. *So she's back on the smokes. Things must be going to ratshit.*

'Here.' He points to the screen. 'This is the footage from the Helios satellite showing the building the team are in. And these' – he indicates the cluster of pulsing orange dots moving through the forest immediately to the west of the building – 'are trouble.'

'Get me Defoe.'

Dan Defoe is the codename Dabrowski uses on the rare occasion he has to speak to anyone at Delaware HQ. He chose the alias himself as a nod to the creator of *Robinson Crusoe*. The story of a man shipwrecked on a desert island had struck a chord. Only Coffey knows his true identity. Within a minute, Coffey has her headset on and has been patched through to the farmhouse in Montana, where the loneliest man in the world says: 'You seeing this?'

'Yes, Dan, I'm seeing it. Is it another biking tour?'

'Perhaps. But I've been watching them since they parked up. They headed straight for the pleasure house. No detours, no deviations.'

'Can we get a visual on the vehicle?' Coffey asks Quintano.

'Hold on.' Quintano keys in a command and a different screen shows a grainy satellite picture of a dark-coloured bus similar to theirs, pulled up to the side of the road about a kilometre to the west of the Maison du Plaisir. Outside, a figure paces, talking on a phone or a radio.

'Zoom in.' Coffey peers at the screen, and though the picture pixelates as it magnifies, it's possible to make out the white bandage around the man's eye.

'Pull them out!' yells Dabrowski, who has followed the same procedure and knows what he's just seen.

Coffey is already on the radio. 'Argylle. You've got company. Abort. Now.'

There is no response, just dead air.

'We lost the connection, boss,' says Quintano, his handsome face troubled. 'Maybe he went underground.'

'Try the rest of them. Someone must still be in range.'

Quintano turns back to his computer, but it's clear from his frown that the news isn't good.

'Come on,' Dabrowski mutters in her earpiece, clearly following the orange dots on the screen as closely as they are.

Coffey's stomach muscles tighten one by one, like she is zipping up a tight jacket. All these lives in her care. Each of them someone's spouse, someone's son, someone's sister.

'Nothing, boss,' says Quintano, grave. 'Either they're all underground or—'

Coffey finishes Quintano's sentence for him. 'Or whoever is in command of those orange dots is jamming our messages. Dan, have you got eyes on the CCTV footage inside the house?'

'I'm on it, boss.'

Quintano glances back at the screen.

'Too late. They've arrived. Our guys are sitting ducks.'

41

WHEN YOU ALLOW YOURSELF TO BECOME COMPLACENT, THAT'S when you're in trouble. Argylle knows this, and yet, making his way up the stairs with the wood panel tucked under his arm, he has a moment of self-congratulation. Mission accomplished.

Casner is agitated when they step through the hidden door.

'I thought I heard something outside.'

They all stop. Listen.

In the distance a plane flying overhead. A bird squawking.

Argylle exhales.

'We're out of here,' he says into his earpiece, but the signal is still dead. 'Carter, can you get us reconnected?' he asks, but he isn't worried. They lost the connection when they went underground and it might take a few moments to get it back, but Coffey will still be watching over the CCTV, he has no doubt.

Coffey doesn't take her eyes off the screen, on which she can see the members of the team proceeding through the Salle de Miroirs, as she tersely instructs a National Security Agency techie to take down whatever scrambling device the Russians are using to block their radio reception. So intently focused is she that at first she doesn't understand what Dabrowski is telling her.

'Smoke alarms.'

'What?'

'We haven't got time to de-scramble the signal. Activate the smoke alarms.'

Her gaze flicks to the monitor, where the live satellite feed shows the orange dots closing in. How many of them are there? Twelve? Fifteen? If the team are ambushed, there'll be a bloodbath.

Within seconds she is on the line to Barney Watterson, director of the CCIE in Frankfurt.

'You've got to set off the alarms,' she tells Watterson.

'But that will also activate the fire shutters. If anyone's inside, they'll be trapped.'

'We'll deal with it. Just do it, Barney. Please.'

The alarm starts shrieking as the team reach the hallway, sending them retreating into the Salle de Miroirs, just as the front door blows open with an almighty bang.

Three men appear in the doorway, dressed all in black, wearing helmets, with face coverings pulled over their mouths and noses. The first flings himself to the ground, raises his rifle to his shoulder and fires in one fluid movement. Argylle, at the rear of the retreating group, waits for the bullet to hit, and is shocked instead by the shattering of a mirror on the central pillar, realizing that the Russian must have mistaken his reflection for him.

To his left Wyatt returns fire, and the gunman falls backwards. But any relief is short-lived as he is replaced by three more troopers, their weapons drawn. The first of Argylle's team has reached the secret doorway at the far end of the room. At the back of the group, Wyatt and Carter have their pistols raised, but they know they are outnumbered and outgunned, particularly as Argylle, holding the wooden panel, is unable to draw his gun.

Another gunman raises his rifle and takes aim, and this time Argylle can tell he isn't going to miss. Just as Argylle drops the panel and reaches into his holster, there's a loud whirring sound and one of the Russians shouts and gestures to the ceiling. Momentarily distracted, his kneeling comrade looks up to see a heavy metal shutter descending at speed. The first man puts a hand on his comrade's shoulder and launches himself, head and shoulders first, under the falling shutter, perhaps hoping to jam it open, or imagining he had time to clear it, only to find himself pinioned to the floor, screaming in agony, when it crashes to the ground on top of him.

The rest of the team have now entered the secret passageway, but the trio bringing up the rear hesitate, transfixed by the writhing Russian, who has stopped making a noise, even though his mouth is still moving. His dark, terrified eyes are fixed on Argylle's face.

'We can't leave him like this,' says Carter.

'Give me a hand, Argylle,' says Wyatt, crossing the room.

When they get close to the man, it's clear he is nearly dead. His face is grey, his still-moving lips are turning blue.

'At least let's get him free of that thing,' says Wyatt, putting his meaty hands under the Russian's armpits.

'I really don't think you should—'

But Argylle's words are swallowed up by Carter's scream as Wyatt pulls the wounded Russian and his top half comes away from the shutter, his legs left behind on the other side of the metal grille.

'Ouch!' Dabrowski exclaims, and Coffey sucks in her breath as the two of them watch through the CCTV as the unfortunate Russian is divided in two.

'Is there another way out of there?' Coffey wants to know.

'Nope. The only exit is back under the shutter and through the front or the back kitchen door, which I believe is sealed up.'

'So they're no better off than they were before we set off the alarm?'

'Except that this time when they make a break for it the element of surprise will be on our side.'

It's not enough, and they both know it.

'Sooner or later we're going to have to shut off the alarm so the shutter goes up and they can get the hell outta there,' says Dabrowski. 'I just wish we could get a message to them so they're ready to go as soon as it lifts.'

Coffey looks down at her monitor, seeing at a glance that the connection is still down.

'I'm afraid they're going to have to work that out on their own.'

*

The team have fled to the basement, which is the only place they can get away from the shrill shriek of the alarm.

'There's no way out from down here. All it needs is for them to lob a grenade in the door and we're all fried,' says Schneider.

'That's why we have to get back up there and be ready with a plan for when those shutters go back up,' says Argylle.

'What makes you so sure they will?'

Argylle glances towards Carter, who explains: 'Because, Schneider, it's obvious Coffey set off that alarm to warn us that we had company. And she'll know we're trapped in here. She may not be able to talk to us, but she's got eyes on us through the CCTV. As soon as we're in position and give her the signal, she'll switch off the alarm.'

'And if she doesn't?' asks Quinn.

'She will.'

Argylle tries to invest his voice with a confidence he is far from feeling. The truth is, Frances Coffey is their only hope. There is no Plan B.

'Good man, Argylle,' mutters Dabrowski as the team reappear in the Salle de Miroirs and take up a formation, with Wyatt, Corcoran and Casner kneeling in the front with their weapons drawn and the others behind. Argylle himself is at the rear, the wooden panel safely under his arm.

Coffey cuts Dabrowski off and gets Quintano to put her back through to the CCIE.

'When I give the order, you need to cut the alarm and get that shutter up . . .'

The team are ready, muscles tensed. To Argylle, who bears the responsibility for leading the mission, every second feels like a lifetime. The alarm is still wailing, reverberating down his nerve endings. His mouth is dry and swallowing seems impossible.

Next to Quinn, Carter's shoulders shake.

And then:

The noise stops and there's a split second of pure silence. Then a rattle alerts them and before the shutter is halfway up, the front row are firing. Caught by surprise, the Russians fire back without thinking and, because they are standing, the bullets ricochet off the ascending metal shutter, one of them rebounding to hit the shooter squarely between his eyes. He falls to the ground, next to the severed legs of his colleague, his mouth a perfect circle of shock.

But by this time the middle row have charged forward and the front row are on their feet.

'Argylle! Move!' Wyatt has turned around to catch Argylle standing still, as if in a daze, clutching the panel in front of him as he gazes at a point to the side. '*Move, goddam it!*'

Jolted out of his reverie, Argylle refocuses. All around him is chaos, with shots fired and scuffles breaking out.

Noah Washington launches into his unique form of combat, his long limbs whirling in all directions, leaping through the air, his front leg extended. When his foot makes contact with a Russian's face there is a crunching noise that cuts right through the shouts and the gunfire. The Russian drops his gun and falls to the floor, rolling around, clutching his hands to the bloody pulp that used to be his nose. Another leap and Argylle doesn't hang around to see where Washington lands, but he hears the piercing shriek that follows.

He rushes towards the doorway, intent on saving the panel at all costs, but a hand clamps on to his arm, trying to pull him back. Without thinking, he swings around and drives the corner of the panel with the jutting rusty nail deep into the neck of the Russian who is trying to wrest it off him. The fountain of blood that sprays out across the room, dripping down the surface of the nearest mirrors, tells him he has hit a carotid artery.

'Look at the satellite picture,' Dabrowski tells Coffey urgently. 'There are two goons stationed out front of the building and more out back. Even if our guys get as far as the front door they're finished the second they step outside.'

'We have to get the Russians away from the front door. Distract them somehow. Any ideas?'

*

'Argylle, I got Coffey!' While the fighting has been going on, Barney Watterson and his team of CCIE hackers have been working out of the US consulate in Frankfurt to override the Russian scrambling software that jammed the team's signal, and finally Carter has re-established contact.

'Aubrey, you need to tell the team to hold back, and then get yourself to the carousel room fast.' Argylle's relief at the sound of Frances Coffey's voice is only partially offset by learning there are two Russians with AK-74s stationed outside the front door.

By now the surviving Russians inside the house have been backed into a corner of the room, their rifles next to useless in close-up combat.

'Wyatt, come and cover me. The rest of you, get ready to run, but not until I give you the signal. We've got company outside.'

The team back out of the Salle de Miroirs and slam shut the grand doors. It will buy them some time, but not much.

Instucted by Coffey, Argylle heads into the opposite room, leaving Wyatt keeping cover on the door and the rest of the team in the hallway, poised to escape.

'Okay, Aubrey, I want you to activate the automaton.'

'But how—'

'Work it out. I know you can.'

Argylle quickly surveys the mechanical box he'd noticed the first time he was here, running his hands around it until he finds a lever on the far side, which he pulls down without stopping to think.

Nothing happens.

'There must be handles, to wind the birds up.'

He opens a door in the front of the box and sees that Coffey's hunch is right. Inside are two wooden handles, which he turns simultaneously. It's hard going. There's a lot of resistance, but he cranks them around until they can go no further.

'Try the lever again.'

This time, there's an immediate response. A loud squawking and whirring coming from the tarpaulin-covered structure outside, and through the slit of a window he sees dents and bulges appearing in the tarpaulin itself as if there is something loose inside. The two

Russians on duty outside the main entrance look alarmed and start talking animatedly to each other.

As Argylle watches through the window, the men turn their backs on the building and approach the tarpaulin, their weapons drawn.

'Go!' he shouts at Wyatt, who sends Quinn, Carter and Washington out through the front door, a finger across his lips signalling the need for silence.

The three team members make it outside just as the Russians each take hold of a corner of the tarpaulin and lift it over the top, revealing an ornately painted man-sized birdcage in which two mechanical birds, one yellow, the other blue, zoom around the cage at speed on a complicated system of tracks, calling to each other as they swoop and dive, missing one another by mere inches. At the precise moment the two startled Spetsnaz open the cage door to investigate further, Quinn and Washington step in to push them inside, locking the door behind them and pulling down the tarpaulin, leaving the Russians trapped in the dark with the automatons, which are still zipping around the cage on their unstoppable course. There follows a series of screams as the tarpaulin bulges in the shape of an elbow or a knee. Then all is quiet.

'Now you get out of there,' Coffey commands.

But when Argylle reaches the doorway, the wood panel back in his grasp, he sees that the Russians who were holed up in the room of mirrors have shot a hole through the doors and, though Corcoran, Schneider and Wyatt are holding them off from the hallway, it's only a matter of time before they are overpowered. He needs to get the panel to safety, but before he can make a dash for it, a Russian who has just broken in through the sealed back door to the kitchen spots him and charges towards him.

Argylle has nowhere to go but back into the room from which he has just emerged, taking shelter behind the carousel. As the Russian approaches he drops the panel and starts the carousel turning by grabbing hold of one of the swings and yanking it around, sending the other three swings flying out, propelled by the centrifugal force. Taken by surprise, the Russian hasn't time to react before the full force of a suspended wooden seat hits him in the face, knocking him to the ground. But now there is another Russian coming, this one taller and broader than the last.

The carousel is still spinning. This time, Argylle leaps into the first bucket seat that swings past and, when it has spun a hundred and eighty degrees, he launches himself out, landing on top of the Russian and knocking him to the ground. His gun shoots out across the floor, and before he has a chance to register what has happened Argylle is standing over him with the barrel inches from his head.

Can he do it? Can he pull the trigger like this when it is a cold-blooded execution?

The moment stretches. Until the Russian reaches into a pouch on his vest and pulls out a grenade and Argylle shoots, grimacing as the blood sprays his face. Then he is running back around the carousel to pick up the panel.

'What are they doing, Glenn? Why are they holding back?'

'I can't get a visual.'

Coffey and Dabrowski are watching through the CCTV camera in the Salle de Miroirs as the remaining Russians huddle over something, their backpacks open on the floor beside them.

One of them gets up and steps back, so that finally they can see what it is they've been putting together.

'Jesus,' says Dabrowski. 'Is that—'

'That's what it looks like.'

'We've gotta drop the shutters again. Right now, and pray to God it's not too late.'

In the hallway, Wyatt is holding open the front door with one foot, leaving his hands free to fire through the broken doors at the Russians still penned in the mirror room. He is flanked by Corcoran and Schneider. Argylle is about to join them when a ball of fire comes barrelling towards the hallway. 'They've got a fucking flame thrower!' yells Schneider. The fireball hits Corcoran, who falls to the ground, blocking the doorway, his clothes ablaze, as two Russians approach from the newly opened back door. One of the Russians is familiar, even with a bandage around one eye. Sergei Denisov.

'Aubrey, I'm dropping the shutters. Get out of there. Now!' Coffey's voice is urgent in his ear.

But there isn't time.

'Go!' Argylle yells to Wyatt, who is on the ground tending to Corcoran. By now the hallway is full of smoke and the alarms once again scream into action. Then three things happen: Wyatt and Schneider drag the slumped body of Corcoran through the front door, slamming it shut behind them just as Denisov's meaty arm reaches out to grab Schneider's shoulder. At the same time the metal shutters slam to the floor, trapping the remaining Russians inside the Salle de Miroirs. As the corresponding shutter simultaneously comes down over the doorway to the carousel room, cutting off his only route of escape, Argylle slides underneath it, in desperation wedging the wooden panel in the shutter's way to buy himself a crucial split second more, scrambling into the carousel room just as the wood is crushed to pieces, splinters flying in all directions.

In the smoke-filled hallway Denisov drops to his knees, scraping up the pieces of whatever it was Argylle was carrying, knowing it's what Federov sent them to recover. Meanwhile, Argylle himself, with a whispered apology to the architects and glassworkers and stonemasons and art lovers and to the Empress Eugénie herself, hurls himself through the rose window of the carousel room, shattering a hundred and fifty years of history and landing sprawled on the gravel in an explosion of stained glass and twisted metal.

42

THE JOURNEY BACK TO THE HÔTEL BEAUX RÊVES TAKES JUST UNDER four hours, and no one says a word.

Tony Corcoran has been rushed to a private hospital on the outskirts of Paris, where a team of doctors are working to save him. He has sustained third-degree burns to his legs and torso, and a bullet wound to his chest. No one knows whether he is going to make it. The oldest in the team, he is still something of a mystery to Argylle. Quiet. Self-contained.

When Argylle crashed through the rose window it was Schneider who'd screamed at him as they raced for the bikes: 'Where's the panel? Where's the fucking map?' And Wyatt, who'd witnessed everything through the window in the hallway, who'd replied: 'He smashed it! He used it to wedge open the shutter and totally crushed it!'

And now no one is speaking, but he hears the accusations in their silence, and they are deafening.

Back in Belgium, they disappear wordlessly off to their individual rooms to wait for the evening's debrief.

At seven, they gather in Meeting Room One.

No one looks at Argylle.

Coffey is taking the debrief from the States, courtesy of Bright Eyes, before boarding the red-eye to join them in Europe tomorrow. She appears on the white wall at the front of the room via a projector connected to Will Hooper's laptop, beaming around at the group from a bland, anonymous office somewhere in Delaware.

'First, I know you'll all be anxious to hear how Tony Corcoran is doing. The good news is he's out of immediate danger.' There is a faint hissing sound as the group collectively exhale.

'We don't yet know his long-term prognosis. He's still in a medically induced coma, but the initial skin graft on his burns has been a success and the bullet missed his vital organs so at least his family can take heart from that.'

His family. The two words drive a splinter into Argylle's heart.

'Second, I want to thank you all for what you did over there in Fontainebleau. I know it was tough. And I want to offer you all, particularly Aubrey, who led the mission, my sincere congratulations on a job well done.'

'Bullshit!' The explosion comes from Schneider, who clearly can no longer hold himself in check. 'Corcoran nearly died. And for what? So that Argylle could destroy the thing we were sent to find just to save his own ass.'

'Be fair, Schneider,' Carter interjects. 'He also stopped it getting into enemy hands. That's gotta be worth something.'

Coffey frowns.

'If you're talking about the map, Matt, we have it right here. Hold on.' She roots around among some papers on the desk next to her, the rustling loud in the computer speakers, before holding up a sheet of A3 paper with clearly identifiable markings.

Wyatt sits up straight. 'But I watched it being smashed to oblivion. The Russians were on their knees scrabbling for the pieces. *I saw it.*'

'Ah, but maybe you missed the part earlier on when Aubrey rather brilliantly held up the map to the CCTV camera, knowing we'd be able to get a still from it. Or, to be completely accurate, he held it up to a mirror that was at exactly the right angle for us to be able to take a still from the reflection and then flip it.'

Woody Wyatt remembers now how the shutter had come up and he'd turned to find Argylle standing as if in a daze. His own surge of frustration. *Well, I'll be . . .*

'How the hell did the Russians know we were there?' Argylle asks abruptly, changing the subject. 'Mount Athos we could just about explain away, but this . . . It seems like everywhere we go, they're right there with us.'

Coffey pauses. Looks around the group. Because her default expression is a smile, when it's not there the absence is striking.

'Did anyone use a sat-phone at any point early on in the mission?'

The team swap sideways glances at each other. *Was it you?* In the end it is Martin Casner who clears his throat.

'I used one in Monaco,' he says defensively. 'It was the only way the rest of us who weren't directly involved in the action could find out what was going on when all the plans suddenly changed.'

Coffey sighs.

'You know better than to use an encrypted line in such a sensitive situation, Martin. You must have realized the Russians would be looking out for any sign of encrypted communication.'

'You might as well walk around with a megaphone, shouting, "Listen to this!" ' says Will Hooper, shaking his head in disgust.

'They'll have logged that line after that, so they'd get an alert the second anyone used it again. Which I'm guessing you have, Martin.'

Now Casner looks positively shamefaced. His voice has rough shards of grit in it when he mumbles, 'Once. On the bus to Fontainebleau this morning.'

'His mom has cancer,' says Washington quietly.

Coffey pauses, feeling her heart fold in on itself, but her expression remains stony.

'I'm truly sorry to hear that, Martin, but there is never an excuse for putting the team at risk. The Russians would have been looking out for that signal. As soon as you switch it on again – *bam* – it's like sending them an open invitation.'

'So you don't think they could have been tipped off by one of us?' asks Argylle.

'What the hell!' Schneider's outburst earns him a withering look from Will Hooper, who is slouching against the wall at the front of the room, moderating the meeting.

'I understand why you might feel offended, Matt,' says Coffey, serene now. 'But you must consider that Aubrey is new to the team and it's perfectly proper for him to ask these questions. The answer is that we are confident there was no leak of information from the inside. With Dabrowski locked up, the team is now watertight. This was a slip-up on our part. Martin should have known better. Nothing more.'

On the way out of the meeting room Schneider jostles past Argylle. 'Nice of you to keep us in the loop, buddy.'

Out in the corridor, Argylle catches up with Carter and Wyatt. 'Are you two mad at me too?'

Carter stops. Gives him a sideways look. 'I gotta admit I'm torn, Argylle. On one hand, I gotta hand it to you, that business with the map and the mirror was smart. But on the other hand . . . how come we're the last to know about it? We're supposed to be your team-mates, and sometimes it feels like you don't trust us at all.'

In his room, Argylle can't stop thinking about what she'd said. *Does* he trust them, these new teammates of his? When they're out on mission, he feels he would trust them with his life – *does* trust them with his life. And yet . . .

He slides out the drawer in the desk where he keeps his journal, unscrews the nib of the heavy silver pen his mum gave him when he first went away to school and shakes into his palm the bullet he rescued from Samra's Quran. Again he goes through the justifications in his head. Just because it exactly matches the bullets from his own Agency-issue Glock doesn't mean anything. Neither does the fact it went through Samra's back. There are easy explanations for both those things.

He ought to throw it away. Striding across to the tiny bathroom with its beige bathroom suite, he lifts the lid on the pedal bin and tosses the bullet inside.

Four and a half minutes later, he fishes it back out.

When your parents – the people you love most in the world – turn out to have lied to you your whole life, you develop an intolerance for trust that never leaves you.

His phone lights up with a text message as he returns the pen to the drawer.

It's from Quinn: *I have a bottle of Courvoisier and a need to get shit-faced. Join me?*

His shoulders relax. Maybe he hasn't alienated *everyone* after all.

Do you need to ask? On my way.

In her office in Delaware, Frances Coffey takes off her rubber-soled shoes and wearily massages her feet while she studies the printout of Henri Dumas's map that was once scratched into a wooden panel and has now been transferred by the miracles of modern technology to a computer drive via a mirror and a CCTV camera lens.

The Agency's top cartographers and geographers have pored over the lines and markings, the scratched words in shaky capital letters, some useful – MONTAGNE, CHEMIN, CHEMIN DE FER, PORTE, GRAND ARBRE (mountain, path, railway, door, big tree) – others less so after over sixty years: CAMP, POTEAU, CASERNE (camp, post, barracks).

Though the prisoners wouldn't have been told place names and locations, Dumas had clearly played a prominent enough role in the design of the project, whatever it was, to gain a fairly comprehensive overview of the site. From the details on his map, the experts have been able to pinpoint the location – a mountain range in Poland called the Tatras, part of a larger ridge of mountains, the Carpathians, that stretches along the spine of Eastern Europe, from the Czech Republic, through Poland and Slovakia, ending in Romania. They even have the name of the nearest town, Zakopane, in the foothills of the High Tatra Mountains, which before the war would just have been establishing itself as the bustling ski resort it is now. Using that as a starting point and following Dumas's map, they've been able to track some eight kilometres from the town around the base of the mountains to a small tourist outpost called Kira Leśnicka, from where the slopes of the mountains start to rise up, with various trails leading through the valleys and over the mountains themselves.

Frustratingly, the missing chip of wood makes it impossible to narrow down the location further and, having called up the satellite view of the area and been confronted with a vast expanse of uninterrupted green, Coffey baulks at the scale of the task in front of her. She doesn't even know what it is she's looking for.

Break it down, she tells herself, as she used to all those years ago when she was sitting in the archives, surrounded by dusty boxes of files and records that hadn't been properly organized since the Agency's inception. *Break it down into its smallest parts.* She divides the screen into a grid of squares and then makes each individual square into a separate full-screen picture and calls up one after the other. Zooming in. Looking for something. Anything. Not knowing what she's looking for, but trusting she'll recognize it when she sees it, she cannot delegate this part to anyone else. Nor would she want to.

Break it down.

It's when she's studying the seventh square that something makes her pause. By this stage, when she's been scrutinizing green treetops for over an hour, she wonders if she is starting to see things that aren't there, like some mirage. But no, the more she looks, the more she is convinced there is something, well, *off*, about the scenery she is looking at. There is nothing concrete. More trees! More rugged rocks! But don't the trees look different from the others in that section? More regular. Fewer dead trunks breaking up the uniformity of the green canopy of foliage.

With her feet up on the desk, she steeples her hands, deep in thought. Then she presses the intercom. 'Mike, I need someone who knows about plants. Who have we got?'

Randall suggests a name from the ecology faculty at Harvard. But gut instinct tells Coffey she doesn't need an academic, she needs someone with earth under their fingernails.

'Where would you go to find the biggest selection of plants in the world, Mike?'

Randall pauses. 'Well, I once visited a place called Kew Gardens in London . . .'

'That's it! You're a genius. Can you get Kew Gardens on the phone for me?'

Gerald Thomlinson has a voice that sounds as solid and steady as the trees to which he has devoted his professional life. Even when he has to call one of the younger reception staff to come to operate the technology for him, Kew Gardens' head of arboriculture doesn't become flustered. 'It's funny, I can remember the names of literally thousands of plants, but ask me my computer password and I go completely blank.'

He is in his office – 'A misnomer, if there ever was one,' he chuckles. 'Airing cupboard would be more accurate.' Then there is a break while he ascertains that Coffey understands what an airing cupboard is. 'One is never quite sure which terms cross the Atlantic, as it were.' Finally he is set up, sitting in Kew looking at the same image as Coffey all those thousands of miles away.

'I just want to know if anything strikes you as odd in this picture. For example—'

'That line of new growth.'

'Pardon?'

'Forgive me for interrupting you, but I assume you're talking about that line where the trees seem more densely packed, without so many gaps? Well, to me that looks like new-growth forest. Where there is old growth, some individual trees will have died over the years, so you'd expect to see breaks in the canopy where there might be a stump or just some debris there on the ground. If you zoom in on the area directly above it, you'll see what I mean.'

Coffey does as instructed and sees that there is a layer of woody debris lying on the ground where a stricken tree has left the forest floor open to the sky.

'But this line here?' She runs a finger along her screen where the trees are more densely packed, no inch of forest floor showing, before remembering he can't see her. Still, instinct tells her they are talking about the same thing.

'Yes, that's very interesting. Can you see how it runs along almost from that hiker's cabin in the Chochołowska valley – do forgive my pronunciation – to the shrine in the Kościeliska valley, but not in this middle part?'

'Where the mountain starts?'

'Exactly. Well, it appears to me like there may have been a train line there at one point, going into the mountain. But the opening must have been blocked up at some time, and the track itself has been disused for so long the vegetation that was planted has grown right over the top of it. Was there mining in that region, do you know?'

There's a feeling Frances Coffey gets when something starts to fall into place that's like a tingling in the very marrow of her bones.

'Yes, there was metal mining along that whole mountain range for centuries. The Germans took over the mines during the war because there's a rich seam of antimony there.'

'I'm afraid you'll have to elucidate – I'm good with plants but woefully ignorant about most other things.'

'I very much doubt that. Antimony is a semi-metallic element found in nature. Ancient civilizations used it in medicine and cosmetics. It can also be added to other metals to strengthen them, and if you add antimony to lead bullets it makes them harder and faster. So you can see why it might have been in pretty high demand during the war. And the Tatra Mountains, which are part of the Polish spur of the Western Carpathians, have it in spades. We believe it's possible there might have been a secret munitions factory there, where the Nazis were manufacturing weapons.'

'Perfect. So there would probably be an existing goods track to get the antimony out of there, and some kind of tunnel system already inside.'

'A train track running into that mountain and out the other side?'

'Exactly.'

'And when the Germans decided to stop using it, they planted trees to disguise the fact it had ever existed.'

'It would seem so.'

After Coffey has thanked Gerald Thomlinson profusely and hung up, she sits still for a moment, while the tingling becomes a buzz that vibrates through her body. Then she logs back into her computer and calls up Google.

'Nazi Gold Train', she types into the search box.

43

WHEN YOU CAN'T LEAVE THE HOUSE AND YOUR FAMILY AND FRIENDS all believe you're banged up in a maximum-security jail, and you've read every book from cover to cover and watched all the videos, and you can't bear to be inside your own head a minute longer, a farmhouse in rural Montana is the most desolate place to be.

As the hot mid-afternoon sun slices like a glittering blade across the baked back lawn and the distant mountains show their barren crowns to the cloudless sky, Glenn Dabrowski is eating a bowl of Cheerios with his feet up on the desk, and keeping busy by watching the CCTV footage from the Hôtel Beaux Rêves. The truth is he finds himself spending more and more time here in his study, watching the screens. He likes feeling connected to something, reminding himself that there is a world out there in which people are going about the business of being alive.

It's just after 11 p.m. in Belgium and the lobby is quiet. Just the mechanic, Jim Ryder, wearily bashing the vending machine that has taken his money but still refuses to dispense his dishwater cappuccino into its white plastic cup. Dabrowski switches to another camera, trained on a corridor whose emptiness uncomfortably echoes his current state of mind. He switches again, sighing when he finds yet another deserted corridor. But just as he is reaching for the mouse to switch to yet another vantage point, a door opens at the end of the corridor and a figure emerges.

Aubrey Argylle, his hair looking decidedly awry.

Dabrowski checks the room plan he has tacked up on the wall next to his monitor to see whose room it is. A smile plays around his mouth. 'Lucky mother,' he mutters out loud.

Argylle disappears through the fire exit at the end of the corridor that leads to the stairwell. As there is no other sign of life, Dabrowski switches to the camera on the ceiling of the first landing stage. Argylle is heading upstairs with his hand on the rail, his shadow looming on the opposite wall.

As Dabrowski gets ready to switch again, his attention is caught by a movement at the bottom of the screen, a dark blur that frustratingly disappears from the camera's viewpoint. He leans forward just as a gloved hand appears on the handrail above. Heading in the same direction as Argylle.

Dabrowski gets an uncomfortable, tight feeling in his ribcage. The shadow on the opposite wall is indistinct and grainy and distorted, revealing nothing. It could be Erin Quinn, he tells himself. Perhaps Argylle left something in her room.

Why would she – or anyone – be wearing gloves on a warm summer's night?

On the next landing, the hidden figure on the stairs stops, its identity still obscured, as if whoever it is knows just where the CCTV cameras are – and how to avoid them. The shadow raises its left arm, elbow bent. It is holding something that at first appears only as a blurred shape, but then sharpens as it moves into the light. Dabrowski sits up straight in his chair. Slams down his half-empty bowl on the desk. The shadow's right hand slickly attaches something to the end of the gun it holds in its left.

Dabrowski has placed enough silencers on weapons over his years with the CIA, and Delta Force before that, to recognize what's happening.

Instantly he is on the line to Coffey's office, only to be told Coffey is in transit and not contactable. 'It's Dan Defoe . . . I need you to get her on her private line . . . I don't care if she *is* about to board a plane,' he tells a flustered Joe Quintano.

*

On board the overnight United Airlines transatlantic flight from Newark to Antwerp, inconspicuous and anonymous among all the other stoic, set-faced passengers, Frances Coffey exchanges a brief smile with her neighbour – the kind of no-eye-contact smile universally recognized as meaning *I'm harmless but please don't talk to me*. The man in question, a thirty-two-year-old tech manager, is relieved. He has already pegged her as a middle-aged mom, possibly travelling to Belgium to meet a new grandchild, and knows, without a doubt, that her conversation would be drearily limited. If you were to ask Coffey what her superpower was, this might well be it. This ability to convince people that they already know everything there is to know about her, that her very ordinariness renders her not worth the trouble of engaging with.

'Ladies and gentlemen, as we are about to take off, we ask you to please turn off your electronic devices,' says the disembodied voice of the chief stewardess.

Coffey reaches into her bag and, after a quick glance at the screen, switches her phone to airline mode – *Ah, bless*, thinks her neighbour, magnanimously, *so anxious to obey the rules* – a sixteenth of a second before an agitated Joe Quintano attempts to make contact.

There's a heavy stone in the pit of Dabrowski's stomach as Quintano tells him the bad news. 'Get on to Hooper,' he commands Quintano. 'And tell him to cram as many cigarettes in his mouth as he can and light them all up at once under the smoke detector in his room.'

'But Hooper doesn't—'

'*Just do it!*'

While he waits nervously, Dabrowski flicks the camera viewpoint to the third-floor corridor. If Argylle has already reached his room, his chances improve. He will at least be able to look through the spyhole in the door to see who his visitor is, though that won't help him if it turns out to be someone he trusts. Which is highly likely.

But Dabrowski's hopes are dashed when he picks up Argylle on the third floor and sees that he has paused to read something on his phone. Something that is causing a small smile to break across his face.

Through his headphones he hears Joe Quintano remonstrating

with someone, then he comes back to him. 'Sorry, Defoe. Hooper says he hasn't got any cigarettes and it's a disgusting habit and he doesn't want to do anything without Coffey's say-so.'

'Tell him to go down to the vending machine in the lobby and buy a packet of smokes.'

'He says if he lights up in the room the alarm will go off.'

Alone in his Montana study, Dabrawski rolls his eyes to the heavens. 'Tell him if he doesn't do this right away, someone is going to fucking die!' So much for staying calm. 'And tell him if that happens, he'll be out of a job and I will make it my life's work to make sure he never gets another one.'

The shadow reaches the second-floor landing, the figure still managing to dodge the CCTV angles. Dabrowski flicks to the other camera, hoping to find the third-floor corridor empty and Argylle safely ensconced in his room. The stone in his stomach grows heavier as he sees Coffey's most promising new recruit still standing exactly where he was before. '*Move, for Chrissakes,*' Dabrowski mutters. '*Just go!*'

Flick. Dabrowski is back on the stairwell watching the shadow reaching the third-floor landing, the gloved hand on the rail.

Flick. Here's Argylle finally replacing his phone in his pocket and moving off down the corridor.

'*Come on.*' Dabrowski no longer sees the bank of screens on his messy desk or the printouts pinned to the walls or the distant mountains through the study's single small window. Instead, his whole being is concentrated on a featureless corridor in a hotel on an industrial estate halfway across the world where a young man with mussed-up hair pauses outside a closed door to fumble for his key just as the fire-escape door at the far end of the corridor swings open.

'He's done it!' Even without Quintano's shout of triumph Dabrowski would have known that the fire alarm had gone off by the reaction of the figure on the screen: Argylle stops in the act of turning his key in the lock and swings his head towards the end of the corridor, where the door that had swung open just moments before now slams abruptly shut.

*

Seven thousand kilometres away, Argylle is not enjoying hearing the sound of a fire alarm again so soon after the traumatic events in the Maison du Plaisir.

'What's going on?' he asks Wyatt as the two of them descend the stairs together.

'Beats me.'

Like any normal hotel guest turfed out of his room late at night, the pair know the most likely explanation is a malfunction or a false alarm, or someone having a crafty cigarette. But they're not normal guests so they can't discount the added possibility of an enemy attack or some other diversionary tactic. They step out into the hotel fore-court, where already a throng is gathered, all with bags slung over their shoulders or across their bodies under their nightclothes. Iden-tification. Handgun. Just the essentials.

Carter is wearing an outsized T-shirt with a canvas tote bag over her shoulder bearing the logo and the dates of the fictitious waste haulage association convention. They were all issued with them when they first arrived at Hôtel Beaux Rêves. Argylle hasn't yet been able to bring himself to use his. He eyes Carter's ensemble. 'If I'd known we were dressing up . . .'

Carter gives him a withering look and says, 'If I'd known we were dumbing down . . .'

Quinn appears, wrapped in a sheet.

'I knew it,' says Schneider.

'Knew what?'

'I knew you were the type to sleep naked.'

'You're such a jerk, Schneider.'

In Montana, Dabrowski is slumped on the desk in relief. Flicking through the different CCTV camera feeds at the Hôtel Beaux Rêves, he watches as doors open and figures emerge, some still dressed, others wearing all manner of strange bed gear. He tries to catch up with the elusive shadow that was stalking Argylle, but it has faded into the sea of people. He switches to the external CCTV with a view of the hotel car park, where, already, the hotel guests have gathered. He recognizes the hulking figure of Alex Kellerman, the explosives expert, and

Brandon Reynolds, wearing pyjamas and looking like he's at a school sleepover rather than on CIA business, and, further away, Matsyuk and Lawler. Scanning the group, he identifies the other members of the squad, who have become by this point more familiar to him than his own brothers and sisters back home. Counts them. Counts them again.

Two people are missing.

'Where's Washington?' asks Will Hooper.

'And Casner?' adds Wyatt, casting around.

Argylle looks up at the third floor of the hotel facade, working out which room is his. There's a light on in his room. Did he leave it like that before he went to see Quinn earlier?

The thought of Erin Quinn brings the blood rushing to his face, and he is glad of the distraction when the lobby door opens and Martin Casner emerges, scowling.

'I knew it would be a false alarm,' Casner says in reply to Hooper's questions. 'Some asshole dicking about.' He glowers at Argylle as he says that, as if holding him personally responsible.

Now the hotel's uPVC front door is opening again, to reveal the unmistakable figure of Noah Washington strolling out, wearing eye-catching silk pyjamas in a paisley print and an eyemask pushed up on the top of his head

'Relax, I just dropped a benzo, that's all,' he tells Wyatt and Argylle. 'Man needs his beauty sleep.'

Ten thousand metres above the Atlantic Ocean, Coffey uses the satellite phone at the rear of the plane to dial into her message service and finds she has missed seven calls from Joe Quintano and one voice message to call Dabrowski. Conscious of the slumbering passengers just feet away, she keys in the number.

'So they're after Argylle?' she says softly, after Dabrowski explains what happened at the Hôtel Beaux Rêves. Her voice is calm and level, betraying nothing of the heavy weight that has strapped itself to her heart at the confirmation of just how much danger her most promising new recruit is in.

'Looks that way. Whatever he's discovered, or thinks he's

discovered, has put a target on his back. I think we should send in extra protection.'

'I'm not sure that's wise. The others will smell a rat, and the person we're looking for will go to ground.'

She hears Dabrowski's deep sigh even through all the thousands of miles of empty air that separate them.

'Okay, but warn him. That's the least we can do.'

44

THE LITTLE BOY IN THE SUPERMAN OUTFIT CLIMBS DOGGEDLY towards the summit of the wooden climbing frame as Frances Coffey takes the plastic lid off her supersized coffee and blows, attempting to get the liquid to a temperature she can drink. She has come straight from the airport and every cell in her body aches with weariness.

It's a clear day and the sun takes the edge off the fresh breeze, which is why, even with her head bent, she notices when someone blocks the light.

'Thank you so much for coming.'

Aubrey Argylle drops down on to the bench next to his boss, pulling a one-sided smile that says, *As if I had a choice.*

'You look tired,' he tells her, and Coffey is startled. It's so rare that anyone gets personal with her. She's the operational head of a huge national organization. Maintaining some sort of distance is vital when you are asking people to potentially lay down their lives. Authority is paramount. Still, perhaps her fatigue makes her less guarded, because she doesn't shut him down.

'You know, Agency people don't usually ask me how I feel or comment on how I look,' she says.

'Maybe they need you not to be human.'

Coffey nods. He's perceptive, this one.

'Anyway, I grabbed some sleep, so I'm fine. Which is more than you, I gather.'

'You heard about the fire alarm, then.'

'I did.'

His steady gaze is fixed on her. Assessing.

'You ordered it to go off, didn't you?'

'I did. Or, to be completely accurate, it was authorized by my office in my absence but with my blessing. The truth is, you're a lucky man, Aubrey. I can't go into specifics, but you have a guardian angel watching over you and, last night, he clocked you were in grave danger and activated the alarm.'

'But why would I be in danger in the hotel, with my teammates?'

Coffey doesn't reply. She knows how smart Argylle is and that he already knows the answer to his own question.

'You took something from Asif Samra's body on the beach at Mount Athos. I believe it was one of our bullets.'

He doesn't hide his surprise. 'But how—'

'It doesn't matter how I know. What matters is why you didn't tell me.'

Now it is Argylle's turn not to answer, so Coffey presses on. 'It's because you don't trust me, isn't it? Because you suspect there's a traitor in the team and you think the betrayal might go all the way to the top?'

Argylle drums his fingers against his leg and says nothing.

'Last night someone with a gun stopped to screw on a noise suppressor and then stalked you through the corridors of the hotel. I think you saw them.'

Argylle shakes his head. Then relents.

'I saw *something*. At the end of the corridor. Just a glimpse of a hand. I couldn't get a clear look. Maybe there was a gun. Maybe not.'

'So why didn't they shoot?'

'Because the fire alarm went off.'

'And why did the fire alarm go off? Do you see what I'm saying, Aubrey? We triggered the alarm because we are on your side. We have your back. And we want what you want – to find out who is betraying the team.'

In front of them, the little boy in the Superman outfit has reached the top of the climbing frame. He turns to wave to his parents, who are seated on the bench opposite Argylle and Coffey, and loses his balance, tumbling to the ground.

Argylle is up in an instant, but Coffey holds him back. It's one thing for them to be sitting here, like a regular mother and son sharing a coffee in the sunshine, but Argylle is an imposing figure, incongruous in a children's playground in rural Belgium. They can't draw attention to themselves.

Instead, it's the parents who rush to the side of the screaming boy, wiping his tears. Coffey is conscious of the intensity of Argylle's gaze, how he is drinking the little family in. She understands all too well that it doesn't matter how old you are, sometimes the fact of being an orphan can hit you like a sledgehammer from the blue, turning you instantly into a bewildered child.

'So when you said in the meeting yesterday that the Russians were monitoring the sat-phone . . .'

'Yes, that was a lie, I'm afraid. Martin shouldn't have used it, that's true, but it isn't what brought the Russians to Fontainebleau. Someone in the team is tipping off the Russians about our every move and we need to smoke them out by making them feel confident enough that the heat is off them that they carry on, giving us a chance to catch them out. Otherwise . . .'

'Otherwise what?'

'Otherwise we'd have to get rid of the whole team and start again, and believe me that's not something I want to do. There are some outstanding operatives in that group who I don't want to lose. Including you.'

'But you already have Dabrowski. Are you telling me there's a second traitor in the team?'

Coffey hesitates, and he gets the feeling she is debating whether to tell him something, something she is holding back.

'I'm afraid that is what I'm saying.'

'So why are you telling me? Why now? Aren't you worried I'll go straight to tell the others?'

Coffey shakes her head. Reaching into her neat brown leather handbag, she withdraws a packet of menthol cigarettes.

'Do you mind?' Argylle shakes his head.

Coffey lights one. Takes a long drag. Grimaces. 'Ugh, I can't stand these things. It's like smoking a toothbrush.'

'So why do it?'

'I'm hoping if I make the experience of smoking unpleasant enough, it'll force me to give up.'

'Going well so far, huh?'

'The truth is, you need to know that you're now a target, Aubrey. Someone must have seen you pick up that bullet and now they're after you. And now I have a moral dilemma. Do I pull you from the team to keep you safe, or do I use you as bait to draw out the traitor?'

'Or do I quit the whole thing. Go back to Thailand. Chill in my hammock and forget I ever met you? No offence.'

'None taken. You could do that, certainly, though I'd advise you hitch your hammock well away from the Sam Gor's patch. But if you did that I would lose someone who is more suited to this life than anyone else I've recruited in my forty years in the Agency.'

'I'm not sure that's a compliment.'

'Not entirely, no. You see, many people have the skills, but not everyone has the temperament. You have a natural detachment that makes you a brilliant operative, though I've been around long enough to know that kind of detachment is dearly bought. And I'm truly sorry for that.

'Not many people find their calling in life, Aubrey. It's both your good fortune and your curse that you've found yours, and that it has turned out to be us.'

The parents of the small boy have stood up, dusting themselves down. They watch as their intrepid child once again turns his attention to the climbing frame, his brush with danger seemingly forgotten.

'Tell me the truth,' Argylle says. 'Is this mission really about the

Amber Room, or is it just a ruse to flush out the traitor in our midst? Because, if so, it seems like an awful lot of trouble to go to for just one person.'

Coffey nods as she flings her half-smoked cigarette to the ground and grinds it under her heel. To his surprise, she then picks up the butt and drops it in a nearby bin.

'After the failed mission in Isfahan I went back to the archives where I started out all those years ago and spent weeks going through the files – old missions, memoirs, journals. I read everything I could find about double agents and the effect they have, and you know something, Aubrey, it only takes one or two rogue individuals to bring down an entire organization. I kept thinking about Philby, Burgess and the other members of the Cambridge Five, and how each of them managed to throw a grenade into the heart of British intelligence from which it has never truly recovered.

'It's every spymaster's greatest fear. But no, the mission isn't a ruse. Vasily Federov is a very real threat to global stability and we're extremely concerned at how much populist support he is garnering among the disaffected voters in Russia and in the former Soviet states. If he succeeds in fulfilling his promise to return the Amber Room, his stock will be sky-high and chances are he will seize power and then use his popularity among the pro-Russia groups in the former territories to try to force a reunion of the Soviet states, through war if necessary. It's vital we stop him.

'But I can't pretend it isn't also a useful veil for us to root out the person who is selling out their teammates and the Agency itself.'

'So, after all this, I *am* a stooge, then?'

His voice has a sharp edge to it, but when Frances Coffey turns towards him, those keen grey eyes searching his face so it feels as if there is nowhere to hide, the bitterness inside him drains away.

'I needed to bring in someone extraordinary, Aubrey. Someone who is outside of the team yet capable of getting right into the heart of it. Someone with enough empathy to encourage loyalty but enough detachment to understand that everyone is a suspect. Someone with courage and integrity and decency.'

'And nothing to lose?'

'Yes. That too.'

The family are packing up now. The boy is tired out, and as the father carries him his head rests on his dad's shoulder. The three of them walk away, and Coffey feels the longing of the man next to her burn as fiercely as a flame.

'Do you have any suspicions about who it might be?' she asks him once they are out of sight.

He shakes his head. 'I'm pretty sure it's not Carter or Wyatt, or Quinn, or Washington either. Even Schneider wouldn't sell out his friends for money.'

'What makes you think it's about money?'

He turns to her, frowning.

'Vasily Federov is a billionaire. What else would it be about?'

'Patriotism. Idealism. You know the Cambridge Five genuinely believed that communism was the only real way to combat fascism. They passed state secrets to the Soviets because they wanted an end to the kind of political system that had given rise to Adolf Hitler. So now think again about your teammates. Can you really tell me none of them are capable of idealism? You don't join the CIA unless you're prepared to lay down your life for a cause greater than you yourself. Well, what if their greater cause just happens to be the opposite of ours?'

As Argylle crosses the car park, heading back to the hotel, he sees Carter and Wyatt huddled round the side of the building.

Wyatt looks up as he approaches and Argylle thinks he reads relief on the big man's face. Carter keeps her face turned towards the ground for as long as she can, but when he says, tentatively, 'Carter? Keira?' she looks up and he sees her eyes are red and puffy.

She has a letter in her hand and his heart sinks as he remembers the letter she'd written to her parents.

'Bad news?'

She nods.

'It's from Mom. She says' – Carter raises the paper so she can read from it, and Argylle sees that her hand is shaking – '*Why did you have to tell us? It's so selfish of you. We might have guessed, but we always had the option not to know. Now you've taken that away from us.'*

'They would rather you'd kept it to yourself so they could look the other way and pretend you were who they wanted you to be? Way to go, Mom and Dad,' says Wyatt.

Argylle feels nauseated. 'I encouraged you to send that letter. I made the wrong call. I'm so sorry, Carter.'

'Back off with that white-straight-male-saviour shit, Argylle. I wrote that letter all by myself and I'm not sorry either. I felt like I was carrying an enormous weight around until I sent it off. Now it's lifted off me and I can stop thinking about it. I wish they'd reacted differently, but I'm still glad I wrote it.'

'She tell you not to come home?'

Carter shakes her head. 'No. But I'm not going back there. Not anytime soon, at least. I'm through with being half a person, just so's my mom doesn't have to answer any awkward questions in her book club.'

Wyatt shakes his head. 'Look at us three. I can't go home because my dad scares the shit out of me. Carter won't go home because her parents think she's selfish for telling them the truth, and Argylle hasn't even got a home, poor bastard.'

'Jesus,' says Carter, looking from one to the other with an expression of dawning horror. 'Don't tell me that means I have to be in some kind of club with you two assholes. Just when I thought my day couldn't get any worse.'

45

'I'VE NEVER EVEN HEARD OF THE CARPATHIAN MOUNTAINS. THEY sound kinda cool.'

Anywhere that wasn't Montana would sound kinda cool.

'I don't suppose you'd think that if you were one of the thousands of men and women who were forced by the Nazis to dig out mile after mile of tunnels underneath them.'

'No, I don't suppose I would,' says Dabrowski softly. Coffey has this way of reminding a person, without saying much at all, of how small you are against the bigger picture; the great tide of human suffering on which you are just the tiniest leaf being tossed around on the surface, hoping not to drown.

They are talking on a secure line, Coffey from her room in the Hôtel Beaux Rêves and Dabrowski in his Montana study. When she'd phoned, she'd apologized for calling so early and promised not to take up too much of his time, and he hadn't had the heart to tell her how little he slept these days and how he wouldn't mind if she talked for hours. He relished the sound of another human voice.

'So tell me more about why the Nazis were so interested in these mountains.'

'Not so much the mountains themselves as what they contained. Gold, silver, iron, coal and antimony.'

Dabrowski has already read up on the little-known element that turns out to be so key to the munitions industry.

'So they literally dug through the mountains to get at this stuff?'

'Most of the mines would already have existed. The Poles had been digging out antimony for centuries. But in order to get the quantities they needed for their war effort, the Nazis would have had to fundamentally extend the tunnel system and infrastructure for the trains to transport it in and out of the mountain.

'There would have been vast underground caverns where the munitions were stored and maybe even manufactured and, from the looks of it, a terminus for the trains. The way they'd do it is to bore out tunnels one on top of the other and then collapse the floor of the upper one, creating huge secret spaces they could use for any purpose they chose – to develop and manufacture weapons, or as underground bunkers. Or storage units for stolen treasures they wanted to keep hidden from the Red Army.'

There is a pause now, and the air itself stills before Dabrowski says, 'Like the Amber Room.'

'It's possible. Treasure hunters have long believed the Nazis might have hidden a trainload of looted treasures in a different mountain range in Poland called the Sowies, or the Owls, where there's an established warren of tunnels and caves known as Project Riese.'

'Sure. The Nazi Gold Train.'

'Got it in one. But since '45, the whole world has been over every last inch of those mountains looking for it and they've yet to find a thing. But what if they've been looking in the wrong place? The wrong mountains? This is an area that has never been properly searched. It had no strategic value beyond its mineral content. It's largely unexplored. There used to be a trainline going from Galicia in Ukraine, which was under Nazi control from 1941, and there were spurs off from it all over the place, going to God knows where. We believe the track on our map might have been just such a spur.'

'And you're really gonna tell the team where they're going? Knowing the mole is going to feed it straight back to Federov?'

'I know it's a risk, Glenn, but our friends at the CCIE have done a brilliant job at harnessing Mainway and Optic Nerve to mount surveillance on the team's phones and laptops.' Coffey feels like she is talking a foreign language sometimes when it comes to the codenames for Agency software and operating programs. 'We may have a chance to catch our traitor before we even leave for Poland.'

'Yeah, but if we don't, it means we're basically racing Federov and his goons to the finish line. Why don't we just feed our guys the wrong information and let them send the Russians off to Siberia or something?'

'It's too late for that. If there really is a traitor in our team, Federov will already know exactly where our temporary HQ is and he'll have eyes on us twenty-four seven. He may not be president yet, but he's got the secret services in his pocket already, thanks to his father-in-law and his billions. He's not going to just take our guy's word for it about where we're heading.'

'He'll track us.'

'Of course.'

'But if we do manage to intercept the message to him, at least we've nailed the traitor.'

Coffey is quiet for a moment, as she paces her small double room. Thoughtful. There's a print on the wall, a seaside scene in various shades of beige, to match the decor.

'I know how much you want this to all be over, Glenn.'

Now it is Dabrowski's turn to lapse into silence, over there in his untidy study in that deadened farmhouse in the back end of nowhere, thousands of miles from the life that used to be his.

'I promise you it will end soon. And your sacrifice won't be forgotten. You have my word.'

'Have you picked up anything, Glenn?'

'Nothing. You?'

'Not a whisper. It's been nearly thirty hours. Our guy has to be using digital steganography, or something.'

'But we're monitoring their emails and mobiles, right?'

'Sure. But they could be sending encrypted files, or slipping out to the library to use a public account. We're keyed into the CCTV in the industrial unit, but we can't track them after that. Or they could have done it under our noses and embedded the message in the meta-data of a photo.'

Frances Coffey still finds it staggering that great swathes of written information can be hidden in the pixels of one innocent-looking image.

'Someone like Carter could do it in her sleep.'

'They all could, Glenn, as you well know. They've all got the know-how. As well as the training they had from us, whoever it is will also have access to the most sophisticated technology Russia has at its disposal. Which means the most sophisticated technology in the world. Don't forget that, as Christopher Clay, Federov made his fortune at the cutting edge of computer science. Our traitor will be learning from the best.'

An hour passes. Then another.

In her hotel room, Coffey feels a crushing sensation on her ribs as the pressure builds. She is sick of sending her best team out to sea, knowing there's a hole in the bottom of their ship, sick of knowing the danger they're in, and having to keep it from them. Sick of spying on the very people she is asking to trust her with their lives. And she knows all too well the toll of what she's asking of Glenn Dabrowski is taking. He is twenty-five pounds lighter than the man who led his team into the hell that was Isfahan. His skin has the translucent pallor of paper held up to the light. But, most damaging of all, she sees how his spirit is draining from him in a steady trickle. Cut off from everything he values, knowing that the people he loves most in the world think the worst of him. He needs to be returned to his wife and his boy. Needs this to be over.

Yet, for now, she needs him more. He's the only one she can trust.

Coffey dozes on her bed, her laptop open by her side, while across the world Dabrowski, eight hours behind, listens on through the hot afternoon.

'Still nothing?' she asks when she wakes fully at around 5 a.m. and sees through the uncovered window the sun rising behind the billboard opposite, spooling ribbons of red and orange across the pale sky.

'Nothing.' His voice is something that has been dried up and hollowed out. But, just moments later, he is back on the line, and now he sounds like a different person.

'Hold on,' he says. 'Bullrun is picking up something coming through.'

Coffey sits up straight, all vestiges of sleep now well and truly gone. Bullrun, the NSA's latest decryption program, has capabilities that go well beyond what ought to be possible when it comes to so-called watertight end-to-end encryption communication. Once you've programmed in a specific key trigger word like 'Carpathian', it can be frighteningly accurate.

'What is it, Glenn? Is it coming from our end? Is one of our team making contact?'

'Hold on.'

While Coffey waits, the very air on the line seems to be holding its breath. But when Dabrowski comes back on she knows instantly the news is bad.

'It wasn't one of ours, it was Federov. He said, "Excellent work. See you in the Carpathians." '

'And no sign of who the message was intended for?'

'No.'

The crushing weight on Coffey's ribcage becomes unbearable. The traitor has slipped through their fingers. The exercise has failed.

'That's it, then. We've run out of options. Looks like we're all heading to Poland.'

46

THE MAN WHO HAD BEEN STRAPPED TO THE CHAIR WHEN FEDEROV last came down to the basement room of his summer palace on the Black Sea coast now lies curled in a corner, a cuff around his ankle chaining him to the wall. Not that he could get very far – both his legs are now broken, the right one in several places, and his spirit has all but left him. He no longer thinks about escape, only about oblivion.

There is no daylight in this hellish place, only the sickly light from the bulb that never goes off, so he has no sense of how much time is passing. It could be days or weeks. Months even. One time a spider made a web in his field of vision and he watched it hungrily, only to feel more desolate than ever when he opened his eyes from sleep to find the web broken and the spider gone.

He has reached a point where even an appearance from the sadist Sergei Denisov would be something to welcome, evidence that the world still exists.

But not Federov.

The prisoner has not forgotten the man who crouched before him in his pale, well-cut suit, while he sat slumped in the chair for who knows how long. Has not forgotten the voice that betrays nothing, or the shudder that passed through him when he finally raised his head to find himself staring into those dead, colourless eyes.

The prisoner yearns for human contact.

But to his pain-addled, dehydrated, fevered mind, there is nothing human about Vasily Federov.

He drifts off into a febrile sleep, awakening some time later to a harsh light. At first he wonders if he is dead at last, and this is heaven – this unforgiving glare. Then it is abruptly extinguished and he sees he is still in the same place, cuffed to the wall by his useless ankle. Except that he isn't alone.

Standing in front of him, looking jaundiced in the thin yellow light of the single bulb, is a woman with long fair hair, and the tight, swollen look of someone who has submitted herself once too often to the surgeon's knife. She holds a hand up to her nose and he realizes how bad he must smell.

For a moment, as she takes in the heap of rags and skin and broken bones he has become, he sees a shadow pass over her face, and hope flares painfully in the heart that he had imagined no longer capable of emotion.

He recognizes this woman as Federov's wife.

'Please,' he says, and his voice is rusty through lack of use. 'Please help me.'

Irina Federova gazes down at him. She is wearing a tennis dress, as if she has just stepped off the court. Its whiteness dazzles him.

'Please,' he tries again.

For a golden, blissful moment he thinks he has got through to her.

Then her cold, surgically lifted eyes slide off him as if he is no more a person than the heating pipe in the corner or the metal chain that links him to the wall, and she turns and walks out without a backward glance. Afterwards he wonders if she was ever really there at all.

PART THREE

47

IT'S NOT THE SAME MINIVAN THEY USED IN FRANCE, BUT IT'S NOT far off. Again they are posing as a group of convention-goers on a team-building exercise, this time a spot of mountaineering. Argylle overheard the hotel night staff talking earlier in Arabic. 'They'd better not try any of that bonding shit on us,' one had said to the other.

Normally he'd have got a kick out of knowing that neither of the hotel workers had a clue he understood every word they said, but right now Argylle is having trouble seeing the funny side of anything. Partly because a raging gale means they've all been pulled from their beds to pile into this van, instead of leaving in the morning from the airport on the twin-engine plane they'd been expecting. But mostly because he can't stop thinking about his conversation with Coffey in the kid's playground. As the bus crosses the German border, he looks around at his fellow passengers. *Is it you?* he thinks. *Or you?*

Now that he has got to know his teammates better, he cannot bring himself to believe any of them capable of the kind of betrayal Coffey hinted at. Once again, he wonders if he can really trust her. He knows she is keeping something back. Something big. So why couldn't she be lying about all of it? It makes as much sense as anything else.

The CIA has long been at the cutting edge of meteorology. Scientists are increasingly looking towards geo-engineering in an attempt either to halt the relentless onslaught of climate change or to weaponize the weather, depending on which side of the political debate you're on. Even as far back as the 1960s, the Americans used cloud seeding in Vietnam, dispersing chemicals into the air to prolong the rainy season and disrupt North Vietnamese manoeuvres and supply chains by making the roads impassable – the so-called 'Make mud, not war' offensive. And yet, here in Europe, it seems they are at the mercy of the weather.

And the weather is shit.

The first official warnings that a storm is on its way came the previous day via Will Hooper, who reported the local and regional weather forecast to them as angrily as if the Europeans had laid on the hostile conditions deliberately to mess with their plans. Already, as they've been driving, Argylle – having lived all over the world and experienced pretty much every type of weather event – has already seen the signs. The easterly winds. The humidity that set the leaves in the trees curling. The blood-orange sky at sunrise. He watches through the window the birds flying low to the ground and the gathering grey clouds.

'Christ, I wish we were flying,' groans Erin Quinn next to him. 'Give me a tiny plane in a ninety-kilometre-an-hour gale, throw in a microburst or wind shear, I don't care. But a fourteen-hour bus journey?'

'You're hurting my feelings.'

'Argylle, Brad Pitt himself could be sitting next to me and I'd still be clamouring to get off this damn thing. I hate road trips. I've always hated them. When I was a kid I'd have to have the window wide open, so everyone else in the car would have to wrap themselves up in scarves and gloves. My dad would sit me in back with a can of Coke in one hand and a barf bag in the other.'

Argylle makes a show of moving away and pressing himself against the window.

'Don't sweat. I'm a lot better now. Although, having said that . . .' She makes a face and swallows hard, before cracking a smile.

Argylle doesn't have long-term relationships. Why would he, after what happened to him? No matter how well you *think* you know

302

another person, the truth is you don't and you can't. Better to get through life alone than risk having your trust betrayed. He likes sex, but is always upfront about the fact he is not looking for intimacy. And the few times women have interpreted that as a challenge, convinced they can change his mind, well, he feels bad for them and wishes they'd taken him at his word, but they can't say they weren't warned.

But ever since he joined the Agency, the hard rope of Argylle's resolve has been softening and fraying. The unexpected kinship with Wyatt and Carter and now these confusing feelings about the woman who sits by his side. The heat of the physical attraction, sure, but something else too, a new awareness of the holes inside him, and a growing suspicion that she might be the one to fill them.

'Your dad sounds like one of the good ones,' he says now.

She nods. 'He was the best. I know everyone probably says that.'

Her fingers go to the delicate gold chain tucked into the neck of her T-shirt.

'I'm guessing your dad gave you that?'

'Yeah. Eighteenth birthday. My parents had already given me their old Chevy on the understanding that was my birthday gift, but my dad was a softie and he couldn't bear for me not to have anything to open on the day. He slipped this into my pocket wrapped in tissue. Mom was so mad.'

Argylle thinks of his own father. His inconsistency – how one day he could be generous and larger than life, the next withdrawn and short-tempered. After Argylle discovered what his parents really did for a living, he better understood his father's changeability, but as a child he had taken it personally.

'Everything I do, I do because of him,' Quinn goes on. 'Everything I am is because of who he was. God, I sound like an asshole.'

By now the storm has well and truly broken. Outside the window, the black clouds release a steady sheet of rain that blurs the windows, washing the world in grey and green. When Argylle looks through the front windscreen, between the wiper blades that send a spray of water shooting into the slipstream of the bus, he sees that the line of trees alongside the autobahn is bending in the wind.

'We must have done something to make God pissed,' says Carter from the seat in front, taking out her earphones and staring at the worsening weather. 'I just heard on the radio that a volcano erupted over in Iceland.'

'All we need now is a plague of locusts,' says Argylle grimly.

'Isn't it weird that the other side of the freeway is so clear?' says Quinn.

Argylle realizes she is right. While their side of the autobahn is full of tail-to-tail traffic, inching through the ever-darkening day, the opposite side is completely empty. Which means . . .

48

'OH SHIT.' DABROWSKI'S VOICE TWISTS WITH FRUSTRATION. 'ARE you seeing what I'm seeing?'

He and Coffey are simultaneously scrutinizing the same footage from both the satellite and the AWACS plane – the airborne early-warning system that circles high above the local weather fronts and can track vehicles on the ground as well as those in the air.

In this way, Dabrowski, in the dead of a mild Montana night, and Coffey – who, along with Mike Randall and some tech guys, has set up a new temporary command post in a disused aerodrome on the flat plain between the villages of Długopole and Krauszów, some thirty-five kilometres from where the team are heading – can keep watch not only on their own people but also on any signs of the Russians approaching.

Coffey flew out late the night before on a Gulfstream IV, more usually used for ferrying captives who don't officially exist to far-flung prisons that also don't officially exist instead of landing in the midst of the kind of turbulence that separates you from your break-fast. Though the eye of the storm hasn't yet hit this very southernmost tip of Poland, it cannot be far off.

The operation has been meticulously planned. A fifteen-strong team of top CIA operatives, including one of the Agency's most experienced engineers, were due to fly in on a Lockheed Hercules direct from Virginia with a cargo of specialized explosives equipment, landing at 11.40 a.m. A convoy of BearCats was on its way from Berlin to pick them up.

The first sign that things were not going to go to plan came early that morning when the worsening forecast meant she'd had to stand down the light aircraft which had been lined up to fly the team from Belgium to within parachuting distance of the Tatra Mountains, hastily organizing the minivan instead, throwing out all the timings she'd worked on.

The second sign came mid-morning with a phone call from one of the BearCat drivers. The storm, which had arrived in Germany with a vengeance, had blown down a power line ahead of them, forcing a coach carrying schoolchildren to slam on its brakes, whereupon the first BearCat went into the back of it, and vehicles two and three each slammed into the back of the vehicle in front. The autobahn was closed, the police were there, the American embassy had been informed. No one was leaving any time soon.

Then, not long after she had finished speaking to the perplexed and none too happy US ambassador to Germany, Joe Quintano called.

'You're not going to like this, boss.'

'If you're calling about the BearCats, I already know.'

'BearCats? No, it's about the ash cloud.'

'The what?'

Quintano's sigh was audible through the crackly line and the thousands of miles that separated them.

'The volcano in Iceland threw up an ash cloud that makes flying impossible. The Lockheed had to turn back.'

And now, as if that's not enough, from their different sides of the world, she and Dabrowski are both scrutinizing the same unwelcome aerial view. It's of the A4 autobahn, on which a forty-ton articulated truck has jackknifed, after its inexperienced driver slammed on the brakes to avoid a car merging from a slip road and his trailer went swinging out across three lanes, sending an overtaking Honda Civic crashing through the central reservation barrier, stopping the traffic in the other direction.

The cars behind the truck have gone ploughing into each other, so that from above the scene is one dark, homogeneous mass of metal, impossible to differentiate one vehicle from another. After that initial clump of wreckage comes the tailback of stationary cars. And half a mile down that unmoving line of cars is the minibus in which the CIA's crack team are travelling.

Or rather, not travelling.

'Any sign of our Russian friends?' asks Coffey.

'Nothing the last time I checked. I'll take another look.'

Dabrowski turns to the monitor that is showing the various FAA radar surveillance feeds from the air towers nearest to the Tatra Mountains. He flicks through, his eyes scanning across the screen. Until . . .

'Glenn? You find something?'

Dabrowski frowns. 'Could be.' He scrutinizes the screen, and then calls up the scheduled flight plans over Polish air space. 'Let me check a coupla things.'

Moments later, he is back. 'Okay. We got trouble. Two Russian Ka-29s, headed straight on course for Zakopane.'

Alone in a small, partitioned office cubicle in the disused aerodrome, Frances Coffey lights up a cigarette and inhales so deeply that, seven thousand kilometres away, Glenn Dabrowski, who smoked his last cigarette nine years ago on the day his son was born, hears it over the line and waits, eyes closed, for the nicotine hit that never comes.

He leaves it a respectful couple of seconds before asking, 'What do we do, boss?'

'We wait for the storm, Glenn, and pray it's a monster.'

49

AFTER HALF AN HOUR WITHOUT MOVING AN INCH, YOU CAN CUT THE atmosphere in the van with a not particularly sharp knife.

'We can't just sit here,' says Schneider for what seems like the hundredth time.

'You wanna get out and walk?' calls Will Hooper from the driver's seat, which he has pushed right back so that he can stretch out his legs, the engine long since switched off. 'You might get there by next week. We'll wave when we drive past you.'

In front of Argylle, Keira Carter is bent over her laptop, her fingers flying over the keyboard. To Argylle, practically the last person on Earth to get a cellphone, her tech proficiency seems as magical and unfathomable as if she were a concert pianist or a skilled portrait painter.

By now, the traffic on the other side of the motorway has resumed, while their side remains gridlocked.

'Multiple casualties,' says Carter grimly, reading from her screen.

'Fricking great,' snarls Schneider.

'They didn't die deliberately to inconvenience you, asshole,' Carter snaps back.

Argylle is staring out of the window at the central reservation, deep in thought.

'You transcendentally meditating there, Argylle?' Wyatt asks, twisting around from the seat next to Carter.

'What kind of vehicle could pull down one of those panels?' he says, indicating the steel barrier running along the middle of the autobahn.

'Why the—' Wyatt's voice tails off as he cottons on. 'Ah, okay. You'd need a four-by-four, with a tow bar.'

'We've got climbing ropes and straps in the trunk for when we get to the mountains,' says Erin Quinn, looking from one to the other with a slow smile.

Two minutes later they have pulled on hi-vis vests and clambered out of the bus and over the central reservation. Spotting a RAV4, Wyatt's hand starts to go up, but Argylle shakes his head. When a Hummer comes into view, they spring into action, flagging down the traffic, which has in any case slowed so that the drivers can rubberneck the carnage on the other carriageway.

The team fan across the road, bringing the three lanes to a halt. The yellow Hummer is in the front of the pack, the driver, a middle-aged man with dyed-black hair and a fake tan, leaning impatiently on his horn, gesticulating angrily to the young blonde woman in the passenger seat. He stops rather abruptly when Wyatt, all two hundred and fifty pounds of him, opens his car door and yanks him out, taking his place behind the wheel. The woman in the passenger seat surveys her new companion with interest.

Even if he hadn't been fluent in German, Argylle couldn't have failed to understand that the ousted driver is not happy. The driver shouts at his passenger to call the police, but she doesn't seem to be in any hurry to do so. Then he stands, gaping, the heavy rain plastering his thinning hair to his scalp, while Wyatt backs his precious car up to the central reservation and Argylle attaches one end of the rope to the rear bumper and the other to one end of one of the steel barrier panels before walking across to do the same to the other end.

Then all of them watch in awed silence as Wyatt revs the engine then slams down on the accelerator. The metal railing groans but doesn't buckle, so he does it again and again, the engine screaming with effort until finally, with a ripping sound, the Hummer lurches forward, taking a four-metre section of crash barrier with it.

Argylle can't be sure, but he thinks he sees the blonde woman and Wyatt exchange a high five.

And now Will Hooper is manoeuvring the minivan through the newly created gap in the central barrier, and, with the team still holding back the traffic, he crosses the three lanes to the hard shoulder. Then all is in motion – Wyatt sprinting from the Hummer, tossing the keys over his head so they land somewhere in the grass of the central reservation, eliciting a roar of fury from the driver. And then the rest of them are breaking formation, racing across the carriageway to the waiting van.

Once in, Hooper floors the accelerator and they screech off down the emergency lane, the oncoming traffic passing just inches away. Quinn groans. 'Jeez, it was bad enough when we were going in the *right* direction.' In the eerie storm light, her skin has a greenish tinge.

Argylle knows time is slipping away from them. Wherever they go, the Russians seem to be one step ahead. And if the Russians are approaching from the east, a far more direct route to the mountains, the chance of the team getting to the Amber Room first is vanishingly slim.

50

'WHAT'S HAPPENING, GLENN? ANY COORDINATES?'

'They're moving too fast, boss. Just flew north of Minsk. At this rate, they'll make Poland in half an hour. Our guys still have at least five hours to go, assuming nothing more goes wrong. They'll never catch them.'

'Have faith, Glenn. This storm is a beast.' As if to prove her point, there's a clap of thunder outside and a barrage of wind rattles the metal shutters of the aerodrome.

Dabrowski gazes through the small window of his study at the still, mild Montana night and the stars he sometimes watches through the telescope in his bedroom. Storm-ravaged Poland seems light years away. His former teammates might as well be on a different planet.

His eyes turn back to the monitor and the radar showing the two moving dots of light that are the Ka-29s. Except . . .

'Boss, something's up.'

Instantly Coffey is alert. 'Where, Glenn? Do you have specifics?'

Dabrowski reads off the coordinates and Coffey gets on to the Mission Integration Directorate, part of the National Reconnaissance Office. Within minutes, her laptop screen is showing her a satellite feed, which, once her eyes have become accustomed to the graininess caused by the storm, makes her clamp her hand to her mouth.

'You got this, Glenn?'

'Yeah. Holy shit. Wind must be raging to blow that thing outta the sky.'

The landscape they are looking at is a densely forested mountainside – unbroken trees stretching as far as the eye can see, apart from a jagged hole in the centre of the canopy where, as Coffey zooms in, she spots the three blades of a helicopter rotor, still spinning idly round, the rest of the craft hidden in the foliage into which it has crashed. She can make out what seem to be bodies, flung clear of the stricken chopper, draped over tree branches.

'What happened to his buddy?' asks Dabrowski, scanning the radar screen. 'Gotcha,' he murmurs under his breath, finding the single flashing dot. 'Looks like he's circling back, boss. Gonna pick up survivors, I'm guessing. Here he comes.'

As if by magic, the whirring blades of a chopper appear on Coffey's screen. The second helicopter attempts to hover over the first in the teeth of the gale, somehow managing to hold position. A door opens from which a rope ladder is lowered, fluttering wildly to and fro. The chopper is still too high, so it circles around again, coming in so low that the blades of the lower coax rotor seem almost to be brushing the tops of the trees, the rope ladder like a banner it trails in the wind. Again the helicopter circles, and now, through the open door comes a figure clad in black who descends on a hoist cable.

'Rather you than me, buddy,' whistles Dabrowski as a huge gust of wind picks up man and rope then drops them down again at force so that they swing like a pendulum through the air. Still he clings on, and the wind retreats enough for him to descend, narrowly avoiding the still lazily turning rotor of the crashed helicopter.

'Brave guy,' comments Coffey. Zooming in further, she sees what she missed earlier, that there are live figures in the area around the helicopter crash. She spots the top half of a man gesticulating, his lower half hidden by foliage. The man on the rope winches himself down and for a moment they are obscured, but then he reappears and is holding on to a second man, whose arm hangs off as if it doesn't belong to him.

For a few minutes, she and Dabrowski watch on in silence. There is an uneasy moment most military personnel recognize, when they come too close to 'the enemy' and what was a homogeneous mass breaks apart, like cells pulling away under a microscope, revealing that all along it was made up of individual humans just like them.

Five times more the Russian descends on his rope, each time plucking a survivor from the wreck.

'Christ, how many of them are there?' asks Dabrowski. On the last time, as the two figures are winched up towards the gaping helicopter door, a fork of lightning cracks open the sky right above them and Coffey is torn between a humanitarian desire not to witness any more deaths and a fervent hope that their mission might end here, her team free to carry on without risk of harm.

But that hope is dashed when, wobbling but still airborne, the second helicopter ascends above the treetops and off into the squally sky, taking its cargo of people and equipment with it.

'At least they took a hit,' says Dabrowski.

'But not enough,' says Coffey. 'Even with the fatalities, they still outnumber us.'

'Where are the guys now?' asks Dabrowski, and there's something about the way he says 'the guys' that speaks of the longing she knows is in his heart.

'Hooper says he thinks they have an hour to go.'

'We'd better hope the wind is against that chopper,' says Dabrowski grimly. 'Or they don't stand a chance in hell.'

51

FIFTY-SEVEN MINUTES LATER, THE TEAM ARRIVE AT THE TATRA Mountains. The flat Polish countryside has been replaced by dramatic Alpine-style scenery with forests of spruce, fir and larch on either side of the road and in the distance the soaring peaks of the High Tatras.

One day I will come back here, Argylle promises himself.

Right now, however, he's finding it hard to enjoy his surroundings. The storm has dogged them every step of the way, dark clouds casting a pewter pall over the winding road ahead. The dense trees seem sinister in the dim light, a black-clad army flanking the bus, swaying dangerously in the wind. For all Argylle knows, a highly trained, heavily armed team of Russian Spetsnaz is out there somewhere, maybe waiting for them at their destination, or else coming up on their heels. And he can't stop thinking about the fact that someone in the team in whose hands he will shortly be putting his life wants him dead.

They drive through a small hamlet, just a handful of houses hidden behind wooden fences, only their high, triangular roofs cresting the treetops that surround them. After the houses comes evidence of logging – a clearing with thick trunks stacked in piles and a forklift truck idly waiting out the storm. Here and there is evidence of the mining that Coffey has briefed them about – a rusting gallows frame in the distance as they round a bend, an overgrown track blocked with a heavy, rusty chain next to a wooden signpost reading *Kopalnia*, the Polish word for mine.

The main road ends at the foot of the mountains, but there is an unmade track stretching ahead. From the signs and the bike rental shack and the rustic benches made from sawn tree trunks, it's clear this is usually a well-used tourist path, but on a day like today there is no one around as the bus proceeds slowly through the narrow valley, between the wooded mountainsides.

Erin Quinn puts her hand out to cover Argylle's and he is taken by surprise until he realizes he's been drumming his fingers against his thigh, that old nervous tic of his, never quite overcome. Wyatt glances over, sees her hand on Argylle's leg. Glances away.

The minivan has now reached unmapped territory. From the airfield, Coffey is using a satellite feed to guide Will Hooper, who has driven the entire fourteen hours single-handedly, refusing to let anyone else take over. She sends them off the main track on to a far more rugged one that takes them deeper and deeper into the forest, the terrain now rising steeply uphill, becoming increasingly uneven until it peters out altogether.

End of the road. Literally.

'Lovely walking weather, guys,' says Hooper, ushering them out into the rain. Hooper is leading them for this final push and Argylle is glad that the more experienced instructor will be taking the helm, rather than one of the team.

Hooper has Coffey in his earpiece delivering instructions, the others following on behind, already soaked to the skin. They are keeping to an even elevation, skirting around the mountain. The terrain is wild and overgrown, and they must hack back vegetation to carve a path through. Forty minutes pass. Just when Argylle is starting to wonder if they might just circle this route indefinitely, they come up against a section of woodland that seems far denser than anything they've been through so far – certainly too dense for them to continue. Now they start to climb, Hooper leading the way until, after a short distance, they come to a small, level, waterlogged clearing cut into the mountainside that is dominated by a towering pile of rocks and rubble.

'Hell yeah!' says Hooper, dropping his heavy pack to the ground. 'We made it. We're here.'

'Where are we, exactly, sir?' Quinn wants to know.

'According to our intel, there's a network of tunnels and storehouses behind all that.' Hooper points at the vast heap of stones. 'Somehow it eventually connects up to the old mine. We think this is where the Nazis hid all that priceless crap they stole. They will have blown the entrance to hide it from the Russkies when they realized they were in danger of getting their asses whipped. The question is, how do we access it?'

'We blow it ourselves,' says Schneider. 'We've got enough charge to blast our way in. Am I right, Kellerman?'

The veteran explosives expert assesses the scene, his forehead furrowed, then shakes his head. 'We do that and we risk bringing the whole mountain down.'

Argylle is thoughtful, looking at the arrangement of the rocks.

'I'm not sure they blew it.'

'So you're an engineer now, Argylle?' Schneider doesn't bother to hide his dislike.

'The Nazis always thought they'd win the war in the end. Sure, they'd have tried to disguise the entrance, but it wouldn't make sense for them to make it impassable, not when they assumed they'd be back just as soon as the Soviets beat a retreat. My guess is that it's been stage-managed to look as if the entrance is completely blocked up with rubble, but if we cleared it away it would probably be only one layer deep.'

'An engineer *and* a mind-reader. Very impressive.'

'Shut up, Schneider,' snaps Hooper.

'That's weird.' Carter is staring at the ground, where the rainwater is pooling at the base of the rocks. 'Check out the water course. The rain is coming down the mountainside above us, and then the laws of physics say it should find a channel between the rocks and disappear into the hillside. But instead, it's staying right where it is.'

'Because something's stopping it,' says Argylle.

'You think they concreted it up?' asks Wyatt.

Argylle shakes his head. 'Not if they were intending to come back any time soon. My guess is that we'll find some doors behind here.'

'I think he could be right,' calls Quinn, who has clambered up the mound of rubble so she can shine her flashlight behind. 'There are some clear gaps between the rocks that aren't filled with debris like you'd expect. It looks as if the rocks have been placed there deliberately.'

Hooper orders Alex Kellerman to set just enough charge to blast aside the front layer of rocks. The chunky Canadian wades through the six-inch-deep water in front of the rocks to set the charges while the rest of them step back with their hands over their ears and their faces turned as the blast goes off.

Then they turn back.

'Sweet Jesus,' says Wyatt.

The blast has revealed a pair of lofty steel doors so tightly closed that the join is hardly visible. The doors are set into a concrete base. But the real reason for Wyatt's exclamation and the open-mouthed stares from the others lies in the way the doors have been decorated. Embossed across the two colossal metal panels, rusted in places after decades under cover but still unmistakable, is the symbolic eagle of Nazi Germany, wings spread wide, clutching a swastika in its claws.

'I think we found it, boss,' Will Hooper says into his microphone, a catch in his voice.

'Glad to hear it, Will,' Coffey tells him. 'But don't stand around congratulating yourselves for too long. You've got company, I'm afraid.'

'The Russians? But how did they—'

'No time for that now. We'll have the inquest when the mission's over.'

'Yes, boss. Understood.'

The doors have shifted something in the mood of the team. Until now, they have talked about the Nazis and the war as if it was something abstract, but here they are, face to face with the proof that it happened. That the evil the Nazis were responsible for existed outside of the history books. The colossal doors with that shocking black-and-red symbol both awe and repel them.

And now this unwelcome news that the Russians have followed them here. While Argylle knew it was likely, to those who'd bought the line about Casner's balls-up with the sat-phone signal it comes as a nasty shock. Some even begin to wonder if the mission is blighted.

Argylle senses the unease that ripples through the team, sees it in the setting of jaws and the tensing of shoulders.

This cavern, whatever it contains, has been sealed from the world for more than sixty years and, once they disturb whatever lies inside, there can be no turning back.

Kellerman is the first to break the silence. 'Want me to blow them open, sir? Seven small ones should do it.'

After a slight hesitation, Hooper nods.

Once again they stand back, but this time Argylle doesn't avert his face. He wants to see that terrible eagle being torn open.

The blast shakes the trees and releases into the air a billowing cloud of foul, stale dust that gets into the team's noses and throats.

The last people to breathe this air were Nazis, Argylle thinks. And the thought makes him dizzy.

Thirty-five kilometres away, Frances Coffey watches the scene through the narrow gap in the cover of trees that the satellite feed allows, and also through the team's bodycams as they wait for the dust cloud to clear. She too feels history breathing heavily on her neck.

Whatever they find under the mountain was hidden for a reason. While she doesn't buy into the idea of a curse, like with King Tut, there's a tiny part of Frances Coffey that believes sometimes the past should stay buried.

'Boss, are you seeing this? Seven hundred metres north-north-east?'

Dabrowski's voice on the encrypted phone line is urgent in her ear.

In her temporary HQ, as the rain ricochets off the tin roof, Coffey moves the angle of the satellite picture until she finds what Dabrowski is looking at. The Russian chopper has arrived. Despite being blown about by the winds, it is managing to maintain position while it disgorges its cargo at the north-east ridge, not twenty minutes from where the team currently stand.

'How many do you think?' Coffey asks, losing track of the personnel milling around on the ground, shouldering backpacks and breaking out weapons.

'I got twenty. At least. Plus all the gear. We're in trouble.'

'Yes, but we're ahead of them, Glenn. That gives us an advantage.'

But as Coffey switches her viewpoint back to the team, who are busy making the opening in the doors big enough to step through, her bravado slips. The Russians are so close behind – and the team have already done all their dirty work for them, leaving the way clear to just waltz on in.

Past the steel doors, the team run along a stuffy tunnel with thick, rough stone walls that opens into a vast concrete antechamber, still draped with Nazi regalia. A row of swastika banners, heavy with dust, their tattered edges blackened with mould, hangs high on one side. Ahead of them, across the concourse, is a second set of doors, just slightly smaller than the last. Some metres in front of them sits a large wooden crate with its lid closed. Argylle's stomach drops with anticlimax. He'd hoped to find the train Coffey told them about, and this isn't it.

'We'll have to blow those doors too,' Hooper tells them. 'Then, once we get through, we'll block them up from the inside.'

Carter, here in her techie capacity to maintain communications between the team in the mountain and Coffey in her makeshift HQ, is in the front of the group, heading for the crate. 'Wow, check this out,' she exclaims, flinging the lid aside. 'There's, like, a whole arsenal of weapons in here.' Argylle, bringing up the rear, is only half listening, his eyes skirting around the chamber – the uneven cement walls, the low ceiling, the floor . . . *Tripwire.*

'Carter, stop!' he yells. 'Stay exactly where you are.' His voice sounds gritted with fear.

Carter, recognizing the pitch of desperation in it, stands motionless. Only her eyes dart around.

'Landmine,' says Hooper softly.

'Yeah, but clearly a dud, sir,' says Schneider, 'or it would have gone off by now.'

Hooper shakes his head. 'Not if it's pressure-release. That thing is primed to go off the second someone shifts the crate. It's how they guarded their asses against anyone coming in here and stealing their shit.'

'But it didn't go off when she stepped on to it. So maybe she can step off it again without triggering the fuse,' says Wyatt.

'Maybe?' whispers Carter. 'I don't like the sound of maybe.'

'Come on,' says Casner. 'We're losing time.'

'We can't just leave her here,' says Quinn.

'The Russkies are right up our asses,' says Schneider. 'We gotta press on.'

Meanwhile, Wyatt has headed back out through the tunnel and the steel doors, and is picking through the debris that was blown aside by the blast. Argylle watches, bemused, as he hefts one huge rock, only to discard it. Then does the same to another.

Now he gets it.

'Carter, how much d'you weigh?'

'What the fuck, Argylle?'

'A hundred pounds? A hundred and twenty?'

'One fifteen.'

Argylle spins around to face the jagged hole in the steel doors through which Wyatt stepped just moments before. 'That one,' he yells, pointing to a rock which is wedged between the concrete base and the top of a tree that came down in the blast.

Wyatt bends and heaves the rock into his arms. Nods to Argylle and makes his laborious way back into the chamber. Seconds later, Argylle has positioned himself on one side of Carter with one arm around her waist, making sure to keep his feet away from the barely visible crack in the cement floor that runs all the way around the base of the crate.

'You ready?' he asks Washington, who is on her other side, and Wyatt, standing, sweating with his boulder, behind them. All three have shrugged off their backpacks so that they are unencumbered.

'Remember, it's about keeping the pressure constant on the mine so it doesn't detect any change in weight.'

'Three.' As Argylle starts the countdown it is as if the very air in the chamber has stopped circulating.

'Two.' His mouth is so dry he can hardly get the words out.

'One.' Someone to the side of him swallows, the sound deafening in the dead silence. When he says 'Now,' two things happen simultaneously: he and Washington lift Carter into the air and at exactly the same instant Wyatt gently places the rock down in the spot where she has been standing.

For a moment time is suspended as they brace for the blast that never comes. Then:

'Jeez, that was *intense*.' Erin Quinn is smiling.

Wyatt reshoulders his backpack, but Argylle stays in position until Carter stops shaking.

In her makeshift bunker, Coffey is listening to . . . well, nothing. Or rather just a static sound where a few moments before she'd been connected to Hooper.

'You still got audio, Glenn?'

'Nothing, boss. The transmitter is down.'

The monitor is still showing the bodycam feeds from the various team members but without an audio connection, there is no chance of giving instructions to the team – or of warning them when they're in danger.

52

KELLERMAN LAYS MORE CHARGES AGAINST THE SECOND SET OF doors. While the rest of the team readies for the explosion, Argylle stares through the tunnel at the jagged mouth in the steel doors behind them, envisaging the arrival of Denisov's meaty head, his dead-fish eyes. The Russians are nearly upon them.

'Down!' shouts Kellerman, but as he hurls himself to the ground Argylle sees, with a twist of his gut, movement through the doors. The Russians are here, their voices echoing in the tunnel.

The explosion from Kellerman's charges momentarily silences the cavern, but before the smoke even clears there is a sound behind them. The team whirl around to see a black-clad Russian with a Kalashnikov fall on to one knee to mount the weapon on his shoulder. As he is about to take aim another soldier shouts out and steps in front of him towards the crate, ignoring the rock that Wyatt so recently deposited there, and begins throwing out the weapons to his teammates.

Argylle holds his breath. How much weight loss will trigger the pressure-release mechanism?

His answer comes soon enough. As the Russian picks up a machine-gun, the ground breaks apart under him, a volcanic column of fire blasting up through his body, sending his limbs cartwheeling in different directions.

In the ensuing confusion, the team pile through the second set of blasted doors before the firing starts up again and cast around for something – anything – to block up the doorway. As the only natural light comes from the hole they've just come through, they have to use their flashlights, the thin beams getting lost in the cavernous space in which they've found themselves.

'There!' yells Hooper, pointing his flashlight at a bulky steel storage unit leaning against the near wall. Wyatt and Casner are already there, jostling the heavy unit into place, blocking the hole left in the doors, just as the machine gun opens fire on the other side. There is a scream and Argylle guesses one of his counterparts on the other side of the metal barrier has been hit by a ricocheting bullet.

This side of the barrier, all is in motion. The team have found a door leading from the main room into a smaller antechamber. And in there, a generator, the biggest Argylle has ever seen.

'Diesel,' reports Hooper. 'But it's bone dry. Fan out, guys. There has to be some diesel lying around here. But watch what you pick up.'

The team carry powerful tactical flashlights, which clip to a holster slung across their vests, but they still struggle to see through the dust thrown up by Kellerman's explosion. All that's clear is that the space they are in is enormous. Too big for them to see how far back or up it stretches. As the temporary barrier they've put in place clangs with the sounds of the Russians using whatever makeshift tools they can find to break it down, the team disperse, flashlights aloft, into the uncharted, cavernous space.

'Here!' Washington has found a forklift truck. Make that two – no, three – forklift trucks lined up neatly in the entrance to a tunnel spurring off the main chamber.

'Don't waste your time,' says Wyatt. 'Any fuel in there will have evaporated years ago.'

'I wouldn't bet on it,' says Carter, who seems to have steadied herself after her near-death experience. 'My brothers are total gearheads. The really old military-grade diesel the Nazis would have used was a lot more robust than the shit we have today. It's worth a shot. Anyone got a hose handy?'

Argylle scans the ground. He knows there's lighting here, once they get the generator working. So there must surely be pipes or hollow cables protecting the electric wires. His beam snags on something. *Gotcha.*

Minutes later, they are pouring diesel into the generator's tank and Washington is wiping his mouth with distaste. 'Put it this way, I ain't gonna be doing no fire-eating when I retire from this, I tell you that for nothing.'

Jim Ryder, the balding mechanic, shines his beam over the workings of the ancient generator then pulls a heavy wooden lever. Nothing. He fiddles with some wires and then tries again. Nothing. Argylle knows the Russians will be setting their own explosives. *Come on*, he urges the monstrous machine silently. *Come on.*

For a third time, Ryder grips hold of the wooden lever and yanks it down. Suddenly, there are flickers of light all around the team as if they are surrounded by fireflies, and then, blindingly, the whole place is flooded with light. Once they've blinked a few times, the team take stock of their environment – a vast, soaring arrival hall with various spurs of tunnel radiating off from it, each containing equipment or box cars or huge metal crates, rusty through non-use. The scale of it is breathtaking. Intimidating. And right in the centre, where once the rail lines would have converged from each side of the mountain, sits a locomotive turntable – an immense circular pit straddled by a rotating steel bridge supported by a central pivot. And there, on the concrete turntable, is . . . nothing.

For a split second, Argylle's stubborn brain superimposes the golden train of his imagination on to the empty turntable. Then the sledgehammer of reality swings in.

'Where's the fricking train?' Schneider's disgust is palpable. Ugly.

'Oh, man.' Wyatt looks defeated. 'All this for nothing.'

'It's underneath,' says Argylle.

Multiple pairs of eyes stare at him blankly.

'Explain,' Hooper demands.

'I've seen something like this before, sir. The Burma Railway built by the Japanese to connect Myanmar and Thailand. Over a hundred thousand people died building it – Asian labourers and Western POWs. There was a section called Hellfire Pass which required the men to cut through the mountainside. Nearby there is a secret cavern just like this, built to hide the trains in the event of the railway falling into enemy hands.'

'Cut the history class, Argylle,' says Schneider. 'If you haven't noticed, everything's gone suspiciously quiet out there, which means any minute the Russkies are about to blow that fucking door.'

It's true that the ferocious clanging has stopped. The silence that has replaced it is chilling.

'Okay. My guess is that this whole hall is designed to dazzle us so that we don't look any further but, actually, this is a fake floor.'

'You think the train might be underneath here?' Hooper sounds sceptical.

'Look at the turntable. See those vertical steel struts? I think the whole circle slides down those to another level. Have a look around. If I'm right, there'll be a control room somewhere close by.'

'There,' Carter's face is animated. 'Look at the power cables – they all lead into that door.'

Jim Ryder is the first one into the control room. 'Christ, I've never seen so many controls. It's like NASA in here.'

'Look for something that seems like it operates hydraulics. A row of valves or levers or something!' shouts Hooper.

'Got it.'

No one really expects the levers to work. Not the first time anyway, and not after Ryder has to run a screwdriver around the base of the mechanism to free it of decades' worth of built-up grease and dirt. But as the heavy gears clang into position there comes a great grinding and creaking from the circular pit, as if a sleeping dragon has been awoken from a deep sleep.

The heavy reinforced floor begins to inch downwards, screeching along the ungreased, vertical steel channels, just as an enormous explosion sounds from the doors to the antechamber where the Russians are grouped.

The team leap on to the groaning, shuddering concrete disc, knowing that once the smoke from the blast clears they'll be sitting ducks.

'Kill the lights!' Hooper yells to Ryder, still in the control room. 'Then get your ass down here.'

They have descended ten feet by this point. Twelve. It is grindingly slow.

Fifteen feet. Eighteen.

There's a commotion from the direction of the doors. Shouting.

'The lights, Ryder, for Chrissakes!' Hooper's voice is hoarse.

Then, suddenly . . . blackness. Shouts from the Russians. A crash somewhere. The sudden plunge into darkness has bought them some time, but if the Russians find them while they're still on this descending floor, there'll be no saving them.

'Come on, Ryder,' mutters Hooper. *Twenty feet. Twenty-five.* 'Come on.'

Now there are footsteps running above their heads and they see the dark shape that is Ryder leaping from the side just as gunfire opens up, strafing his body mid-air. He crashes to the descending floor, landing a direct hit on Mia Matsyuk. When Argylle drops to his knees to turn Ryder over, his fingers disappear into a gaping hole in the man's shoulder. There's another hole in his chest and where his face used to be. Matsyuk, meanwhile, is making a bubbling sound from the back of her throat. She clutches hold of Argylle's arm and he hears how she can't breathe, how her own blood is drowning her, sees how the screwdriver Ryder was still carrying has embedded itself in her chest.

While the others drag the lifeless Ryder away, he bends to whisper in Matsyuk's ear. 'It's okay,' he tells her, and 'You are safe. You are loved,' because he can think of nothing else to offer, and because it occurs to him how very much he wishes he could have told his parents the same.

By the time Ryder's body has been moved, Matsyuk is dead and the platform they've been standing on has touched down on to something solid. '*Syuda!*' comes the shout from above.

They scramble off the platform just as the first bullets hail down from above, illuminated by powerful flashlight beams. A fierce argument breaks out among the Russians standing around the upper rim of the turntable.

'Someone thinks they should jump down, and the others aren't having it,' Argylle translates. Well back from the range of Russian fire, he turns around to take stock of his new surroundings.

At first he can make out very little through the thick, grainy gloom. But as his eyes adjust and the team switch on their flashlights it becomes clear they are in another cavernous space, again with various tunnel entrances spinning off from it, though in this one the air feels closer and more fetid, catching in their noses and throats. As the beams criss-cross the chamber, they pick out various objects – a banner, hanging from the lintel over a tunnel entrance, the words 'Heil Hitler' printed in black beneath the ubiquitous black swastika, a row of religious statues that Argylle momentarily mistakes for living people, his hand grasping for his gun, heart lurching in his chest. There's a pile of wooden trunks in the tunnel spur nearest to them and, after pausing to check for booby traps, Wyatt rips open the first one, revealing a swastika stamped on the inside of the lid.

'Sweet Jesus!' Wyatt's exclamation cuts through the thick air.

Argylle joins him, and they both stare down in stunned silence at the trunk, where dozens of gold bars glint in the yellow beam of their flashlights.

'Oh, *gross!*' The exclamation comes from Erin Quinn, who has tripped over something. Argylle swings his beam around to find his teammate on her back amid a pile of human remains. Skulls and bones, some with strips of mummified skin and tendons still clinging to them.

'Don't think much of your friends, Quinn,' laughs Schneider as he helps her up. The team focus their flashlights on the ground and see what they'd failed to pick up in the first random sweeps of light. The downstairs chamber is littered with skeletons, mostly in heaps like the one Quinn has just fallen into. Mixed in with the bones are boots, the leather hardened to concrete.

'Guessing they got the poor bastards to dig out the tunnels and then wasted them when they didn't need them any more,' says Wyatt.

'And wrote my will across the sky in stars to earn you freedom,' murmurs Argylle softly, remembering Henri Dumas, the sole survivor from the thousand-plus men and women drafted in to make these vast caverns. Are they here, Dumas's comrades who laboured beside him in those barbaric conditions to hollow out an entire mountain? Could some of these bones belong to the construction workers and engineers and architects he might have called friends?

The clothing has almost all deteriorated to unrecognizable scraps. Only the hard seams of things remain intact. Argylle sees a glint of metal resting beside what looks like the seam of a pocket or a hem. Stooping, he finds a wedding band, plain and tarnished in places. He knows POWs and those fleeing persecution sometimes sewed their valuables into the linings of their coats or jackets, hoping to salvage something from their previous life to remind them who they once were. He gently places the ring down next to the bones.

Not all the bones are grouped in clusters and piles. Their beams pick out several intact skeletons lying separate from the rest. These have helmets nearby, and weapons – semi-automatic pistols, it looks like, though Argylle also spots a sub-machine gun.

'The guards,' says Schneider, nudging a skull with the toe of his boot, so that it rolls across the ground.

'No bullets here,' Carter observes. 'I wonder how they died?'

'Grab whatever weapons you can get,' Hooper orders. 'We're going to need more firepower.'

The team brought what weapons they could carry in their packs, but Argylle, Washington and Carter had to ditch theirs in the land-mine rescue, leaving them dangerously exposed.

Casner picks up one of the regulation-issue Mausers, points it at the cement wall and pulls the trigger.

Nothing.

'Take out the clip and reload,' suggests Hooper. But when Casner raises it to fire a second time the muted bang indicates something very wrong.

'Squib load,' mutters Casner, throwing the gun aside.

Closer inspection reveals all the weapons to have been compromised in some way.

Up above, the Russians have now stopped their shooting, perhaps realizing the team are out of range.

Argylle listens to their heated discussion with growing unease. 'They're planning to come down on ropes.'

'Then we'll pick them off as they come down. *Puh-puh-puh*,' says Schneider, miming sniper fire.

'Oh my Lord,' mutters Washington, gazing at something his flashlight has picked up on the rough stone wall.

Argylle squints to make it out.

'They destroyed the operating panel,' he says, recognizing parts of the machinery from the corresponding panel upstairs, the rest having been obliterated by some sort of explosion. Realization twists savagely around his gut.

Hooper whistles under his breath. 'Whoever was the last to go up on that moving floor must have blasted the controls with a grenade launcher or something as they went up.'

'But there were still German soldiers down here,' says Carter, gesturing to the helmets and guns on the ground.

'They couldn't risk anyone who knew about this place giving the game away once they got out,' says Argylle.

'So they sealed them up down here and left them to die?'

In the yellow light, Quinn's face is pale and waxy. 'There's a special place in hell for people like that.'

'Sir! Here! Look!'

Casner is about thirty metres ahead of the others, who hurry to catch up.

'Over there in that tunnel.' Casner's voice, normally a languid Texan drawl, thrums with excitement. Argylle follows the beam of his flashlight and his stomach flips over.

53

A TRAIN. LOOMING UP FROM THE SHADOWS, VAST AND MAGNIFICENT. The face of it, black and curved like the bow of a ship or the head of a monstrous whale, its lack of windows rendering it disturbingly eyeless. A chrome eagle spreads its wings across the bulbous nose, while remnants of Nazi flags, shredded and mildewed, hang in ribbons from the top. The body of it stretches back into the darkness – sleek and black, a giant eel lurking in the rocks waiting for its prey. Even after all these years of hibernation it is spectacular, dwarfing the team standing at the edge of the tunnel.

'Armoured,' whispers Hooper, who for once seems as awestruck as the rest of them. 'Jeez, this thing would have been indestructible.'

Before anyone can respond there's a disturbance from the upper level behind them where the turntable shaft is. And now the ends of rappel ropes come dangling down from the dark chasm above into their line of sight. Not quite a full circle of ropes, Argylle notes.

Schneider's narrow face lights up and he begins sprinting back towards the ropes. 'Come to Mommy!' he yells, getting ready to raise his assault rifle.

'I wouldn't—' Argylle warns him, but his words are lost in a hail of bullets and grenades that rain down from the gap in the circle of ropes, creating a solid field of fire on the nearside of the turntable, with the ropes at the outer edges.

Schneider drops to the ground and, for a moment, Argylle thinks he has been hit, until he starts scrambling backwards on his stomach. The artillery bombardment from above is relentless, leaving no chance of anyone being able to get close enough to return fire.

'They're using tracers,' says Will Hooper breathlessly, watching the bursts of fire that light up the darkness. 'Anyone in their line of sight doesn't stand a chance. Withdraw. We'll regroup on the train.'

The others start moving back. All except Argylle, who realizes that the first Russians down the ropes will pick them off before they get to the train.

'I'll catch you up.'

Hooper, who is already fifty metres away, swings around. 'Argylle, withdraw. That's an—' But Argylle is already racing towards the circular shaft. He tries to empty his mind and blur out the edges of his thoughts as if he is in a tunnel and everything else is happening on the outside of the tunnel and the only thing that matters is the light at the end.

The hail of bullets is that light.

All other thoughts have to be kept out or he will never keep going, never do the reckless, stupid, *suicidal* thing that needs to be done.

He shuts out Hooper's voice yelling at him, closes off the part of him that is scared and doubtful as he charges ahead, grabbing hold of a rope-end in each hand with the bullets raining down around him, and pelts across the circle of fire with his hands raised and the ropes stretched out so that for a split second the figures clinging on lie horizontally, taking the full force of the missiles hailing down from above.

They don't stand a chance.

'You're batshit crazy,' grins Wyatt, who started running just as soon as he realized what Argylle was planning, and now crosses his path, trailing a couple of ropes of his own. By now there are four bodies lying on the ground, riddled with holes as if they've been aerated like a lawn.

But still the Russians keep coming. Too many for them to take down. Argylle risks stepping forward and sees, as a bullet whistles past close enough for his ears to feel a breeze, that there are at least five – make that six, no seven – figures descending on ropes from above.

'Run!'

Wyatt doesn't need telling twice. Picking up their flashlights, they race towards the mouth of the tunnel where the train is. They won't make it in time. As he runs, Argylle casts around looking for something. Anything.

'Wyatt. The statues.'

Reading Argylle's mind, Wyatt helps him grab hold of the religious icons they'd seen earlier – the weeping Virgin Mary with her arms outstretched, the saints with their robes, the Christ figures blessing invisible congregations, and line them up in the path of the advancing Russians, pausing just long enough to fire off a round of bullets around the sides of the plaster figures.

In the darkness, unable to hold both weapons and flashlights, the Russians believe they are under attack and drop to their knees to take aim, blasting the statues with all the firepower at their disposal while, in the confusion, Argylle and Wyatt make their escape. Glancing over his shoulder, Argylle winces as the Madonna loses first her right arm and then her head.

'Get in the train. Now!' Will Hooper is waiting for them by the mouth of the tunnel.

Eric Lawler and Brandon Reynolds have set up position tucked inside the tunnel entrance. The two are sheltering behind a pile of sandbags that had been protecting a pallet-load of paintings. Many of the paintings are in ornate frames, the gold dulled to bronze and heavily tarnished, and Argylle sends the stack a longing look, knowing how many important artworks disappeared during the war. He thinks about Raphael's famous self-portrait and the missing Van Gogh, and the sorrow on his art-lover mother's face when she told him about them and said that if the Nazis could have shut away the sun itself in Hitler or Goering's private collection, they would have done so. What else is on that pallet?

'*Now*, Argylle!'

He pushes past the sandbags, nodding at Reynolds and Lawler, whose job it is to hold off the Russians while the rest of the team enter the train, hoping against hope to find the Amber Room there. There's no question that the two men have drawn the short straw.

And judging by the way Lawler's jaw is grinding and Reynolds is gripping his sniper's rifle, his arm pressing into the canvas covering of the sandbag in front as if he is trying to steady himself, they know it too.

54

OWING TO A BEND IN THE TUNNEL, IT'S IMPOSSIBLE TO SEE HOW FAR back the train stretches, even with flashlights. The team have jimmied open the steel coverings over a window into the first of the sealed-up carriages, and Argylle follows the others inside, surprised to find himself in what resembles a fancy cocktail bar. There are red-velvet-upholstered booths, and curtains with gold-brocade trim. Octagonal art deco-style glass ceiling lights and a rich, swirling carpet. At one end is a horseshoe-shaped bar and behind it glass shelves on which bottles of brandy and vodka are still lined up. Argylle sees on the highest shelf three bottles of *Führerwein*, made on the orders of Hitler himself to celebrate his fifty-fourth birthday, each boasting on the label a picture of the Führer in full military regalia.

A shudder passes over him like a wave.

There are two stools at the bar, with glasses still in front of them, as if they had been set down only a moment ago, and underneath them a pile of bones, including a couple of skulls, and two pairs of remarkably well-preserved jackboots.

'The bastards sat here drinking while the people who bust their asses building this hellhole were out there being shot,' says Wyatt in disgust.

'See if there's an armoury carriage further back,' says Hooper, mindful of their dwindling weapons supply.

They make their way into the next carriage, which is a dining car. Argylle has the disorienting feeling of entering a room where the occupants have stepped outside for a brief moment, the tables still set with fine bone-china plates and crystal wine glasses, a heavy silver spoon resting on the lip of a soup bowl. And yet, the piles of bones on the seats and the floor tell a different story.

'So what killed them?' Carter muses. 'I mean, there they are, partying like it's 1999 – liquor and fancy food – and then *kaboom*.'

'There,' Argylle says, shining his flashlight up to the wood-panelled ceiling, underneath which a row of yellow glass bell-shaped lamps project from the walls to softly light each individual table.

'So they lit them to death?'

'Above the lights, at the top of the walls. Those holes.'

'Heating vents. What of it?' says Schneider.

'I don't think so. I've seen those before. In the Holocaust Memorial Museum.'

'You think they gassed them?'

Argylle nods. 'I'm guessing they pumped the carriages full of Zyklon B or something similar.'

'They killed their own officers? Boy, they really didn't want anyone shooting their mouths off about this place,' says Casner.

'At least it looks like these guys went peacefully,' says Wyatt. 'More's the pity.'

Casner is in the front as they break through the sealed door, heading for the next carriage. 'Sir, I think this next one could be a weapons store.'

'Woo hoo!' Alex Kellerman is jubilant when he sees the skull-and-crossbones symbol and the word VORSICHT stamped in big red letters on the door of the next carriage along, but when he sees Casner raising up his pistol to blow the lock, he hits it away angrily.

'Are you crazy, dude? Do you know what could be on the other side of that door? You trying to kill us?'

So now tools must be assembled from backpacks, and the handle carefully drilled out, but finally they are clear.

Hooper flings the door open. 'It's colder than a witch's tit in here.'

Standing on the threshold, he shines his flashlight around, and Kellerman, who is at his shoulder, whistles.

'Looks like Christmas came early,' says Kellerman as the yellow beam falls on piles of Karabiners and MP 40s, even a clutch of mortars.

Drip, drip, drip.

Hooper angles his flashlight downwards.

'Jesus Christ.' Disappointment flattens his voice. 'There must be a foot of water in here.'

Craning to see over his shoulder, Argylle sees the black liquid on the floor of the carriage, completely immersing the weapons on the bottom half of the stack and almost certainly destabilizing the rest.

'But the train was sealed,' Kellerman is complaining.

Argylle raises his own light to the ceiling, and it becomes clear where the water has come from – a tear in the supposedly impregnable roof of the train. He wades through the water to stand underneath it, training his flashlight upwards.

'What the—' says Wyatt, who has followed him. 'Is that an—'

'Ice stalactite,' Argylle finishes for him.

Directly above the armoury car, the roof of the tunnel has caved in, revealing, way above it, a monstrous growth on the roof of the topmost cave formed of hundreds of sharp spears, many metres long, pointing down towards them, the result of water dripping through the cave roof into the freezing air.

'You reckon one of those mothers fell on here?' asks Wyatt.

'More than one, judging by the amount of liquid.'

From outside through the broken carriage door, there now comes the sound of gunfire. And the answering rat-a-tat-tat of a machine gun far closer by. Argylle thinks of Brandon Reynolds steadying himself on the sandbag in front.

'I say we just grab the guns that seem dry,' Schneider says. 'There have to be some that are still good.'

'Too risky,' says Hooper. 'We can't be sure how badly they've been compromised.'

'So what do we do now?' asks Carter.

'We keep on going till we find the Amber Room,' says Hooper. 'And pray we can pick up some more firepower on the way.'

*

The next carriage contains rows of hard wooden seats. By the sealed side doors there's a pile of bones and two unornamented, bowl-like helmets of the kind ordinary German infantry soldiers would have worn. The polished wood of the door bears hundreds of fine, silvery scratches. Argylle looks up and sees the same vents in the walls above as in the officers' carriages. 'Poor bastards were trying to escape,' he says.

'Poor bastards nothing – look what they did. And please don't tell me they were just obeying orders.' Quinn's expression is unforgiving.

'You think they had a choice, then?'

'Everyone has free will. We have to stand for something.'

Outside, it sounds as though the fighting has intensified, with now hardly any difference in volume between the two sides, meaning the Russians are advancing fast.

Schneider is muttering under his breath, and Argylle notices he has gone against Hooper's orders and is carrying two semi-automatic rifles slung over his shoulder, picked up from the armoury carriage.

As they open the door at the other end, an ear-splitting scream from near the front of the train cuts through the turgid tunnel air. The firing ceases for a beat. Argylle winces, guessing that either young Reynolds is gone, or he is still alive – and now completely alone. He doesn't know which is worse.

Behind the empty carriage, there is one last railcar. The standard door of this one has been removed and replaced with one made from lead, with heavy iron locks all the way up. The tingling along his nerve endings tells Argylle that this is where they'll find the Amber Room. But between that final carriage and the one they have just come through is a flatbed, and on the flatbed sits an anti-aircraft gun, still mounted on its two-wheeled trailer, its long barrel pointing skyward so that it all but grazes the roof of the tunnel.

'Well?' Hooper asks Casner, the team's most experienced firearms operative. 'Can you get it to work?'

'I think so. But I'll need some time.'

'I'll get you three minutes.'

*

Noah Washington isn't thrilled to be sent back to take over from Brandon Reynolds and Eric Lawler, who have been bravely holding off the Russians at the mouth of the tunnel, if indeed either one is still alive. But he knows he's the best marksman and he's been in the Agency long enough to obey orders first and ask questions later.

'Do whatever it takes to delay them,' Hooper urges him.

Hooper needs to buy some time to get the anti-aircraft gun working, and he's running out of options.

Meanwhile, Wyatt has been dispatched, armed with just enough charge to blow the heavy door locks, to check out the final carriage, searching for any crates or boxes that look as if they could have been used to store the Amber Room. 'Make sure your bodycam is recording so the boss gets a clear view – but for Chrissakes don't open anything. For all we know, the whole thing's booby-trapped.'

Washington departs with his usual grace, an HK416 assault rifle slung over his shoulder, grenades collected up from the team's grenade pouches bouncing in his backpack. He prays their pin tapes are secure as he flutters his fingers in a languid farewell, but Argylle sees how stiffly he holds his head, his eyes fixed on a point ahead of him, recognizes that deliberate summoning of focus and purpose, trying to drive out fear.

Washington is a good shot. Probably the best they have. But the Russians are better armed and there are more of them.

Lots more.

In normal life, three minutes is no time at all – not long enough to boil a decent egg, even. But when you are alone, waiting for an assault from multiple invaders, three minutes can feel like a lifetime.

In the flatbed, Casner is on his knees next to the hunk of metal that was last used several decades ago. 'It's a Flak 30. And our German friends have kindly left an unused tracer magazine loaded up.'

'Can you crank down the barrel so that it points straight through the train?' Hooper indicates the open carriage door they've just come through.

'I'm trying, but it won't move. Kellerman, give me a hand.'

But even the two men together can't move the wheel controlling the gun an inch.

'Two minutes left. Can you do it, Casner?'

'I can't, sir, it's stuck fast.'

'We're running out of time.'

On the outside, Coffey's and Dabrowski's attention has been snagged by something on the satellite feed.

'Oh, Christ, are you seeing this, boss?'

'Right with you, Glenn.'

'You think it's reinforcements?'

'It's an Mi-8. But look at the markings. See the gold VF?'

Vasily Federov is known to only fly Russian-built aircraft. Another way of making himself out to be the ultimate patriot.

Though the worst of the storm has abated, the helicopter, with its cream-and-gold livery, is still struggling to land in a small clearing five hundred metres from the mountainside.

'But why would Federov risk being here?'

Dabrowski's question is answered when the helicopter's doors open and a television film crew begin unloading their equipment.

'I don't believe this,' he says. 'He thinks he's going to broadcast the discovery of the Amber Room live.'

'You have to admire his chutzpah,' says Coffey.

'He's gotta get past our team first.'

'I'm guessing he's planning to hold back until he knows the coast is clear and the Amber Room is definitely there, and then sail in like the conquering hero. It's all part of the PR push.'

'The man's a fool.'

'Far from it. As Christopher Clay, working in tech in San Francisco, building his brand, Federov had teams of people analysing how best to present himself in order to sell his product. He recognized the power of storytelling in raising brand awareness. Tell people your new desktop has a groundbreaking processor type, and ninety per cent will glaze over. Tell them it was developed by an orphan who started life in a dumpster, now you have an identity. Federov knows the power of narrative. If he presents the people of Russia with the Amber Room as a fait accompli, they'll be impressed. If they watch him raise it from the dead, they'll do anything he wants. And that's the worst-case scenario for us.'

55

WHILE CASNER STRUGGLES WITH THE FLAK, WYATT RETURNS FROM HIS exploration of the final carriage, flushed with excitement. 'It's full of wooden crates,' he reports. 'And guess what they're stamped with?'

'Königsberg?' asks Hooper, and punches the air when Wyatt nods. But there's little time for celebrating.

'It's still the wrong angle,' Casner complains, his face purple with the effort of wrangling with the ancient gun.

'The wheels,' Hooper says suddenly, indicating the trailer that the gun sits on so it can be towed from battle to battle. 'Take the wheels off. Maybe the whole thing will tip forwards.'

'Worth a try,' says Casner, already unscrewing the left wheel. Kellerman gets to work on the other one. In the background, the gunfire exchange is louder and uglier than ever.

Within seconds, the wheels are off and the heavy metal gun clunks forward.

'Damn, it's too low,' Casner bellows in frustration, but Kellerman is already on it, wedging a metal ammunition box underneath the nozzle of the gun until it is pointing through the open door to the next carriage and squarely down the length of the train.

Casner pushes the safety catch into the 'ready' position and pulls the lever to open the breechblock. 'All set.'

From the corner of his eye Argylle sees one of his teammates detach themselves from the group, dropping silently down on to the platform, next to a safety alcove that houses a rusting fire extinguisher, and disappear around the side of the train. *Interesting*, he thinks.

'Hold off for a second, I'm going to warn Washington,' he calls to Hooper as he sets off in pursuit.

'Argylle, you stay right where you are.'

But Argylle acts like he can't hear.

And maybe he can't.

'You got *two* minutes!' Hooper yells at his back in frustration. 'Then this thing blows – with you or without.'

In the gap between the restaurant car and the cocktail bar, Argylle clambers up on to the train roof, crying out in frustration when his 9mm Glock, his sole remaining weapon, dislodges itself from his holster and clatters on to the tracks below. Even crouching as low as he can, the top of his head brushes the tunnel roof. The air up here is stale, and thick with dust and dirt. Argylle thinks of all the dead bodies in this cave. Wonders what exactly he is breathing in. From here the sound of gunfire is deafening, Argylle's adrenaline-pumped heart jolts with each new explosion.

When he reaches the front of the train, he drops on to his stomach and crawls to the edge, wincing at what he sees. Brandon Reynolds's body slumped over the wall of sandbags, his face – still bearing traces of old acne scars – turned to the side, clear blue eyes open, looking straight at Argylle. He could almost be smiling if it weren't for the fact that half of his forehead is missing. Eric Lawler's body is lying on the ground, next to the sandbag barricade, his finger still bent around the trigger of his assault rifle.

Behind his left shoulder, Argylle's quarry stops momentarily to hunch over a device retrieved from a trouser pocket, before continuing on down the platform towards where Noah Washington, his long body shielded by sandbags, is firing rounds from a sub-machine gun he must have taken from one of the four dead Russians within a five-metre range.

When the magazine empties Washington throws down the gun and picks up an assault rifle from the stack of weapons he has piled next to him. As Argylle watches, hidden, Washington whips around, alerted by a noise behind him. His expression softens into relief and he lowers the rifle.

'My *goodness*, but you're a sight for sore eyes,' he tells the person who has come up from the rear. Then his eyes widen in shock.

'I'm sorry,' says a voice Argylle recognizes. 'Please believe me, I'm so sorry. I have no choice.'

'Holy shit!' Dabrowski fades to silence as the back of the helicopter he and Coffey are watching on their respective screens slides open, disgorging four armed Russian Spetsnaz on scrambler motorbikes, one with a sidecar loaded with cables and lighting and sound equipment.

Only when this is done does a door towards the front of the helicopter open. A set of steps folds down and now an unmistakable figure emerges. Dressed in crisp military fatigues.

As Federov descends to the bottom of the stairs one of the motorbikes pulls up in front of him, the driver clearly expecting him to climb on behind, but instead Federov orders him off and straddles the bike in his place.

'Everything is about image,' says Coffey, half admiring, as the former tech magnate poses for the camera astride the purloined bike.

But though Federov looks the part, he seems in no hurry to get moving. Instead the entire group – Spetsnaz and TV crew – linger by the chopper as its blades slowly grind to a halt.

'What are they waiting for?' murmurs Dabrowski.

Coffey zooms in on Federov and notices his earpiece.

'He's waiting for a signal,' she says flatly.

'From one of ours?'

'I believe so. Some sort of pre-agreed sign, I'd guess, probably a series of electrical pulses or something similar.'

Federov, who has been sitting all this time with his brows knitted in concentration as if listening to something, now rips out the earbuds and says something to the assembled personnel, who all bustle into life, the cameraman riding pillion on the bike behind Federov's, filming his progress.

'Guess he got his signal.'

'They're going to make quick time getting to the cave on those things.' Coffey's voice is strained. 'I just wish we could get a warning to Hooper. Are you any nearer getting the transmitter fixed?'

'I'm working on it, boss.'

While everyone is waiting for Argylle, Carter is off on her own down the far end of the tunnel, busily trying to restore the lost connection to Frances Coffey. They've been relying on ultra-low-frequency transmissions via the compact RF transceivers they brought with them, but even these have stopped working. Now she starts examining the extensive cabling the Germans installed in the tunnel to power the lighting and the locomotive turntable. She is no historian, but she knows even the earliest underground railway networks employed a rudimentary system of telecommunications so the drivers in the tunnels could communicate with the signalmen. Somewhere there'll be a coaxial cable, its casing missing at intervals so the bare copper internal wiring is exposed, allowing the signal to be radiated in or out all along the length of it. She just has to find it . . .

On the train roof, Argylle feels as if he is underwater, the words he just heard distorted, travelling sluggishly along his auditory nerve, arriving late and jumbled in his brain. Several beats pass between him recognizing the voice and comprehending what it said. When he does, something inside him splits clean in two. He leans forwards over the edge of the roof until he sees the speaker, still cherishing a shred of hope that he is mistaken.

He isn't mistaken.

'What the hell—'

A flicker of regret passes over Erin Quinn's face as she spots him up there on the train roof, but still she doesn't lower the semi-automatic pointed at Washington's head.

'They lied to me, Argylle. Your sainted CIA. My dad didn't die in an explosion in Iraq. The commanding officer only assumed that. He was in such a hurry to save his own ass, he lied and said he'd seen him get blown up with his own eyes. They left him behind. Then the Iraqis captured him and passed him on to the Russians.

'Do you know happens to captured CIA agents, Argylle? It's not pretty. Meanwhile, Coffey told us he died a hero. Sent us an empty coffin to bury.'

'That's no excuse for—'

'My dad's still alive, Argylle.' Quinn's voice is gritty with emotion. 'Federov has him. But the only thing *keeping* him alive is me.'

A weight settles on Coffey's chest, crushing the air out of her as she flicks between Erin Quinn's bodycam feed and Argylle's. Quinn's anguished expression, the way the gun shakes in her hand and the shock on Argylle's face. Coffey is glad Dabrowski can't see her. She reaches for her cigarettes but withdraws her hand at the last minute, as if denying herself is the very least thing she can do to make amends for the huge injustice she knows was done in the name of the organization she runs.

'What the . . . ! Is Quinn pointing a gun at Washington? Am I really seeing this? What the hell is going on down there?'

'There's something I need to tell you, Glenn. Jared Quinn was let down by his commander out in Iraq. There's no way to sugar-coat it. There was an ambush. Everything was chaos. The commander made some poor decisions and Quinn was left behind.

'The Iraqis tried to use him as a bargaining chip at first, torturing him, then offering him up in exchange for the release of two hundred captured Iraqi fighters. And when we refused, they told us they shot him. You have to believe we had no idea he'd been passed on to the Russians.'

'But you didn't tell the family?'

'What good would it have done? Jared was dead. We couldn't change that, but we could try to protect his widow and daughter from the truth about how he died, the horrible details that would haunt their dreams.'

'And the empty coffin?'

'They deserved a funeral.'

'I have to do what they say,' says Quinn, without lowering her weapon. 'Otherwise they'll kill my dad. You do see, don't you? First they told me Isfahan was the end of it. I waited months and the bastards never released him and I had to assume he was dead, but three weeks after Monaco, they sent me a video. I wasn't going to, but, oh God, Argylle, the state of him.'

As Quinn is talking to him, Argylle sees five Russian Spetsnaz approaching. His nerves scream as he recognizes the bull-like figure of Sergei Denisov, one eye still bandaged, the other black as a scorch-mark. The Russian in the lead drops to his knee to take aim.

'Don't shoot!' Quinn calls out, just as Washington cries out and pivots, trying to aim one of his lethal Savate kicks at her head. She pulls the trigger before he is even a foot in the air and Washington collapses to the ground.

'I'm sorry,' Quinn says, anguish twisting her features into some-thing unfamiliar. 'I'm so, so sorry.'

Distorted sounds fill Argylle's head, time entering slow motion. By now Denisov is just a few feet away, close enough for Argylle to see the spittle that has collected in the corner of his fleshy mouth. Argylle can't risk any sudden movement, just presses himself to the roof of the train, sure it can only be seconds before Quinn gives him away.

Instead she turns to Denisov, her gun still raised. 'I've done every-thing you asked,' she says. 'Where's my father? You promised to bring him.'

Denisov holds up his hands to show he isn't armed. 'Sure,' he says, and his good eye, sunk into his face, seems like the portal to hell. 'Your dad is just back there. He is very happy to see you.' He ges-tures behind him, and as Quinn turns eagerly to peer into the darkness of the cavern and her hand holding her gun dips, he darts forward with an unexpected agility, and then he is behind her with his meaty elbow hooked around her neck, pressing on her windpipe so that she drops the weapon in order to clutch her hands to his arm, trying to wrench it away.

Argylle raises his head, preparing to move, unable to stand by and watch, but Quinn's eyes lock on to his and widen as if warning him not to be a suicidal idiot.

'Did I say he was here, your daddy?' Denisov says, too intent on Quinn to notice Argylle in the shadows. 'My mistake. He is dead. He died two days ago. On the ground. Like a dog.'

Argylle turns away, knowing that one small twist from Denisov's elbow will snap Quinn's neck like a twig. He braces for the crack, but it never comes.

Instead, when he next dares look, Denisov has released his hold and Quinn slides down to the ground, clutching her throat and gasping. 'I don't kill you when you are such a big help for us. I let your friends do that.'

Denisov laughs and heads off towards the front of the train, followed by his band of heavily armed Spetsnaz fighters.

Now there is just Argylle, there on the train roof. And the woman who, up until a few moments ago, he had thought he might love.

Quinn picks up the gun which she dropped when she struggled with Denisov. Her face is ashen, so that the burn mark on her neck shows up purple and livid. When she raises her eyes to Argylle's, they are wide with shock, and he guesses the enormity of what she has done is only now sinking in.

'Oh God, Argylle,' she says, raising the gun until the barrel is pointing at him. 'I've screwed up everything. I've hurt so many people.'

'Samra. Washington. These were your friends, Quinn. How could you?'

Argylle tries to ignore the gun and focus on her face, which now bears an expression of utter despair.

'My dad is . . . was . . . my hero, Argylle. The Agency abandoned him.'

'And what? You think he'd be proud of what you've done? You think that's what he'd have wanted?'

Quinn slowly shakes her head, but she doesn't lower her weapon. Instead she brings her other hand up to clasp the first and flicks the safety lever.

'I'm sorry, Argylle. I really am.'

The last thought that passes through Argylle's mind before everything goes black is surprise at finding he believes her.

56

AN EXPLOSION OF PAIN BRINGS ARGYLLE BACK TO CONSCIOUSNESS. Instantly his hand goes to a point just below his left collarbone, coming away wet. He tears off the bodycam that is pressing against the wound as two thoughts go through his mind in rapid succession: *I've been hit; I'll survive.* He drags himself upright. No sign of Quinn, just the awful sight of Washington, his long body bent on the ground like a letter Z. Except . . .

He swings his legs over the side of the train and, bracing himself, drops down on to the platform. A red-hot bolt of agony shoots across his closed eyelids and he almost loses consciousness again. His fingers go to his collarbone itself, which is no longer one long continuous bar but several disjointed nubs of bone. The bullet must have shattered it on its way in.

He takes a deep breath and drops down next to Washington, biting down against the pain. He wasn't mistaken, his teammate's chest is definitely moving. Washington is alive, though a quick monitoring of his pulse tells Argylle he might not be for long.

'I'm coming back for you,' he whispers. 'I give you my word.'

Getting to his feet, he staggers along the platform. From inside the train comes the sound of shouting. The Russians have found the artillery car. He arrives at the end in time to hear Hooper yelling, 'There he is! Denisov. Straight ahead. At the end of the carriage. Forget about Argylle. Fire!'

The flatbed comes into view just as Casner discharges the Flak, the ancient weapon creaking briefly into life. Nothing.

'Reload!' Hooper shouts. The Flak is reloaded, but before Casner has a chance to press the button the Russians open fire from the far end of the next carriage. Casner takes a straight hit to the chest, toppling gracefully sideways. Kellerman isn't so lucky. One bullet penetrates his sternum before emerging from his back. Another shoots through his jaw.

Now Schneider charges forward, his rifle raised. Except it isn't his own rifle, which is already out of ammo. It's the Schmeisser he took from the armoury carriage.

'No, Schneider, don't!' But Argylle's warning is lost in the exchange of fire and his teammate pulls the trigger. Argylle's stomach twists as Schneider's faulty weapon malfunctions and his old adversary is engulfed in a fireball.

Taking advantage of the momentary burst of smoke, Wyatt hauls Casner's body aside and slides in behind the Flak, pressing the trigger on its handwheel. This time it works, the noise reverberating through the tunnel as the discharged tracer shell, made to self-destruct after two seconds, blasts low and straight through the open carriage door. Denisov, still charging forward down the carriage aisle, has just enough time to understand what is happening before the shell hits, exploding on impact to create a second fireball. Before he dives into the safety alcove that is recessed into the tunnel wall to the side of the flatbed, Argylle sees the fireball swallow up the various disjointed parts of Denisov that rain like confetti through the air, before barrelling through the train at a hundred miles per hour, destroying everything in its path.

'We're in, boss. Carter must have fixed up some kind of leaky feeder down there. We have a connection.'

Dabrowski's voice is wound tight. He and Coffey have watched the unfolding carnage in horrified silence. Erin Quinn's betrayal. Most of the team wiped out. All this will have to be painfully unpicked and confronted at a later stage. But now there is still a job to be done.

As Dabrowski, in his lonely Montana exile, turns his attention to the monitor which is showing the live broadcast on Channel Rossiya, the Russian TV network owned by Vasily Federov's political running mate, Anatole Poletov, Federov himself approaches the entrance to the cavern. The face of the most dangerous man in the world is set hard, and the TV crew, guarded by armed Spetsnaz, are filming his every reaction. Every now and then the camera accidentally alights on a dead body in Federov's path and swings quickly away, the footage wobbly, as if the camera operator's hand is shaking.

Wyatt has spotted Argylle in the entrance to the alcove. 'Are you hit, dude?' he calls, getting to his feet and climbing out from behind the Flak. 'Hold on, I'm—'

Whatever he was about to say is swallowed up by the sound of boots on concrete and a command shouted out in Russian. Six armed Spetsnaz line up alongside the flatbed, their backs to Argylle, who has shrunk back into the alcove, hidden by shadows. Hooper and Wyatt, taken by surprise and still reeling from the carnage that has just decimated the rest of the team, have no chance. Argylle puts his hand on the rusty fire extinguisher, calculating how he could cause maximum damage, but to his surprise the Russians don't open fire.

Instead the leader orders two of his men to take Wyatt and Hooper back to the main part of the cavern. Argylle's captured teammates don't so much as glance in his direction as they drop down on to the platform and are marched at gunpoint with their hands on their heads back up the tunnel, past the smouldering wreckage of the train.

Meanwhile, the remaining four Russians make their way to the only train carriage still intact, the one at the back of the flatbed with the wooden crates. They are gone for some time, re-emerging just as Argylle is on the point of stepping out of his hiding point, wrestling a wooden crate down from the carriage, followed by a rudimentary wheeled wooden pallet. Once on the platform, there is an interminable delay while they manhandle the crate on to the pallet, and Argylle's stomach knots as he remembers that the Amber Room was reportedly stored in twenty-seven crates. Are they intending to bring each of them out like this? Fortunately, the men seem content with just the one and they wheel it off down the platform, past the fragments of twisted, smoking metal which are all that remain of the front section of the train, towards the main cavern.

When he is sure they're not coming back, Argylle steps out of the alcove and makes his way up the platform. Every time he thinks about what happened to his team in that tunnel – Casner, Schneider, Kellerman and the rest of them all dead, Wyatt and Hooper as good as – an invisible knife twists in his chest, merging with the pain still radiating from his shattered collarbone and the bullet lodged somewhere underneath it. At least Carter wasn't in the flatbed. He tries to focus on the hope that she survived and is hiding somewhere.

Reaching Washington, he drops down to feel his pulse and reassure himself he's still alive. He sags with relief when he feels the faint throb under the pads of his fingers. They are at the mouth of the tunnel, and he can hear a hubbub of Russian voices coming from the cavern just out of sight.

The wall of sandbags is still in place and he crawls towards it, avoiding the fallen bodies of Lawler and Reynolds, every movement prompting another jolt of pain. Peering over the top, he can now see into the main part of the cavern, and the scene in front of him stoppers the breath in his throat.

Coffey and Dabrowski switch in grim silence between two monitors – the one that follows Federov's live broadcast on Russian TV and the one showing a grid of the different feeds from the team's various body-cams, most of these now either cut off or showing a completely static picture. Minutes earlier they had watched breathlessly as Wyatt's bodycam showed them the wooden crates, stamped with the word 'Königsberg' and each one sequentially numbered, but their excitement had turned to horror as the scene on the flatbed unfolded. The transmitter had been reconnected too late to help them warn Hooper, and now he and Wyatt are captured, the others all seemingly dead or wounded. There is nothing to say. All they can do is bear witness.

The vast space has been floodlit – the powerful beams emanating from five portable, pole-mounted, battery-powered arc lamps. A TV crew stride about purposefully; one has a huge camera mounted on his shoulder, another wheels a microphone clamped to a boom arm. Three further crew members seem to be hurriedly dressing the area as if it was a film set. A pair of swastika banners have been found from somewhere and are now suspended over telescopic, retractable aluminium ladders the crew must have brought with them. A towering triptych that could only have come from a grand cathedral is propped up against the cavern wall. The trunks containing the gold bars have been opened and placed under a yellow lamp so that the metal glows. Several vast Persian carpets have been unrolled over the dusty ground, the bones that were there before now unceremoniously swept to the outer edges. Everywhere there are paintings and statues, artefacts and jewels, the overall effect so dazzling that at first Argylle doesn't notice the figure at the centre of it all.

Vasily Federov stands as still as one of the statues that surround him, gazing down at the closed wooden crate in front of him. His focus is absolute as his fingertips trace the swastika stamp on the lid and the black lettering that spells out 'Königsberg' as if in a trance, and the camera hones in on his face.

Argylle notices Wyatt and Hooper over on the far side, their hands still on their heads, even though their guards' attention is, like everyone else's, turned towards the man in the centre of the cavern and the crate in front of him, and whatever that crate might contain. But now there is a buzz passing through the cavern, and a uniformed Spetsnaz approaches Federov to whisper in his ear.

For a moment, Federov remains still, his expression unchanged. Then he gives a curt nod, and the man disappears off to the side, only to reappear seconds later with . . . Behind the sandbag wall, Argylle's whole body jolts as if he's been shot, sending a white-hot spear of pain through him from his shattered collarbone.

'This woman has been feeding us CIA secrets for months,' Federov announces in Russian, turning Erin Quinn around so that the camera can capture her wide grin. 'At first because we'd captured her father, but then because she realized what a corrupt, venal institution the CIA is, tossing their operatives out like garbage once they have no use for them any more.'

Argylle fights back a rush of nausea, seeing how Federov is using Quinn to score propaganda points on live television, boosting his own patriot credentials and underlining how totally he has repudiated his adopted country. Not that she appears concerned about that as the two of them shake hands for the camera, Federov surreptitiously wiping his on his trouser leg afterwards.

Only now does Argylle realize how much he'd been wanting to believe Quinn's tearful protestations of remorse earlier. Had any of it been true? Or had the whole thing about her hostage father been a calculated lie to win him over? Finally, he has to let go of the fairy story he's been secretly clinging to – that she'd purposefully missed when she shot at him earlier. He has to face up to the fact that the Erin Quinn who'd seemed so racked with guilt never existed. This woman cosying up to Federov next to the closed wooden crate is who she really is. He wonders how much Federov is paying her. How much for each of the teammates she has betrayed?

So engrossed in thought is he, Argylle doesn't notice someone coming up behind him. Until it is too late.

With the team's bodycams showing very little, Coffey and Dabrowski are glued to the other monitor, where Federov's live broadcast is going out in Russian with English subtitles for the benefit of the global audience. Word of the unprecedented scenes has spread like wildfire on social media and now people are tuning in from all over the world. On screen, a security guard sweeps the crate with an explosives trace detector. He steps back with a curt nod and now there is a close-up on Federov. Though his expression is as flat as ever, his nostrils are flared and he licks his thin lips. In the background, Quinn gazes up at him, rapt.

'How badly I got this wrong,' Coffey says softly. 'To turn a principled young woman like Erin so fervently against the agency that used to be her life.'

'Plenty of people get let down,' Dabrowski says, harshly. 'But they don't all sell out their friends. Or their country.'

*

'It isn't enough for you that I got shot, you wanna give me a heart attack as well.'

Even while he's speaking, Argylle is thinking it's quite possible he's never been gladder to see anyone in his life than he is to see Keira Carter right now.

Carter drops down beside him, and for a moment he takes comfort from her presence, but then the reality of the scene he is witnessing overwhelms him again.

'I just can't believe it,' says Carter. 'Anyone but Quinn.'

They stop talking as Vasily Federov leaps on top of the crate and launches into a speech.

'The history of Russia in the last century is a history of theft and plunder. Things stolen from us. Recognition stolen, for the twenty-five million people we sacrificed in the Great Patriotic War. Respect stolen, for the power we used to be when we were still the Soviet Union, before our lands were divided up and our own people forced to live under hostile, fascist governments, puppets of the West, who threaten our security on our own borders. And wasn't I stolen also? A Russian baby, ripped from the teat of his motherland to grow up in an alien, morally corrupt society?

'The Amber Room is the symbol of everything that was stolen from us and continues to be stolen from us as the West tries to ally itself with countries in our own sphere of influence. Well, now is the time for restoration and restitution. Now we take back control. In every area where our national security is compromised and our citizens cry out to be back under our protection. The West today is a flapping shark without teeth or fins, drowning in its dependence on Russian oil. This is our moment.

'Just as I have returned home, so I will return every last vestige of what has been stolen from us. Once the votes are counted tomorrow we will start the process of restoring our sovereign lands. And the restoration starts here and now. With the eighth wonder of the world, stolen in 1941 from the Catherine Palace in St Petersburg, and now returned by my hand to my beloved Russia as a pledge of my commitment to Russian glory.'

He jumps from the crate, fuelled by a zeal normally kept in check.

Taking a pistol from a holster at his hip, he raises it theatrically before shooting off the crate's heavy metal padlock.

'Ladies and gentlemen. Fellow patriots. Citizens of Mother Russia. I give you, the Amber Room!'

Carter grips Argylle's arm as Vasily Federov, former foundling, brave new hope of a re-energized, reunified Russian superpower, jimmies open the crate's lid.

It is as if the very air in the cavern stops circulating, as all those present hold their breath at once. Argylle and Carter are at the wrong angle to see inside the crate, but whatever is in there catches the overhead light, creating a peculiar halo effect, as if the crate is glowing from within.

Federov's face, normally devoid of expression, cracks into a smile, his entire being focused on whatever it is that glitters in front of him, reflecting flecks of gold on the underside of his chin. The assembled audience can't tear their eyes from him, which is why no one except Argylle notices Erin Quinn unscrew the battery barrel of the tactical flashlight slung across her body in its holster.

'Wait, is that a . . .?' Carter has followed Argylle's gaze and the two of them stare in disbelief as Quinn takes the pin out of the grenade she has just retrieved.

'Oh Jesus,' mutters Carter, but Argylle is already on his feet and yelling, 'Quinn! No!'

As everyone turns in his direction, Quinn's eyes fleetingly meet his in an expression which somehow seems to encompass both regret and resolve. Then, as Federov's henchmen move towards him, she seizes advantage of the momentary distraction to step forward and toss the live grenade into the open crate.

Carter pulls Argylle back down next to her. For one seemingly endless moment, nothing happens, and it seems like the grenade must be a dud. Then comes an almighty explosion. As Argylle and Carter watch helplessly from behind the sandbags, and Dabrowski and Coffey over their computer monitors, and countless millions of viewers through their TV screens, shards of something brittle and golden shoot out from the crate, blasting into the air like fireworks, one of them slicing through Vasily Federov's neck, separating it cleanly from his body, the blue rag he'd just pulled from his pocket flung wide as he falls.

Of Quinn herself there is no trace at all.

And now, over the sound of screaming and yelling, comes an ominous rumble as the rock that makes up the cavern roof, destabilized by the blast, begins to crumble and rain down on those in the central cavern.

'The whole thing is about to collapse,' says Coffey, staring at the live feed, which the cameraman, who was paid to continue filming at all costs, is still heroically recording. In the chaotic scrum of people trying to escape, they have lost sight of Wyatt and Hooper.

Neither of them can bear to bring up Argylle and Carter, who haven't been heard from for some time.

Incredibly, the live broadcast is still running, the footage juddering as the cameraman runs towards the locomotive turntable, but as he swings the camera around for one final look behind, the ceiling over the main hall gives way, crashing down on top of the beautiful stolen paintings and statues, the jewels and the gold bars, the banners and the open crate, the contents of which are now lost for ever.

The screen goes black.

The moments immediately following the roof collapse come to Argylle in fragments, pain and shock rendering him incapable of holding on to a continuous thread of thought or action. He is staggering through air that is thick with black dust that makes it impossible to see or breathe. There's a weight dragging on his good shoulder, so that the other one screams with every step. Somehow he knows that the weight is Washington and he mustn't let go of him, no matter how agonizing it gets. On Washington's other side is Carter. He doesn't know how he knows this; he just does.

Then they are at the locomotive turntable and Carter leaves, so that he alone is propping Washington up. He tries not to pass out. When Carter returns she is holding something. An aluminium ladder. Where did she get that? No time to ask because she is off again, up the ladder, leaving him once again with Washington. And now he can't stay upright any more, and they are both sliding to the ground.

A grinding noise in the filthy darkness. A monstrous groaning. And now Carter shouting from somewhere above him. 'Quick, Argylle! It's going up.' Belatedly, he realizes she has summoned the turntable itself back into life and it is slowly rising. So now he must haul himself to his feet and somehow find the strength to drag Washington on as the great disc lifts into the foul, swirling air.

Somehow they are on, and approaching the top, and the dust has cleared enough to make out two human shapes there, waiting. Spetsnaz? Has Carter been taken? It's two women from the film crew, sitting there with their heads in their hands. They don't even look up. And somehow he understands that the Spetsnaz themselves have gone.

And now they are emerging out of the cave and into the light and it is so bright, as if those floodlights from the cavern are out here and all pointing at him. 'I think . . .' he begins. And then the world folds in on him.

57

ON THE DIRTY STONE FLOOR OF THAT TERRIBLE HIDDEN ROOM IN the belly of Federov's summer palace, the pile of rags that was once Jared Quinn lies perfectly still. In fact, it hasn't moved in fifty-six hours, not even when Sergei Denisov nudged it with the toe of his Gucci loafer, unwilling to get any closer on account of the stomach-turning stench. Little wonder he assumed his captive was dead. And yet he wasn't. Not then. Rather, Quinn's body had slipped into a peculiar state of stasis where nothing was real, and nothing meant anything. There was no hunger, no loneliness, no fear. No feeling at all. Just being.

But as his breath – slowed so much by the time of Denisov's last visit that the Russian missed it entirely – finally ceases altogether, some awareness fleetingly returns to him.

A memory ripples across the smooth surface of his mind – Federov's hard-faced wife, holding a clean white handkerchief against the smell of him so that her words sound like they come from a long way away. *Your daughter killed my husband. You should be proud.* Did it happen? It no longer matters. Only the feeling matters, a warm net settling over the chilled bones of him. And now a picture of his daughter, Erin, his great love, arrives like a speck in the wasteland of his thoughts and then expands, radiating along his nervous system into his organs, his limbs, until it fills every last cell of him.

Peace comes now. And he welcomes it.

58

Seventy-five hours later

AT THE GOVERNMENT FACILITY IN HARVEY POINT, NORTH CAROLINA, there's a room not many people ever get to see. Sometimes it's used to hold informal meetings that no one else needs to know about; other times it's where bereaved families come to learn more about how their loved ones died. There's a long, soft leather couch with cream scatter cushions and a selection of easy chairs upholstered in easy, neutral linen, a low coffee table with a discreet box of Kleenex. The room's square window looks out on to a garden planted with roses. It is a restful space, and it is here that Coffey has gathered most of what is left of the team just over three days after the events in Poland that have sent shockwaves around the world.

Corcoran is back and looking quite recovered, though forty pounds lighter. Washington is being beamed in on a TV screen from his hospital bed. Though he's out of the danger zone, he is still weak from the surgery to remove the bullet from the left side of his chest, and has a long way to go. Will Hooper sits by the window, along with Mike Randall. And on the couch are Wyatt, Argylle and Carter, Argylle's arm held up at a right angle by the sling that keeps his newly pinned collarbone in position.

Coffey starts by thanking them for their service and saying a few warm words about each of their fallen teammates. Lawler, Schneider,

Casner, Kellerman, Ryder, Matsyak. Tears prick Argylle's eyes when she talks about Brandon Reynolds, who, like him, was on his first mission but, unlike him, never made it back.

When she comes to Erin Quinn, her tone changes.

'The Agency doesn't always get things right. We let down the Quinn family very badly. And while I don't expect any of you to forgive Erin for the things she did, I hope you will try to understand them. She loved her father very much. She was in an impossible situation. The person she loved most in the world was being held hostage, and the only people she trusted enough to ask for help had betrayed her in the worst way.'

'So why shoot Argylle?' Wyatt wants to know. 'There was no one else around. She didn't need to do that.'

'Yeah, she did,' says Argylle flatly. 'Because she'd already decided on her plan and she knew that if she didn't shoot me, I'd stop her.'

'That's right.' Coffey nods. 'Just remember Erin Quinn acted out of desperation to save her dad, and when she came to her senses and realized what she'd done, she sacrificed herself to try to make amends.'

As Argylle listens he fights the impulse to detach himself from what Coffey is saying, emptying his mind so that her words float somewhere out of reach. Over the past months he has been learning to engage with the world again, but the pull of the old numbness is never far away, the tempting relief of not having to feel anything. He knows he needs to force himself to stay present, to feel the things he feels rather than burying them, no matter how painful they are.

Now she is talking about the mission itself. The cavern has been declared unsafe and sealed off. At some point the authorities will start sifting through the wreckage, looking for any remnants of the Amber Room, if indeed it was ever there – the explosion occurred before the TV cameraman had a chance to focus on the crate's contents, so the pictures were tantalizingly inconclusive. CIA experts believe it's unlikely anything survived the catastrophic collapse. The Russian election has been postponed, but it's near certain Vice President Zhuravlev will go through uncontested. While he's as corrupt as his predecessor, at least he doesn't represent the same threat to the world order as Vasily Federov did.

A sharp knock interrupts Coffey's flow, and the door swings open, revealing a man Argylle has never seen before and yet somehow seems to recognize.

Instantly Wyatt is on his feet and clapping the new arrival on the back. 'Dabrowski. My bro.'

A very changed Glenn Dabrowski to the one Frances Coffey visited in Montana. Gone the livid, bruise-coloured shadows under his eyes, gone the sloping shoulders that carried on them the weight of the world.

This Glenn Dabrowski walks taller and has a smile that seems too broad for his cheeks.

On the long journey back from Poland, the team were filled in on the sacrifices Glenn Dabrowski had made to smoke out the real traitor in their midst, but this is the first time they've seen him in person and those who served with him clamour for his attention.

'I never lost faith in you, man,' Wyatt tells him. 'Not once.'

'Are you coming back?' Corcoran wants to know.

Dabrowski shakes his head. 'I've missed enough of my family's life. I don't want to miss a single moment more.'

While the others bombard him with questions, Argylle holds back, feeling suddenly shy with this stranger whose shoes he stepped into. He is taken aback when Dabrowski turns to him.

'You don't know me, but I sure know you. I've been watching over you for months.'

Now it falls into place. 'You're my guardian angel.'

Dabrowski laughs. 'Something like that.

'I wanted to congratulate you,' Dabrowski goes on. 'You did a great job out there.'

Argylle feels unaccountably tongue-tied and Dabrowski, seeming to recognize his awkwardness, unexpectedly steps forward to give him a gentle, one-sided hug. And despite the fact that, gentle or not, it sends fireworks of pain shooting around his body, somehow it's one of the best hugs of Argylle's life.

When he steps back, embarrassed, Wyatt blocks his path. 'If we're all hugging now . . .' he says, cracking his knuckles before opening up his arms to show off biceps that could crack a coconut.

'Don't even think about it, big guy.'

But Argylle is laughing when he takes his place back on the couch between Carter and Wyatt and, for a moment, despite everything that has happened, he feels a warm, pleasant rush of something he can't immediately identify. Only after a few moments does he recognize the unfamiliar feeling as belonging.

Frances Coffey beams around the room. 'You've all given so much and worked so hard. I want you to take some time for yourselves to recharge before I tell you your next mission.'

Argylle's new-found sense of wellbeing dissolves at the prospect of an empty stretch of free time. Where will he go? Then Coffey looks at her watch.

'So shall we say we'll reconvene at five thirty this afternoon?'

Wyatt nudges him. 'Excellent. That gives me just enough time to whip your ass at pool.'

'I guess you've forgotten I've only got one arm?'

Wyatt grins.

'And your point is?'

Carter stands up, gathers her things. 'If this is gonna get ugly, I want a ringside seat.'

Coffey watches the trio leave. She has seen many cohorts of recruits come and go, but she never gets jaded or blasé. It's always a responsibility and an honour to watch them grow and eventually fly. Every last one of them touches her. Even so, she has to admit Aubrey Argylle is special. That lost soul who came wandering out of a Thai jungle and still has no idea of his own potential.

Alone in the room, Coffey fumbles in the bottom of her bag for the cigarette packet she knows is there, and she stares at it for a long time. Then she sighs and puts it back.

Life is fragile and short. Wouldn't she be a fool to make it even shorter?

Mike Randall knocks at the door. 'When you're ready, boss, Taylor Kearney is in reception.'

Kearney is Coffey's newest recruit, plucked from a small-town police department after single-handedly foiling an armed robbery, and still has that wide-eyed rabbit-in-the-headlights look that says, *What am I doing here? I don't belong.*

Still, Coffey has a good feeling about her. And by now, she's a pretty good judge. The teams might be constantly changing, but the threat remains the same, and as long as the Vasily Federovs keep coming, she needs to carry on seeking out more Aubrey Argylles.

'Show her up.'

Epilogue

THE MOSCOW STUDIO OF CHANNEL ROSSIYA BOASTS AN AWARD-winning hair and make-up department, but Irina Federova insisted on bringing her own personal stylist. Having commandeered the studio's largest dressing room, she stares stonily at her reflection while the woman irons her hair smooth, knowing to avoid the tiny blobs of polyurethane that hold Federova's extensions in place.

There's a knock on the door. A production assistant, accompanied by one of the detectives, who has been giving Mrs Federova regular updates about the ongoing investigations into the events in Poland.

'Do you need me to stay, madam?' asks the assistant, hovering in the doorway. Irina wafts her away dismissively with her hand.

'I have brought you some . . . *items* . . . belonging to your late husband that were recovered from the scene,' the detective says once they are alone. 'I thought it might comfort you to have them.'

From his briefcase he produces two clear plastic bags.

Irina reaches into the first bag and pulls out Federov's rimless spectacles, remarkably intact. She suppresses a shudder, remembering how her husband's pale eyes would fix on her through those lenses and she would have a terrible sensation of her soul being sucked clean out of her body.

'How is it these survived when everything else was crushed or buried?'

The detective looks down at his hands and she notices his cheeks flush pink.

'I think you know that his head was . . . um . . . separated from his body. The blast jettisoned it quite some way out from the site of the roof collapse.'

The detective sneaks a glance upwards and is chilled by the lack of emotion on the new widow's face. Later, he will eye his wife thoughtfully over the dinner table and wonder how she'd react if someone handed *her* the glasses that had been taken off his own recently decapitated head.

Twenty minutes later, Irina sits behind a long white table, uncomfortably warm under the studio lights in her black wool Chanel suit, trying to ignore the cameras just inches from her face and the TV crew milling busily around.

She knows she has to pitch this exactly right. Knows that as yet people don't know how to react to what happened. The popular view is that Federov fulfilled half his promise – he found the Amber Room, but then he failed to deliver it. So does that make him a winner or a loser?

She has to convince them of the former if she's to have any chance of achieving her goal.

'My fellow countrymen,' she begins, directly to camera, allowing a tear to trickle down her cheek. 'My late husband was a hero and a patriot. He put duty first, and now so must I. While I long to be left alone to grieve in private, I know that's not what he would have wanted. Which is why tonight I am announcing my intention to run for office in his place. In his honour.'

When she gets back to the dressing room, Irina Federova is flushed with triumph. She could tell by the reaction of the crew that her message has hit home. Finally, after all these years of being someone's daughter, someone's husband, she is about to step into the limelight in her own right. It is her time.

Pouring herself a glass of champagne from the bottle that has been left for her, she sits back down in front of the mirror. Her eye falls on the two plastic evidence bags.

She picks up the second one.

'The soundman found it when he got home, tangled around his equipment,' the detective had told her. 'Apparently, your husband took it from his pocket just before he was . . . just before he died.'

Irina opens the bag and her face twists with disgust as she withdraws the strip of blue-grey rag, grubby with use.

She holds it up between her thumb and forefinger while her other hand reaches into her handbag on the chair beside her.

For a long, still moment, she contemplates the rag, remembering what it meant to her husband and how he kept it close to him always.

Then her fingers close around her lighter and, withdrawing it from her bag, she sets fire to the bottom edge of the strip, dropping it into the wastepaper bin to watch it burn.

Author Apology and Acknowledgements

Though it feels mighty real to me, *Argylle* is a work of fiction. That means that while many of the places and institutions mentioned in it are real, the characters and what they do and say are not. La Chèvre d'Or, Kew Gardens, the Royal Observatory, the archives in Koblenz, the house of Mellerio, the CIA itself – all these exist, and I encourage readers to seek them out (well, maybe not the CIA, unless you want to end up arrested). Just don't ask for the characters by name when you get there, and please don't judge the real-life institutions by the words and deeds of their fictitious personnel. Any errors/outright lies are mine alone.

I apologize for the gross liberties taken with the geography of Mount Athos and the Tatra Mountains, and with the timing of the Icelandic ash cloud, and all the other factual things I have bent and twisted in order to fit my narrative. As far as I know, there is no secret cavern off the Burma Railway, and the taxis in Mount Athos are all operated by monks who would have no reason to accept a CIA bribe. What can I say? Maybe I ought to have been a politician instead of a writer.

Plenty of people have been hugely helpful in the writing of this book, but special thanks go to Ron Munn and Mike Jewett for their insight into the covert intelligence world, and to Dr Robert

Massey, Deputy Executive Director of the Royal Astronomical Society, for his patient explanation of star charts. Again, all mistakes are mine.

Elly Conway, 2023

About the Author

ELLY CONWAY was born and raised in upstate New York. She wrote her first novel about Agent Argylle while working as a waitress in a late night diner.